Anonymous

Anglers' Evenings

Thomas Wallace Knox

Adventures of Two Youths in the Open Polar Sea

ISBN/EAN: 9783337325404

Printed in Europe, USA, Canada, Australia, Japan

Cover: Foto ©Andreas Hilbeck / pixelio.de

More available books at **www.hansebooks.com**

Adventures of Two Youths in the Open Polar Sea

THE VOYAGE OF THE "VIVIAN"

TO

THE NORTH POLE AND BEYOND

By THOMAS W. KNOX

AUTHOR OF

"THE BOY TRAVELLERS IN THE FAR EAST" "THE YOUNG NIMRODS" ETC.

Illustrated

NEW YORK

HARPER & BROTHERS, FRANKLIN SQUARE

1885

PREFACE.

FOR nearly four centuries the arctic regions have been an interesting
field for explorers, and public attention has been frequently drawn to
the voyages and travels that have been made in the zones of ice and snow.
The fresh interest given to polar study by the story of the *Jeannette* and
the work of Lieutenant Greely, on Lady Franklin Bay, has led to the
preparation of the present volume. It is especially intended for youthful
readers, but the author indulges the hope that those of mature years may
find instruction and amusement in its pages. He has pursued the plan
which met with favor in his previous works, and endeavored to present an
array of facts upon a groundwork of fiction, in the same manner as in
"The Boy Travellers in the Far East." He trusts that the youths who followed the fortunes of Frank and Fred in their many wanderings will give
a kindly welcome to "The Voyage of the *Vivian*" and its young heroes.

The ship and its crew are fictitious, but the scenes of the voyage, and
the incidents and adventures herein described, are intended to be realities.
They have been mainly derived from the experiences of explorers, from
the time of Martin Frobisher down to the present date. It was the author's
design to introduce all the important incidents of arctic voyages, together
with the most recent scientific discoveries, into a single narrative. The
portion of the voyage from Herald Island to the North-pole, and thence to
Grant Land, is wholly imaginary. (The writer believes that the sea around
the pole is open in summer, and will yet be reached by a ship fortunate
enough to find an opening through the icy barrier which surrounds it.)
Thus believing, he has permitted the *Vivian* and *Gambetta* to pierce the
barrier, and explore the islands and waters which are as yet concealed
from mortal vision. He asks the literal reader to remember that from
Chapters XII. to XVII., inclusive, the geographical positions of the explorers are not to be regarded as actualities.

Many works of arctic navigators and travellers have been consulted in
the preparation of the book. The history of polar exploration has been

carefully studied, from the voyages of John and Sebastian Cabot, in 1497, down to the most recent publications in England and America. Many of the authorities are given in the text of the book. The author acknowledges his personal obligations to Professor J. E. Nourse, author of "American Explorations in the Ice-zones," and other works; to Lieutenant Lucien Young, of the United States Navy; and to Deputy Inspector-general Robert M'Cormick, of the Royal Navy of England. He is also indebted to the courtesy of his publishers for their kind permission to make use of illustrations that have appeared in their previous publications relative to the arctic regions and the adventures of polar explorers.

With this brief explanation of his motives, and plan of work, the author submits "The Voyage of the *Vivian*" for the inspection of press and public.

T. W. K.

New York, *June*, 1884.

P.S.—The pages of this book had been printed and made ready for binding when, on the 17th of July, the country was electrified with the news of the rescue of Lieutenant Greely, at Cape Sabine, on the 22d of the previous month. Sorrow was mingled with joy when it was learned that out of the twenty-three companions of the heroic explorer only five survived; eighteen had perished of cold and starvation, and if the relief expedition had been forty-eight hours later in arriving at Cape Sabine not one would have been found alive!

Lieutenant Greely's expedition has added materially to the work of previous explorers. The country to the east and west of Lady Franklin Bay has been examined, and a large extent of coast-line carefully surveyed; valuable meteorological observations have been recorded; important additions are made to the map of Northern Greenland and the Polar Basin; and the believers in an open sea around the Pole have received fresh support to their theories. The flag of the United States has floated nearer to the Pole than that of any other nation. In May, 1883, it was unfurled by Lieutenant Lockwood, in latitude 83° 24′ 30″ N., longitude 40° 45′ W. In the friendly contest in polar explorations the honors have been transferred from England to America, but the whole world will share in the additions which have been made to our knowledge of the far North.

T. W. K.

New York, *August* 1, 1884.

CONTENTS.

CHAPTER XII.

CHAPTER XIII.

CHAPTER XIV.

CHAPTER XV.

CHAPTER XVI.

CHAPTER XVII.

CHAPTER XVIII.

CHAPTER XIX.

CHAPTER XX.

THE VOYAGE OF THE "VIVIAN."

CHAPTER I.

THE DEPARTURE.—BOUND FOR THE NORTH.—DESCRIPTION OF THE PARTY.

" ALL ready there ?"

"Ay, ay, sir," was the reply.

" Up with the anchor !"

The capstan went slowly round, propelled by the arms of twenty men; the anchor left its bed at the bottom of San Francisco Bay, and as the cable shortened till it hung straight down from the bows of the vessel, the order " Go ahead slow !" was shouted to the engineer, who stood at his post below. The machinery responded to his touch, and the whirling screw churned a great breadth of discolored foam around the stern of the *Vivian*. Soon she was ploughing her way through the water, turning now to port and now to starboard to avoid collisions with anchored or moving craft in the harbor of the great city by the western sea.

The ships at the docks or in the bay dipped their flags; the steamers, great and small, sounded their whistles pitched to all the notes of the chromatic scale; cannon boomed from their embrasures on Alcatraz Island and the other defences of the city; and a military band

OUTWARD BOUND.

on a steamboat which followed closely in the wake of the *Vivian* filled the air with its music. The decks of the steamboat were black with people who kept up a perpetual waving of handkerchiefs and, in the pauses of the band, replaced the music with shouts and cheers of farewell.

Without a pause the departing vessel held her way to the Golden Gate; then she stopped her engines to permit the departure of the pilot, together with several gentlemen who had accompanied her commander from the anchorage in the harbor. The crowd on the steamboat cheered more loudly than ever; the band played again, its notes growing less

AMONG THE ICEBERGS.

distinct at every pulsation of the engine, as the *Vivian* headed away into the open ocean and left the shores of California fading in the distance. And to many on the deck of the steamboat, as she returned to San Francisco, the query arose, "Shall we ever see her again?"

The *Vivian* was bound on a voyage to the arctic seas; she added a unit to the number of those that have sailed in quest of the North-pole.

It was not her first visit to the regions of ice, although she had never before gone in the character of an explorer. Originally she was built for a whaler: as the whale has been driven from the open ocean, it has been necessary for those who desire his oil to follow him to his retreat in the region of perpetual ice. In the early part of this century, and down to thirty years ago, the huntsmen of the sea found their prey in the broad expanse of the Pacific and Atlantic oceans. But in these latter days the whale is not to be found in his former haunts, and even in the far North he is by no means abundant. The successful hunters must pursue him where ice abounds through the entire year, and only during a few months in summer is it sufficiently open for ships to find a way through it. Frequently the whale-ships are nipped in the ice, and a craft of ordinary construction would be speedily crushed and destroyed.

"She was just as strong as wood and iron could make her," said the former owner of the *Vivian*. "That is, I mean she was one of the strongest whalers ever launched, and that is saying a good deal.

"She is a bark of 490 tons, old measurement; her ribs and all her timbers were the best we could find; her sides were twenty inches thick, and we covered her with extra planking till she looked as though she had put on an ulster overcoat for a sleigh-ride. For ten feet back from her stem the bow was solid oak, and then she was braced all through with timbers, so that no ordinary pressure could break her in.

"We christened her the *Fanny*. She has made five voyages to the Arctic Ocean, and come home every time full of oil, and not a man injured. But she had some narrow chances in the ice, and two or three times it looked as though her crew never would see land again."

We shall hear more of the adventures of this tough little craft, as her former captain is now her sailing-master. When she left San Francisco, as described in our opening lines, she was owned by some wealthy gentlemen of that city, who had subscribed a sufficient amount to purchase and fit her out for a voyage of exploration.

"What shall we call her?" was a question in dispute for several days, as each of her joint-owners had a pet name which he wished to have adopted.

Masculine names were voted out of order on account of the feminine character of a ship. The dictionary was consulted, and also the long list of ships that have been in the arctic regions; finally, it was agreed to call her the *Vivian*.

"Couldn't be better," said Captain Jones, who formerly commanded her, when the result of the deliberation was reported to him. "No ship of that name ever passed the Arctic Circle; besides, you say that *Vivian* means 'lively,' and when she's in a rough sea I don't know of a livelier craft than the old *Fanny*."

In spite of her excellent qualifications for an arctic voyage, it was determined to improve upon them to a considerable extent. The solid bows were extended about five feet farther aft than they were originally; additional braces were placed throughout the hull; the bow was plated with steel half an inch thick to within a foot of the rail, and the rest of the hull received a steel plating three-eighths of an inch thick from the water-line downward. Thus prepared, it was thought she could resist a pressure sufficient to lift her bodily from the water without straining her enough to open her seams and start a leak.

New sails were bent to her yards, and an extra new set was stowed below; in addition to these, she had her old sails, which were laid away in the hold. Thus she was provided with three sets of canvas to guard against accidents; and, even if they were not needed for their legitimate purposes, the sails would come handy to cut up into tents for camping on the ice or on land.

ARCTIC DISCOVERY SHIPS.

Her engines were not intended for steady use at sea; she was to rely on her sails under ordinary circumstances, and only make use of steam when emergencies required. Four hours after she had dropped the pilot at the Golden Gate the engines were stopped, the fires were extinguished, and all canvas was spread to bear the *Vivian* northward to her destination. The wind was blowing down the coast, and almost directly in the track the bark was to follow; consequently, she was obliged to stretch away to the westward and make a long "leg" by which to beat up towards Behring Strait.

Three persons on the deck of the *Vivian* watched intently the receding shore as the bark held her course. Others would have watched with them had they not been occupied with the work of clearing the decks, and arranging sundry packages which were lying inconveniently about. Probably no ship ever sailed from port for a long voyage without having much to put in order as soon as she got away from land.

The trio in which we are specially interested were the commander of the expedition and two young men whom he had selected to accompany him. And, while we are on the subject, we may as well give a brief description of the principal characters in the story we are about to narrate.

First and foremost was the gentleman to whose energy the organization of the expedition was due, Commander Bronson, formerly an officer in the United States Navy. He had already made two voyages to the Arctic Ocean in an effort to reach the pole, and add to the discoveries of other explorers. He was a cousin of Dr. Bronson, with whom some of the readers of this volume may be familiar, and possessed all the good qualities of that indefatigable traveller.*

Second in command was Major Clapp, who had been granted a leave of absence from his regiment, with which he had been fighting Indians on our northern frontier. His army rank was that of first lieutenant, but for the purposes of this expedition he received the commission of a Major of Volunteers from the Governor of California.

Third and fourth were Alfred Chapman and George Bridgman, two young men who had just graduated from college, where they were equally renowned for standing high in their classes and distinguishing themselves in all the athletic sports that were encouraged by the professors. Alfred, or Fred as he was better known, had rowed "stroke" in the last boat-race (wherein the rival college was badly beaten), and George was without a superior in running, leaping, and in the national game of base-ball. They had never visited the far North, but had spent a good deal of time out-of-doors in winter and thereby accustomed themselves to the cold.

As we have before said, the sailing-master was the former captain of the *Vivian* when she rejoiced in the name of the *Fanny*. He was allowed to retain his title, and therefore we shall know him as Captain Jones.

Dr. Tonner was the surgeon and historian of the expedition, and, as he had a fondness for matters of science, he was intrusted with the col-

---

* "The Boy Travellers in the Far East:" Adventures of Two Youths in Japan, China, Siam, Java, the Philippine Islands, Burmah, Ceylon, India, Egypt, the Holy Land, and Central Africa. Five volumes, published by Harper & Brothers, New York.

lection of minerals, plants, and such natural history specimens as might be worth preserving. He was especially cautioned not to waste his time in skinning and stuffing polar bears, arctic foxes, seals, and other well-known products of the far North. "You may bring back the ears of the bears and foxes as trophies," said the commander, "but, as to loading the ship with specimens that abound in all the museums, we won't think of it."

The crew of twenty men had been carefully selected from a great number of applicants. All were comparatively young, and at least twelve of them had been to the North on whaling voyages, and knew something of the dangers and hardships of the journey before them. We shall become better acquainted with the entire party as time goes on.

Major Clapp was occupied with the stowing of the cargo, so that Commander Bronson was left with Fred and George to watch the land and talk of the subject that was uppermost in their minds. Dr. Tonner was busy with the journal of the expedition, and determined to record the incidents of their departure before he had time to forget anything. We are indebted to his notes for much that we shall present in this volume.

"I have not had time to explain fully the plans of the expedition," said the commander, "and we may as well devote our leisure to them now. Dr. Tonner has the whole story in his journal, and as soon as he comes on deck we will have him read it over to us."

Fred and George nodded assent, as they could hardly do otherwise, and the conversation turned to other than arctic topics till the doctor appeared. When the desire of Commander Bronson was made known to him, Dr. Tonner went for his journal and proceeded to read its opening pages. They contained a brief history of arctic and antarctic exploration, and included many names that have become famous in history.

Before beginning to read from his journal, the doctor requested his listeners not to be reluctant about asking questions, as he wished to make every point perfectly clear to all of them. They agreed to the suggestion, and, as it was fully carried out, the perusal of the journal took the form of a dialogue, and resulted in the young men learning a great deal that they did not know before.

"A good many people believe," began the Doctor, "that the discovery of America by Europeans was made from the arctic regions, and not by Columbus in his celebrated voyage from Spain."

"I have read something about it," said Fred, "but had forgotten the fact till this moment."

"Nearly five hundred years before the time of Columbus," continued the Doctor, "a Norwegian voyager came from Iceland to the coast of

THE "OLD STONE MILL" AT NEWPORT.

North America, which he descended as far south as Massachusetts and Rhode Island—at least such is the account. He named the country Vinland, owing to the large number of vines that he found growing wild, and he is credited with the construction of the Old Stone Mill at Newport. There has been a great deal of discussion about the antiquity of the old mill, and its origin is not yet fully settled; but the claim for its construction by the Northmen has a large number of supporters. Whether they built the mill or not, it is pretty certain that they visited the coast of North America, and on their return told what they had seen. About that time the Northmen explored Baffin's Bay, where they built monuments which were discovered in the early part of the present century. They established colonies on the coast of Greenland which existed for several hundred years, and can still be traced in the ruins of buildings where the villages stood.

"They also made settlements on the shores of Spitzbergen, and their expeditions were pushed far to the north in pursuit of whales, seals, and other products of the sea. In the eleventh and twelfth centuries these colonies flourished, and we may credit the Northmen with being the first explorers beyond the Arctic Circle."

One of the youths asked if the Northmen left any history of their discoveries.

"They did not," was the reply, "except a few fragmentary records in some of the old chronicles of Iceland and Norway which tell the adventures of Eric the Red and his sons. Eric planted the colonies in Greenland, and his son Leif made the first voyage to Newfoundland and the coast of New England. The Icelandic chronicles mention other voyages to the same region, and their stories are confirmed by Adam of Bremen and by Nicolo Zeno, a Venetian, who went to Greenland near the end of the fourteenth century, and heard while there about a great country to the west and south. According to one account he visited the country he described; and, if the story is true, the Venetian Zeno stood on the soil of America a century in advance of the Genoese Columbus."

SCENE IN SOUTHERN GREENLAND.

"What a perfect cyclopædia of knowledge the Doctor is," said Fred, in a whisper to George.

"Yes," replied the latter, "and I shouldn't wonder if his cabin is stuffed full of cyclopædias and all the latest works on arctic exploration. I hope so, at any rate, as we can best accomplish the objects of our voyage by knowing what others have done before us."

"The Cabots, John and Sebastian, in 1497, were the next explorers of the arctic seas, as they projected a voyage to the North-pole, and hoped to go around America to the Pacific Ocean. They went beyond the sixty-seventh degree of latitude, having previously visited Labrador, but were turned back by the ice in Davis's Strait. They may be said to have been the first seekers for the north-west passage, and have had many imitators no more successful than themselves."

NORSE RUINS IN GREENLAND.

"I have a long list here," continued Dr. Tonner, "of the early adventurers in the arctic regions, and what they endeavored to accomplish. Unhappily, the story is in many cases a story of disaster, and it is a credit to the courage and persistence of mankind that where many have failed others are always ready to come forward to fill their places. The battle for the pole will never cease till some one has stood on the point where latitude and longitude cease to exist, and has spread his country's flag to the icy breeze.

FROBISHER RELICS.

"About A.D. 1500–02," the Doctor read from his notes, "the Brothers Cortereal made three voyages to the North, but without important results; fifty years later Sir Hugh Willoughby and his crew perished in the effort to find the north-west passage; and in 1576–78 Martin Frobisher made three voyages among the fields of ice, and discovered the strait which bears his name. Relics of Frobisher were found in 1861 by Captain Hall, who sent them to the British Museum. Ten years later came Davis, whose name is preserved in the strait he discovered and explored; and after him were a host of explorers from most of the nations of Europe, all in search of a new road to the Indies by way of the northern sea. English, French, Dutch, and Danes struggled for the prize, but all in vain. Henry Hudson was sent to find a passage around North America to India; and to his failure in this attempt we may attribute his southerly voyage, which resulted in the discovery of the Bay of New York and the river which flows into it from the north, and keeps the name of Hudson fresh in our memory.

"While these and later expeditions were in progress on the east, the Russians were busy on the other side of the Arctic Ocean. The most noted enterprise of the Russians in the last century was commanded by Vitus Behring, who sailed in 1741 from Petropavlovsk, in Kamchatka; the Russian histories say that the sails of his ships were of deer-skins, and the cordage was of thongs of the same material. Nothing important came of his voyage, nor of the expeditions of Shalaroff, Andreyeff, and Captain Billings; the latter an Englishman in the Russian service, who attempted to reach the pole from the mouth of the Kolyma River, in Siberia. The most famous of the Russian expeditions is that of Von Wrangell and Anjou, in 1820–23, which was made over the ice, but got no farther north than latitude 70° 51', where progress was stopped by open water.

"Coming down to the present century," said the Doctor, partly reading and partly in a conversational tone, "we have the expedition of Ross and Parry in 1818, and that of Captain Buchan and Lieutenant (afterwards Sir John) Franklin in the same year. Ross and Parry went in search of the north-west passage, while Buchan and Franklin were ordered to go to the North-pole if possible. It is needless to say that both expeditions were unsuccessful; the one did not find the desired road to India, and the other failed to reach the pole.

SIR JOHN ROSS.

"Captain Ross, who afterwards became Sir John Ross, made three voyages to the arctic regions, the last being in 1850 in search of Sir John Franklin. He must not be confounded with his nephew, Sir James Ross, who sailed with him on his first voyage, and afterwards was an officer under Captain Parry in his four voyages, between 1819 and 1827. In 1839 he went on a voyage of antarctic discovery, and was absent four years in the southern hemisphere."

"Was he the discoverer of the antarctic continent?" one of the youths inquired.

"He was, and he was not," replied the Doctor. "When he reached the antarctic continent, and hoisted the English flag upon it, he supposed he was the first to see that hitherto unknown land. But it happened that a few months earlier Commander Wilkes of the United States Navy had discovered the antarctic continent at a different point, and traced its coast for several hundred miles. The discovery of Captain Ross was entirely independent of that of Commander Wilkes, and neither knew what the other had done until a long time after."

"Is it fully determined," asked Fred, "that the South-pole is surrounded by land?"

"Exploration in that direction has been so limited that it would be rash to assert that there is an antarctic continent of any great extent. Commander Wilkes saw the land at only a few points, as he was separated from it by an immense field of ice; and it is quite possible that what he regarded as the coast-line was nothing more than a series of islands. At the point reached by Captain Ross there were mountains ten or twelve thousand feet high; one of them was an active volcano, which he named Mount Erebus in honor of the ship he commanded.

"There has been," added the Doctor, "very little exploration of the antarctic regions compared with the attempts to reach the North-pole; but it is the general belief of geographers that the South-pole is surrounded by land, and the quantity of ice there is much greater than at the north. Thus far nothing resembling an open sea has been discovered there, and every explorer has been stopped by immense fields of ice. On the other hand, open water has been found as far north as most of the explorers have ever been, and many geographers believe that the pole is surrounded by an iceless sea, easy to navigate if we could only get to it."

"And what is really the case?"

"That is what we want to find out," replied the Doctor with a smile, as he closed his journal and promised to give them another talk on the subject of arctic discovery at a later date. "Is it polynia or paleocrystic?"

"Polynia means an iceless sea around the pole," continued Dr. Tomner, "and the name was given by the Russians. Paleocrystic means a sea of ancient ice, and is the term used by those who believe that the pole is surrounded by an area of ice that never melts, but is piled up in enormous masses quite impassable by man. The advocates of each theory are able to give sound reasons for their belief; let us hope that we may prove which is the correct one."

CHAPTER II.

AT SEA.—STORIES FROM THE ARCTIC REGIONS.

ALL who were not required for duty on board the *Vivian* retired early on the first night at sea. There had been little sleep on shore the night before, as the officers were entertained at a dinner given in their honor at the Palace Hotel by the gentlemen who had contributed to the enterprise, and the dinner had lasted until long after midnight. Fred and George consoled themselves for their late hours with the reflection that it would be a long while before they could sit down to a similar feast, and it was well to make the most of it.

In accordance with the nautical custom, Captain Jones had divided the crew into watches; at eight o'clock the starboard watch was set, and the men off duty went below. The night was clear, and the *Vivian* sped along under full sail, heading into the wind as much as possible in the effort to beat to the north. As the sun went down the land was visible on the eastern horizon, but by morning all trace of it had disappeared, and the bark was in the open ocean, with nothing but sea and sky within the line of vision.

Fred and George were on deck soon after six o'clock, and the freshness of their faces showed that they had made up for previous loss of sleep. Neither had been disturbed in the least by the motion of the vessel, and as it was their first sea-voyage, each congratulated the other on the prospect of their becoming good sailors.

"I suppose, though," said George, "that we have not been tried yet, as we have had very little rolling and pitching since we left port. Every day of this sort of weather increases the chance that we will not be sea-sick at all, and if it keeps up a week or so without change, we shall then be ready for a blow."

"Don't feel too confident," said Captain Jones, who joined them from below. "I've known men who were not disturbed in their digestion for nearly a month, but became the most sea-sick of mortals when they caught a strong gale from the north. This part of the Pacific is well enough, but when you get above the fiftieth parallel you'll often find it as bad as the Atlantic."

Then the captain amused them with stories of his experiences as a whaler among the icebergs until seven o'clock, when breakfast was announced. Descending to the cabin they met the commander and Major Clapp, and soon after they were seated at table the Doctor made his appearance. He was not habitually an early riser, and often came late to breakfast, always making the excuse that his appetite was light in the morning, and a very little food would be sufficient for his purpose.

After the usual greetings had been made, the conversation naturally turned upon the object of their voyage, and their hopes and fears for its result.

George asked how many arctic expeditions had been sent out.

"Nearly three hundred in all," replied the Doctor, "if we include those which have gone by land in America and Russia, instead of proceeding by sea."

"And how many of these expeditions have been lost altogether?" Fred inquired.

"Less than you would suppose," the Doctor replied. "Only two expeditions have been completely lost, and their destruction was due to ignorance of facts which have since been demonstrated. More than three hundred years ago Sir Hugh Willoughby and all his companions died of starvation on the coast of Lapland, within a short distance of a native settlement where there were plenty of reindeer. The expedition was poorly provided, and totally unfitted for the severity of an arctic winter. It was fitted out by an association of merchants, who hoped to reach India by the north-west passage; and out of the entire company of one hundred and thirty-six there were eighteen merchants engaged in the venture.

"The other expedition, which has been entirely lost, was, as you are well aware, that of Sir John Franklin, consisting of the ships *Erebus* and *Terror*, the latter commanded by Captain Crozier. The expedition sailed from England in May, 1845, and was last seen by a whaler in Baffin's Bay, on the 26th of July of the same year. The ships were then moored to an iceberg, waiting for an opportunity to enter Lancaster Sound. For a long time the fate of the ships and their crews was a mystery, but it is now clearly known.

"The disappearance of the *Erebus* and *Terror*, gave an impetus to arctic exploration, as it led to more than twenty search expeditions, some on Government account, and others by private subscriptions. In a single year (1850) no less than twelve vessels went to the polar regions in search of Sir John Franklin, in addition to several sledging parties and land expeditions. No traces of the missing ships and their crews were found, but the search was continued at various intervals until quite recently.

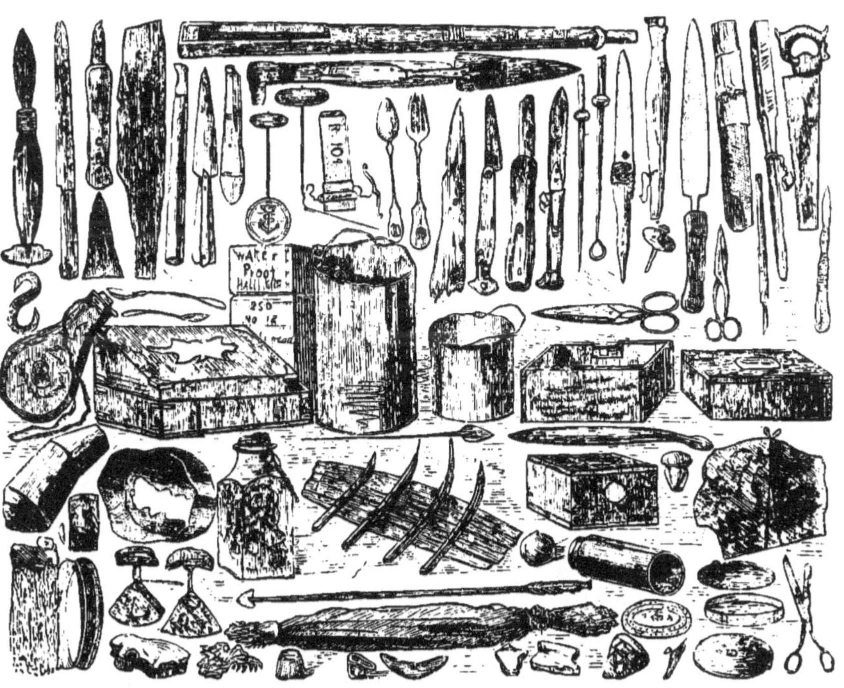

RELICS OF SIR JOHN FRANKLIN'S EXPEDITION.

"The mystery was solved by M‘Clintock's expedition in 1859, which discovered records showing that Franklin died June 11, 1847, and that the crews had been forced to abandon the ships, which were crushed by the ice. The natives reported that the party went southward over the ice, with their boats mounted on sledges, and that many of the men fell and died on the way."

One of the youths asked if the records found by Captain M‘Clintock gave a history of the expedition down to the time the ships were abandoned.

"They did not," was the reply. "The records consisted of a slip of paper enclosed in a tin case. There were two memoranda, one dated May 28, 1847, on board the ships, and the other April 25, 1848, on the same slip of paper as the other, but in a different handwriting. The latter said the ships were abandoned April 22, 1848, having been beset in the ice since September 12, 1846. It mentioned the date of Sir John Franklin's death, and said that, down to the writing of the record, out of a total of one hundred and twenty-nine persons, twenty-four had died.

"A few days before the records were found, Captain M'Clintock discovered a boat fitted to a sledge and containing two skeletons, some guns and ammunition, Sir John Franklin's silver tea-set, some tea, chocolate, tobacco, and other things. Many other relics of the expedition were found in the neighborhood or bought from the natives, and from the accounts given by the latter it was evident that the entire party had perished.

"Captain Hall, an American explorer, who made three voyages to the Arctic Ocean and died in Greenland in 1871, discovered additional traces and relics of Sir John Franklin's expedition, but made no material addition to its history. He was an enthusiast on the subject, and entertained the belief that some of the Franklin party remained alive for ten or twelve years after the loss of the ships. His first voyage covered a period

CAPTAIN HALL AMONG THE ESKIMOS.

of two years, and on his second visit he remained five years among the Eskimos, learning their language and becoming familiar with their ways. He adopted their dress and mode of life, and at length became so accustomed to the food of the natives that he preferred it to the dishes of civilization.

"He had a relish for raw seal-meat, which he pronounced superior to the finest beefsteak ever cooked, and he was perfectly happy when sitting down to dinner in an Eskimo hut — a performance that would not result agreeably to the stomach of an ordinary man. In the account of his travels he describes one of these parties, where a whole family, including half a dozen dogs, entertained him with a feast which began with raw seal and frozen fish, and terminated with stewed seal, cooked in a pot that had no other cleaning than what it received from the tongues of the dogs. Probably his appetite was sharpened by hunger, which in all ages has been pronounced the best sauce.

"But we are wandering from the searches for Sir John Franklin, which we may as well finish before we go on to other topics.

DISCOVERY OF A BOAT OF THE FRANKLIN EXPEDITION.

"After it was definitely ascertained that all the members of the Franklin expedition had perished, there was a great desire to find its records. Information came from time to time concerning books which the retreating explorers carried with them after leaving the ships, and some of the natives said these books had been buried in a cairn of stones which the white men erected. The most definite statement came in 1876. A party of Eskimos were visiting the bark *A. Houghton*, which was wintering near Marble Island; one of the natives was looking at the captain's logbook, and said that the great white man who visited them years before had kept a similar book. Having said this he produced a spoon on which the word 'Franklin' was engraved, and thus made it evident that the book he had seen was that of the missing explorer.

"These bits of information attracted the attention of Lieutenant Schwatka of the United States Army, and led him to organize an expedition for the purpose of finding the missing records. He sailed from New York in the summer of 1878. The history of his journey has been published under the title of "Schwatka's Search," and was written by Mr. W. H. Gilder, who went with him as second in command.

"Quite likely we shall have occasion to speak again of Lieutenant Schwatka and his expedition. To put it briefly, the lieutenant and Mr. Gilder made the most remarkable sledge journey on record, having been absent from their base of supplies an entire year, lacking only a few days. In this time they travelled a distance of 3251 statute miles, or 2819 geographical miles, nearly all of it over an unexplored region, and in one of the coldest seasons known in the arctic regions for many years. Once the thermometer showed the temperature to be 71° below zero, Fahrenheit; there were sixteen days averaging 100° below the freezing point, and twenty-seven days when it was more than 90° below it. During all this time the expedition was travelling, and its historian says it never stopped at all on account of the cold."

"But you haven't told us what Schwatka learned about the records of the Franklin expedition," said the commander with a smile.

"I was just getting to that," answered the Doctor. "He found that the books had been destroyed by the natives; not maliciously, but because they were quite ignorant of the value of the property. They gave some of the volumes to their children for playthings, and no doubt the Eskimo urchins had a great deal of fun with them. The rest of the books were left on the rocks until they were destroyed by the wind and storms: they had originally been deposited in a tin case, which the natives broke open in the expectation of finding something valuable. Of course

the books were of no use to them, and it seems a great pity that the officers had not informed them that the records would bring a great price
if carried to where white men could see them.

"Schwatka brought back quite a collection of relics of the Franklin
expedition, and buried the bones of many of the men, which had been
lying exposed for years. The grave of one officer, Lieutenant Irving, was
found, and his remains were removed and sent to England. All the other
graves of officers had been opened by the natives and the contents scattered about: that of Lieutenant Irving was opened like the rest, and a
portion of the bones had disappeared; those that remained were gathered
as carefully as possible, and were identified by a silver medal awarded to
John Irving at the Royal Naval College, England, in 1830. The medal
was lying on a stone near by, where it was probably placed by the natives
when they robbed the grave, and was forgotten by accident."

The conversation which we have recorded was frequently interrupted
by the movements of the steward, who was busy with the work of serving
breakfast, and as the cabin was narrow he was obliged to display a good
deal of skill to avoid accidents. Once he upset the coffee-pot at the edge
of the table, but managed to catch it before the entire contents were
spilt. A few minutes later he allowed a fried egg to slip inside the col-
lar of George's coat, just as that young gentleman was leaning forward
to help himself to a sea-biscuit; consequently, George left the table for
a short period, and missed a part of the Doctor's lecture. He consoled
himself with the double reflection that the Doctor's fund of informa-

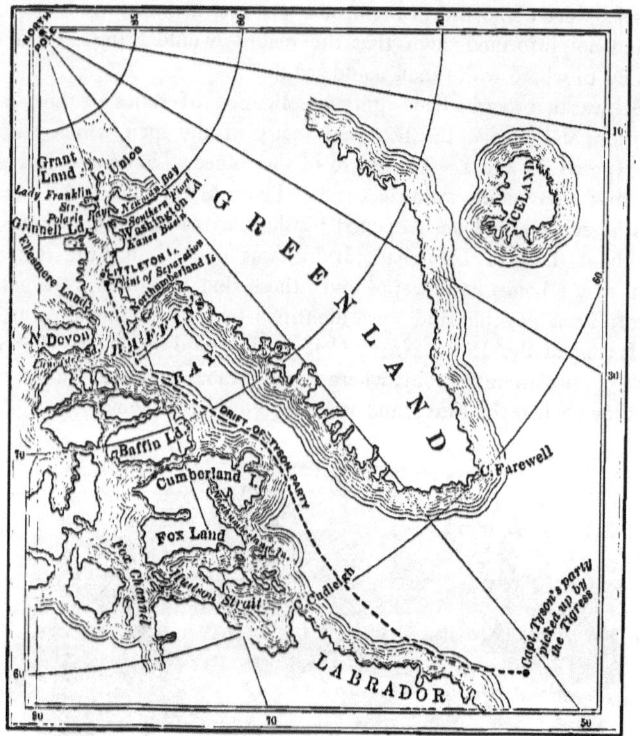

ICE-DRIFT OF THE TYSON PARTY.

tion was by no means exhausted, but the store of fresh eggs would soon give out.

After breakfast there was an inspection of the list of provisions that had been brought along for the use of the party in the North. Previous to the. inspection the commander explained to the youths the plan of the voyage, and his reasons for preferring San Francisco to New York as a point of departure.

"To make it clear to you," said he, "I must first tell about the polar currents.

"Most of the navigators who have entered the Arctic Ocean by way of Davis's Strait and Baffin's Bay have found themselves opposed by the currents flowing down to the south. Frequently, when their ships are enclosed in the ice, they have been carried slowly but steadily along over the very track by which they ascended to the North, and without any power to resist the movement.

"There are many instances of this on record. Captain Tyson, on his escape from the *Polaris* in October, 1872, drifted south nearly two thousand miles on a large floe of ice, from which he was rescued by the steamer *Tigress*. In 1827 Captain Parry made a sledge journey over the ice, but found that he drifted to the south nearly as fast as his sledges carried him northward. Captain M'Clintock, in the steam-yacht *Fox*, had a similar experience: the *Fox* was locked in the ice in Baffin's Bay, August 17, 1857, and was carried back on her course until April 25th of the following year; when released she had drifted one thousand three hundred and ninety-five miles southward.

THE CABIN OF THE "RESOLUTE."

"In 1854 Sir Edward Belcher, with a fleet of five ships, was caught in the ice near Beechy Island; the ships were abandoned, and given up as totally lost. Sixteen months later one of the officers of the whaling ship *George Henry* saw a vessel in the ice near the west shore of Baffin's Bay, in latitude 67°. Making his way to her with some difficulty, he found she was the *Resolute*, one of Sir Edward Belcher's abandoned ships, perfectly sound and sea-worthy, though locked fast in the ice. The cabin was mouldy and musty in appearance, but everything was in order, showing that she had not been visited by the natives. Some decanters of wine were on the table, and the discoverers helped themselves to the beverage which they had fairly earned by their long tramp over the ice.

"The prize was a valuable one, and the captain of the *George Henry* decided to go home with her as soon as he could get her free from the ice. He divided his crew between the two vessels, going on board the *Resolute* in person and leaving the *George Henry* in charge of his first mate. It was rather a curious circumstance that in a day or two after he had done so the *Resolute* was free and the *George Henry* frozen in. She got free, however, shortly after, and the two vessels made the best of their way to New London. The *Resolute* was bought by the United States Government, and, after being thoroughly refitted, was sent to England as a present to the Queen. The British Government accepted the gift, but immediately dismantled the ship, and laid her up in the Woolwich dock-yard.

"From the time she was abandoned until picked up by the *George Henry*, the *Resolute* had drifted a thousand miles, entirely by the force of the current. Other instances of the steady drift of the currents could be given, but those I have cited are sufficient."

One of the boys asked how the currents were made, and whether they were the same throughout the whole year.

"The currents are generally stronger in winter than in the warm months, but such is not always the case. They are formed by the Gulf Stream, in the Atlantic Ocean, and the *Kuro Siwo*, or Japan current, in the Pacific. The Gulf Stream, as you know, flows from the Gulf of Mexico northward and eastward till it reaches the coast of Northern Europe, passes the North Cape, and strikes the western shore of Nova Zembla. Portions of it flow northward towards the pole, and naturally create a counter current which sweeps down the coast of Greenland to the south. It is this current which brings the icebergs that are one of the dangers of navigation in the North Atlantic."

"I know them very well," said George. "When I came home from Europe in the steamer *Arizona* last year, we passed ten or twelve icebergs in a single day. Captain Brooks, who commanded the *Arizona*, said they had come from Greenland, and were brought down by the current; and he said they sometimes went as low as forty degrees north latitude before they were melted by the warmth of the atmosphere."

"The other stream," continued Commander Bronson, "is the *Kuro*

Siwa, and flows from the coast of Japan northward through Behring Strait. It greatly resembles the Gulf Stream, only it is much smaller, the narrowness of the strait preventing the passage of a great body of water; still it is sufficiently extensive to sweep away the ice from that part of the Arctic Ocean in ordinary summers, and give an entrance for whalers and other ships. Many scientists have thought that this current would furnish the best mode of reaching the pole, and some of them believe that it flows directly over it. While many explorers have sought to reach the pole by the Greenland route, and been carried back by the currents, others have argued that the true way to get there is to take advantage of the current through Behring Strait. Nine-tenths of the sailing or steaming expeditions to the arctic regions have been by the Greenland or the Spitzbergen route; only a few have tried the other approach, and consequently its capabilities have not been tested.

"It is my opinion that the gateway to the pole is through Behring Strait; for that reason I wished to sail from San Francisco rather than from New York. Perhaps we may be caught in the ice and drifted across the pole by the Japan current; then we may be brought down with the ice along the coast of Greenland or by Spitzbergen, and so make our way to New York by the Atlantic route. Who can say that we shall not?

"Only a few years ago a whale-ship that had entered the Arctic Ocean through Behring Strait, found open water farther than it had ever been seen before. She sailed more than a hundred miles

AN ICEBERG FROM GREENLAND.

along this water in pursuit of whales, but found none. As she was not on a scientific voyage, she turned to the south and lost a valuable opportunity. It is not impossible that there was an open way to the pole, caused by a combination of the winds and currents; and if to the pole, why may it not have continued southward on the other side? Of course

THE BARRIER OF ICE.

it is all conjecture, but where everything is guesswork, the guess of one
is as good as that of another."

"Do you think there is water at the pole," said one of the youths, "or
perhaps solid land ?"

"That is one of the vexed questions," replied the commander, with a
smile, "and it cannot be answered until somebody has actually been to
the pole and seen for himself. I have already told you of the discussions
relative to the sea at the pole (supposing there is a sea there), whether it
is polynia or paleocrystic, open or eternally closed. All that the expeditions have accomplished towards reaching the pole is to get within about
five hundred miles of it ; ten hours of an express train on a railway might
finish the journey, but, unhappily, the railway has not been extended to it,
and Pullman cars are unavailable. Certainly the pole is surrounded by
an icy barrier, which does not remain the same at all times. One expedition finds open water where another, a few years earlier or later, discov-
ers only solid ice ; and this experience has been repeated again and again.
The barrier of ice has been indented in a few places, but, practically, there
is an area of two and a half million square miles around the pole where
the foot of man has never trod."

"It seems to me," said one of the youths, "that the cold must increase
as we go towards the pole, and where there is so much ice at every point
four or five hundred miles from it, there must be a great deal more ice at
the pole itself."

"Evidently you adhere to the paleocrystic theory," was the reply, "but on one question you are wrong. The point of greatest cold is not at the pole itself, but away to the south; observation shows that there are two points of greatest cold, one in Northern Siberia and the other on Parry Island, on the American side of the globe. North of these points the temperature decreases as we approach the pole, but our progress is impeded by the ice barrier already mentioned, and which has been such a hinderance to every explorer in that direction.

"The North-pole is not the magnetic pole any more than it is the pole of greatest cold. Sir James Ross, in 1832, fixed the magnetic pole in latitude 70° 5′ 17″ N., longitude 96° 46′ 45″ W. It is there the needle of the mariner's compass points, and not to the spot over which the North-star is supposed to hang perpetually."

"What are the arguments in favor of an arctic continent?" was the next inquiry.

"Here is the opinion of Lieutenant Lucien Young," was the reply; and so saying, Commander Bronson drew from his pocket a slip cut from a newspaper. "He has given much time to the study of arctic exploration, and his theory is the result of careful deliberation.

ARCTIC BIRDS.

"'The wild-fowl of the higher arctic regions,' says Lieutenant Young, 'when winter comes on, do not go south, but north. There, somewhere in the unknown, mysterious regions, they build their nests and hatch their young, returning south in the spring. These birds do not build their nests on ice and snow, and are fond of vegetable substances. Again, the Gulf Stream, as is well known, after leaving the coast of America, divides into three currents. One of them breaks on the British Isles, and gives them the temperature of New York; another goes along the northern coast of Europe and Siberia; and a third sweeps northward along the eastern coast of Greenland until it meets a cold current of greater specific gravity coming from the north, when it sinks and becomes an undercurrent, still running northward. Now it is only when the waters of the Gulf Stream meet with a resistance that they give out their latent heat. For instance, they pass by the Grand Bank of Newfoundland, and do not materially raise the temperature there, but when the resistance of the British Isles is encountered, the heat is given off.'

"'Now,' continues Lieutenant Young, 'may not the portion of the Gulf Stream running north meet with the obstruction of land around the pole, and, coming to the surface and giving off its heat, raise the temperature of the region very materially? In support of this theory we find Gulf Stream water in Smith's Strait running south. I believe there is land at the pole, and immortality for the man who shall place his foot upon it.'"

Commander Bronson folded the paper and carefully replaced it in his pocket.

"I can understand the benefits of the currents flowing from the pole," said one of the youths. "They bring away the ice and thus prevent a vast accumulation. If it were not for the currents there would be a great increase every year."

"Quite true," replied the commander, "but, in spite of the currents, it is generally believed that the quantity of ice at the pole is increasing every year. Here comes the Doctor; let us ask him to explain his theory of the grand cataclysm."

The query was made, and the Doctor readily assented to the proposal.

"My theory," said he, "is not by any means my own; it was propounded years ago by M. Adhemar, a celebrated French mathematician, and is supported partly or altogether by Lyell, Darwin, Hebert, Hon, and others.

"Briefly stated, it is that the centre of gravity of the earth is changed at certain epochs by the accumulation of ice at one of the poles, until its balance is lost. When this happens, the earth turns over: that is, it changes its position in the heavens, so that what is now the North-star hangs over the present South-pole. There is a grand cataclysm, or rush of waters, making the inundations of which we see the traces all over the globe, and forming the deposits that compose the different strata of the earth's surface."

"How often do these upsets occur?" Fred inquired,

"About once in every twenty-one thousand years," replied the Doctor. "The last is supposed to have been the Deluge, which is described in the Genesis of the Bible. You needn't be alarmed for our present safety, he added, "as the next cataclysm is not expected for at least ten thousand years!"

"But I don't understand how it all comes about," said George. "What is it sets the cataclysm going?"

"According to the geologists," the Doctor explained, "there is a difference in the amount of heat and cold in the two hemispheres. In the first part of one of these great cycles of twenty-one thousand years there will be more heat in one hemisphere than in the other, while at the last half of the cycle the conditions are reversed. Humboldt estimated that at the present time there are eight days more of winter in the South-pole than at the North, and consequently eight days less of summer. It follows, therefore, that there is an accumulation of ice and snow at the South-pole which increases slightly, but surely, every year. Thousands of years hence the weight of ice, snow, and water there will be so great that the centre of gravity will be changed, and then will come one of those terrible inundations already mentioned. According to this theory we are now a little past the middle of the cycle. Ten thousand years ago the North-pole was a warm region, and the mammoth and kindred animals roamed through its forests. Since that time the temperature has fallen in the Southern Hemisphere; all the explorers in the direction of the South-pole say there is a greater quantity of ice there than in the North, and the hinderances to travel are everywhere insurmountable."

"Then, if we wait a few thousand years," said one of the youths, "we can have a better chance than now of getting to the North-pole, since the cataclysm will sweep everything away, and there will be no ice to hinder us."

"Quite likely," responded the Doctor; "but we won't make this a reason for giving up our present expedition."

CHAPTER III.

PROVISIONS FOR AN ARCTIC VOYAGE.—WHALES AND WHALERS.

WE have observed that the inspection of the list of provisions was interrupted by the talk concerning the exploration of the arctic regions and the searches for Sir John Franklin; then came the dissertation of the Doctor on the grand cataclysm which should change the relation of the poles and derange things generally, coupled with the re-assuring assertion that it was not likely to come off immediately. Quiet having been restored, as the reporters say, the list of provisions was produced.

"We are provisioned for two years," said the commander, "and of course we have the usual stores of a ship for a long voyage. They include salted meats, both dry and wet—the former carefully wrapped in canvas, and the latter in strong casks. Then we have a liberal stock of flour, meal, dried fruit, preserved vegetables of different kinds, canned meats and fruits, and tea, coffee, and chocolate. Hard bread or sea-biscuit has not been forgotten, as it is generally the first item in a ship's list of provisions.

The Doctor remarked that the hardships of long sea-voyages had been diminished by the abundance of canned goods, which were almost unknown in the time of Sir John Franklin, and even at a much later date.

"As to that," said Commander Bronson, "we are less fortunate than you might suppose, as there are many qualities of canned provisions which will not bear transportation to the arctic regions. All articles that contain water are undesirable, as they are injured by freezing, and, besides, it is not well to carry water where every ounce of weight is of serious consequence. Our canned provisions have been specially prepared for us, and contain the least possible amount of moisture.

"We have horseradish and lime-juice, in large quantities, to prevent the disease called scurvy; it has frequently impaired the efficiency of arctic expeditions, and in some instances has been the direct cause of failure. I have had our lime-juice prepared in a new form, partly to facilitate transportation, and partly to make it easier of distribution when wanted. Instead of being in liquid shape it is in the form of lozenges, and in sticks like candy. When we are on the march over the ice we can more easily distribute it than if it were frozen solid in bottles.

"Our pemmican was made by a man who thoroughly understands its preparation, and we have a liberal supply of it."

One of the youths asked what pemmican was, and the commander proceeded to enlighten him.

"Pemmican," said he, "is an important article of supply at the posts of the Hudson's Bay Company and all through the northern regions. There are two forms, raw and cooked; for the former, lean meat is cut into thin strips and dried, and for the latter the meat is boiled before cutting and drying. In either case the meat is reduced to powder, and this is mixed with melted fat. A little seasoning is added, and in some parts of the North the powder of certain leaves is introduced. When thoroughly mixed, the substance is poured into a bag of green hide, the end of the bag tightly sewed, and as the hide shrinks in drying it compresses the contents into a mass nearly as hard as a brick. The pemmican is preserved from injury by its hide envelope, and is so solid that it must be cut out with a hatchet or a stout knife.

"As an article of food it is admirably adapted to expeditions over the ice, or in regions of intense cold; the great quantity of fat contained in it supplies the carbon required by the system for resisting the effects of a low temperature, and it is so well protected by its covering that it may lie for hours in the rain, or be immersed in salt-water, without injury.

"I have tried an experiment," the commander continued, "or, rather, I have repeated an experiment that was made by a recent English expedition, and found to work successfully."

"What is that?"

"I have mixed lime-juice with the pemmican in such a proportion that it will not be necessary to keep the anti-scorbutic medicine always at hand. At least, I think the result will be that our men will keep in good health without the necessity of frequent rations of lime-juice.

"So much for the food provisions," he added, "and with care they will be all we need, in addition, of course, to the game we hope to kill from time to time.

"For killing our game we are well provided with arms and ammunition. We have several rifles of the latest pattern, and we have revolvers sufficient to set up a small shop, in case we want to make a trading venture. We have a few rifles that can be loaded with loose powder and ball, but the most of our weapons use fixed ammunition; the shells can be

OVER THE ICE.

reloaded if we happen to run short, or are in danger of doing so, and there is an abundance of material for reloading.

"There are only two sizes of fixed ammunition—one for the rifles and one for the revolvers. Perhaps I might express it better by saying that our weapons have only two calibres—the rifles one and the revolvers another.

"We have an abundance of warm clothing, both for under and outer wear; it will serve us in ordinary times very satisfactorily, but on long journeys over the ice, or in the dead of winter, we shall adopt the native dress, of which we will learn more by-and-by. You remember the old adage, 'when with the Romans, do as the Romans do;' apply it to our case, and when with the Hyperboreans, dress as the Hyperboreans dress. They wear thick furs and skins, and so must we if we would escape freezing in the arctic winter.

"For fuel we have coal—as much as we can stow away in the ship's bunkers; and we may be able to replenish our stock at one of the international depots recently established in the arctic regions."

"I had not heard of them," said the Doctor; "when were they established?"

"I made a suggestion three or four years ago," was the reply. "It was favorably received by our government, and the Secretary of the Navy proceeded to act upon it. My suggestion was that every whaler, or other ship, proceeding to the Arctic Ocean under sail alone, and having spare room in her hold, should carry a quantity of coal, to be left at certain designated points, for the use of any explorer who might need it. An exploring ship of any nation might use this coal under certain restrictions, reporting through her own admiralty the number of tons taken, so that compensation could be made to the government that sent it out. It is

NATIVE AND EUROPEAN DRESS CONTRASTED.

not necessary to trouble you with all the details of my scheme; it was accepted, and communicated to the governments of England, France, Germany, Denmark, Sweden, and other nations interested in polar explorations, and there ought to be by this time several coal depots in the Arctic Ocean, where an explorer should be reasonably sure of finding enough to supply his wants."

"But won't the natives steal the coal, as they do everything else?" one of the youths inquired.

"Undoubtedly, if it could be of any use to them," was the reply, "but thus far they have not found out how to utilize it. They look with wonder on the white man's ability to burn 'black stones,' but have not learned how to perform the feat themselves. As long as they have no stoves, and are not taught how to create a draft through the coal, they will respect the heaps which we shall make on the barren rocks at East Cape, Littleton Island, Point Barrow, and the other places selected for our depots. Then, too, these depots will be convenient post-offices for the interchange of news and information. I suggested that at each depot a mark should be made on some prominent rock, indicating the spot where letters were concealed a short distance away. The distances should be in yards, and the direction magnetic by compass; or it might be shown by an arrow, cut or painted on the rock. Thus "N.E. 22" would mean that a box had been buried twenty-two yards away, in a north-easterly direction; " —— 27" would show that the direction of the arrow must be followed twenty-seven yards to find the place of concealment. The position of the deposits would be according to the character of the ground, the drift of the snows, and the liability to discovery by the natives.

"It is of very little use," he continued, "to deposit papers under cairns of stones, as the natives invariably dig into the cairns and break open the cases containing the papers. This was the fate of the records of the Franklin expedition, as we have already seen. Now, if the records had been buried in a dry spot, and all trace of the digging of the ground obliterated, future explorers might have been directed to the place by marks on the rocks some distance away."

"But some of the natives—two or three that have been to the United States and England—have learned to read," said Fred, "and one of these natives could discover the place of deposit."

"Quite likely," said the Doctor, "but he would be intelligent enough to know that the records would bring a handsome reward to whoever found them, and there could be no danger from such a cause. Suppose there had been a native of King William Land able to read when the Franklin records were lying about in the hands of the children, or exposed to the winds on the rocks. Every scrap of paper would have been carefully collected and carried to one of the stations on Hudson's Bay; instead of waiting more than ten years for definite information, we should have known the fate of the expedition in a couple of years at farthest, and the history of its work would have been preserved."

"But to return to the subject of coal," said the Doctor; "there is plenty of coal in the far North, I believe, but it has never been utilized, partly owing to the difficulties of mining it, and partly because it is of very poor quality."

"Unless I am misinformed," responded Commander Bronson, "the most of the coal found in the islands and along the coast of the far North —with the exception of a large seam of anthracite at Lady Franklin Bay —contains so much sulphur that it is dangerous to burn it in the furnaces of steamships, on account of its eating away the iron of the flues."

"Yes," answered the Doctor; "one summer when I was in Alaska we made a trip to the Aleutian Islands. On one of the islands there is a fine bed of coal, so close to the water that it is an easy matter to get it out. We stopped there a couple of days, and filled our bunkers, and then steamed off in high spirits. But we soon found that the sulphur in the coal was destroying our flues, and the unconsumed stuff was pitched overboard. We made the discovery just in time: our engineer said that if we had gone on with it another day there would have been danger of setting fire to the ship. When we returned to Sitka it was necessary to replace nearly all the flues with new ones, but we were consoled by learning that others had made the same mistake."

"There she blows!" said Captain Jones, pointing rather excitedly at the spout of a whale a few hundred yards to windward.

The conversation relative to the Arctic Ocean came to a sudden stop, and the entire party rushed to the rail to see the "monster of the deep."

"Eighty barrels of oil in him," said the captain. "Wouldn't he give us a fine stock for winter evenings at the North-pole?"

"Then we wouldn't have so much occasion for the coal depots we have just heard about," exclaimed George.

"Let's capture him," said Fred, "and cut up his blubber for the engine-room. Wouldn't the propeller send us along, with such stuff as that for fuel!"

Evidently the whale was not at all frightened, and perhaps he mistook the ship for one of his own family. He slowly came up, until he was not fifty yards away, and then made a complete circuit of the *Vivian*. Fred wanted to shoot at him, "just for fun," and started below for a rifle; Captain Jones called him back, and said the shooting could not be allowed, and with that the youth resumed his place at the rail.

"It would have done no good to shoot at him," said the captain, "and might have done harm. Perhaps he would have dived after getting your shot, and come up a long distance away, and perhaps he might have come up directly beneath the ship, and given us a shock that would have strained us severely, or possibly sent us to the bottom.   Such things have happened, and there are several instances of whales having attacked ships, breaking in their sides and converting them into helpless wrecks.   The whale-ship *Essex* was destroyed by a whale in this way, and so was the *Union;* other ships have been attacked, and there is no good in taking a shot 'just for fun,' as you say."

Fred assented readily to the captain's suggestion, and concluded that a shot at anything for mere sport, whether on land or sea, was not to be recommended.   He inwardly resolved that the lesson should not be lost on him, and to strengthen his resolution he imparted it to George, who promptly agreed with him.

Soon another whale, and in a little while another, were reported in sight, somewhat to the discomfort of Captain Jones, who regretted passing such magnificent game without trying to capture it.

"Why didn't we rig the ship for a whaling cruise as well as for an arctic exploration?" said one of the youths; "then we could have had the sport of killing whales, and made a nice profit from the oil."

"Very good in theory," remarked the Doctor, "but the practice would not have been so good.   Whaling would delay our explorations, and perhaps ruin them altogether; you can't put science and commerce quite so close together without making one or both of them suffer. A better way would be to make one cruise entirely as a whaler, and another in the interests of science; then you wouldn't run the risk of getting things mixed."

"A voyage after whales would be an excellent preparation for a scientific one," remarked the captain, as he overheard the conversation between the Doctor and the youths. "You make an intimate acquaintance with the ice-fields, bergs, floes, and packs, and what a man doesn't know about ice after a few whaling voyages is hardly worth finding out.

"The best whale-fishing is now close in upon the ice, and very often you go for your game where the bergs and packs are thick. The first whale I ever struck in the Arctic Ocean was along-side of a great berg, like a mountain, and when we hit him he tried to get under the ice to escape us.

"We sighted him from the berg, where some of the sailors had been sent to try to find fresh water, the ship meantime standing on and off under full sail. Of course when they saw the whale they dropped all idea of water and went for the prize; he cost us more than three hours hard fighting, and at one time it looked as though he would get off in spite of us. He doubled around the point of the berg with the harpoon in him, and if he had cut the line against the ice we should have lost him. In one way the ice helped us, as he finally went into a little nook or (cove), in the berg, where he got bewildered, and gave us a chance to finish him up.

LOOKOUT ON AN ICEBERG.

"I once saw a whale caught in an iceberg," the captain continued; "or, rather, he was pretty well up towards the top of it."

"How did that happen?" said one of the listeners.

"I'll tell you," responded the mariner. "I was in the *Robert Gibbs*, of New Bedford, off the southern end of Greenland, and we hadn't seen a whale for several days. But we kept a sharp lookout all the time, partly for whales and partly to steer clear of the ice. One day we were sailing along within a mile or so of a big berg that was drifting south with the current, and seemed to have everything its own way. I was up in the crow's-nest, and had my eyes on the berg, when suddenly about a third of it broke off from one side with a report like thunder, and went crashing and splashing into the water.

"The part that broke off changed the balance of the rest, so that the berg turned about half-way over. One side went under water, while the other came out, and the side that came out brought a whale along with it, and lifted him nearly a hundred feet into the air. He was in a hollow in the berg, not large enough for him to swim in, but high enough in the sides to keep him from getting over.

"He splashed about and made things lively, and the more he thrashed the less water there was for him to live in. I shouted, 'there she blows!' and pointed to the iceberg, and away went a boat to capture him.

"The boat made fast to the berg, and the boat-steerer went on the ice with a lance, though he had a hard time getting up the slippery side. But he got to the whale after a while and finished him with the lance, and then we wondered what to do with him.

"It wasn't exactly safe to go to chopping the ice enough to make a channel for the whale to slip through to the water, as our blows would be likely to split the berg again, and let us into the ocean among the falling ice. Then it would be a long job to cut off the blubber where he was, and carry it away in the boats, after sliding the pieces into the water, and nobody could tell what minute the berg might turn over again.

"It wasn't a large whale—about fifty barrels or so—but it was too good to be lost. The captain looked the business all over, and then hit on a plan which we at once carried out.

"We rove ropes around a dozen empty casks, and fastened the ends of 'em together, so that the lot looked like a bunch of toy balloons which the peddlers sell on Broadway. Then we towed the casks along-side the berg, close to where the whale was, and carried up the rope that held the bunch.

"We made it fast to his flukes to prevent its working loose, and then we went back to the ship.

"The boats were all hauled in, and then we made sail and brought the ship within about five hundred yards of the perpendicular side of the berg. We fired several times at the berg with a small cannon, in the hope that the concussion might shatter it and make it turn over again; but though we brought off some large pieces it didn't turn as we wanted.

"Then we went back with one of the boats, taking along some powder in a tin canister, a long piece of safety-fuse, and the tools we needed for making a deep hole in the ice. We drilled a big hole just back of the whale; then we put down the canister of powder, with the fuse attached, and filled the hole up with the fine ice we had chiselled out of it. When all was ready, everybody but one man went back to the boat, and then he lit the fuse and followed too. You can be sure he made the best of time down the slope, and the boat's crew never did better pulling than when they were getting away from that berg.

"We got to the ship's side before the powder blew up. It split off a great piece of the berg and let the whale down into the water, where he was kept from sinking by the casks tied to his tail. When the commotion was over we went and picked him up, and in a little while had his carcass along-side, and were cutting him in. I reckon that was about the only whale ever killed on the top of an iceberg.

"Talking about mixing up the whaling business with arctic exploration," continued Captain Jones, "you'll find we are indebted to the whalers for a great deal that has been learned about the polar regions. For instance, there was Captain Scoresby, who flourished in the early part of this century; he combined the capture of whales with the pursuit of science, and when he was not busy with the chase of a whale, he was making observations on the ice-packs and currents.

"Scoresby made more than thirty voyages to the arctic regions; he believed in the open polar sea, and in 1806, when whales were scarce, he endeavored to prove the correctness of his theory. He sailed into the ice-barrier, and reached latitude 81° 30' N. before he was compelled to return. Hendrik Hudson had previously reached the same latitude in the Spitzbergen seas, but the record of Scoresby was the best made by a whaler down to that time. Altogether he was full of adventure, as he passed the 80th parallel in fifteen of his voyages, surpassing everybody else before or since his time.

"He was full of courage in his fights with the whales, and had many narrow escapes. Once his ship was in a bay that had been freshly frozen over; the ice was so thin that it would not bear the weight of a man, and too thick to be broken by rowing a boat through it. Whales were in the bay, and there were holes where they came up to breathe, and Scoresby wanted to get at them.

"He went to work and made what he called 'ice-shoes;' they were of thin plank, six feet long by a foot wide, and in the centre of each plank he made a place where his foot could be held by straps. With these shoes he slid along the ice to the holes where the whales came up to breathe, and there he harpooned them at his convenience.

"But after he had struck the harpoon into a whale the rough part of the business came. The creature dived, and by-and-by came up to breathe, and when he rose he wasn't particular whether he came to a hole or made a new one with his back. Scoresby followed on his ice-shoes to where he thought the whale would come up, and if he made a good guess, he generally succeeded in finishing him off.

CAPTAIN SCORESBY.

"Once he calculated a little too closely, for the whale came up right under where he stood, and sent the old captain into the air, ice-shoes and all. But there happened to be some strong ice close by, so he skipped out of his ice-shoes and made for the solid ice, where he could stand in safety."

"There were two Scoresbys," said the Doctor, "and I presume it is of the elder you are speaking."

"Yes," answered Captain Jones; "I forgot to say there were two of them, father and son. Both were named William: the father did not begin his seafaring life till 1790, when he was thirty years old, and he died in 1829. The son ran away to sea in one of the father's ships when he was only ten years old, and six years later he had risen to the rank of first mate. The elder Scoresby made many improvements in whaling, and it was he that invented and used the ice-shoes I told about. He commanded the ship *Resolution*, when she made the northward voyage in 1806 to latitude 81° 30', and at that time his son was second officer under him. The son was the first to make scientific observations on the electricity of the polar regions, and he made so many contributions to the geography of the far North that his work has been long regarded as a high authority."

"He had a good deal of correspondence with Sir Joseph Banks," the Doctor remarked, "and it was this correspondence, and the various reports of Captain Scoresby, that led to the equipment of several important expeditions by the British Government."

"We doff our caps to the Scoresbys," said Commander Bronson, "and they are worthy of all the honor their successors can give them."

The attention of the party was called to an object on the water almost ahead of the ship, and, as they neared it, the eyes of the youths were strained to their utmost to make out the strange sight. Flocks of birds were circling about, or settling on the waves, and there was a commotion in the water that resembled a small whirlpool.

"There she doesn't blow!" said the captain, as soon as he turned his gaze in that direction.

Then he explained that what they saw was nothing but the stripped carcass of a whale. "Some whaler has had hold of him," said the captain, "and his blubber is now being converted into oil, somewhere beyond the horizon.

A NIMROD OF THE SEA.

"The birds are having a rare feast on what the huntsmen of the sea have left, and that is why you see so many of them. The sharks are in for their share as well, and they are kicking up a lively commotion in the water. They are dangerous customers for the birds; anything is game for them that they can get hold of, and if you were near enough you would see a bird go under every few minutes, and become food for a shark.

"The sharks make it risky sometimes for the men who are cutting in a whale. A man has to go down on the whale's back to start the strip of blubber, and if he misses his footing while there, and slips into the water, he runs a great chance of being swallowed by a shark. The back of a whale isn't the best footing in the world; you must have spikes in your boots, or woollen stockings over them, and even then, when a ship is rolling and the whale is bobbing about, there is great danger of slipping. After the strip is started the man climbs into 'the chains,' where he has a better footing, and can chop away with the spade as fast as the blubber is unrolled."

As the *Vivian* passed the drifting carcass some of the birds flew away, but their places were promptly filled by others, and there was no decrease in the number. The captain said that sometimes the carcass of a whale floated after being stripped and cast adrift, while at others it sank instantly. Why it should float at one time and sink at another was a mystery nobody had been able to explain. And he further said that, sometimes when a whale is on the surface of the water, he will sink as rapidly as a stone, without any apparent motion of fins or tail.

The conversation continued for some time, and touched a variety of topics, until dinner was announced. The next day and the next there were more stories about the whale-fishery, and for a week or more Captain Jones contributed freely to the amusement of the youths.

One day he was describing an adventure with a sperm-whale in the South Pacific; just as he was in the middle of his story, it was suddenly interrupted by the announcement of a sail ahead, which threw everybody into a state of excitement.

A CARCASS ADRIFT.

CHAPTER IV.

MEETING A STRANGER.—SOMETHING ABOUT KAMCHATKA.

GEORGE and Fred looked for the sail that had been sighted, but it was some time before they could make it out. Even when they did see it there was little more than a speck on the horizon, but it was clearly distinguishable to the experienced eyes of the commander and the captain. The latter declared it was a bark, even before he brought his glass to bear upon it; after a long look at the stranger, he said it was probably the *Behring*, on her way from Petropavlovsk to San Francisco. The youths had a suspicion that the latter announcement was entirely guess-work, and based upon the captain's knowledge that the *Behring* was on her way southward, and was due about that time. Whether they were right or wrong in their supposition, they had no way, for the present at least, of finding out.

On the course they were sailing they were not likely to come very near the stranger, as she was a long distance to leeward. Captain Jones ordered the *Vivian* to change her bearing, and thus the two vessels gradually approached each other. An hour or so before sunset they were within signalling distance, and the guess of Captain Jones turned out to be correct. For the last two hours pens had been busy on board the *Vivian*, and letters were ready for despatch to San Francisco. George and Fred wrote brief accounts of their voyage, for the benefit of friends at home, and Commander Bronson embraced the opportunity to say what he thought best to the owners of the *Vivian*. The most that any of the party could say was that everybody was well, the voyage had been delightful thus far, the ship was all that could be desired, and the stores, so far as they had been examined, were in excellent condition.

The signal, " we desire to communicate," was hoisted by the *Vivian*, and the *Behring* responded by announcing that she would heave to. Then the *Vivian* signalled, " we will send a boat." As soon as the two vessels were hove to away went the boat from the *Vivian's* side, in charge of the second officer. The captain suggested that one of the youths might go in the boat: there was a passage of politeness between Fred and George, each urging that the other should have the honor and novelty of the expedition, and as they could not decide upon it, the question was submitted to the commander. The latter promptly declared that the elder of the twain should go, and without another word Fred descended the rope-ladder and took his seat in the boat.

She danced rapidly over the waves, and in a quarter of an hour Fred was on the deck of the *Behring*, exchanging salutations with her captain. He was nearly knocked over by a large dog, that showed a desire to be familiar without the formality of an introduction, and the brute continued his attentions until dragged away by one of the sailors. The captain explained that the dog was from Kamchatka, and had never been used to polite society; he was on his way to San Francisco, where it was hoped his manners would be improved. Fred observed that the animal was identical with what he had seen in the pictures of the Esquimaux dog, and the captain confirmed his opinion by declaring that the Esquimaux and Kamchatka dogs are precisely the same.

Fred delivered the package of letters for San Francisco, and gave the captain several newspapers of recent date. Then the second officer handed over a small parcel addressed to "the bark *Behring;*" it contained letters that had been sent from San Francisco, on the chance that the *Vivian* might meet her, or be able to leave the missives where they could be delivered. On the way back to the *Vivian* the officer explained to Fred that it is the custom to send letters in this way by every ship leaving port for a direction in which another is supposed to be.

"My father," said he, "was the captain of a whaler in the old times, when they sailed from New Bedford and came home again, three or four years later, with the ship filled with oil and bone. My mother used to write by every ship that sailed for the Pacific Ocean; not more than one letter in twenty ever reached my father, but of course that one was welcome enough to be a consolation for the loss of the rest."

The *Behring* had sailed from Petropavlovsk, in Kamchatka, and was on her way to San Francisco, and her captain had nothing of consequence to report. He invited our friends below, and of course they accepted the invitation, but did not stay long, as it was getting late and there was no occasion for further delay. Just as they were leaving the cabin he remarked that the officials at Petropavlovsk were preparing to receive a French ship, which was shortly expected on its way to the Arctic Ocean. Letters had been received from the French Government for the officers of the ship, and with it came a message that the Gallic explorers had been instructed to stop at Petropavlovsk for their final instructions. He could not give the name of the ship, nor tell anything further than that such a craft was expected.

The *Behring* filled away on her course for San Francisco, and her crew joined in a farewell cheer to the *Vivian*, as the boat of the latter started on its return. Just as the sun went below the horizon the boat was hoisted in, and the *Vivian* turned her sails to the breeze that bore her to the northward. Fred was overjoyed at his part in the incident of visiting a ship at sea, and George was not far behind in excitement. Only those who have made long sea voyages can appreciate the feelings of the youths. A meeting at sea is a great relief to the monotony of sailing over the wide expanse of waters, and every incident, however trivial, becomes an event of the greatest importance.

When Fred made his report to Commander Bronson, he caused some perplexity to that gentleman. The story was a confirmation of what he had heard while the *Vivian's* preparations were going on—that a French expedition was on its way to the Arctic Ocean by way of Behring Strait. He desired to co-operate in a friendly way with any expedition to the polar seas, without regard to its nationality, and when the report reached him he wrote at once to the American minister in Paris for any information he could obtain concerning it. The latter could learn nothing definite on the subject, as the French are very reluctant to let their neighbors know what they are doing in the line of explorations, and so the commander had pretty nearly dismissed it from his thoughts.

The information derived from the captain of the *Behring* had thrown new light upon the subject, and he at once thought it would be of advantage to meet the French ship at Petropavlovsk, with a view to co-operation.

"How much would it take us out of the direct course to Behring Strait," he inquired of Captain Jones, "if we should touch at Petropavlovsk?"

"About a thousand miles," was the reply. "I can tell you almost to a mile by measuring on our charts."

"Never mind for the present," responded the commander; "perhaps I will ask you more on the subject to-morrow."

"As we are now steering," the captain explained, "we shall go through the Oonimak Passage of the Aleutian Islands, and enter Behring Sea. If we steer for Petropavlovsk, we shall leave the whole Aleutian chain to the northward, and go several degrees farther west than we expect to at present."

Commander Bronson made no reply; the captain discreetly ventured

PETROPAVLOVSK, KAMCHATKA.

a remark about the weather, and walked to the binnacle to see how the ship was headed.

The commander went to his cabin, but the youths remained on deck and began to discuss the probabilities of their visiting Petropavlovsk. George remarked that Petropavlovsk was the principal settlement of the peninsula of Kamchatka, and he was sure it would be a very interesting place.

Dr. Tonner joined them, and to the question as to whether he had ever been in Kamchatka, he gave, to their delight, an affirmative answer.

"I was there several years ago," said he, "and probably the country has not changed in any appreciable degree since my visit. There is nothing to change, or but very little, as the population is small, and does not devote itself to building railways or otherwise making improvements."

"Please tell us something about Kamchatka, and what you saw there," said George. "If we go there the information will be useful, and if we do not visit Petropavlovsk, or any other port, we shall have learned something at any rate."

"Well," replied the Doctor, settling himself into a deck-chair, and evidently making preparations for a long dissertation, "Kamchatka is at the north-western extremity of Asia, as you can see by a glance at the map.

"It is not by any means as cold as you might suppose, from its position so far to the north. In fact, it is too warm to allow the inhabitants to raise wheat."

The youths looked at each other with surprise, but were too well-bred to indicate a disbelief in the Doctor's assertion.

"That statement requires explanation," continued Dr. Tonner, "and it is simple enough when you understand it. Kamchatka is a country of volcanoes and earthquakes; three volcanoes, two of them extinct, and the third only acting sluggishly, are in sight from Petropavlovsk, and there are others in more distant parts of the peninsula. The underground fires make the earth warmer than it should be for agricultural purposes, and when I landed in Kamchatka, and asked why they did not make their own flour, they told me the summers were too short for the cultivation of spring wheat; and as for winter wheat it was invariably killed, because the warmth of the earth caused it to sprout before the snow melted.

"They have had no severe earthquakes for a long time, but there are several mild shocks every year. When I was there I was invited to dine with the governor; we were about half through with our dinner when there came a shock of an earthquake that threw down the chimney of the house, and shook the building so violently that it nearly overturned the table where we sat. I don't like dining under such circumstances, and we

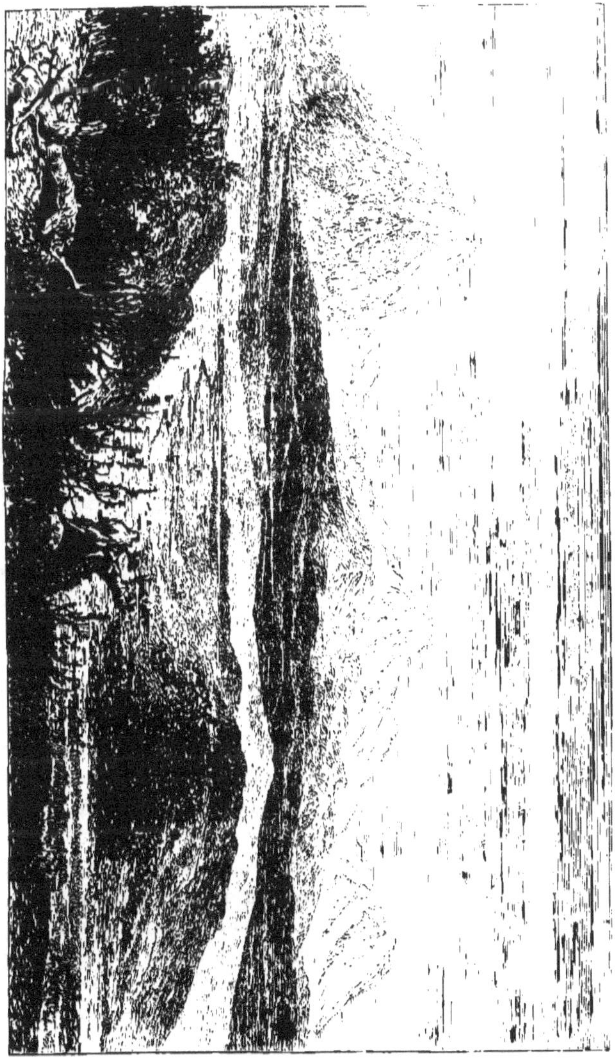

VOLCANOES OF KORIATSKI, AVATCHA, AND KOSELDSKAI.

didn't finish the meal. The governor apologized, and I tried to laugh over the occurrence, but the fact is, I was too scared to do so. The captain of our ship was of the party, and as he lived in San Francisco when not at sea he was able to take things coolly, and declared that he always had an earthquake for the third or fourth course at dinner.

"Petropavlovsk is one of the prettiest places, so far as the situation is concerned, that you ever saw. It is on a great bay, nearly circular and twenty miles across, with an entrance two miles wide from the ocean. The bay is surrounded by mountains, and as you enter it the most majestic of them all is directly in front. The mountain gives its name to the bay, or the bay to the mountain, I don't know which. At all events, the expanse of water is called Avatcha Bay, and the mountain is Avatcha Mountain. It is a magnificent landmark, and can be seen through a clear atmosphere nearly a hundred miles at sea.

"I shall never forget the scene as we entered the bay on a bright morning in July. The tops of the mountains were white with snow; half-way down their sides the color changed to a barren brown, while the base of every hill was covered with a thick growth of forest which half suggested the tropics. The dark green of the forest was in several places relieved by a strip of white beach, which separated it from the waters of the bay, so that altogether the picture had a great deal of variety. Around the bay there are some little harbors — eight in all — completely landlocked, and furnishing admirable shelter to ships that seek them. On one of these harbors Petropavlovsk is situated; the anchorage is enclosed like a pond, and the only winds that a ship has any occasion to fear are the sharp blasts that come down from the mountains.

"We sailed into the great bay with the breeze that was blowing in from the ocean, but as we approached the little harbor it was necessary to move with caution. Our sails were furled one by one, and for the last mile or more we sent a line on shore and were warped to our anchorage. All the population came out to meet us, and our line was grasped by dozens of willing hands. Ordinarily, not more than half a dozen ships enter Petropavlovsk in a year, so that an arrival is an event of importance.

"From the time of Captain Cook and his fellow-explorers Petropavlovsk has been famous for its hospitality, and all travellers who have been there are warm in its praise. Our party was kept in constant activity during our stay, and the number of dinners and parties that were made in our honor is frightful to contemplate. It was in the middle of summer, with the thermometer generally above 70°, and by the end of the first week I was pretty well used up."

Fred asked if Petropavlovsk was a large town, and what it lived upon.

"It is not a large town, from our point of view," responded Dr. Tonner, "but it is the largest in Kamchatka, and is the capital of the peninsula. Before the Crimean War it had nearly two thousand inhabitants, the most of them being laborers and sailors connected with the government service. It was attacked twice by the combined English and French fleets; in the first attack the fleet was repulsed, but in the following year seventeen ships were too much for it and the town was abandoned, and thereby hangs an amusing story.

"The Russian authorities knew of the immense preparations for the second assault, and sent orders for the inhabitants to retire when the fleet arrived, and allow it to land without opposition. The fleet came into Avatcha Bay, and the town was deserted; but the people left behind them their dogs, which they use in winter for dragging their sledges. There was one man, an American, in the town, and more than five hundred dogs.

FORT ST. MICHAEL'S, OR MICHAELOVSKI.

The brutes kept up a perpetual howling, and the commanders of the fleet concluded that there must be a very large garrison in Petropavlovsk to keep so many watch-dogs; and so the seventeen English and French ships waited a whole day before venturing to send a boat on shore to a deserted town! When they did so, they had the consciousness of being beautifully 'sold.'

"The principal business of Kamchatka, in fact the only business amounting to anything, is the fur trade, and the chief contributor of furs is the sable. The animal is caught in a variety of ways, and the annual catch is about six thousand. The *yessak*, or poll-tax, of the natives is payable in sable-skins—one skin to every four persons—and once a year the governor makes the tour of the country and collects the tax. The trade is on the barter principle, as there is very little money in the country; the people bring their furs to the stores of the merchants, and exchange them for whatever commodities they want."

KAMCHATKA SABLES.

George asked if they did not get a good many bear-skins, and the skins of foxes and others, in addition to the sable-skins.

"Yes," replied the Doctor, "they do, but the sable is the animal of greatest consequence. They get about a thousand common fox-skins, and a few silver foxes and sea-otters, and once in a while they get a curiosity in the shape of a black fox.

"The government claims every black fox as the property of the emperor, and when the governor learns that one has been taken he requires it to be surrendered, as a present to his imperial master."

"And does the emperor get it?" one of the youths inquired.

"He is more fortunate than I think he is if he does," said the Doctor, in answer to the question. "Siberian governors are human, and it is not impossible that the skin which should be sent to the emperor is privately sold to an American, or other foreign merchant, and sent out of the country. The emperor is not likely to hear anything about it—and even if he does, the governor can declare that it is a long time since a real black fox was caught.

"The silver fox and the black fox are both liable to be demanded for the emperor," he continued, "and the result is that the governor doesn't usually hear about them. When a native catches a silver fox, or by great good-luck a black one, he conceals the fact, and also the skin. Then he goes to one of the foreign merchants, and pledges him to secrecy before admitting what he has to sell.

"As the merchant has a chance to buy the skin for about half its value, he is easily induced to be silent, especially as he might be compelled to give up the prize if the story should reach the ears of the governor. Thus it happens that the silver and gray foxes do not adorn the neck of the emperor as often as they might, if the subjects of the Imperial Government were better treated. They would be willing to sell it to the government at a fair price, but to give it up for little or nothing is not in accordance with the feelings of human nature."

"But about the bears?" queried George again.

"They have great numbers of bears in Kamchatka," replied the Doctor, "but their skins are not used for exportation. The beasts grow very large, and they are not agreeable companions when one meets them in the woods. The bears are brown or black; I have seen their skins more than six feet long, and been assured that the animals they originally belonged to were not considered at all extraordinary. Bear-hunting is one of the amusements of the country, but there is a good deal of danger to it. I went out on a bear-hunt one day with some friends, a few miles from Petropavlovsk, and was not at all sorry that we returned without seeing any game. I remembered the story of the California hunter who followed the track of a grizzly bear for nearly two days, and then gave it up because it was getting a little too fresh. As long as the bear is far off I enjoy a hunt, which I can't say always when he is close at hand.

"They told me a story of a cow coming home, a year or two before my visit, with a bear on her back. She had made his acquaintance a short distance back of the town, and probably concluded that, as a dutiful cow, she should take him to her master. She was not much hurt by the performance, but it was observed afterwards that she preferred to do her grazing in the vicinity of her own stable. Formerly she had been addicted to wandering in the woods, but her habits were completely changed by her adventure."

The Doctor rambled on with his experiences of Kamchatka till it was time to go to bed. The youths had a good many questions to ask, and were by no means slow to ask them, and before the party broke up they had accumulated knowledge enough for the production of a newspaper article on this odd corner of the world. They learned that the country had an aboriginal population of about six thousand, and less than a thousand Russian inhabitants—the latter being pretty evenly divided between Cossacks and the descendants of exiles. The Doctor explained that there were no exiles in the country, as none had been sent there since 1830, and all these had been pardoned long ago. Hardly any of the original exiles are living at present, but their children are often mentioned as exiles, to distinguish them from the Cossack or native population.

MOUNTED COSSACKS.

"What is a Cossack?" Fred inquired, "and in what does he differ from the soldier and the peasant?"

"I will try to explain," the Doctor answered, "and perhaps the best way for beginning is to compare the Cossack to a militiaman in the United States. He is sort of half soldier, half peasant; he lives with his family, and is engaged in agricultural or other occupations, but is required to give a certain number of days every year to the service of the government. In some parts of Russia the Cossack is required to serve on horseback, providing his own horse and equipments, but this is not the case in Kamchatka. In war he becomes a soldier, and does excellent service in annoying the enemy; in ordinary times he does any kind of work the government may require. He may be called on to row a boat, drive a team, build roads, cut forests, tend the governor's garden, or possibly take his children out to walk.

"To show the authority of the government over the Cossacks I will give you an illustration: In 1856 it was determined to colonize the valley of the Amoor River in Siberia. There was a Cossack population in Eastern Siberia, and the governor-general gave orders that a hundred villages should be transferred to the Amoor.

"The order was carried out without delay. In each case the old village was abandoned for the new one, a thousand miles away; the people, with their household goods, cattle, and other portable possessions, were floated on rafts down the Amoor to the points that had been selected for their homes. In the new village each family found itself with the same neighbors as of old, and everything went on as before. The government supplied them with food, and paid a part of the expense of building new houses, but of course the move was a severe loss to the people, as they abandoned the fields they had cultivated, and were forced to make new ones in the country to which they were carried. The ordinary peasant population of Russia cannot be moved about in this way, but the government can do pretty much as it pleases with the Cossacks."

A VILLAGE ON THE AMOOR RIVER.

"Haven't I read somewhere," said one of the youths, "that a Cossack is a robber?"

"Quite likely you have," was the reply, "and in many cases you are not so far out of the way. In some parts of Russia the Cossacks indulge in robbery to an extent greater than accords with our notions of honesty, and this is particularly the case along the frontier of Central Asia. The word 'kazak' in Turkish means robber, but its Tartar interpretation is the equivalent of soldier. Most of the inhabitants of Eastern Siberia are Cossacks; the whole country was originally explored and settled by Cossacks escaping from punishment which had been decreed for some improper conduct on the banks of the river Don. Their leader, Yermak, received an imperial pardon for himself and his men, in consideration of the addition they had made to the empire, and for this reason the Cossacks of Siberia are naturally proud of their ancestry.

"The Cossack, in many parts of Russia though not in all, has a dress peculiar to himself. He wears a tall hat of sheepskin with the wool outside; sometimes its color is jet black, but more frequently it is of a dingy white, caused by the contact of the wool with a good deal of dirt. He has wide trousers and a flowing coat; he carries his cartridges in a row across his breast, and his arms consist of a lance, a carbine, and, generally, a pair of huge pistols stuck in his waist; if he is a mounted soldier, he has a small but very tough horse. When an army is on the retreat, in Russia, the Cossacks are a terror, as they pick off all the stragglers and make sudden attacks in unexpected places. If you have read the story of Napoleon's retreat from Moscow, you will remember what devastation was caused by the Cossacks during the march."

With this desultory lecture on Kamchatka and its people the evening came to an end.

RUSSIAN CARPENTERS.

CHAPTER V.

A VISIT TO KAMCHATKA.

THERE was a long conference the next morning between Commander Bronson and Captain Jones relative to the movements of the *Vivian.* It was held in the cabin immediately after breakfast, and required frequent consultation of the chart of the North Pacific Ocean. The chart was spread on the table, and several real or imaginary courses of the ship were pencilled upon it.

"We shall have more sailing to do," said the captain, "if we go to Kamchatka instead of steering directly for Behring Strait; but if the wind continues to blow from the north, we shall make better headway by going farther to the west than if we keep directly towards the strait. At present it is almost a head-wind, and by steering more westerly we shall have it on the beam.

"We shall be pretty certain to lose time at the Aleutian Islands on account of the fogs. I have been a week getting through the Oonimak Passage; the fog was so thick I could not get an observation, and it is dangerous to beat around in that region without knowing exactly where you are. I have known ships to be kept there a fortnight, waiting for a good chance to pass the Aleutian Islands. Once, when I was second mate of the *Rover,* we sailed through the passage and were shut in by the fog immediately after. The fog lasted three days, without any wind, and when it lifted we found we had been carried back by the current, and had to make the passage over again."

The captain paused while Commander Bronson made a calculation on a slip of paper. As soon as it was concluded, he went on with the "pros and cons" of the direct and indirect voyages to Behring Strait.

The result of the calculation was, that there would be a loss of about ten days altogether in case the *Vivian* went to Petropavlovsk instead of proceeding directly to the strait. Even with this loss there would be ample time to get into the Arctic Ocean in season to take advantage of the summer; consequently, Commander Bronson decided in favor of the indirect voyage.

The course of the ship was immediately changed, and it was announced to all on board that Petropavlovsk would be their first port.

There were light winds and fogs, fogs and light winds, with now and then a corner of a gale, for the rest of the way across the Pacific. Not a sail was seen, and there was little to break the monotony; occasionally

AVATCHA MOUNTAIN.

the *Vivian* passed through schools of whales; there was hardly a day when she was not surrounded by sea-birds; and several times the youths found their attention drawn to seals swimming close to the track of the ship. The captain said it was not unusual to find these amphibious creatures three or four hundred miles from land. They appear every summer on the Fur Seal Islands, in or near the Aleutian chain, and after raising their families close to the habitations of men they go away, nobody knows where.

One day the captain made his observation at noon, and after figuring out his position, announced that they ought to see Avatcha Mountain about four in the afternoon. At that hour everybody was on the lookout; and not five minutes after eight bells had been struck, the captain pointed out something on the horizon closely resembling a cloud.

"That is Avatcha Mountain," said he, "and it is about eighty miles from us."

It was two or three minutes before George and Fred could determine the position of the mountain, which lay almost dead ahead on their course. Even when they made it out, they were not altogether certain till they compared it with the picture on the chart, and satisfied themselves it was not a conical cloud.

The ship sailed slowly along during the night, and by morning was within twenty miles of the coast. At nine o'clock fires were kindled under the boilers, and by noon they were steaming inside the entrance to the bay, and heading for the anchorage in front of the little town. Captain Jones said that the sailing directions for reaching the harbor were practically the same as made by the officers of Captain Cook's famous expedition more than a century ago. Avatcha Bay and the harbor of Petropavlovsk were surveyed by Lieutenant Bligh, who accompanied Captain Cook, and afterwards became known to the world for his connection with the romantic story of the mutiny of the *Bounty*. "From all accounts," said the captain, "Bligh was an admirable navigator and a detestable brute. He has left a record of splendid seamanship and the most heartless tyranny. The mutiny of the *Bounty* was the natural result of his brutal treatment of her officers and crew, and his escape from the perils of a voyage of four thousand miles in an open boat illustrates his skill as a sailor."

The red roof of the little church at Petropavlovsk was a prominent object in the picture before our friends as the *Vivian* steamed to her anchorage. George brought his glass to bear on the church, and discovered that the building, though crowned with a dome, had no belfry; by looking closely he made out that the bells were hung under a little roof at one end of the church, and quite apart from it. Commander Bronson explained that it was not at all uncommon in Russia for the churches to have their bell-towers entirely apart from the structure. Fred asked the reason for it, but the conundrum was not answered.

The Russian flag floated from the staff in front of the governor's house,

CHURCH AT PETROPAVLOVSK.

and a cannon at the little wharf near by boomed out its welcome. Several
boats put off from shore, the first bringing the Captain of the Port, an
official without whose authority it was impossible to go on shore or do anything else.   He was a portly individual, wearing the uniform of his rank,
and decorated along his breast with a row of stars and crosses. Captain
Jones whispered to the youths that there is no country in the world where
the officers have so many decorations as in Russia, and they need not be
surprised to meet a young lieutenant, hardly out of his majority, wearing
at least half a dozen decorations which had been given for services in time
of peace.   What a war might give him, provided he lived through it, was
hardly to be computed.

As soon as the Captain of the Port had completed his inspection and
retired there was liberty for others to come on board, or for the officers of
the *Vivian* to go on shore.   Two or three resident merchants, and the
captain of an American ship lying at anchor in the harbor, were soon on
her deck to make the acquaintance of the strangers, and invite them to the
hospitalities of the place; last came an officer from a French bark which
lay just beyond the sand-spit marking the entrance of the harbor, and
which Commander Bronson had rightly conjectured to be the craft which

he wished to see. Excusing himself from the others, he turned his attention to the latest visitor, and learned that the Gallic explorer was the bark *Gambetta*, and had arrived only three days before. It was her commander's intention to remain two or three days longer: he had been informed of the voyage of the *Vivian*, and hoped she would visit Petropavlovsk before his departure.

Captain Jones and Major Clapp, with the assistance of the Doctor and our young friends, did the honors to the other visitors, and in a little while the commander went on shore to pay his respects to the governor; he was accompanied by the major and the Doctor. Fred and George embraced the opportunity to have a stroll around the town, and on the hills near the harbor, and we can be sure it was a great pleasure for them to set foot on solid earth after nearly a month on board ship. George declared that his steps were unsteady for the first half mile or so, and Fred could not resist an inclination to adjust himself to meet an expected rolling or pitching every time he raised a foot.

DOG-SLEDGING IN KAMCHATKA.

But they soon forgot all about their month at sea with the novelty of the sights around them. They realized what they had been told of the dogs of the place, as they encountered some of those animals at every turn, and were rarely out of sound of their howls. They did not have a high opinion of the courage of the dogs, as the most of them ran away as soon as they caught sight of the strangers; occasionally one would stop a moment to gaze, but he generally concluded to put a good distance between himself and possible harm. Near the edge of the town a dozen or more dogs were tied to a long pole supported on posts. Fred said the place was either a stable or a dog boarding-house, and he was inclined to the latter opinion from the smell of fish that rose from it.

One of the resident merchants who had visited them at the ship joined them in their promenade, and explained some of the things they could not understand. Fred asked about the dogs, and the gentleman said his theory was correct. "The dogs," said he, "are generally tied up in summer, or kept in pens; if allowed to run at large they get lost or injured, as they are fond of fighting and can get into a quarrel without half trying. We tie them up as you saw them, and each dog gets one fish daily as his ration. In New York it would be extravagant to feed dogs on salmon, but here it is the cheapest article of food. The only cost of salmon is the trouble of catching it. When we buy these fish we pay two or three cents apiece, and if I agreed to take all that would be caught, and pay one cent each, I should have half the population at work for me. Ordinarily, in winter, there are about two thousand dogs in and around Petropavlovsk, as everybody has his dog-team, and many of us keep several teams for carrying freight. In summer most of the dogs are sent to the country, so that there are only four or five hundred of them around here at present.

"This place is just like New York," he continued. "The fashionable part of the population passes the summer in the country or by the sea-side. Board is cheaper there than here, as the streams in the interior abound in salmon; sometimes they are so thick that they fill up the stream altogether and drive out the water, and a friend of mine says he has walked on them as on a pile of shingles or a heap of potatoes!

"Perhaps you may think that statement is too strong, and I won't dispute you; but they really are so abundant that the bears and dogs catch their own fish out of the brooks, and the bears soon get so dainty that they will only eat the backs of those they catch. The fish keep on going up the stream till their tails are worn off against the rocks, and I have repeatedly seen them taken from the water with nothing but the bone protruding where the tail ought to be!

"And perhaps you may be sceptical about the dogs catching their own fish? Look there!"

As he spoke he pointed to where a couple of dogs were standing in the water at the edge of the bay, and evidently waiting for something to turn up. They were so far out that little more than their backs were visible, and they held their noses just on a level with the surface of the water. They were standing perfectly motionless, like sporting-dogs on a "point," and the gentleman said they were foraging for their breakfast and waiting for salmon.

Suddenly one of the dogs darted his head under water with the rapidity of a flash, and there was a lively commotion for a minute or more. It ended in favor of the dog, who came up triumphant with a salmon of his own catching in his jaws, and brought him safely to shore.

DOGS CATCHING FISH.

"Even the cows and horses eat salmon," said their guide, "but they never imitate the example of the dogs, and catch their own food. It is proper to explain that they prefer grass, and generally stick to it when it can be obtained. We give them dried salmon in winter, and if we run short of hay they soon get accustomed to this odd food. There is one cow here that will leave grass in summer and make a meal off fresh salmon; but she is an exception, and not a rule.

"We feed the dogs on fish the whole year round; they eat it in every shape—fresh, dry, putrid, boiled, smoked, or any other form you can imagine. One fish a day is a dog's ration; when he is travelling he only gets half that amount, and the day before he starts on a journey he gets nothing at all."

"It seems cruel to treat them so," one of the youths remarked, "but of course you know from experience what is best for them."

"Yes," was the reply. "When I first came here I thought it was very hard on the dogs to be only half fed while at work, and determined to treat mine differently; but I soon found I did not get so much out of them. They did not travel as fast and far as teams that were kept in the old way, were sooner broken down, and were in worse condition when the summer came around again, so I concluded to do for the future as the natives did.

"Perhaps you've heard enough about dogs?" he continued, "and if so, we'll talk about something else."

George assured him that they had not begun to get enough of the subject, as they were likely to make an intimate acquaintance with dogs in their arctic expedition, and the sooner they knew about them the better.

"Well, then," said their informant, "let me give you a piece of advice at the outset. When you get among the dogs, and are going to use them for travel, the first thing to do is to make their intimate acquaintance. You must feed them yourself, and give them all the care they require: have them understand that you are their master in every sense of the word. When they do wrong, don't fail to punish them at once; and when they do well, you must be just as prompt to reward them. You won't be able to get up much affection for them, and they will obey you more from fear than from love. They have treacherous dispositions, and are not usually capable of warm attachments. You know what a reputation the spitz dog bears in New York and elsewhere; well, the spitz is first cousin to the Kamchadale dog, and his name comes from Spitzbergen, whence his ancestors were imported. He has improved by domestication, but is yet the most undesirable of family dogs.

"You must drive your own dogs as well as feed them, and when you begin to practice dog-driving you will find it is no sport. The dogs will take the first and every opportunity to run away. We harness them with thongs of deer-skin, and they go in pairs with a leader, so that a team always consists of an odd number. A great deal depends on the leader; he is selected for his intelligence and docility, and a good leader is worth four or five times as much as an ordinary team-dog. He turns to the right or left at the order of his driver, and frequently when the team is tired out, and drags slowly along, the leader will rouse them by barking, and pretending that he is on the track of a wild animal. This will stir them up, and the brutes forget their weariness in the excitement of the chase.

"There are two kinds of sledges that we use, one for travel and the other for freight. The travelling sledge weighs about twenty-five pounds, and is just large enough to carry one person with a little baggage. The driver sits with his feet hanging over the side, and clings to a bow that rises in front. In one hand he holds an iron-pointed staff called an *ostoll*, which he uses as a brake to retard the sledge while descending hills, or to bring it to a halt. If you drop the *ostoll* the dogs know it as quickly as you do, and take the opportunity to run away or upset the sledge, and even the leader is apt to join in the sport.

"The freight sledge is much heavier than the other, and sometimes as many as twenty-one dogs are harnessed to it. The team for a freight sledge is not trained to high speed like the travelling team, and it is never well to allow your travelling dogs to be used for freighting purposes, as it is very hard to get them to run rapidly when they have once practised a slower gait. An ordinary team for travelling is five dogs—two pairs and a leader—but very often we use only three dogs in a team."

GETTING READY FOR THE ROAD.

Fred asked how fast the dogs could travel, and what distances they usually made in a day.

"That depends on the length of the journey and the condition of the snow," was the reply. "For a week or ten days we are satisfied with forty or fifty miles a day, if the snow is good, and for two or three days' travel under the same conditions we make fifty or sixty miles daily. I have gone a hundred miles in little more than a day with a single team, and once a team travelled from Bolcheretsk to Petropavlovsk—a hundred and twenty-five miles—in twenty-three hours. It made three or four halts of not more than fifteen minutes each time. The snow was excellent, and the dogs were in the very best condition, while the driver was a small man and had no baggage of any kind. He was a messenger bringing news of the declaration of the Crimean War.

"We don't use the dogs for sledging in summer, as I told you before, but occasionally some of the natives harness them up for towing boats along the shore of the bay just to keep them in practice."

BOAT TOWED BY DOGS.

He pointed, as he spoke, to a boat which was coming along the shore, and the youths saw that it was propelled in the manner described. Four persons were in the boat, one of whom steered it, while another attended to the tow-line; two others were seated nearly amidships, and evidently had nothing to do with the management of the craft. The team was walking along the bank, under the guidance of a man armed with a stick, and whenever they showed a disposition to lag he impelled them forward with his voice and occasional blows.

George said it was certainly a novel mode of travelling, and a reminder of the old days of going west by canal.

"In North-eastern Siberia," said their guide, " they use dogs for ascending the rivers in summer in the way you see. From Ghijiga light-house to the village of that name they follow the river a part of the way, and the journey is not at all disagreeable. Occasionally the path shifts from one bank of the stream to the other, and then the dogs and driver are taken in the boat to be ferried over. At such times the dogs amuse themselves by shaking the mud and water from their shaggy coats, and it is well for a passenger to wear his worst clothes on such journeys.

"The best dogs in Siberia are in the neighborhood of Ghijiga and around Penjinsk Gulf, which is an arm of the Okhotsk Sea. Most of the Russians buy their dogs from the natives, and there are several villages where the raising of these animals is the main business. Like everything else of value that we use, the price is regulated by the laws of supply and demand; sometimes dogs are very cheap, and at others very dear."

Fred asked if the dogs of Kamchatka were subject to the same diseases as the canines of civilized life.

"Quite as much," said their informant; "and perhaps we may say that they are more so. They suffer greatly from hydrophobia, and every few years thousands of them are carried off by epidemics. The cause of these epidemics is unknown, and it has happened that all the dogs in a village will die off in the course of a fortnight without any apparent reason. Some of the native tribes make sacrifices to their deities, and invariably take their best dogs for the purpose. We have tried to convince them that the old and useless, or even the dead dogs, would do just as well, but they refuse to believe us. They show their faith in the power of the evil spirits by offering up the best of their possessions."

George asked if there were any reindeer around Petropavlovsk, and said if there were he would like to see them.

"We don't have reindeer in these parts," was the reply. "You will see plenty of them on the shores of the Arctic Ocean when you have passed Behring Strait. They are the principal possession of the Chuckchees, the tribe that occupies that part of the country; and when you ask how much a man is worth, they state the amount in reindeer, just as you state it in dollars in New York."

Then the conversation shifted to a variety of topics. The youths learned that the place was named Petropavlovsk in honor of saints Peter and Paul, but they could not ascertain how it happened to have two names when one would have been quite enough. As before stated, it had nearly two thousand inhabitants previous to the Crimean War, but since that time the government has transferred its arsenal and naval depot to Nicolayeff and Vladivostok, farther to the south, and the port of St. Peter and St. Paul is shorn of its importance. It now has about three hundred inhabitants, including a garrison of fifty soldiers and half a dozen officials.

In the grounds of the residence of the Captain of the Port there is a monument in honor of Vitus Behring, whose name is preserved in the strait between America and Asia. On a tongue of land is another monu-

MONUMENT TO BEHRING, PETROPAVLOVSK.

ment, but without an inscription; it is known as the monument to La Perouse, and the story goes that a French ship-of-war was once at Petropavlovsk, and her captain was invited to dine with the governor. During dinner the Frenchman said he supposed there was a monument there to La Perouse, as that navigator visited the place on the voyage which resulted in the destruction of his ships and their entire company.

"Certainly there is," answered the Russian, "and I will show it to you to-morrow."

He had the monument made and set up during the night. The next morning he invited the French captain to go with him to see it. Of course the latter was delighted, and it is to be hoped he did not observe the newness of the construction. The memorial to Behring was paid for by the officers of a Russian ship, and was made in St. Petersburg; the other is of sheet-iron, nailed over a frame of wood, and was evidently constructed in a few hours. Fred remarked that it was riddled with bullet-holes, and learned that it was a favorite target for the practice of anybody who chose to take a shot at it.

For the next two or three days the strangers had an excellent opportunity to learn the extent of Russian hospitality, which has been already mentioned. There was an endless succession of breakfasts, dinners, luncheons, and suppers; and on the latter occasions it was not unusual for the party to sit down at the table considerably past midnight. Not only did they have all the meals above enumerated, but whenever they entered a Russian house, no matter how humble, and remained more than five minutes, they were greeted with a steaming tea-urn and cups or glasses of tea. Here is the diary made by George of the repasts of a single day:

> " Breakfast on board ship.
>   Two cups of tea with Mr. Pfluger.
>   One cup of tea with Mr. Pierce.
>   Do.   do.   with Captain Hunter.
>   Do.   do.   at a Russian house (owner's name unpronounceable.)
>   Do.   do.   do.   do.   do.   do.   do.
>   Luncheon with the Captain of the Port.
>   Cup of tea at each of three houses where we called.
>   Dinner at the governor's house.
>   Tea at intervals of fifteen minutes during the evening.
>   Supper of broiled partridges at 11.30.
>   More tea.
>   P. S.—Headache next morning."

One day there was a picnic arranged by the ladies and gentlemen of
Petropavlovsk for the entertainment of the visitors. The latter included,
in addition to our friends, the officers of the *Gambetta* and the officers of
an American merchant-ship then in port. The entertainment was held in
a little grove about a mile from town—a short distance from the spot
where the Russians repulsed the men that landed from the allied fleet
during the Crimean War. The picnickers sat on the grass under the trees,
after the custom of picnics all over the world, and our friends voted that
they had a jolly time.

George said it might be called a polyglot picnic, on account of the
nationalities represented. The entertainers were Russians and Americans,
while the guests were Americans and French, with the addition of an
Italian, a Swede, and a Dane. Conversation was somewhat restricted, as
none of the American or French visitors were fluent in Russian, and several of the entertainers could speak nothing else. But what they lacked
in lingual facility was made up in good-will, and there was many a hearty
laugh over the difficulties of being understood. George and Fred made a
mental note of the strange dishes at the feast, though they had already
seen most of them at the dinner-tables of their hosts. There were several *pirogs*, or pies, quite unknown to the American table, and some of
them were voted excellent. One was made of salmon and eggs, with a
crust above and below; another was composed of the marrow of the backbone of the sturgeon; while a third was filled with partridges, cut in
halves and alternated with slices of bacon. Of course they had tea in
abundance, and it was accompanied by numerous odds and ends of cakes
and patties, so that there was no danger of any one going away hungry.
In fact, when they returned to the ship for dinner all our friends confessed
their inability to do justice to the repast which their cook had prepared.

A return entertainment was given on board the *Vivian*, and another on the *Gambetta*, the latter vessel sailing a few hours after the last of her guests had left. The next day the *Vivian* followed her example, and continued her voyage to the northward. They passed the rocks known as "The Three Brothers," in front of the light-house at the entrance of Avatcha Bay, and were once more on the broad waters of the Pacific. The fires were extinguished, and as the ship spread her sails to the favoring wind Fred made a hasty sketch of the rocks, as a souvenir of his visit to a remote but exceedingly friendly port.

"THE THREE BROTHERS."

CHAPTER VI.

BEHRING'S ISLAND AND BEHRING'S VOYAGES.—AMONG THE CHUCKCHEES.

SAILING north from Avatcha Bay the *Vivian* passed Behring's Island, in the Sea of Kamchatka. The name of the island naturally caused the youths to ask several questions concerning it, and they were promptly answered by Dr. Tonner.

"In that island," said the Doctor, as he pointed to one of its rocky headlands, "the brave old navigator after whom it was named died and was buried, but the location of his grave is unknown. He deserves much renown for his arctic explorations, and is worthy of additional fame, as he is one of the discoverers of America."

Fred and George were not a little surprised at this announcement, as they had never heard the name of Behring associated with that of Columbus or Americus Vespucius. The Doctor went on with his story, which was about as follows:

"Peter the Great formed a project for making discoveries in the ocean beyond Kamchatka, and several explorers were sent to the eastern part of Asia with that object in view. Very little was accomplished in the lifetime of that monarch, but his plans were carried out by his successors.

THE ERMINE.

"Behring sailed from Avatcha Bay in June, 1741, and steered to the eastward. 'On the 16th of July,' says Steller, the historian and naturalist who accompanied Behring, 'we saw a mountain whose height was so great that it was visible at the distance of sixteen Dutch miles. The coast of the continent was much broken, and indented with bays and harbors.'

"This discovery was made on the day of St. Elias, and accordingly the mountain was named in honor of that saint. If you wish to become familiar with its location you can look for Mount St. Elias on the map of North America.

"Behring sailed a short distance along the coast, and visited several islands. Then he steered for Kamchatka; but it was his destiny never to get there. In the latter part of the voyage he was confined to his cabin by illness, and the crew suffered severely from scurvy. Steller says that at one time only ten persons were fit for duty, and they were so weak that

A SIBERIAN FOX-TRAP.

they could not furl the sails. The ship was thus left almost at the mercy of the winds, and in this condition it was drifted on a rocky island — the one now before us. It was dashed to pieces on the rocks, but not until all the crew had reached the land in safety.

"There were no human inhabitants on the island, but there were a great many foxes, and they seemed to have no fear of the shipwrecked mariners. Steller says, 'We killed many of them with our hatchets and knives. They annoyed us greatly, and we were unable to keep them from entering our shelters and stealing our clothing and food.'

"Many of the crew died soon after they got on shore, but on the whole the life on land seems to have diminished the ravages of scurvy among those who were not already far gone with the disease. Behring died on the 8th of December, and was buried in the trench where he lay. The survivors of the party built a small vessel from the pieces of the wreck, and managed to reach Avatcha Bay with it. On their arrival they learned that they had been given up for dead, and the property they had left in Kamchatka had been appropriated by strangers.

"The report of the large number of fur-bearing animals on Behring's

Island and elsewhere stimulated several adventurers to fit out expeditions in the hope of making a handsome profit. The ships were built in Kamchatka, or in the ports of the Okhotsk Sea; they were of the rudest construction, the timbers being fastened with wooden pins, owing to the scarcity or entire absence of metal nails, and in some cases they were tied together with leathern thongs. The crevices were calked with moss, the sails were of reindeer skins, and the rigging was made of thongs of the same material. A good many of these ships were wrecked, but others made the voyage safely and brought back loads of furs.

"Out of these expeditions grew the Russian-American Company, which received the administration and control of North-western America, and had the exclusive right to the commerce of a vast territory. The company occupied Russian America and the Aleutian and Kurile Islands, and pushed its traffic into the Arctic Ocean. It had a monopoly of trade, law, and everything else; it reduced the inhabitants to a condition little better than slavery, by compelling them to labor for the company at any time they were wanted, and at whatever prices the company chose to pay, and it managed to control them by keeping them always in debt.

"The company's centre of operations was at Sitka, but it was not established without considerable opposition by the natives. At one time the natives were victorious; the Russians were driven from Sitka, and the fort they had erected was destroyed. But the invaders came back and established themselves firmly; complaints of their tyranny and abuses reached St. Petersburg, and a commission was sent to investigate them. After that time affairs went along more smoothly, the profits from the trade in furs were large, and the company made fine dividends. But the fur-bearing animals, principally the fur seal, were killed off too rapidly, the profits diminished, the company's affairs ran down, and finally its title was extinguished, and the country was sold by Russia to the United States.

"There, you have a whole page of history," said the Doctor, "and it all grew out of our interest in the island we are passing. Perhaps you knew it before, but a repetition will do no great harm. Sitka is now an American town, and the flag of the United States floats over the former residence of the Russian governor, on a high rock at the foot of Mount Edgecombe. The fur trade is in the hands of an American company, which is said to make much larger dividends to its stockholders than the old Russian company was ever able to give."

"But what is Alaska good for, now that we have it?" was the very natural and practical query of one of the youths.

"That question was very freely discussed at the time we bought the country," the Doctor answered. "We acquired a good deal of ice, polar bears, and similar property with our purchase, and as an investment of money it is doubtful if the speculation was a profitable one. From a patriotic point of view it was better, as it gave us a large area of territory and removed the possibility of trouble between ourselves and Russia at some future time. It is a protection to the fisheries in the North Pacific Ocean, and since the purchase they have grown to considerable importance. Gold has been discovered in several places, but gold mining can hardly be carried on with profit, on account of the long winters and the deep snows that lie on the ground for so large a part of the year. It is possible that some exceptionally rich mines may be found, similar to those in Siberia, but up to the present time they have not been discovered.

"But the American eagle can scream more loudly than before we bought Alaska, as there is more for him to scream about; and as the lungs of that bird require to be well exercised, we are not so badly off as we might be in the possession of this frigid region."

It was arranged between the commanders of the *Vivian* and the *Gambetta* that the ships would meet at East Cape, the most north-easterly point of Asia, and forming one side of Behring Strait. Each was to make a direct course under sail, and the first at the rendezvous would wait three days for the other before proceeding. In case of her departure she would leave a memorandum where it could be found by the other. There was usually a summer encampment of Chuckchees at that point, but they could not be relied on to be there; in case there should be such an encampment, the memorandum would be intrusted to its chief.

There was no incident of consequence during the voyage from Petropavlovsk to East Cape, but there was enough to do in reading up the history of arctic research, and observing the peculiarities of the high northern latitude, to prevent time hanging heavy on the hands of our young friends. Every hour they were coming nearer to the Polar Circle; the days lengthened, till it seemed as though there would soon be no night, the air was perceptibly cooler, the sea-birds were more numerous than in the direct voyage across the Pacific, whales and seals abounded in the waters, and the shore, whenever they passed near enough to discern its character, was a scene of desolation. Entering the strait and passing around the cape, the captain said they were within the Arctic Circle, and had reached the regions of the midnight sun.

The *Gambetta* was at anchor in a little bay, sheltered from all winds except from the north and east; on the shore was an encampment of

SITKA, OR NEW ARCHANGEL.

natives, and in the waters around the *Gambetta* several of the native boats were plying.

As soon as the *Vivian* had dropped her anchor Commander Bronson and Major Clapp went on board the *Gambetta*, while Dr. Tonner, with Fred and George, proceeded to the shore. The youths were anxious to visit the native village, and the good Doctor was by no means loath to accompany them.

A Chuckchee boat preceded them, and on the way to the shore George made a sketch of the strange craft. Arrived at the land, the native boat was drawn up along-side their own, and the youths examined it critically.

Here is the description which George entered in his note-book:

"The Chuckchee boat is unlike anything I ever saw in the waters around New York. Its native name is *bydara*, and it consists of a frame-work of wood, over which a covering of deer-skins is stretched. The skins are sewn together very tightly, and, when properly made and handled, these boats are said to leak very rarely. In getting into the boat you must be careful not to step on the bottom, or you might put your foot through the skins, which are often kept in use until quite tender.

"They have a short mast, carrying a square sail which is also made from deer-skins, unless the owner is lucky enough to get a piece of old canvas from a whaling ship. On each side of the *bydara* they generally carry a seal-skin blown up like a bladder and securely fastened to the boat at each end; these seal-skins serve to buoy the craft in case she heels over from the effect of the wind or the waves, or is tipped by the clumsy movement of an occupant.

"They carry heavy burdens in these boats, and venture fearlessly out into the open sea. Occasionally they cross to the North American continent for the purpose of trading with the Eskimos, but their favorite plan is to meet the Eskimos on Diomede Island, about midway between the continents, so that neither is within the territory of the other."

Lying on the bank not far from the boat was an inflated seal-skin, attached to a line ten or twelve feet long; the other end of the line was tied to a harpoon, and the youths naturally wondered what was the use of the apparatus.

"That is what they use for catching walrus and whales," said the Doctor. "The way they do it is this:

"They fill the boat with as many men as it will hold, and in addition to their paddles they carry long slips of whalebone, which are flat at the end like a piece of board. They paddle to the spot where a walrus has been seen to dive, and then half the men pound on the water with the whale-bones in such a way as to make a peculiar cracking sound. This rouses the curiosity of the walrus, and he comes up to see what it all means. If they are near enough to throw the harpoon it is darted by the man in the bow; another in the middle of the boat polses the seal-skin and throws it simultaneously with the harpoon. If they are lucky enough to hit the walrus he drags the seal-skin after him as he dives; it pulls steadily on the harpoon, and after a while brings him to the surface, where he gets another harpoon, and then another and another.

A CHUCKCHEE BOAT.

"The old adage that 'it is the first step which costs,' is well illustrated by the Chuckchee mode of catching the walrus. A great many efforts are made to get the *first* harpoon into him, and sometimes a whole day will be passed in continuous failures. But when a harpoon is properly fastened into one of these animals he can be easily traced by the floating seal-skin, and the rest of the job is comparatively easy."

"And did you say they catch whales in the same way?" one of the youths asked.

"Certainly," was the reply, "but they need a great many floats to hold him up, so that he cannot dive. It is only when a whale or a walrus is prevented from diving by the number of floats attached to him, that they can lance and kill him. Half a dozen will suffice for an ordinary walrus, and a dozen for a large one, but in the case of a whale a great many are needed. He has to be stuck full of harpoons, and the seal-skins and bladders almost hide his body from sight. The capture of a whale is a matter of great importance to this people, as you will realize when you know something of their habits and mode of life."

While our friends were examining the boat, and talking about it, they were surrounded by a group of natives, who looked at them with a good deal of curiosity, but without any rudeness of manner. They wore a dress of deer-skins from which the hair had been stripped. Dr. Tonner explained to the youths that this was the summer costume, the clothing for winter being much heavier and lined with fur. The costume was a simple one, as it consisted of a tunic, like a shirt, which came nearly to the knee, while the lower limbs were encased in garments which fitted rather more closely than the trousers of civilization.

Fred noticed that all the strangers had the crown of the head shaven smooth, and asked the Doctor if they were members of a priestly order. Dr. Tonner replied that it is the custom of this people, and also of some other tribes in Siberia, to shave the head, and they are very careful in its observance. Why they did so he could not say, except that it was the fashion. Fashion rules as imperiously among savages all over the world as in the extreme of civilization, and whatever she commands is obeyed. A Chuckchee would no more think of rebelling against the shaving practices of his tribe than would a society man of New York venture to disregard the rules of etiquette prevailing in that city.

"They have strange customs relative to the disposal of their old and infirm people," said the Doctor. "According to the statements of several who have been among them, they have a practice of killing the aged members of their tribe, and the curious thing about it is, that the victims are always entirely reconciled to being thus put away, and the sacrifice is generally at their request. There seems to be no doubt that such is the case; one gentleman (Mr. Richard J. Bush), who has written a book about this country, visited a spot where one of these executions was about to take place."

"Did he stay to witness it?" George inquired.

"Not by any means," replied the Doctor — "partly because he was greatly disinclined to do so, and partly because the natives did not seem willing to go on with the ceremony in the presence of a stranger. When you go back to the ship you had better read what Mr. Bush tells on the subject."

George promised to do so, and faithfully kept his promise. Here is what he read, on page 439 of " Reindeer, Dogs, and Snowshoes : "

"During one of our visits to the lower end of the bay we saw quite a large group of natives assembled at a spot on the rugged mountain-side, about half a mile back of the village, and being

WALRUS-HUNTING AMONG THE CHECKCHEES.

curious to know what they were about, a boat was lowered and a party of us started for shore. We had to make an ascent of a few hundred feet over the loose, jagged fragments of rock, and it was not without some difficulty that we reached the place. On all sides, scattered over the rocks, were crushed human skulls and other bones, and we at once decided that this was the spot where they killed the old and disabled of their tribe. Our first impression was that we were to witness one of these acts of barbarity, and I confess to a feeling of reluctance and sick-heartedness as we approached the group; but their lively chattering and occasional laughter disarmed our suspicions.

"There were about forty persons present, from old men and women down to mere babes, all of whom appeared to be in the best of spirits. We thought they were about to make an offering to their gods, and calling aside Naukum, one of the natives who had learned to speak a little English from intercourse with whalers and traders, we began to question him about it. Pointing to one in the group, he replied, 'See old man—no got eyes—bimeby kill um.' Looking where he pointed, we beheld an old blind man seated upon a rock among the other natives, but his face wore an expression of such perfect calmness and unconcern that I looked elsewhere to find the victim, thinking I was mistaken in the person pointed to. No one was showing him any kind of attention, neither was there anything in his appearance, nor in the actions of his companions, to lead to the suspicion that he was so soon to be ushered into the next world. . . .

"We had some difficulty in making out Naukum's explanation of the matter, but at length comprehended that it was by the old man's request they were going to kill him. He had plenty of deer, and was beyond want, but the previous year he had lost his only son, whom he loved very much, since which time life had become a burden to him, and he wanted his tribe to put him out of existence. The day had been once before fixed, but his little grandson begged so piteously that the old man consented to live for his grandson's sake. But he had again changed his mind, and his wishes were now about to be gratified."

The natives were unwilling to proceed with the sacrifice until the white men had gone; the latter had no desire to remain, and consequently returned to their boat. Naukum afterwards said the old man again postponed his execution out of deference to the wishes of his grandson, but Mr. Bush thought the tribe wished to defer it till after the ships had left the bay.

From where they landed our friends walked back a hundred yards or so to the crest of a ridge, where the natives had their summer residence. The group that had surrounded them walked with them and kept up a continual chattering and laughter, not at all in accordance with the solemnity of many savage tribes. Dr. Tonner explained to the youths that the Chuckchees are generally friendly with the whites, but sometimes they have trouble with whalers and other traders, growing out of disputes in commercial transactions. As far as can be ascertained, the fault is quite as much that of the white men as of the natives, and generally a good deal more so.

The natives have been demoralized by the whalers, who sell them ardent spirits in exchange for furs, whalebone, walrus-ivory, and other commodities. The use of fire-water leads to trouble, and it is a great pity that it cannot be suppressed altogether. Apropos of this subject, a good

SCENERY NEAR EAST CAPE.

story is told by the officers of the expedition that was in North-eastern Siberia in 1865–66, endeavoring to build a telegraph line from Europe to America by way of Asia.

One party was landed near Behring Strait, and another at Ghijiga, near the head of the bay of that name, and on the northern shore of the Okhotsk Sea. During the winter the natives brought a report to Ghijiga that there was a party of white men near Behring Sea who burned black stones in a box, and had the most wonderful whiskey ever known.

The party at Ghijiga joined the other towards the end of winter, and through all the journey across North-eastern Siberia the principal news that came to them was the astonishment of the natives at the wonderful whiskey in the possession of the white men. Nothing of the kind had ever been seen before; the liquid which the whalers sold was of no consequence whatever in comparison with the new sort.

The sequel was interesting. It turned out that when the party landed the natives began at once to beg for whiskey. Their demand was refused, and they were told the white men had not brought any of the vile stuff. To refute this assertion the natives pointed to several barrels that had been piled in the camp, and were known to be full of liquid of some kind or other. To put an end to their demands, some of it was given to them.

The natives drank and were delighted; they had heard of the white man's beverage called fire-water, but never before had they found the genuine article. Certainly this was the fire-water they had heard of; there could be no doubt of its character, as it burned and blistered their throats, and a little of it went a great way. This whiskey, that became so famous through the land, was nothing more than very strong pepper-sauce, which was intended for the preservation of meat.

Dr. Tonner told the youths there was a curious custom among the Chuckchees which was not likely to be adopted in America or England—certainly not in a hurry. He had been told that when a Chuckchee trader, on a voyage to or from the Diomede Islands, or elsewhere, was caught in a storm and found it necessary to lighten his boat, he proceeded to throw overboard the crew instead of the cargo. Goods are valuable, and cannot be dropped into the sea without loss, but men are abundant, and a fresh crew can be engaged at any time. The Doctor further stated that his informant said the men made no objection to this novel process of salvage, but went over the side of the boat when ordered, under the full conviction that they were simply discharging their duty to their employer.*

At the edge of the village several men were at work on the erection of a house, and of course George and Fred stopped to have a look at them. Though the men were interesting, the house was a great deal more so, as it was of a material entirely new to the young travellers.

"You remember I told you how valuable the whale is to the Chuckchees," said the Doctor. "This house illustrates what I was saying."

The frame of the house was made of ribs of the whale and walrus, and a good deal of ingenuity was shown in arranging it. Two or three poles of wood that had been brought from Kamchatka, or some region far to the south, served to support the ends of the ribs and other bones that formed the sides, while the covering of the roof was kept in place by long strips of whalebone. One by one the bones were put in their places, and then the covering was stretched over it. The latter was like a piece of patchwork on an American quilt; it was composed principally of deer-skins, but there were a good many sections of walrus hide among them, and one or two strips of sail which had been begged or otherwise obtained from the whalers that frequent this region. This covering serves its purpose admirably, though it is apt to let in water in case of a long rain; it is fastened carefully, to prevent its disappearing in the *poorgas*, or high winds, that prevail in these northern latitudes.

---

* This story was told in all seriousness to the writer of this volume by Governor Bilzukavitch, at Ghijiga, in 1866, and was confirmed by another Russian official present at the interview.

Dr. Tonner said the Chuckchee house was not a comfortable one for a European, but it met fully all the desires of the natives. On the score of ventilation there was much to be desired, as there was no chimney, and the best exit for the smoke was through a hole in the roof. Sometimes it is necessary to close even this hole, on account of the weather, and then the smoke has a hard time in getting out. The natives live, without apparent inconvenience, in an atmosphere that would stifle a civilized being in half an hour.

ERECTING A CHUCKCHEE SUMMER-HOUSE.

A short distance back of the village a herd of reindeer was grazing, and after a glance at the house our friends went in their direction. They were scattered over a considerable area, under the watchful eyes of several natives who kept them from straying.

Nearly all were standing, and while some continued to pluck the moss and other vegetation from the ground, others raised their heads and gave an inquiring look at the strangers. One old deer, with a magnificent pair of antlers, was lying on the ground in the front of the group, and retained his position with an air of content and independence.

"The reindeer is even more important to these people than the whale," said the Doctor, "at least to the majority of them. The whale can only be taken in summer, but the reindeer is with them through the whole year; his skin supplies the material for clothing, and for the coverings of the tents, his flesh is an important article of food, his bones form the handles of knives and the heads of lances, his sinews are an excellent substitute for thread, and his antlers are used for the runners and frame-work of the sledges.

"Deer are the circulating medium of the country, and values are reckoned in them; a man with a hundred deer is in comfortable circumstances, one with five hundred is 'well to do,' and one with a thousand looks complacently on the future. When we go beyond a thousand we are among the nabobs or millionaires, though the latter are not fairly reached till we pass ten thousand. The wealthiest native of North-western Siberia is the owner of forty thousand deer; he is regarded as a Vanderbilt or an Astor by his neighbors, and takes quite as much pleasure in life as do the heads of the families I have just named."

"What an enormous herd of deer!" said one of the youths. "Forty thousand together! I should like to see them."

"It is doubtful if you ever have the opportunity," replied Dr. Tonner, "and I hardly believe the owner has ever seen them together. Where a man has a very great number of deer he divides them into herds of a thousand or twelve hundred each, and then scatters them over a large area of country. He is obliged to do this in order to find pasturage for them; if they were all assembled in a single drove it would be very difficult to support them."

George asked what was the food of the reindeer. The Doctor replied that the animal fed in summer on the scanty grass and shrubs that grow in the valleys of the streams, and in the portions of the *tundras* or plains that are least exposed; in winter he lives altogether on moss, which he searches for beneath the snow, and displays a wonderful instinct in finding it. Nature has adapted his nose to turning the snow in search of food, and when he digs for moss he rarely fails to get it.

George wanted to mount one of the deer and take a ride. The Doctor explained his wishes as well as he could to the natives in charge of the herd, and one of them ran off to his tent and brought a saddle, and also a long staff like a stout broom-handle.

The saddle was placed across the back of one of the animals, just behind his shoulders; it was a pad like an ordinary racing saddle, but very roughly made and without stirrups. George thought the man had forgotten the stirrups, and motioned for him to go back for them, but the Doctor explained that they were not used in riding the reindeer.

Both the youths shook their heads at the prospect of being mounted in this fashion. While they hesitated, the native took the staff in one hand to support himself and then swung into the saddle; the instant he was seated the animal started off for a graceful circuit of a hundred yards

A GROUP OF REINDEER.

or so, and then came back to the starting-point. The native dismounted, and George endeavored to imitate his movements.

He supported himself with the staff, as he had seen the native do, and then vaulted into the saddle; the result was that he went over, and fell on the other side, more to Fred's amusement than his own. He repeated the effort with no better success, and as Fred continued to laugh at his misfortunes, George resigned in the latter's favor.

Fred did exactly what George had done, and then the laugh was the other way. Then the native assisted him for a few moments, and as soon as the youth could find his balance he got along very well. Dr. Tonner explained that nearly every novice in mounting a deer goes over to the other side, and for the first day or so he spends most of his time in falling off. The back of the deer is very weak, and consequently the weight of rider or other burden must be placed over the shoulders; a weight of fifty pounds, placed as a horse is loaded, would permanently disable a strong reindeer.

The shoulders of the deer slide against each other as the animal walks, and this makes the pad sway from one side to the other at every step. As the rider has no stirrups he must keep his balance or run the risk of falling off, and to prevent this he uses the *polka* or staff. Many persons on beginning their experience with reindeer use two of these *polkas*, one on each side, but even with this protection they get a good many falls. The *polka* has a bag or net of deer thongs at the lower end to keep it from sinking too deep in the snow; the foot of the deer spreads out as he steps on snow or on marshy soil, and is evidently admirably adapted to its purpose. A horse would not be able to walk at all where a reindeer can proceed with ease.

A very little riding of the sort we have described was enough for our young friends, and the inspection of the herd of deer did not require a long time. On the way back to the landing-place the Doctor described the sledges used in winter in North-eastern Siberia. He said they were similar to the dog-sledges, there being some for light travel, and others for transporting freight. The deer were harnessed with straps or belts around their necks, and to these straps leather thongs were attached that extended back to the sledge. The animals were generally driven in pairs, and as each had a separate harness, the one that went slowest was in danger of having the sledge dragged on his heels.

The reins are fastened to the horns of the beasts, and the whip consists of a long stick or rod with which the animals can be enlivened when they grow weary. The sledge is made so that its body is at least a foot above the snow, and the greatest care is taken to have the runners slide as easily as possible. They are usually made of the antlers of deer, or of bones of the whale, and polished so that they shine like ivory. Where strips of ash timber can be obtained they are preferred, on account of their elasticity which renders them less liable to be broken than bone.

Ordinarily the pace of the reindeer is not rapid, but the animals for the travelling sledges are trained to move with a speed which justifies the reputation they have received in story-books. Instances are on record of reindeer having gone at the rate of nineteen miles an hour for three or four hours, and a single pair has been driven one hundred and fifty miles in twenty hours. On such occasions they take a steady trot at starting, and if the roads are good they rarely break from it until they have gone a dozen or twenty miles. In many parts of Siberia they are preferred to dogs, as they find their own food; but on the other hand the traveller must follow a route where food is known to exist, or his team will break down. When reindeer are wearied they stop, and refuse to move until rested; if urged to go on they lie down, and no whipping in the power of man to administer can induce them to rise and proceed.

A REINDEER SLED.

CHAPTER VII.

CHUCKCHEES AND KORAKS.—INTERNATIONAL FESTIVITIES.

COMMANDER BRONSON found the captain of the *Gambetta* ready to receive him, and talk over the plans of their expeditions. Both had the same purpose—to get as near as possible to the pole.

All the latest maps of the polar regions were spread on the table in the cabin, and the two explorers sat for some time in consultation over them. Commander Bronson pointed to the discoveries of Wrangell and Anjou in the early part of the century, and to those of De Long and others in recent times.

"Wrangell was stopped at latitude 72° 2' north," said he, "not by ice, but by open water. He had travelled to that point on sledges, and had no boats with which he could proceed. Since his time the land which he endeavored to reach has been visited, and found to be a large island, to which his name has been given. The natives of the Siberian coast had been there before him, but of course their stories concerning it could not be relied upon."

"It was almost directly north of Wrangell Island," said Captain Girard, of the *Gambetta*, "that De Long was beset in the ice on the 4th of September, 1879. From that point he drifted, helplessly, till his ship was crushed and sunk nearly two years later. He went five degrees nearer to the pole than Wrangell had been able to get, and found solid ice where the Russian discovered open water."

"The drift of the *Jeannette*," replied Commander Bronson, "shows that the current, at that time at least, was setting northward and westward. Now it is my intention to seek a more easterly direction, by keeping nearer to the American coast. From this point where we are now anchored I shall keep as close as I can to the 170th meridian of longitude until I have crossed the 70th parallel. We may then expect to encounter the ice, but we shall hope for the best, and keep a sharp watch for lanes of open water to carry us towards the pole."

Captain Girard said the route was so near what he had planned for his own, that he would be pleased to have the ships proceed in company. They could doubtless be of mutual assistance in the ice, and if an accident occurred to one of them she could be aided by the other, and perhaps her crew relieved from danger. "Of course," he added, "we understand that each of us is at liberty to make the best of his way where the condition of the seas will permit. All new discoveries shall belong to the one who makes them. If we find an island not laid down on the charts, it shall be named by the man that first sets foot upon it; and if neither ship is able to send anybody to it, the discovery shall belong to the first who saw the land and announced it by signal to the other."

BARON VON WRANGELL.

Commander Bronson agreed to this proposal, and said he should try to put the flag of his country in advance of the banner of the French. Captain Girard smilingly replied that the tri-color would be first at the pole, and with these good-natured expressions of patriotism the interview came to an end. Commander Bronson invited Captain Girard to dinner on board the *Vivian;* the invitation was promptly accepted, and the commander hastened back to his ship to give the necessary orders, and to recall the Doctor and our young friends from their trip on shore.

Soon after the signal was hoisted the boat came dancing over the waves, and the Doctor and his companions went to their cabins to dress for dinner. The cook was instructed to do his best, as the occasion was a momentous one: none of the party had ever entertained guests at dinner in the Arctic Ocean, and as they could not determine what the etiquette of the country was, they agreed to stick to that of the civilized world.

The French captain came at the appointed time, wearing the full uniform of his rank. He was accompanied by the surgeon of his ship, who had also been invited to the festivity; very cordial was the greeting between the latter and Dr. Tonner, as they had discovered in Kamchatka that they were students together in Paris, and had met frequently while promenading the hospitals. The French surgeon spoke very little English, while the American doctor was decidedly rusty in the language of Paris; there was a good deal of blundering in their conversation, and occasionally each managed to misunderstand completely what the other said. However, they managed to get along, and the meeting was a real pleasure to both. Their comparison of notes was interesting, as they found they had been doing the same things in different parts of the world. While Dr. Tonner was in the service of the American Army in Arizona and New Mexico his fellow-student had been in similar employment in Algeria; in the same year that the former had started in private practice in San Francisco the latter had set up for himself in Marseilles, and almost in the same week that the American went from San Francisco to reside in New York the Frenchman emigrated from Marseilles to Paris.

"*Les extrêmes se touchent*," remarked the surgeon of the *Gambetta* when their comparison of notes was ended.

"Yes," was the reply, "extremes meet, and perhaps we shall continue on the same lines for the future. We may follow different roads and both reach the pole."

The eyes of the Frenchman sparkled at the suggestion. He began to say something, and suddenly checked himself; then he made a remark about the hazards of a journey in the arctic regions, and closed with the suggestion that he certainly hoped to reach the North-pole.

Then he wanted to make a wager that the French flag would be the first to float over the pole, and warming with excitement he next proposed to double his wager and make it on behalf of his own ship.

Dr. Tonner grew interested, and asked why he was so confident of success where all before had failed.

"*Nous verrons*," was the reply; "or, as you says in Eengleesh, 'we shall see.'"

Then the conversation changed to other topics, and was interrupted by the announcement that dinner was ready. In a few minutes entertainers and guests were in their places, and the party did ample justice to the products of the skill of the cook. The guests were loud in their praises of the number and quality of the dishes, and paid a high compliment to the skill of the Americans in preserving fresh meat and vegetables.

"You have carried the science of 'canning' to a higher degree than any other country," said Captain Girard, "and have made long voyages comparatively easy, so far as the health of the men is concerned."

LOCKED IN THE ICE.

"But we have taken lessons from your nation in the science of cookery," was the polite response of the American commander; "and without good cooking our efforts in the preserving line would be of comparatively little use. The first must be perfect, or the second will fail."

"For a comparison between the new way and the old," replied Captain Girard, "let us take the voyage of the *Jeannette* and place it by the side of almost any long voyage of half a century ago. In old times nearly every crew imprisoned for a single winter in the ice was disabled by scurvy; the *Jeannette* passed two winters among the bergs and floes, and after the sinking of the ship her crew was three months on the ice before reaching Siberia, but they were in good condition when the vessel sank, and even when they landed at the mouth of the Lena. They were weakened by hardship and exposure, it is true, but they suffered almost nothing from the diseases formerly inseparable from an arctic voyage."

Commander Bronson then told about the arrangements for the distribution of lime-juice to his men when unable to procure fresh provisions, and gave other details of their preparation for the voyage. His guest replied by detailing whatever was new in the mode of outfitting the *Gambetta*, and by the end of dinner a good deal of information had been exchanged.

The party sat for some time after the dinner had been completed, and finally the hour came for the guests to return to their ship. The crew of Captain Girard's boat had been entertained by the sailors of the *Vivian*, and a spectator of the affair would have had an amusing story to tell. One man of the *Vivian's* crew could speak a little French, but only a little, while not a man from the *Gambetta's* boat knew a word of English. Conversation was carried on in pantomime for a while, but this could not last long; then the boatswain of the *Vivian* suggested a song and dance, and the idea was immediately carried out.

Among the *Vivian's* men there were three musicians: one played the violin, the second the flute, and the third had a high rank on the accordion. A quartette had been formed by adding a drummer, and on the voyage up from San Francisco a drum was manufactured by the carpenter which served its purpose very fairly. The violinist, known as " Fiddler Jack," had been chosen leader of the band, and a good deal of his watch below was devoted to the training of the musicians under his control. Their knowledge of what the professors call *technique* was very limited, but they made up for it in the vigor of their execution. Nearly all the crew could sing after the nautical fashion, and altogether the *Vivian* was well equipped for a season of arctic opera.

Jack mustered his band, and several American airs were played, accompanied with variations which are not found in the scores of fashionable performers. Then the crew sang " Hail Columbia " and " The Star-spangled Banner," followed by " The Old Folks at Home " and " Nancy Lee." All these songs were assisted by the band, the drum included. Fiddler Jack suggested in a mild way that the drum had no business in " The Old Folks at Home," though it might be all right for the rest.

One of the French sailors then hummed " The Marseillaise," in the hope that Fiddler Jack could play it, but the latter shook his head and said he was not up to foreign music anyhow. The drummer thought he might be able to beat the time on his drum, but the Frenchmen concluded that no instrumentation was needed, and sang " The Marseillaise " without assistance.

One of them gave the solo, and the rest joined in the chorus with a zest that showed they were no strangers to the song. The boatswain of the *Vivian* said it was lucky there was no more of the frog-eaters, or they would raise the ship's deck and start all the timbers down to the water-line. This song was followed by a love ditty or two, and then by a nautical air corresponding to "Tom Bowline" or "Nancy Dawson." Then came a dance, in which the Yankees gave their French visitors a sample of the "double shuffle" and other dances peculiar to America, to which the latter responded by an "All Hands Round" and some lofty kicking which threatened the safety of the deck more than did the singing.

When this was over Jack tuned his violin and sounded some of the notes of "Pinafore." This brought one of the Frenchmen to his feet and led to a discovery!

Though the crews of the two ships had no language in common, and their national airs were unlike, they had a mutual acquaintance through the music of this operetta, which had gone out from England and invaded both France and America. Its nautical character had caused it to be received with favor by the sailors of both nations, and a little investigation showed that the crews of the *Vivian* and *Gambetta* were equally "up" in their knowledge of it.

Jack and his attendant performers (the drum included) essayed the music of the sailors' chorus in "Pinafore," and when the air had been played through to the satisfaction of all concerned he announced, "Now we'll sing."

"*Chantons! chantons!*" shouted the Frenchmen in unison, and the sailors of two nationalities joined in the performance with such energy of action and volume of sound that the boatswain declared you couldn't tell which was which.

While the Americans roared out, in fair time with the instruments,

> "For he's the captain of the *Viv-i-an*,
> And a right good captain too,"

the Frenchmen were equally earnest in proclaiming,

> "*Car il est capitaine du Gam-bet-ta,
> Et très bon capitaine lui.*"

Just as they had finished the song, and were wiping the perspiration from their foreheads, there was a call from the deck for the *Gambetta's* crew, and with hand-shakes and embraces between those who had had a good time in spite of their lingual difficulties, the evening's entertainment came to an end. In a few minutes the visitors had gone, and the *Vivian* resumed her wonted quiet.

The next day most of the officers of both ships were on shore, and the little village of Chuckchees had quite a foreign aspect. Reindeer meat was purchased in considerable quantities, and the crews of the *Vivian* and *Gambetta* were treated to Siberian venison with great liberality. The Chuckchees almost uniformly refuse to sell live deer, on account of a belief that they will bring misfortune on themselves by so doing, but they have no objection to slaughtering the animals and selling the meat.

The purchases were paid for with beads, tobacco, hatchets, knives, and kindred things; rum was asked for, but refused in every instance, and the orders of both the French and American commanders were strictly obeyed, to give no opportunity for trouble. In bartering with the natives the cost of a deer was not more than fifty cents; and as the animals weighed from eighty to a hundred pounds when dressed, the strangers had no occasion to complain, while the natives seemed perfectly satisfied. George remarked that deer at that price could not be considered dear; he was informed that the joke had been made by every English-speaking visitor to that region for the last hundred years.

Commander Bronson's first inquiry was for a village where he could purchase dogs for sledging purposes; both he and Captain Girard had intended to buy dogs in Petropavlovsk, but had been advised not to take them from that place, as they could be procured in the vicinity of East Cape or Cape Szerdze Kamen. The Chuckchees formerly had no dogs, but a few years previous to the date of which we are speaking they made a friendly arrangement with the Koraks by which the latter had a settlement in the Chuckchee country on payment of a tribute to the owners of the land. The Koraks had an abundance of dogs, while the Chuckchees possessed thousands of reindeer: there was a Korak village close to a Chuckchee one, and at these villages it was possible to purchase dogs for arctic travel, and plenty of meat on which to feed them.

The villages were about ten miles from where the ships were anchored, and a guide was easily procured to lead the way to them. Major Clapp and one of the French officers set out at once, accompanied by Fred and a youth of about his age from the *Gambetta*. They were mounted on reindeer from the herd our friends had visited the day before, and Fred estimated that they made not less than half a dozen tumbles to the mile for the first half of the journey. On arriving at the villages they began negotiations for dogs, assisted by their guide, who could speak enough English to make himself understood in conducting a bargain.

It is easier to begin to talk business with these people than to finish it. There was a vexatious delay in bringing them to terms, and the major found that his hope of returning to the ships the same day was not to be realized. They were invited to partake of the native hospitality, but the interior of the Korak tents was so uninviting that they retreated outside in a very short time, and concluded to sleep in the open air. Through the exertions of the guide a temporary tent was erected, and beds of deer and bear skins were provided. The strangers shunned the stewpots of the natives, and supped on steaks of deermeat cooked over the fire by themselves.

A PORTRAIT.

Fortunately they had a good supply of biscuits and tea from the ships.

But if the Korak tent in summer was unendurable by the strangers, what would they have thought of the *yourt*, or winter residence of these people? While Fred was relating his experience on his return to the ship, Dr. Touner proceeded to enlighten him further on the subject.

"I spent a winter in Siberia, as you know," said the Doctor, "and a part of my experience was to travel among the Koraks. It used to give me a shudder to think of entering a *yourt*, but there was often no help for it, and I had to go in and do my best. These buildings are of logs or poles, banked around with earth, and made flat or tunnel-shaped on top. They are half sunk in the ground, so that it is no great effort to reach the roof

A KORAK BEAU.

from the outside. A hole in the centre of the roof serves as a chimney and door, and a pole, notched like a fence-post, forms a ladder.

"You descend directly over the fire, shutting your eyes and trusting to luck. The heat and smoke are blinding and stifling, so that you are very apt to lose your way. When you think you are near the floor you jump from the ladder; you should try to jump away from the fire, but sometimes you go straight into it, or possibly into the kettle in which the dinner is stewing. The smoke has no exit except through the hole mentioned, and the interior of the *yourt* is dimly lighted by some oil burning in a basin. The dogs hang about the hole above you, attracted by the heat and the smell of food; they are constantly quarrelling, and every little while one of them drops through and tumbles into the fire or the dinner-kettle. In either event he is flung outside, but the dinner is not spoiled by his intrusion. As the Koraks cook the whole of a reindeer except the hide and horns, they are not at all troubled by the presence of a few handfuls of dog's hair in their soup."

Bargaining went on very well on the second day, and forty dogs were procured for each ship, together with sledges and harness. Four drivers were also engaged, two for each ship, and the party returned in high spirits. It was not considered safe to come back without the dogs, for fear the natives might interpose, therefore the animals and their drivers headed the procession on its return to the landing-place. The whole party was immediately taken on board, and the major and Fred were congratulated on the success of their enterprise.

The rest of the officers had not been idle; they had purchased all the fur clothing the Chuckchees would sell, and all dressed deer-skins the market afforded. These would be made up by the sailors on board the ships after leaving the coast, and with the native garments as models they would have no difficulty in performing the work. At Petropavlovsk they bought a supply of *kuklankers*, together with fur boots and trousers, but as the French officers and sailors had been there ahead of them, they did not get all they wanted. The *kuklanker* is a sort of frock with a hood, and has to be put on over the head, like the ordinary shirt of civilized life. In warm weather the hood hangs over the shoulders, but in the intense cold of an arctic winter it is drawn over the head, and forms an admirable protection. The best quality of this garment is made of deer-skin, with the hair outside, and has a lining of the skins of very young deer or some cheap fur. Trousers of the same material, with deer-skin boots, complete the costume for the far North.

They were also fortunate in finding a supply of dried fish for dog's-food on sledge journeys; it was carefully stowed away where the animals could not reach it, and for the present they were fed on deer-meat. As soon as the dogs were quartered on board, it was evident that the ship would be far less peaceful than before their arrival. The brutes had the run of the deck, and were constantly fighting; George said they were never at peace unless they were having a quarrel, and the only way to keep them quiet was to let them fight whenever they wished. In the night they howled almost constantly, and it was not easy to sleep, on account of their noise. Luckily, they did not hurt each other much in their fights, and their drivers had plenty of occupation in beating them whenever they deserved punishment.

Two sledges were bought from the natives, and also a complete outfit of harness for the dogs. Then there were three sledges which had been made in

A KORAK BELLE.

San Francisco from the arctic models; but, with all the skill of the American carpenter who constructed them, they were nearly twice as heavy as the sledges of the Koraks. The drivers, Alexy and Petroff, were not favorably inclined to the American sledges, and before the ship sailed they obtained the necessary materials from their people on shore, and offered to construct sledges on their own models.

In a couple of days after the return from the purchase of the dogs the ships were ready to sail in search of the pole. As before arranged, it was understood that they were to keep in company as long as possible and

A BALL ON SHIPBOARD.

convenient, but each was at liberty to seek its own course, and say "good-bye" whenever it chose to do so. The evening before their departure was marked by an event of considerable interest to our young heroes.

Captain Girard returned the compliment of Commander Bronson by inviting him to dine on board the *Gambetta*, accompanied by Major Clapp and Dr. Tonner, and also by Fred and George. The crew of the *Gambetta* had obtained permission to get up an international ball, to which the crew of the *Vivian* was invited, and also some of the Chuck-chees from the village on shore. The French sailors decked their ship with all the flags they possessed, and so many of them dressed in fancy costume that the affair took the form of a masked ball instead of a plain one. As there were no ladies on board either ship, and the native belles were not accus-

"ALL HANDS ROUND."

tomed to European dances, several of the French
sailors got themselves up in feminine dress, and
played their parts admirably.

A spectator at the dance would have been easily deceived by several of the couples and quar-
tettes as they balanced to each other, keeping time
to the music of the violins in the hands of the performers, who were on a platform of boards placed
over a couple of barrels. The disguise was excellent, and would have done credit to actors made
up for the stage. One of the young sailors was

"BALANCE."

dressed as a flower-girl, and went around pretending to sell bouquets made from moss and
shrubs among which artificial flowers were deft-
ly woven. Closely following the flower-girl was
a cook with a basket on her arm, and her head
neatly covered with the cap which is the badge
of her occupation at home. Then came a stout
old sailor disguised as a fish-woman, and another
who pretended to be a peddler of cakes and
sweetmeats. Occasionally these perambulating
characters laid aside their baskets and other im-
pedimenta to join in the dance, which was as
lively as the music would permit. Some of the

FLOWER-GIRL.

dances were arranged for the accommodation of
the visitors, and at such times the Americans did
their best to make a name for their country.

Fiddler Jack was there with his band, and supplied the music for the performance whenever it
was desired to relieve the French violinists. Consequently there was no lack of entertainment for
the Americans, and though they did not become as
excited as their hosts in the execution of the figures, they managed to work themselves into a condition of great warmth.

The dinner in the cabin was over while the ball
was under way, and the gentlemen went on deck
to enjoy it. Jack's band happened to be playing

FISH-WOMAN.

when they appeared, and at once the music was shifted to the strains of
"Pinafore:" the sailors of both ships took the hint, and at once the song

was picked up, and echoed far over the waters of the Arctic Ocean, and along the desolate shore of North-eastern Siberia :

"For he's the captain of the *Viv-i-an*,
Car il est capitaine du Gam-bet-ta,
And a very good captain, too.
Et tres bon capitaine, lui."

At ten o'clock the ball came to an end, and the officers, and crew of the *Vivian* returned to their ship.   The sun was still above the horizon, and consequently many of the attendants at the ball were unwilling to close the performance.   George suggested that it was not a good place for singing the popular air "We won't go Home till Morning," since the movements of the sun would compel them to keep up a month or two, to comply with the suggestion of the chorus.   Candles were of little use in such a latitude, and nobody was inclined to look forward to the arctic winter, when darkness would be as continuous as was then the daylight.

THE COOK.

CHAPTER VIII.

FROM SIBERIA TO WRANGELL ISLAND.—ICEBERGS AND A BEAR-HUNT.

AT the appointed time the two exploring ships sailed from the coast and headed to the north. A few hours before their departure a whaler came to anchor near their moorings; Commander Bronson sent Captain Jones, accompanied by Fred and George, to ascertain if there was any news of importance.

The whaler reported ice in small patches to the north and east, and said another whaler had told him there was an extensive barrier of ice between the coast of Siberia and Wrangell Island. There were several whalers at work there, and they had met with very good luck. Two of them were nearly full, and would complete their cargoes before the end of summer, when they would sail directly for the Sandwich Islands or San Francisco. One whaler had lost a boat in a battle with a whale, but the crew was saved, so that the accident was of little consequence. Another whaler had been nipped in the ice, and got off without much damage; on the whole the season's work was satisfactory, and the whalers were happy.

A GOTHIC ICEBERG.

"I hope they'll get out of the Arctic Ocean before the ice comes down," said Captain Jones, as the boat was returning to the *Vivian.*

"Every few years some of them get caught by the ice before they pass the capes, and when it comes down with full force it crushes them like egg-shells. In 1871 thirty-three whaling ships, almost in sight of each other, were caught, and crushed between the ice and the shore; the wind was against them, and the ice drifted faster than they could work ahead."

One of the youths asked how it happened that so many of them were enclosed at once.

"They were chasing a large school of whales," was the reply, "and went farther than it was safe to go.   Finding the ice was closing on them, and that a part of the fleet would certainly be lost, the captains decided to abandon the ships that were in the most dangerous positions, and go on board those which had the best chance of escaping. A few had already been crushed between the ice and the shore before this decision was made, but happily no lives were lost. Some of the ships were nearly full of oil, and the loss of property was estimated at a million and a half of dollars."

"The whalers have had a hard time in this part of the world," said one of the youths. "I was reading yesterday how the rebel steamer *Shenandoah* came here during the civil war and burned all the whale-ships she could find."

"You are not exactly right on that point," replied the captain.   "The *Shenandoah* came to the Arctic Ocean in 1865, at the close of the rebellion, and destroyed all the whaling ships she could find; I was here at the time, and my ship barely escaped destruction. I left Plover Bay one night, and sailed out into Behring Sea, and the next day the *Shenandoah* came in and burned ten whalers. All the captains knew that the war was over, and showed newspapers and letters to confirm their assertion to the captain of the *Shenandoah*, but he refused to believe them. Altogether he destroyed thirty whale-ships. The captain of an English whaler, the *Robert Tawns*, warned some of the Americans of their danger, and enabled them to escape, and was consequently threatened by the *Shenandoah*.

"It's an old story now," he continued, "but every whaleman feels a grudge against Waddell, the captain of the *Shenandoah*, and will hold it as long as he lives. As the *Shenandoah* was an English ship, fitted out in Liverpool, and well known to be bound on a piratical enterprise, we don't feel very kindly towards England in consequence; especially so when she was allowed to recruit a crew openly in Melbourne, and received facilities in that and other ports which were denied to United States ships. But here we are at the *Vivian's* side, and in half an hour we'll be on our way to sea."

The ships went under sail, and did not even light their fires to get away from land. The wind was blowing off the shore, and the breeze was fair towards the north.

The course was laid for Herald Island, in latitude 72° north, longitude 175° west. The youths supposed it had been named after the *New York*

Herald, but learned, on reference to the books, that it was discovered and named by Captain Kellett, of the British ship *Herald*, in 1849. Other navigators claimed to have seen it before Captain Kellett, but the latter was the first to land on its shores.

The day after leaving the coast Captain Jones ordered the crow's-nest to be rigged on the foremast. Fred and George watched the operation with a good deal of interest, as they had already seen the crow's-nest on some of the whalers, but had been too busy to investigate its construction.

Captain Jones told them that the crow's-nest was an invention of Captain Scoresby, or at all events he had the credit of it. Ordinarily a man is stationed aloft to watch for whales, and as the air is very cold he is apt to become benumbed, and runs the risk of falling off. To protect him from danger and from the cold a cask is rigged aloft, and in this cask he stands when on duty. Its sides shelter him from the wind, and in case he is benumbed he cannot fall to the deck; there is a trap-door in the bottom for entering it, but no sailor who respects himself would think of getting in that way. He invariably clambers over the side, unless he has been so chilled as to partially lose the use of his limbs.

"The crow's-nest is a point of observation when we are looking for whales," said the captain, "and also when we are in the ice. We are not going to chase whales now," he continued, "but we must keep a sharp eye on the ice to preserve the ship from injury.

"And now that we are in the region of ice, I may as well tell you some of its peculiarities.

"There are two kinds of ice in the Arctic Ocean—that which comes from the rivers, and is made from fresh-water, while the other is formed from the salt-water of the sea.

"All the rivers that flow into the Arctic Ocean bring down large quantities of ice at their annual floods. This amount of ice would alone be enough to fill up the entire regions within thirty degrees of the pole, in the course of a few centuries, if it were not melted by the heat of summer or drifted away by the currents.

"The ice brought down by the flowing rivers, such as the Lena, Kolyma, Yenisei, Mackenzie, and others, is in great floes, such as you may see in the rivers of the Northern States of America in the spring of the year. But there are other rivers, exactly similar to the glaciers of Switzerland, that bring down masses of ice in the form of bergs. Greenland has great numbers of glaciers, and they are the sources of the bergs which float south in the Atlantic Ocean, and in May and June lie in the track of the steamers between America and Europe. If you want to know about them in detail I advise you to read 'The Land of Desolation,' by Dr. Hayes."

The youths promised to do so as soon as their talk was ended, but meantime they wanted to know about the ice of the Polar Sea.

VIEW OF ICEBERGS.

"Well," continued the captain, "the whalemen have distinct names for all the varieties of polar ice. Of course all the salt-water ice is flat, as it is formed by freezing the surface of the sea; it never forms a berg, and whenever you see a berg you may know that the ice is fresh. If the salt-water ice spreads over a large area it is called a *field*, and if it is a field broken into smaller expanses, each one of these is called a *floe*. A field or floe broken into smaller pieces, not more than forty or fifty yards in diameter, is called a *pack*, and the fragments composing a pack are crowded together by the action of the wind and waves, so that their surface is often exceedingly difficult to cross. A broad pack is a *patch*, and a long and narrow pack is a *stream ;* when the pieces of the pack are sufficiently separated to allow a ship to sail through, it is *drift-ice*, and is said to be *loose* or *open ;* when it is greatly broken up, it is *brush-ice ;* and when the pieces crowd each other, so as to force some of them to rise higher than the rest, the elevated portions are called *hummocks*. In heavy packs there are often a great many hummocks, and I have seen them not less than thirty feet high. They are very pretty to look at, but are the dread of all who are obliged to travel among them, as they greatly hinder progress, whether on sledges or on foot."

Fred asked what the *ice-blink* was, as the captain paused after his description of the different kinds of ice.

"That," replied the captain, "is the name given by the Dutch sailors to the singular appearance of the horizon where it is bounded by the ice. It is a stratum of lucid whiteness, occasioned by the glare of light reflected against the atmosphere from the surface of the ice; it is generally in the form of a shining streak, and always looks brightest in clear weather. An experienced navigator knows by the ice-blink when he is approaching ice, even when it is twenty or thirty miles beyond the line of direct vision. He can even make out the quality of the ice: the blink from the packs appears of a pure white, while that from snow-fields has a tinge of yellow. Many a ship has been saved from danger by the ice-blink, which warned her commander what to do while he had plenty of sea-room before him."

ON AN ICE-PACK.

Just then the captain's attention was required in another part of the ship, and the interview was abruptly terminated. The youths went below to look up the book which Captain Jones had recommended for their perusal.

They learned from it that the glaciers from which the icebergs are formed are sometimes several miles in width and hundreds of feet high;

they fill many of the valleys running down to the sea, and as their progress is slow, it often takes many months for the formation of a single berg. But so many of the glaciers are at work that the aggregate number of bergs annually born and set afloat is very large.

This is the process: the glacier flows slowly along, its rate varying according to the season of the year and the temperature of the atmosphere. Sometimes it may be only an inch or two daily, and at others it may advance ten or twelve inches in the same time. As it reaches the sea the end is pushed out into the water, and gradually sinks beneath it; after a time the buoyancy of the water, lifting on the immense mass of ice, causes it to break off and float away. Thus the iceberg is formed.

Fresh ice floating in sea-water has seven-eighths of its body below the surface and one-eighth above; consequently, before the lifting force of the water can be exerted on the end of the glacier, more than seven-eighths of it must be forced out beneath the surface of the sea, or of the narrow bay where the glacier frequently has its termination. When the break occurs the commotion is like that of an earthquake, and the position of a ship or boat in front of the glacier is full of danger. Dr. Hayes describes an incident of this sort where a party from his ship had gone on shore to take photographic views of the glacier and the mountains around it. The ship was anchored in the bay, some distance below the glacier, and her captain thought she was in no danger.

The boat reached the shore without difficulty, and the party proceeded to set up their instruments on the rocks, some distance above the landing-place. Those on the ship were busy with their ordinary work, or loitering around, when they heard some loud reports which indicated the breaking off of pieces of the glacier. The fragments fell into the sea; the commotion they created caused the ship to roll at her anchor, and waves of considerable extent broke on the rocks.

While they were regarding the strange occurrence, and thinking it was all over, there was a report louder than all the others, followed by the fall of a great mass of ice, at least half a mile long and a quarter of a mile in width; simultaneously another mass, equally large, rose from beneath the bay, and then the whole front of the glacier seemed to crumble and fall.

Wonder at the magnificent spectacle was changed to thoughts of the peril of the ship; the waves rolled up with tremendous force, one greater than all the rest sweeping from the front of the glacier down the bay in the direction of the ship.

As it passed beneath her she was lifted on its surface and borne to-

WHERE AN ICEBERG IS FORMED.

wards the rocks; but fortunately her anchor held, and she swung back to her place uninjured. The wave broke on the cliffs above the ship, its force being so great that the spectators estimated its height at a hundred feet; the top of the wave, as it struck the rocks, curled backward and fell on the deck of the ship, which it deluged with water, but not enough to sink her. Another wave followed, and then another and another, but each was less violent than its predecessor, and after a while the bay resumed its wonted quiet.

The party on shore had quite as narrow an escape as those on the ship. They were a short distance from the beach when the wave reached them, but by throwing themselves flat on the rocks, and clinging with all their might, they managed to hold on. One of them lost his grasp and was thrown several yards by the wave, but though considerably bruised, he seized another rock and was saved. They lost all their implements, and if they had been on the beach when the wave swept down the bay, it is probable that not one would have escaped.

VERTICAL SECTION OF A GLACIER.

Bergs are sometimes seen two or three miles long and several hundred feet high floating in the Atlantic; remember that only one-eighth of their mass is visible, and then think how enormous must be the quantity concealed below. Frequently several large bergs will be found close together, which were evidently from the same glacier and broken off at the same time. When the convulsion took place by which they were thrown from the front of the glacier it was split asunder, and thus their escape was facilitated. In some places where the glaciers come down to the sea, the water is too shallow to allow the bergs to float off; they become crowded together, and as the heat of the sun is not sufficient to melt them they lie for years close to the place of their formation.

For the present we will drop the consideration of the iceberg, and its parent the glacier, and return to our friends on the *Vivian*.

Captain Jones did not put his crow's-nest in order any too soon, for not more than an hour after it had been completed, the lookout forward reported fragments of ice dead ahead. In a little while the ship was among

IN FRONT OF A GREENLAND GLACIER.

them, but they were neither numerous nor large; beyond indicating what might be expected before long, they were of no particular consequence. Captain Jones caused a piece to be fished up as they sailed slowly along, and on examination he pronounced it pack-ice that had probably drifted from the eastward. Orders were given to shorten sail during the night, and to keep a sharp lookout lest they might suddenly be brought against something more serious than the fragments they had thus far encountered.

The air was perceptibly colder than the day before, although the wind blew from the south, and had not changed its direction a single point since their departure from land. The next day the scene was unchanged, with the exception that the drift-ice was somewhat more abundant, and the lookout thought there was an indication of an ice-blink on the horizon, betokening serious work before them.

Both vessels held their course for Herald Island, and it was agreed that if they were separated during the night from any cause, they would endeavor to meet at its eastern extremity. There was no special glory in landing there, as the island had been several times visited since Captain Kellett's exploration, but it contained an arctic post - office, where Commander Bronson desired to leave letters for future ships.

The ice increased as the ships advanced, and by the next morning there was "more ice than ocean," as Captain Jones expressed it. On the eastern horizon there was an appearance of a solid pack, while to the west only loose ice was visible. The signal-flags were set at work between the *Gambetta* and *Vivian*, and it was agreed that they would steer to the northwest, and probably sight Wrangell Island if the condition of the ice remained unchanged. At the time this agreement was made they were exactly on the 70th parallel of latitude, and Wrangell Island was thought to be about one hundred miles away, in a north-westerly direction. As they changed their course the wind died out, and there was not enough breeze to fill the sails.

An hour or so after the signalling was over the man aloft called out,

"Bear on the ice on the port bow!"

Of course there was a rush to that side of the ship. Fred ran below for his glass, and speedily returned. It did not take long to discover the bear, who was sitting on the ice as though wondering how he got there. George remarked that the brute was evidently monarch of all he surveyed, to which Fred retorted that he couldn't be much of a surveyor, as his domain was not more than a hundred feet from side to side.

A boat was lowered to go in pursuit of the game; Major Clapp and Dr. Tonner formed the hunting party, each armed with a heavy rifle with

THE BEAR AT BAY.

which to do effective work on the occupant of the floe. The boat had no easy task before it, as the sea was pretty well filled with loose ice, and it was highly desirable to avoid coming in violent contact with any of the floating cakes. The Doctor acted as ice-pilot, and performed his work very well; standing in the bow he directed the course of the boat, keeping the bear steadily in view, except when he was hidden by hummocks of ice. They had about a mile to go in a direct line, but so tortuous was the course that it took them a full hour to reach the floe where the bear had his summer residence.

As they drew near, Bruin came close to the edge of his domain, as though intending to dispute its possession. The major raised his rifle to fire when within a hundred yards, but with a wave of his hand the Doctor restrained him.

"Don't fire as long as he stands there," whispered the Doctor. "The closer we can get, the better will be our chance of dropping him."

The major saw the force of Dr. Tonner's suggestion, and allowed the boat to proceed, but he held his rifle ready for action at the first movement of the beast. Evidently the bear was not accustomed to the sight of boats, and looked upon the new-comer as an inhabitant of the waters whose acquaintance he had not yet made.

He allowed the boat to approach within twenty yards, and then the major told the men to stop rowing. As the boat reduced its speed the rifle sent a bullet directly into the breast of the bear; he gave a leap backward and fell heavily on his side, but was up in a few seconds.

It was now the Doctor's turn, and he was quick to embrace it. The major had a front view of the bear when he fired; as the animal rose, it looked as though he intended to seek safety in flight, and present only a rear view to the Doctor. But the beast was not devoid of curiosity, and this was fatal to him.

He turned to look at his assailants, and as he did so the Doctor fired as closely to the heart as he was able to aim. Instead of the ordinary bullet he used an explosive one; as it struck the bear's side, and was fairly embedded in the flesh, it exploded, tearing a hole large enough for the insertion of one's hand. By this time the major had a fresh cartridge in his Remington rifle, and sent another bullet not more than two or three seconds behind the Doctor's. Down went the bear. The boat was now at the edge of the ice; one of the men held it with an ice-hook, and the Doctor sprang on the floe, closely followed by the major.

Both thought the bear was dead, but they had learned prudence from experience. "Always approach a dead mule by the head," said the Doctor, "and a dead bear by the side. A dead mule has been known to kick, and a dead bear will rise and bite." As they put fresh cartridges in their rifles the bear suddenly rose again; he was not more than a dozen feet from his assailants, and as they were standing opposite his side they had an excellent mark.

The two bullets brought him to the ground again, or rather to the ice, and the major said he ought to be killed by this time. An oar was brought from the boat, and one of the sailors prodded the recumbent beast with it, while the hunters stood ready to shoot in case he stirred. There was no movement, and the game was evidently theirs; but to make assurance doubly sure, the Doctor sent a solid bullet through the animal's skull, re-marking as he did so, that probably such a thing never entered the bear's head before.

It was a full-grown arctic bear, in excellent condition, and estimated to weigh not far from twelve hundred pounds. The next thing to consider was the question of removal: it was not easy to handle such a burden and place it in the boat, and it would be a difficult matter to tow it back to the ship. The major decided to skin and divide the animal where he lay, and as each sailor was provided with a knife, and the Doctor had brought along a pair of sharp blades for use in case of need, the operation was quickly accomplished.

Of course the party had been carefully watched from the ship, and the death of the bear was known there as soon as it occurred. Meantime the course of the ship had been changed, so as to bring it within less than half a mile of the floe where the prize was taken; another boat was sent to assist in bringing home the provisions, and in little more than an hour from the time the first shot was fired, the entire party was back again. The major and the Doctor received the congratulations of their friends at the success of the hunt, which had been a pleasant episode, and supplied fresh meat for the table. The signal "we wish to communicate" was hoisted; the *Gambetta* was a couple of miles to windward, and on seeing the signal she bore down to come nearer her consort. The breeze con-tinued light, and it was some time before she was near enough for the *Vivian's* purpose. When the ships were about half a mile apart a boat was sent to Captain Girard with one of the quarters of the bear, accompa-nied by the compliments of Commander Bronson, and those of the two heroes of the fray.

In the cabin of the *Vivian* they had steaks of polar bear for dinner, and the party was unanimous in declaring it equal to the best beefsteak they had ever tasted. The Doctor intimated that the fatness of the bear, and probably his youth, had a good deal to do with the favorable opinion passed upon him. "If he had happened to be old and lean," said the man of medicine, "we should have heard a different story. I have tried to eat the flesh of the polar bear when it was like devouring a section of a boot-sole."

Fred asked what was the proper name of the animal: should he be called white, polar, or arctic bear?

"As to that," replied the Doctor, "there is a difference of opinion. Scientifically he is *Ursus maritimus*, or 'bear of the sea;' his home is on the ice of the northern seas, and the name fits him perfectly. He is a good swimmer, and takes readily to the water when occasion requires; when he lives on land it is rather from necessity than choice, as his food comes mostly from the sea, or the bays that empty into it. His chief prey is the seal, and one of these days we may see the ingenuity of the bear in securing his dinner.

"He is a dingy yellow, rather than white, and therefore 'white bear' does not properly describe him; we don't know whether he is found at the North-pole or not, and consequently 'polar bear' may be a misnomer; his home is in the arctic regions, and you may call him 'arctic bear' without fear of contradiction. But if you employ any other of the names already mentioned, none of us will dispute you; language was made for the use of man, and not man for language, and nobody should lose his digestion if our prize of to-day is set down as a white or a polar bear. *Ursus maritimus* is too long for practical service."

The crew was regaled on bear-meat, and so were the dogs; the former took their allowance in peace, but not so the four-footed members of the ship's company. The scent of the meat excited them, and they came near eating up their drivers in their eagerness to get at their allowance of the new food. In spite of all efforts to restrain them, they had as many fights as there were dogs in the party, with several extra quarrels thrown in to keep things lively.

The morning after the incident of the bear-hunt the lookout reported land in sight, and the commander mounted to the cross-trees to inspect it. There were mountains in the background, and the coast was fringed with ice, which threatened to be an effectual barrier to a near approach. The position on the chart indicated that they were in sight of Wrangell Island, and the ships were headed for it as directly as possible. As the *Vivian* approached the land a strip of gravelly beach was made out, but there were no signs of vegetation or animal life, greatly to the disappointment of our young friends.

The ice was not so abundant as on the previous day, but the floes were larger, and Captain Jones proceeded with caution, through fear of springing a leak in the sides of his craft. Frequently it was necessary to shorten sail, and so much time was lost in this way that the long arctic day was drawing to a close when they were yet a dozen miles from shore.

SCENE IN FRONT OF THE ISLAND.

Following the charts, and the directions laid down in Mr. Gilder's "Ice-pack and Tundra," the two ships, early the next morning, headed for the southern end of the island, and entered the harbor where the *Rodgers* anchored on her cruise in search of the *Jeannette*. They found plenty of water and good anchorage, just as Mr. Gilder described, though the bay was encumbered with ice that had evidently been blown there by the wind. As there were two ships, it required considerable manœuvring to get them properly anchored where there was no danger of their interfering with each other; the best part of the forenoon was gone before this work was over, and Captain Jones decided not to send a boat on shore until the men had eaten their dinners.

The captain of the *Gambetta* was less considerate, as his ship had not settled to rest after dropping her anchor before a boat was seen stealing away from her side and heading for the land. The French flag waved over her stern, and it was evident that the explorers intended to hoist the tricolor in advance of the stars and stripes.

Fred and George wanted to start at once and get ahead of their rival, but their proposal was promptly checked by the commander.

"Never mind what they do now," said he; "the island has been visited before, and so nobody can discover it.   American whalers have been here, and so have American exploring ships.   The revenue cutter *Corwin* was here in 1881, a month or more in advance of the *Rodgers*, and they both hoisted the American flag over Wrangell Island and left records of their visit.   Let the Frenchmen enjoy themselves.   Think of what the people of Florida say of the Northerners who go to that State and shoot at the alligators: 'The Northerners are amused, and the alligators don't mind it.'"

WINTER-QUARTERS OF BARENTZ THREE HUNDRED YEARS AGO.

CHAPTER IX

A VISIT TO WRANGELL ISLAND.—HUNTING SEALS, WALRUSES, AND POLAR BEARS.

IT was no easy matter for the French boat to push through the cakes of ice, but the effort was successful; and just as the men of the *Vivian* were called to dinner the French flag was seen waving on a rock just above the shore. As soon as dinner was over a boat was sent off from the *Vivian*, carrying the two youths, with the major and Doctor. A lane through the ice at one side of the bay had slowly opened since the *Gambetta's* boat made its journey, and enabled the Americans to reach the land much more rapidly than their rivals.

Meantime the French party had wandered off to the northward, leaving two men in charge of their boat; most of them were out of sight beyond the rocks, and just as the Americans reached the shore the report of a rifle was heard, followed quickly by another and another. Fred and George started in the direction of the sounds, but before they had gone a dozen yards one of the French officers appeared from behind a large rock and waved his handkerchief, so that it could be seen from the ships.

"They've probably killed a bear," said George, "and he wants a boat to carry the prize on board."

The signal was answered from the *Gambetta*, and in a few minutes a boat was on its way from that ship to the land. The officer then disappeared the way he had come, and the youths concluded not to follow him. "Let them have their bear all to themselves," said Fred; "and if we get one they won't have any excuse for interfering with us."

They rejoined the major and the Doctor, and accompanied by two sailors from the boat, the four explorers started in a direction different from that taken by the Frenchmen. It led them along the beach for half a mile or more, where the ice lay piled up in great winrows, with here and there a few open lanes. At the highest point where the tide rose there were many pieces of driftwood, and our friends were able to corroborate the testimony of Mr. Gilder, that the coast of Wrangell Island is strewn with fragments of logs which have been borne thither by the currents. Mr. Gilder says that the *Rodgers* party found many utensils of wood here that were made by the natives of the Siberian and American coasts, some of them presenting a very ancient appearance. Occasionally there are articles of civilized manufacture, but no one can tell whether they came from wrecks of ships or were dropped overboard from whalers. Fred looked for a portion of a spar mentioned by that gentleman, and found it lying apparently undisturbed since the visit of the *Rodgers*. "There could be very little reason for its absence," said Fred, as he touched the spar with his foot, "as there is no record that any ship has been here since the *Rodgers*, and the natives are not in the habit of venturing as far as this from the coast."

Moralizing on the origin of the driftwood on Wrangell Island resulted in the conclusion that it had been brought there from America and Siberia, principally the former. It is evident that the prevailing tendency of the currents is towards the west, and this theory was confirmed by observation of the masses of ice that ground against the headlands protecting the harbor where the *Vivian* and *Gambetta* were lying. Even when the wind blew from the east the flow of the ice was westward. Mr. Gilder had previously recorded a similar circumstance, and said that sometimes when the people of the *Rodgers* went to bed, while they lay at Wrangell Island, they would see pack-ice filling the sea as far as the eye could reach; and when they went on deck next morning there was a vast expanse of open water, with only a cake of ice floating here and there on the surface. Quite as often they found the solid pack in the morning where it was clear water the night before; these sudden changes had given rise to a theory which prevails among the whalers, that the ice sinks and rises in obedience to some unknown law of nature.

After a time our friends left the beach and ascended to the higher ground. Major Clapp was a little in advance, when he suddenly waved his hand and intimated that there was fun ahead. Guns were set at half-cock, and the hunting blood was apparently high. As the rest of the party reached the major's side the reason for his action was apparent.

Two bears, one of goodly size and the other a partly-grown cub, were walking leisurely among the rocks on their way to the sea-shore, where they evidently hoped to pick up a breakfast. They had not seen the intruders in their domain, or at all events did not indicate any alarm. It was decided that the major and the Doctor would attend to the old bear, while Fred and George looked after the cub. "And as the cub will stick by his parent," said the major, "you had better let us do our part of the work first."

Keeping among the rocks as much as possible, the party edged in the

FEMALE BEAR AND CUBS.

direction of the bears, and soon had them at short range. The Doctor fired first; the effect of his shot was to bring the old bear on her haunches, and cause her to look around to discover the source of the attack; then the major put in a bullet, and as all occasion for further concealment was over, the whole party rushed forward, the two hunters taking the lead.

Evidently the bear was severely wounded, but not enough to prevent her turning on her assailants with a savage roar. The major told the youths to fire, and they did so without hesitation; the older hands added their leaden contribution, and together their efforts brought the bear to the ground.

"Now go forward and finish the work," said the major, as he handed his rifle to Fred. "Step close up and put a bullet through the skull, but be ready to spring out of her way in case she rises suddenly."

Fred obeyed the instructions, and the bear was a prize to the hunters from the *Vivian*.

The cub did not attempt to run away, but stood as though quite dazed at the whole business. It seemed a pity to shoot the innocent little fellow, and George proposed that he should be captured, and carried on board the ship. Fred seconded the suggestion, but the major and Doctor explained to the youths that it would not be feasible to do as they wished. "We have no place for him," said the major; "and even if we had, his presence would excite our dogs so that their fury could not be restrained. They would be more difficult than ever to manage, and we could not have even the semblance of peace until he was killed and devoured. The best way out of the perplexity is to shoot him as mercifully as possible, and we shall doubtless find his flesh an agreeable addition to our table supplies."

The cub was promptly despatched, skinned, dressed, quartered, and carried to the boat, and the skin of the old one was also taken along as a trophy. While the work was going on, Dr. Tonner told the youths of an incident in the experience of the author of "Seasons with the Sea-horses," when hunting bears in Spitzbergen.

This gentleman and his friend one day saw a bear and two cubs on the shore, and started in pursuit of them. He says it was touching to see the devotion of the old bear to her young; she could have escaped with ease had it not been for the cubs, who did not seem to realize their danger, and needed constant assistance to get over the rough places in their way.

The hunters could move faster than the cubs, and at length they overtook the group and succeeded in killing the old bear. When they came up to where she lay, the cubs growled viciously, and would not allow themselves to be touched till the men brought lines from the boat and lassoed the little fellows. They were tied together, like dogs in a leash; on finding themselves fast they began to fight viciously, and evidently each regarded the other as the cause of his misfortune. It was no small task to get them to the boat, and then to the ship, as they resisted at every step and used their teeth freely. A cage was made for them, and they fought against entering it; they embraced every opportunity to escape, and one day one of them got out of his cage and jumped overboard. A boat was lowered for his recapture, and he wounded one of the sailors quite severely while being restored to his old quarters. With a good deal of trouble their owners brought them to civilization, and deposited them in a public garden, where they received much admiration.

Birds were numerous, and easy of approach; evidently visitors were rare in that locality, and the birds had not learned to beware of the white man and his means of destruction. No more bears were in sight, and it was decided to bag a few ducks and other game-birds for the table. For this purpose the shot-guns of Fred and George were better adapted than the rifles of the major and Doctor; the latter suggested that the youths would have a good time for practice by providing the birds for the table, and might take easy lessons where the prey was so tame.

Ducks and plover were the principal attractions, and our friends succeeded so well that in less than an hour they had all that were needed for the day. The two sailors acted as retrievers to bring in the game, and when they started for the boat with the proceeds of the shooting they had all they wanted to carry. The ducks proved to be tender, and of delicious flavor, and evidently had not changed their character since the visit of the *Rodgers*. The Doctor was excellent authority on birds, and after dinner was over he declared that the plover of Wrangell Island surpassed anything of the kind he had ever seen. He murmured something about Taft's, at Point Shirley, but the whole of his remark was inaudible to the rest of the party.

While the youths were busy among the game-birds the elders of the shore party occupied themselves with searches for the trace of previous visitors. At the head of the little harbor was a cairn of stones, which they reached a few minutes in advance of one of the French officers, who was evidently chagrined that the Americans were ahead of him. Removing the stones of the cairn one by one, a wooden box was found, and in the box was a bottle carefully corked and sealed. Inside the bottle was a roll of paper which proved on examination to be the record of the visit of the *Corwin* in August, 1881, and of the *Rodgers* a month later. Bottle and paper were taken on board the *Vivian*, and returned the next day to the cairn, with a record of the visit of that ship and the *Gambetta* attached to the original paper.

The rocks near the sea were covered with water-fowl, and each report of the guns sent hundreds of them flying into the air. The youths wanted to shoot some of them, but were restrained by the Doctor, who said they were of no use as food, and it would be a waste of ammunition to kill them. There were several varieties of these birds; among them were the mollemoke, and the great and little auk, the latter a comical looking fellow who sat upright on the shore, and held his wings as though they were intended for hands. The auk is well known to all arctic travellers in the regions of Greenland and Spitzbergen; he lives upon fish, and his diet gives his flesh a flavor not at all to the taste of the European.

It was getting late in the afternoon, and the major ordered a return to the ship. During their absence the ice had drifted out of the bay, so that they had an easier journey than when coming ashore; the French boat started back at the same time, and they had a friendly race for a part of the distance, which was won by the latter.

THE AUK AT HOME.

During the afternoon the lookout espied several seals on the rocks a little farther down the bay, and a boat was sent in pursuit of them. The second mate of the *Vivian* had been in the Greenland seal-fishery, and consequently the expedition was placed in his charge; he carried a couple of rifles, but his chief reliance was on some clubs, which he pronounced far more effective. "You must kill them at short range," said he, "and when you come to close quarters the club is a better weapon than the rifle. You don't have to stop to put in fresh cartridges every minute, and besides, when you hit one there's no report to frighten the rest."

The boat reached the shore in such a position as to cut off the retreat of the seals to the water. The mate sprang on shore, followed by two of the sailors, all armed with clubs; with no other weapons they rushed among the seals, and in a short time a dozen or more had been killed. A violent blow on the nose is fatal to the seal, but it is not easy to hit him in the right spot, as he does not stand still, and besides, he shows fight when in close quarters. The male seal is particularly fierce, and will make a stout defence; woe be to the assailant who slips on the rocks and gives one of these fellows a chance for a bite on arm or leg. He can sever an arm at a single movement of his jaws, and can break the bone of a man's leg without much effort.

No accident happened to the sealers, and they returned with a full load of meat as the reward of their exertions. Not only was the boat laden as low as was safe to fill her, but several of the seals were towed astern, and had to be hoisted in with a tackle at the end of one of the spars. The flesh of the seal is excellent eating, and sailors generally prefer it to beef.

A FIGHT WITH THE SEALS.

The crew were liberally provided with it, and so were the dogs; what with young bear, ducks, and plover, in the cabin and wardroom, and seal-meat in the forecastle, there was no scarcity of fresh provisions on board the *Vivian*. The *Gambetta* had followed her consort's example and sent a boat among the seals, but evidently her men were not skilful in the pursuit of that amphibious game, as they secured less than half as many as the other boat.

"As fat as a seal" is an old saying in the eastern States, and certainly it is an expressive one. The seal is usually in excellent condition, and at certain seasons of the year contains so much oil that he is a valuable prize to his captors. The seal-fisheries of Greenland employ great numbers of men, principally from Newfoundland and Nova Scotia, and also from Iceland, Norway, and Denmark. Some of the seals are taken for their skins, but the main purpose of capture is for the oil. We have already heard of the fur seal of the north-west coast of America, who is quite different from his cousin of Greenland, and far more valuable. Fur seals abound in only a few localities on the surface of the globe, and if they were not protected by stringent laws they would soon disappear.

During the evening Commander Bronson went on board the *Gambetta* for a conference with Captain Girard. It was decided to remain a day or two longer at Wrangell Island, to lay in a plentiful store of food for the dogs, and to make observations that might be of advantage to themselves or future navigators. A boat was to go from each ship in pursuit of seals and walruses; as the *Vivian's* mate was an experienced hunter after this game, he was placed in command of the joint expedition, and while he and his crew attended to securing the prizes, the Frenchmen were to look after the transportation. Then each ship was to send out an exploring party, the Frenchmen going to the north, while the Americans took a southerly course.

Fred went with the sealers, while George was with the exploring party. The former were off before six in the morning, and within two hours they had killed nearly thirty seals. While waiting for the French sailors to remove the game to the shore, and thence to the ships, they espied some walruses on the ice, beyond a point of land which formed one side of the bay, and away they went in chase. They were screened from the view of their game by the intervening point of land, and managed to get quite close to the ice without being perceived.

"We'll shoot one, and perhaps two of them," said the mate, "and then we'll take to the harpoons."

Fred asked why they did not rely altogether on shooting, as it ought to be quicker work than with the harpoon. The mate explained that the vulnerable part of a walrus is about the size of an orange, and unless you hit him on that spot your shot goes for nothing. "We may be able to get

HUNTING THE WALRUS.

one or two of them in that way before they take alarm," said he, "but after that it's hard work to hit 'em. You'll know more about walrus hunting an hour from now, and then you'll see the reason of our relying on the harpoon."

Fred was willing to wait and be instructed. They reached the edge of the floe where half a dozen walruses were taking the sun, and all unconscious of the impending danger. The side of the floe was about five feet above the water, and so the boat and its occupants were quite out of sight as they lay along-side.

With a repeating rifle in his hand, the mate stood up in the bow of the boat, while the men held it as steady as they could with the ice-hooks against the floe. One, two, three shots were fired almost as quickly as you could count, and each bullet went crashing into the skull of a walrus.

Then the rifle was passed back to one of the men, and the mate seized the harpoon. As he did so, the frightened animals that had not been touched by the bullets went sliding from the floe into the water.

To the surprise of Fred, the mate threw the harpoon into the smallest of the herd, a little fellow less than half the size of any of the others. He began to cry immediately, and then his mother came to his relief, and with her several others. They showed their tusks, and threatened to attack the boat; four of them were killed, and then the cub was slaughtered, and as soon as he ceased crying the rest went away. The mate said the walrus hunters always did this when they had the opportunity, as the mother will stay by her young, and the rest will come to assist her to defend it. At such times the walruses are very fierce, and they have been known to attack and sink a boat; they come along-side and hook their tusks over the gunwales, and when they get a good hold something must go.

Fred thought that seven walruses were enough for a day's catch, but the mate said they must make it eight, in order to have no trouble about division between the ships. They waited near the ice-floe for some time, and finally a walrus came to the surface close to the boat; the mate threw a harpoon and caught him, and in a little while he was finished with the lance. Then signal was made to the ship to send another boat, and meantime they started off with two of the prizes in tow. Slow progress was made, and before they rounded the point they met the boat from the *Vivian*, and also one from the *Gambetta*. All the game of the morning was brought in before nightfall, and Fred was congratulated on the part he had borne in the affair. He declared he had only been a spectator, to which Commander Bronson replied that a good spectator was not always easy to find.

The land party had a more wearisome journey than did the seal and walrus hunters, with less excitement to sustain them. George was ambitious to plant the American flag higher than the French had placed the tricolor the day before, and consequently fixed his eye on a hill about a thousand feet high, at least a couple of miles back from the head of the bay. He carried ashore a small flag, with its staff, and started as soon as they were landed for the hill in question, accompanied by one of the sailors. The French boat was close behind them, and as the sailor was a better climber than George, he ran ahead and planted the flag at the top of the hill before the Frenchmen had reached its base. The latter stopped, and gave three cheers for the Americans, who had got ahead of them, and then made for another hill farther inland.

There was not much to be seen on the hill, as the country was destitute of vegetation save a few patches of moss, and now and then some tiny shrubs that evidently had a hard struggle for existence. George

HOISTING THE FLAG.

found an enormous bone, which Dr. Tonner pronounced to be the bone of a mammoth; other bones were found in the vicinity, and they looked around for the tusk of the animal. No tusk could be found, and they concluded it had fallen to the possession of some previous visitor.

Later in the day the tusk of a mammoth was discovered, and it was so large that two men found it a heavy burden. They were sent to the boat to bring an oar, and some cords for lashing it, but near the landing they found a slender pole, which seemed better for the purpose, and it was taken along. The pole had drifted across the Arctic Ocean; whether it grew on the banks of an American or a Siberian river nobody could tell, but in either case the forest of its origin was many hundreds of miles away. The tusk when weighed on shipboard was found to tip the beam at a hundred and fifteen pounds, and it was afterwards ascertained that the people from the *Gambetta* had found a tusk weighing a hundred and six pounds. America was therefore nine pounds ahead!

The incident naturally led to a conversation of which the mammoth was the chief topic. Dr. Tonner said so many mammoths' tusks had been

THE SIBERIAN MAMMOTH.

found in Siberia that they had become a regular article of commerce for more than a century, though in recent years the number had somewhat diminished.

"The scientific name of the animal," said he, "is *Elephas primigenius*, and he was in his time the elephant of the period. He was somewhat larger than the elephant of to-day, but not much; his body was heavier and clumsier, and covered with hair that enabled him to live in a colder climate than the natural home of the elephant we are familiar with."

Fred asked if any living mammoth had been known in modern times.

"No," was the reply; "but as the bones have been found with marks upon them, it is conjectured that they lived with man during the Stone Age. The climate of Siberia was evidently warmer than it is now, probably like that of New York or Pennsylvania, and the mammoth found plenty of food to eat. He had three kinds of hair: one long and coarse, a second of finer quality, and a third like wool. The first was like horsehair, and measured twelve or fifteen inches; the second resembled the hair of a deer, and was nine or ten inches long; and the third was woolly, and four or five inches thick. So you see he could stand the cold a great deal better than the modern elephant, which has to be housed in the winter of our northern climate.

"You may wonder how we know all this. In the year 1799 a Tungusian fisherman discovered a mammoth frozen into a bank of earth near the river Lena. He kept the discovery to himself, and after a time removed the tusks and sold them; the wolves, bears, and foxes fed upon the flesh of the dead animal which had been so wonderfully preserved, and when the spot was visited in 1805 by Adams, an English naturalist, not even the whole skeleton remained. One fore-leg had disappeared, and a few of the other bones were gone, but the brains were in the skull and the eyes in their sockets. A good deal of the skin and hair was found: as much as possible was gathered and taken to St. Petersburg, where the skeleton now is.

"Elephant remains are found in America, where the extinct animal is called the mastodon. They have also been discovered in England and all over Europe, especially in Germany, and the evidence is very conclusive that this animal had the range of a large part of the globe ages and ages ago."

"But how did that one get frozen into the bank where the fisherman found him?" one of the youths inquired.

"Probably in the grand cataclysm we were talking about some time ago," replied the Doctor. "The earth cooled suddenly, or rather this part of it did, and the mammoth was caught in the congelation in the same way that fishes are sometimes found frozen in the ice of rivers. There was this difference, though, that the fishes are frozen in their natural habitation, while the mammoth was doubtless drowned by the upheaval of the waters, and then covered with the drift of earth, where he lay for thousands of years until brought to light in the way I have described."

THE MAMMOTH RESTORED.

CHAPTER X.

HERALD ISLAND.—CAUGHT IN THE ICE.—A NARROW ESCAPE.

IT was not deemed advisable to devote any time to the exploration of the coast of Wrangell Island, nor to make long excursions into the interior, as that work had already been performed by the officers of the *Rodgers* in 1881. So, on the third day after their arrival, the two ships left the bay where they had been anchored, and headed for Herald Island as directly as the drifting ice would permit.

The visit of the *Rodgers* demonstrated that Wrangell was not a continent but an island, and contained two ranges of mountains whose highest peaks were less than three thousand feet high. One of these ranges lies

EXPLORING THE COAST.

along the southern coast, and the other near the centre of the island, from east to west; north of the backbone, or central range, there is a rolling land, with occasional detached peaks, and along the entire coast line there are numerous sand-bars which render navigation both difficult and dangerous. As before stated, there is very little vegetation, and the animal life is confined to polar bears, seals, walruses, and numerous water-fowl.

Before they lost sight of Wrangell Island our friends had Herald Island in full view, so that there was no necessity of an observation except for verifying or correcting the figures of previous navigators. Near the coast of Herald Island they met a whaling ship, and sent a boat on board; it returned shortly, with the announcement that the whaler had been successful and was nearly full of oil; one whale more would complete the cargo, and then she would steer for San Francisco. This annonncement led to a hasty completion of letters and despatches, which were sealed in a bag and despatched to America. The *Gambetta* also sent a bag of letters, and as soon as they were on board, the whaler filled away and steered to the southward. Her captain was confident that in a few days his cargo would be complete, and he hoped soon to be out of the Arctic Ocean, and headed for home.

ON SHORE IN THE FAR NORTH.

The approach to Herald Island was rendered difficult by masses of floating ice, and also by a reef which extended about two miles from its south-western extremity. There was no sign of a harbor, and so the ships lay-to off the shore, while each sent a boat inside the reef, where a small strip of beach afforded a convenient landing-place. The party from the *Vivian* included the Doctor and the major, together with George and Fred; they got off a little ahead of the *Gambetta's* boat, and by energetic pulling were the first on shore. The major and George climbed to the top of the island, while the Doctor and Fred busied themselves with the inspection of the beach.

The climbers did not have an easy time of it, as the rock was loose, and liable to break off at any moment, while the sides of the ascent were very steep. George said they made the most of their upward journey "coon-fashion," and the return "sled-fashion." They had to go up on hands and feet, clinging to the projections and running the risk of a tumble; they came down the same way to where the broken shale lay piled up, like the cinders on Mount Vesuvius. On this they sat down and coasted, to the detriment of their garments, especially as they acquired a rapid rate of progress before reaching the beach. The major estimated the central elevation at about six hundred feet, and said the whole island was visible from it. He described the island as a ridge about six miles long and less than half a mile wide, without a harbor where ships could anchor. Wrangell Island was visible, but no other land could be seen in any direction.

The beach party did not fatigue themselves with climbing, but were by no means idle. They found drift-wood abundant, and proceeded to light a fire, and then they looked about for records of previous visits. None were discovered, although it is certain that several ships had touched there at different times. A cairn of stones was found at the western extremity of the island, but it had evidently been despoiled, as it contained nothing to reveal its origin, and there was no mark on the rocks in the neighborhood. They looked for the plank erected by the *Rodgers*, but it had disappeared. Assisted by the men from the *Gambetta*, our friends erected a cairn in which they placed a bottle containing a record of the visit, and to make sure that it should be seen, a cross formed of two pieces of drift-wood was placed above it. No bears or other quadrupeds were visible, but there was an abundance of water-fowl similar to those on Wrangell Island. The rifles were of little use, but there was abundant occupation for the shot-guns in killing ducks and plover for the cabin table. Dr. Tonner killed a duck which he pronounced an eider, the producer of the down famous the world over for its usefulness in filling quilts. Whether the duck belonged on the island or was only there by accident no one could tell.

The best part of the day was spent in the visit to Herald Island, and when the boats returned to the ship the travellers were weary and hungry. Major Clapp reported ice to the north of Herald Island as the result of his observation from the summit, but said it did not appear to be very thick. While the boats were on shore, the two commanders had met in the cabin of the *Gambetta*, and decided to steer to the north-east, unless prevented by circumstances then unforeseen. When the boats were hoisted in, the ships filled their sails with the southerly breeze and steered as agreed upon.

They were now in the domains of the midnight sun, and it was not always easy to keep the time; as Fred expressed it, "you couldn't say whether it was to-day or to-morrow." The sun did not go below the

UNDER THE MIDNIGHT SUN.

horizon at midnight, though it just touched it, and the assertion that the sun rises in the east and sets in the west had lost its correctness. The uses of a clock on which the hours are marked from one to twenty-four became apparent, and Fred and George adopted the plan of dividing the day in

NEAR THE ICE-PACK.

that way. "Eighteen o'clock" served to indicate six in the afternoon, and "twenty-three o'clock" meant eleven at night. It was rather trying to go to bed in broad daylight, but they soon got used to it. Fred said he couldn't think of staying awake for three months, and then sleeping for the same length of time, and so he accepted the situation without a single break.

As they sailed away from Herald Island, with the prow of the *Vivian* in the direction of the pole, Commander Bronson recalled the fate of the *Jeannette.*

"We are now," said he, "almost at the point where the *Jeannette* was beset in the ice on the 6th of September, 1879. She never escaped from it until she sank to the depths of the Arctic Ocean, nearly two years later, and left her crew to the perils of a journey over ice and open water to the shores of Siberia."

"Yes," responded the Doctor, "and who can tell how soon we shall be enclosed in the icy walls, and compelled to drift wherever the currents may take us?"

"There was one remarkable feature of the drift of the *Jeannette*," said the major. "It was not on a reasonably direct line, as though driven by a steady current, like what we find on the coast of Greenland. The *Jeannette* seemed to move as though propelled by shifting currents, and her track was very irregular. On the published chart it is in the form of zig-zags, and crosses itself repeatedly. This was the case soon after she was frozen in near Herald Island; she drifted north, then east, and then south-west, and then to the westward. On the 3d of November, 1880, she was in almost exactly the same position as on the 26th of the previous April, but in the mean time she had drifted, or rather had been borne by the ice to every point of the compass, and her wanderings covered fully ten degrees of longitude."

"What was the rate of the drift?" one of the listeners inquired.

"It varied considerably," was the reply. "Some days it was as high as twenty miles or more, and at other times not more than half a mile. Occasionally the ship was almost stationary for days together; this happened in the coldest weather, and showed that at such times there was very little current.

CABIN SCENE IN AN ARCTIC WINTER.

"Captain De Long was of the opinion," the major continued, "that even the lightest winds caused a movement of the ice, except when it was of great thickness. We shall probably have occasion to make practical observations on this point before many days; we'll drop the subject now, and follow the *Jeannette* in her monotonous career after she was enclosed in the ice.

"From the time she was frozen in, the life on shipboard was full of dreariness. For more than a year she moved in the zigzags I have described to the north of Herald and Wrangell Islands, and then drifted slowly to the westward. Sometimes the ice broke, and promised to set them free; when the hopes of Captain De Long and his companions were thus raised the ice closed again, and escape was as far off as ever. As the winter came on, the cold increased and the ice thickened. Terrible gales

EDGE OF THE ICE-PACK.

swept over the surface of the Arctic Ocean, and caused a continual grinding and crushing of the great floes, which threatened the instant destruction of the ship.

"The captain in his journal gives a vivid description of the noise caused by these movements of the ice. There were loud crashes as the floes broke against each other, mingled with the peculiar grinding sounds of the attrition of the smaller pieces, and the roar of the wind as it impinged on the roughened surface. Frequently they were called from their beds at night, in momentary expectation that the ship would be crushed, and for months and months together everything was kept in readiness for sudden departure. The sledges and boats were on the ice near the ship, where the floes seemed to promise the greatest security. The dogs were quartered there, though they came aboard the ship whenever they liked, and quantities of provisions were stored near the boats or on the sledges.

"The first serious alarm occurred on the 19th of January, 1880, an hour or so past midnight. The captain was seated in his room, when he heard a sound as though some of the ship's timbers were cracking; he ran out and found there was no movement of the ice, and after looking around and discovering no cause for the sound, he went to bed under the impression that nothing more had happened than a bolt drawn by the extreme cold. About eight o'clock in the morning the wind suddenly shifted from north to north-west, and the ice began to move; it came with tremendous force against the bow, and piled up large masses in front of the ship; but as that was the strongest part of the *Jeannette*, it was thought she could stand the strain without injury.

"But when the men went below to serve out coal for the day's use, they found a stream pouring in through a crack in the fore-foot; there were three feet of water in the fore-hold, and a corresponding amount in the store-room and fire-room. All the crew was called, and while some worked at the pumps the rest removed the stores from the part of the ship that was most seriously threatened.

"From that day until she disappeared beneath the waters the *Jeannette* was constantly leaking, and it required the steady attention and exertion of her crew to keep her afloat. The supply of coal was exhausted in working the steam-pumps, so that if the ship had been released from the ice she would have been compelled to work under sail alone. After this incident orders were given to have the sledges packed ready for instant departure, and during the gales everybody lay down to rest with his knapsack on his back or by his side. Captain De Long described their situation 'like living over a powder magazine, with a train laid for instant firing.' The excitement growing out of their constant peril, varied with occasional hunts after bears and walruses, were the only variations to the monotony of their existence, and everybody suffered from the enforced inactivity.

ICE IN MOTION.

"Of course they hoped to be released during the summer of 1880, and have an opportunity to add to the discoveries of previous explorers. But the Ice-king did not relent, and they remained in their prison until winter came again. Then followed the long darkness, then the arctic spring and summer, with the sun at midnight, and it was in this second period of continuous day that the great calamity occurred to the *Jeannette*.

"The ice opened, and for some time the ship was afloat; then it closed again, crushing her sides as though they had been of pasteboard, but holding her firmly in their grasp. She remained afloat nearly twelve hours, so that there was time for everybody to escape to the ice, with a fairly good stock of provisions. Then followed the preparations for the journey to the Siberian coast, and seven days after the sinking of the ship the march began to the southward.

"The boats were on sledges drawn by the men and dogs, and there was a stock of provisions sufficient for reaching the Siberian coast. The journey occupied more than three months, including a rest of eight days on Bennett Island, where the sledges were abandoned and the boats launched in the water, which had become sufficiently open for navigation.

"The party landed on one of the islands of the New Siberia group, and afterwards on Semenovski Island. They were separated by a gale on the 12th of September, and one of the boats, commanded by Lieutenant Chipp, was never heard from. Another, commanded by Engineer Melville, reached the coast safely, and her party soon fell in with the natives and were saved from starvation. The other boat, in which were Commander De Long and thirteen others, was less fortunate than that of the engineer; it reached one of the mouths of the Lena, which it ascended as far as the ice would permit, and there the crew went on shore. It was necessary to abandon many things on leaving the boat; when they reached the land the stock of provisions was very small, and there was but a limited amount of clothing for the weary and frost-bitten men. Two sailors, Nindermann and Noros, were sent away to procure help, and when nearly dead with fatigue and starvation fell in with some wandering natives. They could not induce these people to go with them to relieve the shipwrecked crew, and so all of their party that had been left behind died of hunger and cold on the banks of the Lena. The two sailors were taken to a Russian village, where they met Mr. Melville, their old officer; he did everything in his power for the rescue of De Long and his companions, but all in vain. The records which were afterwards found by the side of De Long at the spot where he died showed that before Melville started on his search the whole party had perished.

"In the following spring an expedition was sent to the mouth of the Lena to find the last camp of the explorers, and secure the records of the voyage of the *Jeannette*. All the papers were found and preserved, the

IN AN ARCTIC GALE.

bodies were buried, and a monument was erected over their grave. One by one the survivors returned to the United States; and finally, in the early part of 1884, the bodies of De Long and those who died with him were brought home for burial in their native land. The story of the *Jeannette* is one of the most pathetic that has been given to us in the annals of arctic exploration."

As the major ended his account of the adventures of De Long and his companions, there was not a dry eye among his group of listeners. Not a word was spoken, but silently, one by one, they sought the deck, and did not revert to the subject of the conversation.

"The ice is growing thicker in the north," said the Doctor, as he waved his hand in the direction indicated. "The wind seems to be pressing the floes together, and I should not be surprised if the pack closes in upon us before another twenty hours."

Hour by hour the ice became more abundant, and the Doctor's prediction was verified. Within twenty hours from the time he made it, they were surrounded by drifting ice, so closely that it was practically turned into a pack. Here and there lanes of water were open, and the ships pressed through them to make as much northing as possible before their progress was arrested. The lanes narrowed, and finally disappeared altogether, and the ships were enclosed where both sails and steam were powerless. It was not deemed advisable to light the fires and use the engines until there should be a prospect of reaching open water by so doing.

Where the ice came from that closed in behind them after their progress was arrested nobody could tell. In ten hours from the time they stopped, the entire horizon to the south had changed from water to ice, with an appearance of solidity which was anything but encouraging. The wind was variable, as it shifted from south to east, then to southwest, and afterwards to south-east, all within a few hours; the change of wind caused an irregular motion to the ice-fields, and the crashing and grinding of the floes and cakes was continuous.

Fred and George asked permission to go out on the ice, but their request was denied. Captain Jones explained that there might be a breakup at any moment, and they would run great risk of being cut off from their floating home. "The pack," said he, "is not yet solidly closed, however much it may appear so; a change of wind may open long lanes of water, and you might suddenly find yourself with one of these lanes between you and the ship. We could not send a boat for you, as it would be impossible to launch one, and your only chance would be to swim across the lanes and clamber over the cakes and floes."

Such a risk was not to be thought of for a moment, and they contented themselves with looking at the ice from the deck of the *Vivian*. George had a glass in his hand, and was endeavoring to find a space of open water when he suddenly caught sight of a bear.

The animal was at least two miles away, and coming towards the ship, as though desirous of investigating it and ascertaining its character. Rifles were brought, and everybody was ready for a shot in case there was a chance for it. Captain Jones said that, if the bear came near enough, the hunters might go out on the ice in pursuit of him; but they must be under strict orders to return at a signal from the ship.

The bear continued to approach, and when he was within half a mile of the *Vivian* the captain gave his permission, and the Doctor and major went over the side and down upon the ice, accompanied, or rather followed, by Fred and George. Screening themselves as well as possible behind the hummocks scattered over the ice-pack, they got along very well, and were soon within range of the game. Evidently the bear was suspicious; he stopped in his advance and stood erect, in order to take in as wide a field of view as possible. This gave an excellent mark for the rifles, and the major took a shot at the denizen of the ice. The Doctor followed his example almost at the same instant; the bullets went true to their mark, and the bear fell to the ice apparently dead.

The hunters advanced cautiously, and it was well they did so. The bear rose to his feet when they were not more than half a dozen yards away, and sprang directly towards them; already his paws seemed to be within reach of the major's face, when the Doctor fired again and brought him down once more. The shot was fatal, and there was no further sign of life.

The major drew his handkerchief and waved it, as an intimation that they had killed their bear and wanted help to carry it on board. As he did so, a rifle was fired on the deck of the *Vivian:* it was the signal agreed upon for their return, and indicated danger.

There was no delay in attempting to save the bear, though all the party regretted leaving such a prize to be eaten by wolves or to sink beneath the waves. They knew that the signal would not have been given without good reason, and possibly they might be in great peril without knowing it.

Wherever the condition of the ice permitted, they ran at the top of their speed; but there were many places where running was impossible, owing to the roughness of the way. To prevent accidents with their weapons, the major ordered that all cartridges should be removed, and on no account was one of the party to stop to shoot at anything except in self-defence. They were near their ship, and the only bear they had seen was dead; consequently, there was not much likelihood of their falling into temptation.

They were about half-way to the ship when two shots were fired in quick succession. They naturally looked in the *Vivian's* direction, and saw one of the officers standing at the gangway waving a small flag. The movements of the flag indicated that they were to make a detour to the right and reach the ship near her bows. They turned as indicated, and the flag ceased its motion.

HUMMOCKS AFLOAT.

"There's open water between us and the ship," said the major, "and we must go about to weather it."

Again the flag waved, and another shot was fired.

"We're in great danger," said the Doctor. "Run for your lives!"

The pace was quickened, the major taking the lead.

A hundred yards from the ship they reached a great fissure or lane, at least twenty feet across, with bits of ice floating at intervals of a yard or two. These cakes were too small to render it safe to try to jump from one to another, and the only way of escape was to pass around the end of the lane. To their dismay, the lane extended perhaps an eighth of a mile, and was widening and lengthening every moment.

There was a commotion below the surface which indicated a general disruption of the pack. Every few minutes an upheaval threw pieces of ice into the air with the sound of an explosion, and formed a hummock like the top of a miniature volcano. What if the mass should separate altogether while they were on its surface!

Faster than ever they ran along the side of the lane till they neared its end. There was a width of four or five feet over which the major sprang with the agility of a deer; he turned to catch the Doctor, who narrowly escaped a fall, and then the two men received Fred and George without accident. Each of the party clung to his rifle; the major admitted afterwards that he was too scared to think of dropping his burden, his whole thought being to waste no time in getting to the ship.

They approached the ship under her bowsprit. Their coming was provided for, as the captain had ordered rope-ladders lowered from the bows, so that the time of going as far aft as the gangway was saved. The major and Fred sprang to one of the ladders, while the Doctor and George seized the other. In a few seconds they were on the deck of the *Vivian*, and safe from their peril.

The lane of water continued to widen and lengthen, and the commotion below the ice increased. While our friends were still panting from the fatigue of their enforced run over the ice, the floes came together with great violence, and formed a huge winrow of irregular blocks and fragments, perhaps a dozen feet high. Then it opened again, and in a few minutes the floes were separated and water was visible in a dozen directions. The ice around the ship gave way and she floated free. With the aid of the glass they could see that the same disturbance was going on in the vicinity of the *Gambetta*.

The latter vessel had been lying with her prow to the westward, but she was gradually turned by the ice until she headed due north. Then she spread her foresail to catch the breeze, and soon was forging slowly ahead.

"She's determined to sail to the pole," said the Doctor.

"Yes," answered Major Clapp, "and so are we."

As he spoke he pointed to the foresail of the *Vivian*, which was following the example of the Frenchman. Captain Jones was aloft in the crow's-nest, and his quick eye had noted the movement of the *Gambetta*. As her men were ascending the rigging he gave the necessary order, and was evidently determined not to be left behind.

HOW A HUMMOCK IS FORMED.

CHAPTER XI.

FAST IN THE ICE.—GOING INTO WINTER QUARTERS.

OBSERVATION at noon showed the ships to be in latitude 72° 15′ north, longitude 176° 20′ west; the lookout reported signs of open water to the eastward, and after a short dialogue with the signal-flags the ships were headed in that direction, the *Vivian* leading. In a couple of hours the course was changed to the north-east, and the promise of open water was increased, since there was no indication of ice-blink on the horizon towards which they were steering. Between seven and eight o'clock, or, as Fred expressed it, "at half-past nineteen," the open water was distinctly visible eight or ten miles ahead of their position, and by midnight they were practically free of the ice.

Just as they had reached clear sailing a fog set in, and it was necessary to proceed with great caution. Very little way was made by either ship, as it was impossible to determine when the ice would be reached again, and it would be a serious matter to run against a floe while proceeding at the rate of five or six knots an hour. Sail was shortened to little more than the extent of a pocket-handkerchief, and the *Vivian* and *Gambetta* drifted along, and literally felt their way. They did not make more than a mile an hour in this sort of progress, and it was especially tantalizing, as there was a favoring breeze that would have borne them merrily along if circumstances permitted. The wisdom of their precaution was shown when a huge floe appeared through the fog and effectually barred their way. The captain ordered an ice-anchor to be put out, and in a little while the *Vivian* was moored to the floe, and the *Gambetta* followed her example.

The fog lifted after a time, and showed that the floe was of great extent; it embraced several small icebergs, the first they had seen, and as soon as it was considered safe to do so a party went off to examine them. The largest of the bergs was about a hundred feet high and five hundred yards long, and the ice of which it was composed was remarkably clear for the product of a glacier. Captain Jones said he thought it must have

MOORED TO AN ICE-FLOE.

come from the American coast, though possibly it may have originated in one of the islands discovered by Captain De Long on his retreat southward, after the sinking of the *Jeannette*. In the journal from which the account of his voyage was written, he says that he saw on Bennett Island one glacier which was three miles across at its front, and another, somewhat smaller, a little farther along the coast.

Several blocks were cut from the berg and taken on board the *Vivian;* they melted one of these blocks, and the water obtained from it was perfectly fresh; this proved unmistakably that it was from a glacier. Floe-ice is formed by the freezing of salt-water, but occasionally cakes and fragments are found which have drifted down from Siberian or American rivers, and are therefore fresh. In the heat of summer the surface of a floe is often covered in many places with water two or three inches deep; sometimes this water comes from the melting of the surface of the ice, and occasionally it is blown there by the action of the wind; in either case it is salt, and can never be mistaken for the product of a berg.

Fred took an ice-auger and endeavored to ascertain the thickness of the floe, but after boring to a depth of eleven feet he gave up the attempt. Captain Jones said he might easily go down twenty feet without finding bottom, and George reminded him that arctic explorers had found ice upward of forty feet thick. Weyprecht and Payer, in the voyage of the *Tegethoff,* reported a depth of forty-seven feet in the ice which surrounded the ship in her last winter in the North; this great thickness shows the effect of long continued and intense cold. If the congelation sets in early in the beginning of an arctic winter, and the weather is steadily cold, without wind, the water becomes chilled to such an extent that a few more weeks and a few more degrees of cold would convert the entire ocean around the pole into a solid mass.

Liberty was given to half the crew to go out on the ice and amuse themselves in any way they liked; but it was understood that they should return with all speed at a signal from the ship. They had a good time, chasing each other like school-boys at play, climbing on the iceberg, sliding wherever there was a smooth surface favorable to that amusement, and searching for shells and pieces of drift-wood. The latter sport was mainly left to Fred and George, as it was more scientific than exciting, and the sailors were not specially interested in it. George picked up a piece of drift-wood similar to what had been found on Herald and Wrangell Islands, and with the help of one of the men carried it to the ship. Commander Bronson said it demonstrated that the ice was formed in the part of the Arctic Ocean west of Behring Strait; its position, together with the iceberg imbedded in it, was an indication of an easterly current which might prove exactly what they wanted to find.

While George was busy with the drift-wood, Fred, who had abandoned the ice-auger, proceeded to investigate the berg from which the blocks had already been cut and carried to the ship. With considerable difficulty he climbed to the top, cutting steps for his feet at every advance and narrowly escaping a serious fall. A few minutes after he stood upon the summit, and waved his hat as a signal of triumph, a large slice broke from the farther end of the berg and slid down with a tremendous crash. This was a warning of the peril of his position, and he prudently descended to the surface of the floe. Safely at the bottom, he realized the force of what he had heard and read, that an iceberg is not to be depended on at any time, and should be approached and mounted with caution.

A commotion among the men who had strayed to the farther end of the berg attracted the youth's attention, and he hastened to ascertain the cause. He had not long to wait.

"A bear! a bear!" said one of the sailors who came running from the group.

"And a big one, too!" said another, who was following close behind his comrade.

None of the sailors had any weapons, and Fred was without his gun. The major and the Doctor, together with the commander, were walking on the ice not far from the ship, engaged in investigating it, and not one of them had anything to shoot with.

"Bring the rifles!" shouted all three of the gentlemen at nearly the same instant. Soon the rifles were in their hands, and they started for the game.

The bear seemed to understand the situation, and gave them a long chase. He could move faster than his biped pursuers, and every minute the distance between them increased. Finding there was no hope of overtaking him, Commander Bronson dropped on one knee and took a long shot, but without perceptible effect. The bear kept on as though nothing had happened, and the chase was abandoned at the end of half a mile. The Doctor said he was reminded of a similar chase after a bear on the ice near the Siberian coast, a few years before; he followed the animal for at least five miles, and the brute seemed to lead him on for the purpose of tantalizing him.

Whenever he stopped and gave up the chase, the bear halted and came towards him, almost within range. Then the bear would stop and look at him; the Doctor would creep forward, and when about ready for a shot, the bear invariably turned and made off. Then the Doctor followed on a while; when he stopped the bear stopped; and thus the performance was repeated several times. Finally he took a long shot, with little expectation of hitting his object; he aimed high, to allow for the course of the bullet, and to his surprise brought the bear to the ice and disabled him. Then he followed up and finished the bear with a shot through the skull. The first bullet had broken a fore-leg and opened one of the large veins, but in spite of the severe wound the bear rushed at him as he approached, and was only stopped by the final shot.

Our friends looked about for seals and walruses, but none were to be seen. It is probable that, if any were in the vicinity, they had been scared off by the noise on the ice, as these creatures are very wary and must be pursued in silence. There's an old saying, " you don't hunt ducks with a brass band," and it may well apply to seals and walruses. Quiet must be observed when pursuing these animals on the ice, as they slip into the water at the least sound. When you have a walrus harpooned you may shout as much as you please, and you can do the same thing when killing seals with a club, after their retreat to the water is cut off.

A gun from the ship drew attention to the signal at the peak, and everybody went on board without delay. The dogs had been let out for a run on the ice, and there was some trouble in getting them in again; they resisted all control, until one of the drivers came to the gang-plank and threw out a few pieces of seal-meat. The whole drove then went aboard with a rush, and had their usual quarrel over the repast on the ship's deck.

The recall had been made in consequence of the clearing up of the fog and the prospect of being able to make a farther advance. When all were safe on board, the *Vivian* cast off from the floe and the *Gambetta* followed her example. A few scattered cakes and floes were visible in the north-east, but there was none as large as the one to which they had been fastened, and the captain considered the opportunity too good to be lost.

The ships made about thirty-five or forty miles on their course, and then the drift-ice became so thick as to necessitate caution. The captain mounted to the crow's-nest, and in an hour or so he announced that he could make out the ice-blink filling the horizon in the distance. It extended so far that he thought it indicated an end of their progress under sail for the present.

Steadily the ice increased, and in ten or twelve hours after the blink was discovered they found themselves hemmed in on all sides. The floes were large, and the lanes became so narrow that sailing was out of the

CHASING A BEAR ON THE ICE.

question. Once more the ships were tied up, and as a matter of precaution Captain Jones ordered the *Vivian* to be warped into a little nook on one side of a floe, where the chances of being "nipped" were greatly diminished.

"We are now," said the captain, "about as far to the north as we can expect to get by sailing. In a few hours we shall probably be frozen in, and must trust to the currents to carry us on our way. The wind is in our favor, and I think the ice is carrying us towards the pole."

Then he ordered soundings to be made on the side of the ship farthest from the ice. The lead showed forty-five fathoms of water, with muddy bottom; after the depth had been ascertained the lead was again cast, in order to ascertain the drift of the ice, and consequently of the ship. This proved to be north-east; the wind was blowing from the south, and consequently the drift was not exactly in accordance with the wind, and showed the existence of a current.

During the night the ice closed in more firmly than before, and the drift to the north-east continued. Observation at noon the next day showed their position, latitude 74° 20' north, longitude 172° 18' west; and it was practically at this point they were enclosed by the ice and held firmly in its grasp.

And now began a period of monotony which we will not attempt to record day by day. Such a narrative would be tedious, and could not differ materially from the stories that many navigators have given us in the accounts of their hibernation in the arctic regions. Our friends followed the example of Kane, Parry, De Long, M'Clintock, and other arctic explorers, and proceeded to make their preparations for the season of long-continued cold. Lumber was brought from below for building a house over the deck; the structure was made as close as possible, in order to keep out the cold, and a sufficient pitch was given to the roof to let the snow slide off as fast as it fell. In the centre the roof was supported by stout rafters, and the space was made so roomy that it virtually added another deck to the ship. The dogs were allowed the run of this enclosed space at certain hours of the day, but the most of their time was passed on the ice, where shelters were erected for them. They were not long in finding out the hour for meals. It was the custom to feed them at four in the afternoon, and when the marine signal of eight bells was given they walked up the gang-plank and indicated their readiness for duty. Had they been the patrons of a well-regulated boarding-house they could not have been more prompt.

The dog-shelters were made of boards, like the housing of the deck.

A VILLAGE OF SNOW-HUTS.

Fred and George wanted to have some huts of snow or ice, and with the assistance of the dog-drivers they constructed some. It required a good deal of engineering, as the Chukchees are not to be compared with the Eskimos in this kind of work; in fact, the Eskimo snow-hut is the finest dwelling of the kind in the whole world. Fred and George made use of the drawings given by Captain Hall, and others familiar with the Eskimos, and then projected their edifices as an architect makes his plans. Every block was hewn from the ice, as a block of stone is cut for a building; the joints were cemented with water; a tunnel was made for the entrance, on the same plan as in Greenland; and altogether the huts, when completed, were highly creditable to the builders.

We will describe the mode of construction of the Eskimo snow-hut by telling how our friends made theirs.

They levelled a space on the ice to form the floor, and in order to have as little transportation as possible for their material they selected a spot close to a solid hummock. The Eskimos use blocks of snow which have been packed hard by the wind, but as these were not available, our friends used ice, which they quarried from the hummock. As before stated, each block was carefully shaped before being set in its place; George attended to the cutting of the blocks, assisted by one of the drivers, while Fred and the other driver performed the work on the hut.

The first hut they built was about ten feet in diameter at the base, and was intended to be six feet clear on the inside. Of course the centre of the dome was the only point where this height was maintained. Opposite the entrance the floor was raised about six inches higher than in the other half of the hut; this raised space was understood to be parlor and bed-room, while the other was more practical in its uses, and served as kitchen, and a lodging for the dogs when they chose to come in. The dogs, by-the-way, seemed to understand from the outset that they were prohibited from mounting to the parlor, and only on a few occasions did they ever attempt it.

The first row of blocks was laid with mathematical accuracy, the circle having been formed by means of a string fastened to a peg in the centre of the prepared floor; then the second row was laid a little inside the line of the first; and then the rows followed in regular succession till the top was reached. Three holes for windows were left at different elevations; two of these were covered with plates of clear ice an inch or more in thickness, while the third was closed with the membrane of the stomach of a deer. It was found that these windows admitted sufficient light for all practical purposes, but the ice-windows were not to be relied on during the period that the sun came above the horizon.

The youths made a ludicrous blunder in their first effort at building a hut. Fred was on the inside, assisting in laying the blocks in place; his attendant native was outside the hut, engaged in handing up the blocks as they were received from George and his assistant. As they were about to put the final block on the top it occurred to George that they had quite forgotten to make a door for entrance. They had planned it originally, but in the excitement of laying out the circle the door had been omitted, and was not again thought of. And there was Fred, almost walled up inside without means of escape!

The ice-axes soon remedied this oversight, and Fred was able to come to daylight, after assisting in covering the dome with its cap. Then the tunnel leading up to the door was finished, and the youths were ready for the inspection of their work.

They held a reception the next day at noon. Calls were made by all the officers of the ship, and each visitor was regaled with a cup of hot tea from a kettle prepared on shipboard, and kept at the right temperature by an alcohol lamp. George said they were not quite up to the native custom of burning oil in a stone lamp, but they might come to it in time.

George was ready to answer all inquiries relative to the construction of huts of this sort; he said they were peculiar to the arctic regions, and were rarely, if ever, seen in the

torrid zone; Stanley and other African explorers made no mention of them, and therefore it was to be inferred that snow-huts were not built in the dark continent. Even in the far North they do not last through the summer, as the sun quickly destroys them; the snow-hut is only a winter residence, and the Eskimos take to skin tents during the warm months.

The winter huts of the Eskimos are usually on the ice, or near it, on account of the convenience of fishing or sealing, but their summer tents are on the land. For a winter residence they select a bay where the ice is not likely to drift, and the nearer they can get to the haunts of the seal the better they like it. It not unfrequently happens that the ice under a village breaks up in a storm; in such case the occupants must run for safety, and they are not always able to do this, especially if a severe gale

is blowing, and there is a general disruption of the floe.   In some instances whole villages have been swept away, and in others only a few
individuals escaped to tell how the rest were lost.

A HUT SUBMERGED.

Fred and George spent the most of the afternoon in their ice-hut to
receive the congratulations of their friends and become accustomed to the
novelty of the situation.   When evening came they abandoned it to the
dog-drivers, and on the next day it was the object of much interest to the
sailors, who were allowed to visit it in small parties till all had been given
an opportunity of inspection and criticism.

Evidently the youths were not in a hurry to occupy the new house they
had built, and they frankly admitted that the cabin of the *Vivian* was
greatly to be preferred.   "But we'll build more of them," said Fred, " in
case they are needed for sheltering the dogs, or for any other purpose.
We've got our hands in now, and can turn them off very quickly.   We can
make a whole village of these huts, and connect them by short galleries, as
the Eskimos do, so that we may step from one to another without going
out-of-doors."

The early part of the hibernation of the ships was not at all dangerous,
as the ice-floes were not crowding each other, and there were no gales to

break up the fields and create the commotions that we have already mentioned. Sometimes the wind shifted suddenly, but in most cases there was a calm interval of a few hours. The weather steadily increased in coldness, and by the middle of September the thermometer at night was frequently below zero.

Every day the dog-teams were harnessed for sledge journeys over the ice as far as practicable. Visits were exchanged with the officers of the *Gambetta*, and both ships made preparations for long explorations as soon as circumstances favored. Fred and George tried their hands at driving the dogs, and had many overturns and mishaps. No serious accident occurred, however, and they counted their bruises as the honorable scars of their warfare with the regions of ice.

Bears and seals were occasionally seen, and when seen they were pursued with varying success. One day a returning dog-team reported walruses on the ice near some open water six or eight miles to the south; of course there was a desire on the part of everybody to go in pursuit of them, and early next morning a party was off. Two dog-teams were taken, and it was arranged that if any walruses were killed the other teams should be sent out as soon as intelligence could be brought to the ship.

They succeeded in killing three walruses out of a dozen or more that were making themselves comfortable on the surface of a floe. The sledges were loaded with the meat, and Fred started back with them; a sharp lookout had been kept on board ship for the hunters, so that Fred and his sledges were discovered before he had made half the distance homeward. The flag of the *Vivian* was dipped three times, as had been arranged, and then the youth mounted to the top of a hummock, and with the small flag that he carried he told the result of the day's sport. In a few minutes the extra teams were off, and making the best of their way in the direction of the hunting region. The dogs enjoyed the run immensely, and needed no urging; in many places the ice was rough, but by making occasional detours the sledges found a fairly good road.

Fred did not return to where the walruses were killed, as it was too late in the day when he reached the ship to make a second journey. The sledges were loaded with all they could carry, and by dark all were safely at the side of the *Vivian*. The Doctor said they had been obliged to leave several hundred pounds of walrus-meat, and hoped to be able to bring it in the next morning; Captain Jones thought there would be very little use in going for it, as the flesh could be scented a long distance by the bears, and the chances were in favor of their devouring every ounce of it before the hunters could get around to the spot.

"If that's the case," said George, "we'll go for it anyway, and if the bears have eaten up the meat they will be likely to stay around for more, and we can have the fun of a bear-hunt."

The suggestion was accepted as a sensible one, and early in the morning the party was off. It consisted of the major, with George and Fred, and they agreed that, as the suggestion came from George, he should have the first shot at the bear in case they encountered one.

As they approached the scene of the previous day's sport they proceeded very cautiously; every few minutes the youths mounted to the summit of a hummock and swept the horizon with a glass, in the hope of discovering a bear. Their patience was rewarded, as a bear was revealed where the dead walrus lay; he was so busy with his breakfast that he did not look up for an instant, and the major thought it would be easy to approach him.

The sledge was left with the dogs behind a hummock; the animals had not seen or scented the bear, otherwise it would have been a difficult matter to keep them quiet. The three hunters went forward with their rifles, George taking the lead in accordance with the agreement.

They crept along, shielding themselves as best they could, though there was little need of precaution, since the bear was so intently occupied with his feast of walrus-meat. Keeping the wind in their favor, so that he should not discover their presence by his sense of smell, they reached a little hummock not more than twenty yards from where the bear stood.

"Don't be in a hurry," whispered the major; "get a good aim at his heart, and rest your rifle against the hummock to steady it. Wait till you have a first-rate chance, as he won't be in a hurry to move off."

George obeyed the major's directions, and secured an excellent aim before firing.

As the report of his rifle rang out, the major and Fred sprang from their concealment, and were ready to give their assistance in case it was wanted.

The bear fell on his side, but was up in an instant. He rose to his hind-feet, and thus gave the opportunity for George's companions. They fired almost simultaneously, and the bear dropped once more. Then George ran forward and smashed the skull of the brute with another bullet. The brief and brilliant encounter was over, and the party had exchanged the meat of the walrus for that of the bear.

While they were engaged in skinning their prize and preparing it for the homeward journey, Fred discovered a large bear on the ice not more than a quarter of a mile away. The youth desired to go on another hunt,

WALRUSES ON THE ICE.

but was restrained by the major, who argued that they already had as much game as they could take care of; and if they killed another bear they would be obliged to leave him for his brethren and the wolves to devour.

"Do bears eat each other?" said Fred, in a tone of surprise.

"Certainly they do," was the reply; "they kill and devour one another in their battles, and if a bear is killed by a hunter, and abandoned, he will be speedily devoured by his kindred. They are not at all fastidious in their tastes, and if the thing was not a physical inconvenience, I believe a bear would eat himself up, and pick all his bones so clean that there wouldn't be enough flesh on them to bait a mouse-trap with.

"And if the bears didn't come around, the wolves would be sure to find their way here before many hours. The meat that an arctic wolf will decline to devour hasn't yet been discovered."

So the solitary bear on the ice was left to himself, and no doubt he fared sumptuously on what the hunters left on their return to the ship.

ARCTIC WOLVES.

CHAPTER XII.

DISAPPEARANCE OF THE SUN. — INCIDENTS OF HIBERNATION. — THE AURORA
BOREALIS.

THE ships continued day by day to drift with the ice as it was borne by the wind and currents. A good deal depended on the wind, and fortunately it was mostly from the southern quarter of the horizon; sometimes, when not a breath was blowing, soundings were made through the ice in order to ascertain the force of the current. At such times the lead was dropped to the bottom, and allowed to remain there until the slope of the line became so great that it was time to take it in. Commander Bronson applied one of the problems of Euclid to the demonstration on the drift of the ship, and perhaps the knowledge of his system may be of use to others.

In the first place, the lead was dropped perpendicularly to the bottom, and the length of line paid out was carefully noted. Then, as the ship drifted with the ice, the observations were made at a hole through the ice. The line was run out until it sloped off at an angle of forty-five degrees. The additional line given out was noted, and thus the perpendicular and the hypothenuse were known, together with the angle between them. Henceforth it was easy enough to find the length of the base; the latter represented the distance over which they had travelled, and as the time occupied was carefully kept, the daily drift of the ship could be averaged.

It could not be exactly obtained in this way, as the drift might vary from one hour to another, but it was near enough for all practical purposes. Similar observations were made on board the *Gambetta*, and at hours different from those of the *Vivian;* the result of the observations was exchanged from time to time, and careful comparisons were made. The truth of the old adage that "two heads are better than one" was well exemplified in this case.

Sounding leads and dredges were frequently used for ascertaining the character of the bottom of the ocean, and the results of the dredging were sometimes quite interesting. Usually the dredge brought up nothing but soft mud, but once in a while it revealed curious forms of marine shells, the most of them so small as to need a microscope for their investigation. One day a tiny branch of coral was secured, but whether it was formed where they found it, or had been drifted northward from warmer regions, nobody could tell. No fishes were caught, but for all that there might have been an abundance of them in the water. It would require a good deal of stupidity as well as sluggishness for a fish to be taken in a dredge which was moving so slowly as to seem almost at rest. Fred tried several times to catch something on a hook which he lowered through a hole drilled in the ice, after carefully baiting it with a piece of seal-fat. But his efforts were not rewarded with a bite, nor even a nibble.

IN WINTER QUARTERS.

The depth of water varied from thirty-five to fifty fathoms, being rarely less than the former figure or more than the latter. The observations on the depth of water corresponded very nearly with those made on the *Jeannette*. It is probable that the Arctic Ocean is nowhere of the great depth of the Atlantic or the Pacific, though it may have been much deeper than at present in ages long gone by. The mud that forms the bottom has been drifted down from the numerous rivers flowing into the Arctic Sea, and has gradually accumulated, just as the mud of the Mississippi River has partially filled the Gulf of Mexico.

Fred and George were anxious to emulate the examples of other navigators and domesticate young seals and walruses, but they did not have the opportunity. It is doubtful if they could have kept these strange pets for any length of time, as their surroundings were not favorable. A walrus or

PERILS OF THE POLAR SEA.

seal in the cabin would not have been an agreeable companion, while outside it would have been liable to escape, or be eaten up by the dogs.

Next to having one of these creatures, George concluded he would like the skin of a bear without a bullet-hole in it. Now the way has not been found for shooting a bear without breaking his skin, and the youth determined, with the proper authority, to set a trap for one. Permission was readily given, on condition that the trap should be far enough from the ship to be out of reach of the dogs. It was thought that a mile and a half would be a sufficient distance, and the trap was set accordingly.

It was one of the largest bear-traps sold in the San Francisco market, and required all the strength of two men to press the spring downward far enough to bring the catch into its place. It was baited with a piece of seal-meat; the snow and ice around it were arranged to appear as innocent and undisturbed as possible, and then the trappers returned to the ship.

The next morning word was brought to George that a bear was in the trap, and that young gentleman, accompanied by Fred, lost no time in going to look at it. Sure enough, a bear had been taken, but he had also taken the trap and walked off with it. There was a strong chain, about two yards long, attached to the trap, and at the end of the chain was a "grapple," or three-pronged hook, like the anchor for a row-boat. They could see where the chain had been dragged over the ice, and had frequently caught and compelled the bear to stop to disengage it.

They followed up the trail of the chain with no great difficulty; sometimes they lost it for a few minutes, but soon discovered it again through the marks made by the hook, and also through occasional drops of blood. About two miles from where the trap had been set they came up to the bear, who had become badly entangled and was tugging violently at the chain with his free foot. He had been caught by the right fore-foot; evidently he had stepped fully upon the trap, and gave the jaws an excellent chance for closing in on him.

When they approached him he growled furiously, and pulled harder than ever in his efforts to escape. Thus pulling, he succeeded in loosening the chain from the ice, and as soon as he had done so he performed one of those feats of intelligence for which the polar bear is famous.

Recognizing that the chain was the cause of his frequent detentions, he stood upright on his hind-feet and gave the confined paw a twirl which wound the chain around it close to the trap. A foot or more of the chain hung down, and this he seized in his mouth and then started off over the ice as fast as his three unencumbered feet would carry him.

GREENLAND NATIVE WATCHING FOR A SEAL.

Our young friends looked on in astonishment at this manifestation of sagacity; for at least a minute neither of them spoke or moved.

Fred broke silence by asking George what he would do with the skin of that bear.

"Better catch it first," was the reply; "and we're evidently a long way yet from doing so."

"I don't see how he can be taken without making a hole in his skin," said Fred; "and unless we're quick about it we shall lose our trap."

They followed as fast as they could, and luckily for them the bear could not make good progress with one leg disabled. But they had a chase of at least half an hour before coming up to him; he rose to growl his defiance at them, and this caused him to drop the chain, so that at his very next step forward the hook caught on the ice and held him.

"Never mind the whole skin," said George; "let us finish him as quick as we can, and unless the holes are too bad we can sew them up."

The trap, with its hook caught in the ice, served the very important purpose of preventing the bear from running away, and also of rushing on his assailants. Thus protected from danger, the young sportsmen made quick work with their rifles at short range, and gave an agreeable addition to the stock of provisions on the ship.

On the way back over the ice George repeated a story, which was first told by Sir Francis M'Clintock, of a native of Western Greenland who was out one day examining his seal-nets. He found a seal in one of the nets, and while stooping on the ice over his prize he received a heavy slap on the back. He supposed it was from his companion, and paid no attention to it; a second and harder slap made him look around, when he found that instead of his companion it was a grim old bear. The bear took no further notice of the man, but proceeded to tear the seal out of the net and eat it; the native did not stay to see the end of the meal, through fear that the bear might not be averse to human flesh, and he had no wish to serve as an ursine *pièce de resistance*.

They met the dog-sledges when about half-way to the ship. Their movements had been watched from the cross-trees, and as soon as they had despatched the bear the order had been given for the sledges to start to bring in the meat. Of course there was no lack of bear-meat as long as the catch of the morning lasted; before it was gone another bear was taken, and from that time onward they were fairly supplied with fresh provisions. There were bears, seals, and walruses in almost regular rotation, though the youths thought that sometimes they stuck too long to a single kind without change; but you cannot always have your hunting as you would

SUNSET SCENE IN THE ARCTIC CIRCLE.

like it, and in this respect they were far better off than many arctic voyagers who preceded them—thanks to the improved weapons for pursuing large game.

Each day the sun remained below the horizon longer than on the preceding one, and in a little while the nights were longer than the days. The decrease continued, and by-and-by came the time when the sun only peered above the line of ice for a moment, and then sank below it. Everybody was on deck to see it, as they all knew the sun would not re-appear again for nearly two months. The next day there was a flush of light on the horizon, and Fred thought he caught a glimpse of the upper edge of the orb's disc, but according to the Doctor's calculation he was mistaken.

Even after the sun failed to appear there was a period of light every day for more than a fortnight. It was the 17th of November when they had their last view of the sun, and the observations showed that they were very near the 77th parallel of latitude.

"The farther north you go," said the Doctor to the youths, "the sooner will the sun disappear in the autumn, and the later will he return in the spring. For example, when Captain Tyson was wintering on board the *Polaris*, in latitude 81° 38', the sun disappeared October 17th, and was not visible for one hundred and thirty-five days. The following year, while he was drifting south on the ice-floe, and was about latitude 70°, the sun re-appeared January 19th, after an absence of eighty-three days. He does not record the day of its disappearance, which must have been farther to the north, as the ice-floe was drifting steadily southward."

"The popular idea," said George, "is that they have six months of day and six months of night at the North-pole every year."

"At the pole itself," replied the Doctor, "the sun would have but two motions to the spectator, and the popular idea might not be so far out of the way. For six months of the year the sun would be moving in a series of circles in the heavens, and then for six months it would make a similar series of circles below the horizon. There have been interminable discussions on this subject, and much divergence of opinion, and the only way to settle the question will be for somebody to go to the pole and make an observation."

"I remember," said Fred, "a classmate of mine at college who was constantly bringing up a perplexing question for discussion. One of his theories was that there could not be 'sound' where there was no ear to hear it; and he used to argue that if a tree should fall in a forest a hundred miles from anything with ears no sound would be produced.

CAPTAIN C. F. HALL, WITH TWO ESKIMO COMPANIONS.

"He would argue that question at great length, and whenever he got anybody to agree with him he would shift to the other side and have the discussion over again. Another question he used to ask was,

"What would be the latitude and longitude of a man at the North-pole, and his points of compass?

"No matter what answer you made he would dispute its correctness, and proceed to demonstrate your error. He said he did all this talking in order to make himself ready in debate, and he kept it up so constantly that we all set him down as a nuisance. We used to hope he would go to the North-pole and see for himself, and nobody ever wished him to hurry in coming back."

"But how would we recognize the pole in case we were there?" George inquired.

"That could be done," was the Doctor's reply, "by means of scientific instruments, though some astronomers think otherwise. Captain Hall was confident of reaching the pole when he sailed on his last expedition, and in reply to the questions on this subject he used to say, 'on reaching that point called the North-pole the North-star will be directly overhead. Without an instrument, with merely the eye, a man can define his position when there. Some astronomers tell me I will find a difficulty in determining my position. It will be the easiest thing in the world. Suppose I arrive at the North-pole, and the sun has descended. Suppose there is an island at the North-pole; around it is the sea. I see a star upon the horizon. If I were to remain a thousand years at the pole, that star will remain on the horizon without varying one iota in height. Then, again, when I am at the pole, on the 23d of June, I take the latitude of the sun: just $23\frac{1}{2}°$ high at one and all hours. Five days before the 24th of June, and five days after, with the finest instruments we have, you cannot determine one iota of change. Therefore, you will see that it is the easiest thing in the world to determine when you arrive at the North-pole. The phenomena displayed there will be deeply interesting, provided there is land there; and I am satisfied, from the traditions I have learned from the Eskimos, that I will find land there.'

"Captain Hall had not the slightest doubt that he would be able to recognize the geographical pole if he once reached it, and other explorers have been equally certain of doing so. The measurements of the angles of certain stars with each other, and with the sun and moon, would be the first necessities, and the position of the North-star should be carefully observed. But the North-star would not be directly overhead, as asserted by Captain Hall, at least not for the astronomer, though it might suffice for the man unprovided with instruments, or ignorant of their use."

One of the youths asked what was the exact position of the North-star.

"That depends upon the time of the year and the relative positions of the sun and earth," was the reply. "The polar star is one of the thirty-six fundamental stars used for observations by astronomers and navigators, and its position at any time of the year is shown in the "Nautical Almanac." The old astronomers made long catalogues of the stars. Hipparchus, one hundred and thirty years before the Christian Era, and without any instruments to aid him, composed a catalogue showing the positions of nearly eleven hundred stars, with their ascension and declension. Ptolemy, two hundred and sixty-seven years later, made a similar and larger catalogue, and this was extended by Albatcngi, an Arab astronomer, seven hundred and eighty-three years after Ptolemy. Three or four other catalogues appeared from that time until 1712, when the catalogue of Flamsteed, an English astronomer, came out, with an exact location of two thousand nine hundred and nineteen stars. Since Flamsteed's time a good many catalogues have been made, and now we have the positions of nearly a hundred thousand stars in both hemispheres. But, as I before said, the astronomers and navigators have settled upon thirty-six stars which are sufficient for their purposes; every year the nautical and astronomical almanacs publish the positions, variations, ascensions, and longitudes of these stars, so that they are ready for use at any moment. This number is quite sufficient for the purposes of science all over the globe, or at any rate to all parts where man has been able to go."

"Suppose you drop stellar science and come to lunch," said the major, whose mind had a practical turn. Prompt assent was given to his suggestion by a simultaneous movement in the direction of the cabin.

Before the sun went altogether below the horizon for his hibernation, Fred and George, with the assistance of two of the younger officers of the *Gambetta*, erected a telegraph line between the ships, for convenience of communication in case of accident during the prolonged night. A complete apparatus for the telephone and telegraph had been brought by both ships; each had a good supply of the kind of wire used by armies in the field, and it was arranged so that it could be strung very rapidly on light poles specially prepared for the purpose. The ships were about a mile apart, and the line was easily set up by fastening the poles in the tops of hummocks along the way. Holes were cut in the ice to the depth of three or four inches, and then each pole was firmly fixed in its place by tamping the fine ice into the hole and pouring water upon it. The telephone was used in preference to the telegraph, and it was found that in the dry air of the arctic winter the insulation was perfect. Occasionally the atmospheric electricity gave them some trouble, and doubtless if the line had been a long one, the difficulties from this cause would have been great.

The electrical conditions of the atmosphere were dependent on the aurora; when the latter was fine there was a great deal of disturbance, and when there was no aurora there was rarely any electricity perceptible. The Doctor said this was the case in all parts of the world, and established beyond question the cause of the aurora. Long before the invention of

AN ARCTIC AURORA.

the telegraph it had been attributed to electrical causes by scientific men; this idea had been ridiculed by many, but since the spread of the wires over the globe, and the observations in consequence, all opposition to it had ceased.

Sometimes for days together there was no aurora, and then again it would be almost continuous for a week or more. Naturally our young friends desired to investigate this phenomenon, and asked the Doctor about it.

"I am not an authority on the aurora borealis, or northern lights," was his reply, "and can only give you what others have said on the subject.

For centuries it has been studied by scientific men, and there is no longer any doubt that it comes from electricity."

"I suppose it is the electric light passing through the air," said one of the youths. "It goes irregularly, and makes the waves and flashes that we see."

"According to Professor Loomis and others you are wrong," replied the Doctor. "The professor says that the light is rarely within forty-five miles of the earth, and usually is from one hundred to five hundred miles from it; consequently it is beyond our atmosphere, or only touches the most rarefied part of it. He describes one aurora that filled all the space above the earth, beginning at forty-five miles distance and ending at five hundred miles."

"How do they find that out?"

"By observing the points from which an aurora is visible at the same time. These observations, when carefully noted and the result computed, will show the height and extent of the aurora. For example, the display of August 28, 1859, was observed simultaneously at a great many points; calculations showed that it was everywhere forty-six miles from the earth, and it extended to a height of five hundred and thirty-four miles. The luminous beams of light in this aurora were five hundred miles long, and from five to fifty miles in diameter. Other auroras have been measured in the same way, and the average height assigned to them is four hundred and fifty miles."

"But I've seen the aurora behind the hills at home," said Fred, "and even here we see it close to the horizon."

"Yes," replied the Doctor, "and you see the sun on the horizon, or setting or rising behind the hills. But do you suppose it is any nearer the earth for that reason than when it is high in the heavens?"

Fred admitted that his argument was fallacious, and that the appearance of the aurora near the earth was in appearance only. The Doctor explained, however, that sometimes on rare occasions the aurora might come within a few miles of the earth, but thus far no observer had ever discovered it within the highest range of the clouds.

"The farther north you go," said Dr. Tonner, "the more brilliant are the auroras, at least in the Western Hemisphere. The phenomena prevail more in America than in Northern Europe and Asia; they cover a large area of the heavens, but seem to be more numerous in the region of the magnetic pole than anywhere else. In the Southern Hemisphere there is a similar display known as the aurora australis.

"As to their electrical origin we have other proofs than the effect on

the magnetic needle and the telegraph wires. The auroral flashes are the
same as those of a spark of electricity sent through rarefied air or through

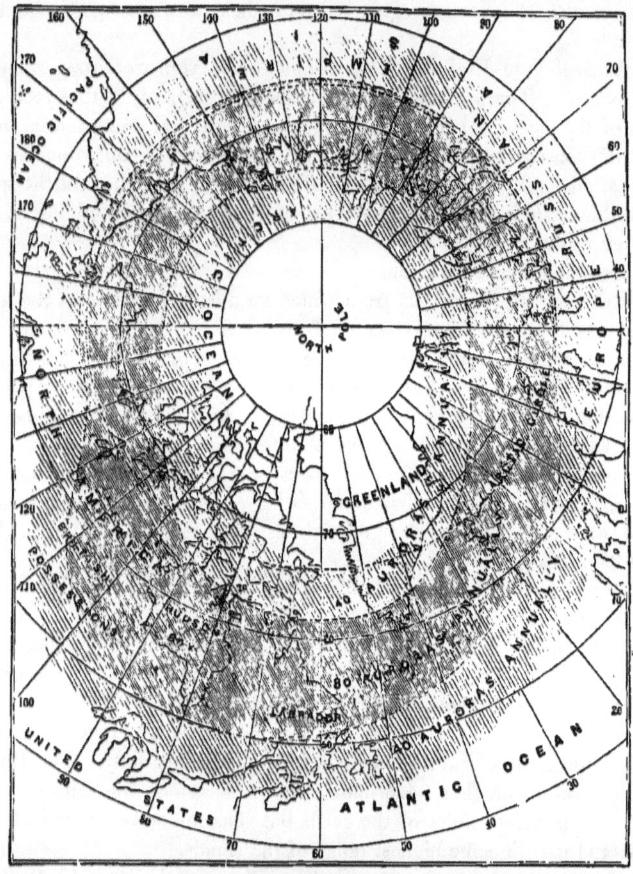

GEOGRAPHICAL DISTRIBUTION OF AURORAS.

a vacuum. The fluorescence of the electric light is repeated in the aurora,
and also—"

"I beg pardon for interrupting," said George, "but what is meant by
fluorescence?"

"There are certain substances," was the reply, "that seem perfectly
transparent when seen in the solar light, but if you illumine them with an

electric spark they appear to be self-luminous. When these substances are illumined by the auroral light they present the same appearance as though charged from an electrical machine. This property is called fluorescence.

"Electricity develops heat," continued the Doctor, "when it passes through poor conductors, like wood and paper. In several instances the auroral influence has set fire to these substances, and the experiment has been made so often as to be well known to all scientists. In fact, all the effects of electricity have been obtained from the aurora—such as working telegraph instruments, making sparks of light, giving shocks to the animal system, and developing magnetism in soft iron."

"But where does this electricity come from?" inquired one of the listeners. "There must be a vast storehouse or factory for it somewhere."

"That is yet a conundrum," the Doctor answered. "Some have supposed that the earth becomes charged with electricity to such a degree that it cannot longer retain it; the surplus is thrown off, and it is the discharge of this electricity that makes the aurora. It has been observed that the prevalence of auroras is in exact proportion to the presence or absence of spots on the sun; when there are many spots there are numerous auroras,

and when the sun is free of spots there are few or none of them. Then, too, the influence of the positions of other planets has been noted, and the whole subject is full of mysteries and speculations."

"We are getting into deep water," said George, "or rather we should be if there was less ice about us. When we have time to spare we will set about devising a machine whereby the electricity of the

FRED'S ELECTRIC NURSERY.

aurora borealis may be harnessed, and made to do duty in a practical way. We will make it run the dynamos to supply our houses and streets with electric light; it shall propel our machinery, and thus take the place of steam; it shall be used for forcing our gardens, in the way that electricity is supposed to make plants grow; and it shall develop the brains of our statesmen and legislators, to make them wiser and better and of more practical use than they are at present. Hens shall lay more eggs, cows must give cream in place of milk, trees shall bear fruit of gold or silver, tear-drops shall be diamonds, and the rocks of the fields shall become alabaster or amber. Wonderful things will be done when we get the electricity of the aurora under our control."

"Yes," responded Fred, "babies shall be taken from the nursery and reared on electricity, which will be far more nutritious than their ordinary food. When the world is filled with giants nourished from the aurora, the ordinary mortal will tremble. We'll think it over, and see what we can do."

And with this cautious suggestion the conversation was changed to a more commonplace topic.

ARCHES OF AURORAL LIGHT.

CHAPTER XIII.

CHRISTMAS AND NEW-YEAR FESTIVITIES.—MUSICAL ENTERTAINMENTS.—THE "GAMBETTA" ON FIRE.

FORTUNE favored our friends in wind and weather. The beginning of the arctic winter was a period of intense cold, but unaccompanied by winds; consequently the ice formed to a great depth, and was perfectly solid for many miles around. For two or three weeks after they entered the ice, and before it attained its winter thickness, there were frequent alarms that the floes were crushing and grinding together; but before the beginning of December there was little fear on this account. Holes were drilled in many places within a mile or more of the ships, for the purpose of ascertaining the thickness of the ice; in no place was it less than thirty feet, and in several localities it measured nearly forty. Fred thought there was not the least danger of breaking through, and he regretted greatly that the surface was not smooth enough for skating, even if the intense cold would render that amusement possible.

Observatories were established a little distance from the ship, and on each side of it, in order to keep a record of the cold. At each observatory there was a thermometer, graduated to tenths of a degree, and an anemometer by which the direction and velocity of the wind could be noted. Both observatories were visited every four hours, and this duty was divided between the major and the Doctor—the former assisted by George and the latter by Fred. A lantern of the "bull's-eye" pattern was carried by the observer on his round, and the rays of this lantern, projected on the scale of the thermometer, enabled him to read it without approaching near enough to affect the instrument by his presence. It was not an easy matter to make entries in a note-book when clad in heavy furs, and with the hands encased in mittens, and Fred set his wits to work to devise a more convenient mode of making his records.

Taking an alpenstock, or ice-staff, he marked upon it the degrees which were likely to comprise all the variations of the thermometer, and also a single degree divided into tenths. Then he arranged sliding rings or hoops which could move freely up or down the staff, but were held firmly in place by means of little knobs on the inside, passing through a slot in the wood.   Similar rings were arranged for the points of compass and the velocity of the wind, and by means of these rings the whole record of a visit to one of the observatories could be taken.   A staff was arranged for each observatory, but it was found rather burdensome to carry two of these aids to the memory, and they settled down upon one.   For the thermometrical readings a third ring was added, to show the variation between the

A POLAR BEAR FAILING TO SEE THE POINT.

two instruments, which rarely exceeded one or two tenths of a degree, while the record of the anemometer was made on a shorter staff, that was carried at the waist like a policeman's club.   The staff, or alpenstock, was of material assistance in going over the ice in the arctic darkness, and it might serve as a weapon of defence, better than nothing at all, in case of interference by a bear.

"In case you meet a bear," said the Doctor, "and he shows no disposition to retreat, your best plan will be to hold your alpenstock like a spear, and let him come on. Many a bear has rushed to his death in this way. It requires a good deal of nerve to meet him with no better weapon than this, and I sincerely hope the emergency may never occur.

"It is one of the favorite methods of hunting the bear in Norway; the principal danger arises from the ability of the animal to turn the spear aside, which he can do with a single blow of his tremendous paw. The Norwegian hunter generally manages to get him so enraged that he is wholly occupied with rushing upon his intended victim, regardless of the consequences."

Fresh water for the use of the ship's company was obtained by melting snow, and great care was exercised to prevent its mingling with the salt of the ice. Whenever there was a fresh fall of snow all hands were set to work to pile it up for future use, and for this purpose all that gathered on the roof of the deck-house and away from the floe-ice was preserved. Snow in the arctic regions is generally like fine sand; the intense cold causes the moisture to congeal in the smallest particles, and not in the form in which we usually find it in the Northern States. "Goose-feather snow" is unusual in the Arctic Circle, except in the summer months.

The uses of steam on board the *Vivian* were various. The cabin and the quarters of the men were warmed by it, the ship having been fitted with steam-pipes and radiators for this purpose. When it had performed this work, it escaped into a large tub that was always kept full of snow to be melted, as already mentioned; another tub, where the steam was occasionally turned, was used for softening the food of the dogs, and there is no doubt that the brutes would have passed a vote of thanks to the engineer of the *Vivian* if the subject had been brought to their comprehension. The last of the walruses which were taken before the ice closed for the winter were piled up near the ship, and from time to time huge chunks were chopped out with axes and taken to the softening tub for the dogs. In its frozen

THE OLD WAY OF MELTING SNOW.

condition, and with the skin perfectly solid, it was safe from their attacks. A frozen walrus hide is about as easy of penetration as a plate of iron, and the dogs never attempted to gnaw it; but they kept a careful watch over the deposit, and whenever the men went to chop out a supply of food for them, they were in a state of great impatience until it was served.

Visits were frequently exchanged between the *Vivian* and *Gambetta*, and the telephone was in daily use. As the end of December approached, preparations were made for celebrating that event, and also for a festivity on New-year's Day. It was arranged that Captain Girard and some of his officers would eat their Christmas dinner on the *Vivian*, and that they should give a return entertainment on New-year's Eve.

In spite of the disadvantages of the surroundings, Fred and George determined to have a Christmas-tree, and readily obtained the permission of Commander Bronson to get it up. Trees were not to be found near their residence, and the forest was too far off to be invaded. George thought the best trees they could get would be the cross-trees; but these were unhappily too high in air for their purpose. They managed to improvise a tree by providing limbs for a small log recently found on the ice and brought to the ship by one of the hunting parties. Holes were bored in the log for the insertion of sticks which served as limbs; the ends of the sticks were festooned with strips of bear and seal skin, together with bits of canvas and kindred things. George had prepared some oakum from old rope, which would have decorated the tree very well, but he was restrained by Captain Jones from using such inflammable material. The captain had a wholesome and proper dread of fire, and was not slow to see the risk they would run in trimming their Christmas-tree with oakum pickings; hence the less dangerous substances, although less picturesque.

The number of candles was limited to twelve, and as a matter of precaution a man was stationed by the tree with a bucket of water, to be thrown over it in case of fire. Presents were hung to the limbs or piled at the foot of the tree, which was set in a thick plank at the end of the *Vivian's* cabin. Everybody received something, and to make the occasion as much as possible like a Christmas at home, a box of goods originally intended for trading purposes among the Indians was opened and distributed. Gaudy handkerchiefs were received by several of the men, and sheath-knives, pocket-mirrors, combs, and kindred things by others. Christmas cards were sent to Commander Bronson, Major Clapp, and the Doctor, while Captain Jones was made happy with a picture of part of the upper rigging of a ship with the crow's-nest. On the sails of the ship were in-

THE CAPTAIN'S SOUVENIR OF CHRISTMAS.

scribed the words, "Voyage in Search of Sir John Franklin;" the captain having frequently remarked that they hoped to come upon fresh traces of the work of that unfortunate navigator of the arctic regions.

Jack and his fellow-musicians played their liveliest airs as the curtain was removed from the tree, and George, in the character of Santa Claus, distributed the gifts. All the officers of the *Vivian*, with the exception of the one in charge of the deck, were present at the unveiling of the tree; the men were admitted in groups of four to receive what the youths had prepared for them. At four o'clock the ceremonies ended, and then the cabin was cleared, as the guests from the *Gambetta* were due an hour later.

Christmas cards were hung on the tree for the visitors, and then the veil was drawn again. As the guests arrived, each was provided with a button-hole bouquet made of tissue-paper and fastened to a wooden toothpick.

Dinner passed off pleasantly, and there was a great deal of conversation about home and home scenes at that time of the year. At a signal from the captain the musicians were slipped into their places so quietly that the guests did not see them.

"What a pity it is," said Captain Girard, "that we have no forest here, and cannot have an *arbre de Noël*, what you call 'Christmas-tree.'"

"Yes," replied Commander Bronson, "but we can't expect the comforts of the civilized world while shut up here in the ice."

George and Fred had carelessly left their seats a moment before, and waited a sign from their chief. As the latter finished his response to the French captain he nodded.

Down came the curtain, the candles were lighted in a few seconds, the music struck up a lively air, and to the astonishment of the visitors they had an *arbre de Noël* before them!

The Frenchmen rose from their seats and gave a ringing plaudit for the Christmas-tree, which had taken them so completely by surprise. Then the cards that had been prepared for them were handed around; each card bore the post-mark of Paris only one day before, and consequently the enthusiasm of the recipients increased.

Then there were songs in French and songs in English, and songs in both languages at once. One of the Frenchmen recited some verses of Béranger, and another gave a selection from one of the stately poems of Victor Hugo. The Christmas punch was brought in by the steward, and as it was placed on the table, George recited a portion of the lines of Dr. Holmes, "On Lending a Punch-bowl." He began with the stanza,

> " 'Twas on a dreary winter's eve, the night was closing dim,
> When old Miles Standish took the bowl and filled it to the brim.
> The little captain stood and stirred the posset with his sword,
> And all his sturdy men-at-arms were ranged around the board."

In this way the Christmas in the Arctic Ocean was prolonged to a late hour. When the officers of the *Gambetta* returned to the ship it required several minutes to muster the sailors who had accompanied them; the Christmas in the forecastle had been quite as jolly as the one in the cabin, and the men of two nations were in no hurry to separate.

For another week things went on quietly enough, and then came the festivity on board the *Gambetta*. All who had taken part in the entertainment of the officers of the French ship were invited to dinner, and it was announced that there would be a musical entertainment afterwards, for which Captain Jones was requested to grant leave to as many of his crew as could be spared from duty.

The dinner must have taxed the genius of the steward and cook of the

Gambetta; under the circumstances it was a gastronomic surprise, and evoked the admiration of all the guests.   Out of the materials at their command they had made a dinner which would do honor to Vefour or the *Café Riche,* and so neatly had they disguised the familiar bear and seal that nobody could guess at their character.   Commander Bronson remarked that

if good dinners could take an explorer to the pole, the French would have discovered it long ago.

The entertainment was given in the house on deck, as there was not room for it anywhere below.   The deck-house was lighted with lanterns and festooned with flags, and there was an attempt to represent trees by means of green cloth stretched over fantastic frames.   Two of the officers of the *Gambetta* were quite skilful with the pencil and brush, and had prepared some drawings on a large scale, which were fastened to the walls wherever the light was best. They represented home scenes of the New Year, and absorbed the attention of the visitors for several minutes.

Of course it was impossible to heat the deck-house like the cabin below, and therefore the whole party donned its furs before going there. Seats had been placed for entertainers and guests in front of the stage, which consisted of a raised platform close to the main-mast; the rest of the space was devoted to "standing-room only" for the crews of the two ships.

Inasmuch as only a few of the visitors understood French, and therefore dialogue would be tedious, the entertainment was a musical one; it consisted of a light operetta ("*Un Jour de Fête*") of one act and four characters, the latter played by three of the junior officers and one of the younger sailors. The sailor was made up as a girl, whose mother was personated by one of the officers; considering all the disadvantages of the situation, the "make-up" was quite successful. The feminine costume was donned outside a suit of fur; but the latter had been made of squirrel-skin and fitted closely, so that it did not add to the stoutness of the wearers to any disagreeable extent. The masculine costumes were also filled with furs, and as their wearers were naturally of goodly size the effect was ludicrous; but since the operetta was a comic one, anything that added to the hilarity was not objectionable.

The thermometer was about ten degrees below zero, Fahrenheit, in the temporary theatre, and the breath of the audience rose like a cloud of steam. Frost gathered on the lips of the performers, and several times it choked their utterance; the girl in the play carried a fan, but she had little use for it, and the same was the case with the parasol in her mother's hands. Mother and daughter kissed once in the course of the performance, and their lips ran a narrow risk of being frozen together. The audience applauded freely, perhaps from a desire to keep warm, and altogether the performance went off merrily. The quartette of voices was by no means a bad one, and our friends of the *Vivian* felt themselves more than repaid for their efforts at Christmas.

The operetta was soon over, and then followed a dance. There was no fear of being overheated, and everybody exercised to the full ability of his limbs. It was so late that we dare not tell the hour when the boatswain called "Vivians away!" and the visitors returned to their ship.

A week later the officers and part of the crew of the *Gambetta* were invited to an entertainment on board the *Vivian*. They accepted, and came promptly to find the deck-house decorated and lighted as their own had been on the New-year festivities, and, fortunately for them, a fall in the temperature had made the place quite comfortable. The entertainment comprised a minstrel performance, in which our young friends had a prominent part and were assisted by the vocal and instrumental musicians of the crew. Then two of the sailors who had been trained to acrobatic

PERFORMANCE ON THE "VIVIAN."

performances amused the company by turning somersaults, balancing cannon-shot on their arms and heads, and going through other evolutions peculiar to the circus. A joke arranged by Fred was perpetrated at the close of the "ground and lofty tumbling" which produced a momentary panic, and then set everybody in a roar of laughter.

Part of the performance consisted in handling a fifty-six pound weight as though it were the merest trifle; and to prove that there was no decep-

tion, the weight was passed around in the audience before and after being
handled by the acrobat.

When he was through with the weight, the performer allowed it to fall
on the stage with a heavy thud, close to the screen at one side; then he
threw a somersault, while his companion essayed certain tricks with the
cannon-ball.   Attention being thus drawn from the fifty-six pound weight,
it was skilfully removed and a pasteboard imitation took its place.

Then the performer picked up the weight again and tied a small rope
to it; by means of the rope he whirled it in the air precisely as though it
had been a solid mass of iron; then, as if by accident, it slipped from his

GEORGE'S "PUNCH AND JUDY."

hand and went flying over the audience.   Heads were "ducked," and
there was a sigh of alarm from several mouths; the sigh was changed to
laughter when the weight was returned to its place by means of the rope,
in which a strip of India-rubber had been concealed.   Nobody was hurt
except by the expansion of ribs, produced by excessive mirth.

Then George gave a short exhibition of a Punch and Judy show.   His
imitation of the time-honored amusement of London children was admirable, and as a part of it was given in French, he secured the earnest ap-
plause of all the visitors.   Then there was a dance, and after two hours of
fun the audience dispersed.

The next week there was a return entertainment on the *Gambetta*, and every week during their hibernation when the weather permitted, and as long as communication was feasible over the ice, there was something amusing on one of the ships. There was a good-natured rivalry between them, and each tried to have something that would interest the other; it was not easy to do this when the difficulties of language were to be considered, and the success of the enterprise showed a great deal of ingenuity on the part of all concerned. Music, jugglery, and pantomime were the principal features of the performances, and to these may be added displays of the magic lantern and occasional experiments in chemistry.

One night, while the people of the *Vivian* were entertaining their friends from the *Gambetta*, there was a sudden interruption.

The bell of the telephone sounded, and the cabin steward called Fred to see what was wanted. As soon as he had placed his ear to the instrument he heard the appalling words,

"*Le Gambetta est en feu!*"—("The *Gambetta* is on fire!")

Fred ran to Commander Bronson with the news, and the latter immediately informed his visitors. Of course the performance closed at once, the men went to their quarters, and Captain Girard and his officers and crew started with all speed for their ship. Commander Bronson tendered the services of his men, and at once prepared to follow to the endangered vessel.

Everything was done in order, and without any excitement whatever. There was excellent discipline on board both the ships, and every man fell at once into his place. The relief party included Commander Bronson, the first officer of the *Vivian*, two petty officers, Dr. Tonner and George, together with ten men from the crew. They followed closely on the steps of the *Gambetta's* men, and were at the side of that ship not more than a couple of minutes behind them. The men brought axes and fire-buckets from the *Vivian*, and Dr. Tonner was provided with whatever might be needed for the relief of the men of either crew who should be overcome by the smoke or flame, or exhausted in the efforts of controlling the fire.

Smoke was pouring from the ventilating shaft in the top of the deck-house, and as they entered the door-way leading from the gang-plank into the covered space on deck, the cloud was of almost stifling thickness. Captain Girard and his party were already below.

The deck was in charge of a petty officer and one man, all the rest being below endeavoring to suppress the conflagration. Commander Bronson sent his compliments to Captain Girard, and asked if he and his men could be of service; the answer was returned that they could do nothing below for the moment, as the *Gambetta's* crew was filling all the working space. As a matter of precaution it was desirable to remove the stores that were kept always ready in the deck-house, and the *Vivian's* party proceeded at once to perform this service.

Boxes and barrels were thrown down the gang-plank by some of the men, while the others slid them along the ice to a place of safety, in case the ship should be burned. The work was performed with great rapidity, and in a quarter of an hour the deck was pretty well cleared. The packages had been previously arranged in such a manner that they could be hastily removed in case of necessity. The same precaution was observed on the *Vivian*, and in thus acting, the commanders were only following the example of their predecessors in arctic exploration.

As the last of the packages was deposited on the ice, word was brought from below that the fire was under control and would shortly be extinguished. In another quarter of an hour the danger was over, and Captain Girard invited Commander Bronson and his officers to join him in the cabin. With the politeness of his nation he apologized for having kept them waiting on deck, and explained that he had been extremely occupied since his return from the delightful entertainment on the *Vivian*.

Then he told the story of the fire, and the narration fell upon interested ears.

The watch below were in their bunks, having laid aside their furs on descending from the deck, as was their invariable custom, and donned their ordinary clothing. All were asleep except two; one of the waking ones thought he detected the smell of smoke, and after a few minutes of hesitation mentioned it to the other. The latter was of the same mind; and while one roused their companions, the other went to report the discovery to the officer on duty. Of course the matter was immediately investigated.

The smoke was found to be issuing from a store-room just forward of the men's quarters; the partition was torn away to gain an entrance to the store-room, which was so densely filled with smoke that the men who entered it were nearly stifled. By creeping close to the deck and holding a sponge to his nose, one of the officers found the source of the smoke, which was below.

There was no hatch in the immediate vicinity, and so a hole was cut in the deck for the admission of water. By this time a hose was ready from the donkey-engine, and a stream was directed to the locality of the fire; buckets were brought into requisition, and the first supply of water was obtained from a tank which was kept constantly full, for use in just such an emergency as this. Then a hose was passed outside to draw water from a hole in the ice; this hole was opened daily, partly in order to take soundings, and partly to have a supply of water in case of fire, since only a limited amount could be kept on board. Of course it froze over almost as soon as it was opened, but it was not a serious matter to drill it clear again. There was one man in each watch whose duty it was to open this hole whenever an alarm of fire was given; in the present instance the man on duty was promptly at his post, so that the water-supply was ready the moment the hose was brought outside.

A FIRE ON SHIPBOARD.

The fire had not gained much head-way, and when Captain Girard reached the *Gambetta* on his return from the *Vivian* the water was pouring steadily into the hold and subduing the smoke. As soon as it was thought safe to do so, one of the officers descended, having taken the precaution to tie a sponge in front of his nose and mouth to prevent inhaling the smoke. Carrying the end of the hose, he directed it against the fire wherever it was visible, and in a little while it was extinguished. The *Gambetta* was saved, and her crew were spared the horror of being driven from their home in the middle of an arctic night to seek shelter with their American friends.

Of course the extent of the damage could only be ascertained by a thorough investigation, and this could not be made until the hold was free from smoke. A careful watch was kept to see that the fire did not break out afresh, and in the course of some twenty hours or more it was announced that all the smoke had disappeared. The party from the *Vivian* returned to their ship at the end of their interview with Captain Girard; George had already told Fred, by means of the telephone, that the fire had been subdued, and when Commander Bronson and his companions reached the *Vivian's* side, they were greeted with three cheers by the assembled officers and crew.

The origin of the fire was a good deal of a mystery, but it was finally attributed to the spontaneous combustion of some articles stored in the fore-hold. It could be accounted for in no other way, as there was no means of reaching the spot with a spark from outside, and no lamp or candle had been carried there for some time. If it had been in the vicinity of the donkey-engine, it might have been caused by the heating of the pipes and the charring of the timbers, as in the case of the *Rodgers* in the winter of 1881; but from the position of the engine this was not possible. Some of the French sailors were superstitious, and thought the fire originated from supernatural causes; one of them solemnly declared that it must have been the work of the Ice-king, who was angry at the invasion of his dominions. Sailors of all nations have many superstitions, and the French mariner is not behind his brother navigator in this respect.

"It is the peculiarity of fire," said Commander Bronson, "that it destroys the evidence of its origin. For this reason the cause of a fire is frequently a mystery, and it will always be so until the habits of conflagrations are changed."

A little while after the return from the *Gambetta* everybody who was not required for duty was safely in bed. There was not much sleep, however, as most of the company had dreams of fire and the perils that accompany it. Fred was the victim of a nightmare, in which he imagined the *Vivian* to be on fire and her crew escaping to the ice. He waked with a scream that startled his companions; he apologized for disturbing them, but explained that he was in the act of carrying the hose to the fore-hatch, where the fire was burning fiercely, when he slipped on the ladder and went tumbling headlong below. Naturally enough he jumped for safety, and found himself outside his bunk, and sitting on the cold floor of the cabin.

At the very outset of the voyage the fire-watch on the *Vivian* was carefully arranged, and every possible precaution taken against the destruction of the ship by fire. To ensure the proper training of the crew, after the accident on the *Gambetta*, alarms were given at frequent intervals; every man ran to his post of duty at these alarms, and it was felt that a serious fire could not occur on the *Vivian* except under the most extraordinary circumstances.

FROZEN IN.

CHAPTER XIV.

ARCTIC NEWSPAPERS AND COMEDIES.—DRIFTING WITH THE ICE.—SLEDGE JOURNEYS.—DISCOVERING LAND.

AMATEUR theatricals and musical entertainments were not by any means the sole amusements of the parties on the *Vivian* and *Gambetta*. In arctic hibernation it is necessary to have both mind and body occupied, and only by doing so can disease be kept from making its ravages among the crew. The prolonged darkness has a depressing effect on the mental organization, and not infrequently the results are disastrous. This is particularly the case with the men in the forecastle, as the officers are more or less occupied with scientific observations and the care of the ship. The crew have little regular work to do, and consequently are liable to become despondent, quarrelsome, and insubordinate, and cases of insanity are not uncommon. To prevent such a calamity, a prudent commander will devise employments and amusements for the men; the officers of the *Vivian* and *Gambetta* had a clear understanding on this point, and encouraged in every way the occasional interchanges of courtesies at the entertainments we have described.

On each ship schools were organized for the instruction of the sailors, and though the proposition was not favorably received at first, the men soon entered enthusiastically into the plans for their mental improvement. Fred and George were the managers of the schools on the *Vivian;* they received a good deal of assistance from the Doctor and the major, together with all the other officers of the ship. They had classes in mathematics, geography, astronomy, and navigation, and once a week there was a lecture by one of the officers in the house on deck. The lectures covered a variety of topics, and the programme which was prepared by the youths announced that it was the celebrated "North-star Course: to be delivered in Vivian Hall, corner of Bear Street and Walrus Avenue. Admission free. Holders of tickets requested not to appear in evening dress."

The lecturing was performed under disadvantages, as both speakers and audience were clad in furs, and their breath often filled the enclosed space like a cloud of steam. Some of the lectures were original, but as the season went on the speakers helped themselves to whatever material they had on hand. Dr. Tonner gave an amusing account of his experiences among the Indians of Arizona, and subsequently made a decided hit with an abridgment of John Phœnix's Lectures on Astronomy. Major Clapp was eloquent over the mysteries of Ichthyology, and gave a good many facts about the habits of the blue-fish, and other products of the sea-shore, in the vicinity of New York, but he was mortified to find that the sailors laughed more heartily at his reading of Artemus Ward's "Sixty Minutes in Africa." George and Fred tried their hands at lecturing, and they also gave readings and recitations whenever the occasion required. They had a liberal repertoire, and altogether the season may be said to have passed off brilliantly. Prizes were given in the schools for the pupils who made the greatest progress, and there was not a sailor in the ship who did not add materially to his stock of knowledge before the winter was over.

The physical amusements included skating, sliding, and other athletic exercise on the ice. When the weather permitted, the men indulged in the construction of snow forts and monuments, and some of them carved grotesque figures out of the never-ending supply of material under their feet and around them. As the sun returned, and the ships were retained in their icy prison, the short period of daylight was frequently utilized by giving half the crew of each ship liberty on the ice, and stimulating them to get up international matches of various kinds. They had running races in different forms—sometimes on the roads they had laid out, and at others over the roughest ice that could be found. The "tug-of-war," where an equal number from each ship pulled at a rope, was one of their favorite sports; the Americans were most frequently the victors at this game, but when it came to running on a smooth road they were usually left behind by the more agile Frenchmen.

Fred announced one day that no society could be complete without a newspaper; everybody shared his opinion, and the result was that the "Arctic Journal Publishing Company" was organized, with limited capital and liability, but unlimited ability, as the prospectus described it. Fred was appointed editor, under the restriction of not being allowed to suppress anything, but to give every correspondent the fullest liberty to say what he pleased. In the prospectus he announced that all communications would be used and not paid for, and that advertisers must invariably pay in advance. The paper was issued fortnightly, or rather it was read from manuscript by the editor and his assistant, George. It was made up of comments on the occurrences of the day, speculation on the prospect of reaching the pole, social, political, and scientific intelligence, together with jokes and advertisements. The paper was a pleasant diversion to all on board the *Vivian*, and after the first number appeared a similar publication was started on the *Gambetta*.

In his first issue the editor of the *Arctic Journal* paid a handsome tribute to the memory of his predecessors in this field of literary work. He said that the first paper of the kind was called the *Winter Chronicle, or the North Georgian Gazette*, and was edited by Captain Sabine on board the *Hecla*, in Parry's second expedition to the polar seas. It was in manuscript, like the *Arctic Journal*, and appeared every Monday during the five winter months of 1820: the first number is still in existence, and contains a column of miscellanies, including a list of "Arctic Miseries." Among them is the following: "To go out in the morning for an airing, and when setting foot out of the vessel to find a frozen bath in the cook's hut. To go out with a piece of soft bread in your pocket, and when you feel hungry to find it so hardened by the frost that, instead of breaking under the teeth, it is rather they that are broken. To give yourself up to deep and useful meditations when out on a walk, and then to be suddenly awakened from your perplexities by the hug of a bear."

George endeavored to rival Fred's efforts by composing a comedy for performance by the company of the *Vivian*. It was voted that he might imitate the example of other and more gifted dramatic authors by making "adaptations" from the French without credit. He immediately opened negotiations with one of the younger officers of the *Gambetta*, with the result that he was liberally supplied with French comedies from which he might steal with a clear conscience. In less than a week he completed his comedy and submitted it to himself; as he was one of the managers of the theatre, it was entirely proper that he should examine his own work, and it is hardly necessary to add that the play was promptly accepted, and underlined for production.

The play was entitled "Parry and Paris; or, The Search for the Pole." When Captain Parry was in the Arctic Circle, endeavoring to get to the North-pole, he received a despatch from his government offering him an important position as soon as he reached home. It seems that the Russian Government was anxious to capture one Carolus Slyfoxsky, a Polish refugee, who was giving them a great deal of trouble, and as the English navigator had got nearer the arctic pole than anybody else, they wanted him to try his skill on this Pole from Warsaw. The first act was supposed to occur on board the *Hecla*, in her winter quarters, the second was located in Paris, and the third in Parry's last journey in the arctic regions, where

he was seeking the North-pole with Slyfoxsky as one of his crew. As suggested by the title, the play was largely made up of puns, and the young
author felt confident of success.

Tickets were freely distributed for the first night, and in this respect
the affair was not unlike an initial performance in Paris or New York.

There was not the array of hair-
less heads in the front rows
which one sees at a first night
in New York, and as there was
only one editor present, he was
unable to congregate in the lob-
by, and discuss the points of
the play with his fellow-critics.
Fred had received a ticket for
a "box," but in consequence of
the distance from home he was
unaccompanied by the ladies of
his family; perhaps it was just
as well, since his ticket only entitled him to an empty candle-
box that was utilized as a seat.
Chairs were scarce on board the
Vivian, and everything which
could serve as a substitute was
brought into use.

CAPTAIN PARRY.

In order that Fred might be entirely without bias in writing his criticism of the play, George invited the young editor to supper immediately
after the performance. The supper was the best that the Delmonico of
the *Vivian* could get up, and when it was over, Fred was clearly of opinion
that the author of "Parry and Paris" was the most gifted dramatist of
the age. "The play that shall move the world to laughter and tears, and
to all the emotions ever found in the human heart or in 'Webster's Una-
bridged Dictionary,' will come from his talented pen. 'Parry and Paris'
gives promise of future greatness; it contains passages surpassing those of
'Richelieu' and 'The Lady of Lyons,' and there are scenes and situations
such as Shakspeare never incorporated in his plays; and we will add that
Shakspeare never gave such a supper to the editor after the play was over,
and we have yet to learn of mince-pies made of pemmican, and steaks of
seal-meat on toast."

George's play was repeated for the benefit of the officers of the *Gam-*

betta, and the example of the young dramatist was followed by the gentleman who had furnished him with part of the material for "Parry and Paris." The American play was given once on board the *Gambetta,* while the French one was transferred, "for one night only," to the boards of the *Vivian.* In this way everybody had an opportunity of seeing both productions, and it was a noticeable fact that there was a full attendance on all occasions, and nobody went out between the acts. In the matter of scenery both ships were sadly deficient, and there was a placard in front of the stage requesting the audience to imagine a forest, a town, or an ice-field, according to the conditions of the play.

CAROLUS SLYFOXSKY.

So the winter passed away. On and on they drifted, eastward and northward; sometimes they moved so slowly that it was difficult to discover any movement at all, and at other times their progress was from twenty to thirty miles a day. The cold at times was intense; the thermometer fell to $-74°$ Fahrenheit on several occasions, and once it reached $-81°$, or a hundred and thirteen degrees below the freezing-point of fresh water. Ordinarily the winter temperature was from ten to twenty degrees below zero; our friends soon became accustomed to these figures, but when the lowest points of the scale were reached they were very cautious about exposing themselves to the weather. They were all agreed on one point, that a temperature of fifty degrees below zero, with the air perfectly still, is easier to endure than twelve or fifteen degrees below zero with the wind blowing. At such times nobody ventured out except on urgent duty, and all communication between the ships ceased except through the telephone.

A CHARACTER.

Fred and George made note of the curious effects of intense cold. One day the former incautiously touched his rifle barrel with his naked hand when the thermometer stood at $-70°$. His hand was blistered as though the iron had been red hot; the youth did not repeat the experiment, and ever afterwards he handled cold iron with his mittens on. Fresh bread exposed to the cold became solid as stone, and could only be cut with a hatchet, and as for beef, it resembled red granite. The moisture in the cans of preserved meat and vegetables caused them to become a solid mass, from which the tin was chopped, leaving the contents like a section from a geological specimen. If it was desired to soften the contents before opening the can, it was placed in the steam-box and gradually thawed into a condition of malleability. Those articles suffered least that had the smallest amount of moisture in them, as there was less to be frozen. Hard - tack, or sea - biscuit, was therefore better for carrying outside than fresh bread, and dried beef was preferable to the canned article.

Arctic explorers have recorded that, on their expeditions over the ice, the supply of brandy and rum which they carried became frozen solid, and the only thing that did not congeal was the alcohol used for making

A CHARACTER IN THE FRENCH PLAY.

coffee and tea, or melting snow in order to procure water. Pemmican and hard bread are the best articles of food for a sledging party in severe weather, as they contain little moisture, and will yield more readily than other substances to the efforts of the hungry man to devour them. In the severest weather the wind on the face has the same feeling as would be produced by the blows of a small whip, and the victim feels as though the flesh were being peeled off in shreds. This sensation is followed by numbness, and then by the blood leaving the exposed places; then the skin becomes blue, which is an indication that freezing is about to commence. If the face turns white it is a sure sign that it is frozen, and unless it is violently rubbed with snow, to bring the blood back again, the consequences are disastrous.

The face cannot be kept entirely covered, as the congelation of the breath on the furs that surround it will speedily cause the formation of a mass of ice. Inexperienced travellers who have covered their faces with wrappers and mufflers are sometimes unable to remove them, as they become converted into muzzles and collars as hard and stiff as iron; the best way of avoiding trouble, and at the same time to protect the face, is to hold the hood with one hand, allowing the breath to pass outside, and leaving a narrow opening for the eyes to see the way. In the severest weather it is next to impossible to move at all; and if a storm arises the most prudent course is to wait in the best attainable shelter until it ceases.

With every storm there were fears that the ice-fields might be broken up and the ships threatened with destruction. Preparations for retreat in case of accident had been made early in the winter, but everybody knew how small was the chance of escape in case of the loss of their floating homes. The ice-field in which they were enclosed was of immense extent and great thickness, so that it was not affected by ordinary winds; on two or three occasions the winds rose to the force of gales, and then the ice rocked visibly beneath them, and the ships groaned and creaked in their beds. The snow flew in blinding masses, and the wind blew with such force that it was impossible to stand up against it. If the fields had broken, and the ships gone down in one of these gales, it is not likely that any trace of the expedition would ever have reached us. Travel over the broken ice would have been slow at best, and it was far indeed to the nearest land where assistance could be obtained.

As the spring advanced, and the sun each day remained longer and longer above the horizon, there was great anxiety to find a release from the icy prison. Early in April, observation showed that they were in latitude 80° 23' north, and longitude 120° west. This placed them to the northward of the Parry Archipelago, in a part of the polar sea not hitherto visited by any explorers; by the end of April they were five degrees farther to the east, and two degrees nearer the pole; not only were they progressing in the direction they desired to go, but they had another motion which showed that some new force was at work. In the last nine days of April the ice-field turned nearly one quarter around; the bows of the ships had pointed towards the north, but were now directed to the west. As they drifted with the ice, they might be said to be sailing very nearly stern foremost.

Naturally the new movement of the ships was discussed by the officers, and various theories were advanced.

"Perhaps the motion of the ice-field is caused by currents opposed to each other," the major suggested. "If there is an easterly current to the north of us, and a westerly one to the south, it would tend to give the ice-field a circular motion."

All the party agreed that the major's ground was well taken.

"What is more probable," said Commander Bronson, "is that there is land on one side of us, and the ice has grounded against it. Explorations have shown that there is an extensive archipelago to the north of the American continent; we know we are to the northward of the Parry Isles, and the probabilities are that we are among islands not yet known to the geographers.

"Thus far," he continued, "we cannot say whether the land on which our ice-field impinges is to the north or south of our position. We must find that out by observation, and as soon as our minds are made up we will go in search of it."

Then the commander detailed his plans for observing the movement of the ice.

Sledging parties were to go from the ship as far as a single day's travel would carry them, one to the north and the other to the south. There they were to observe the drift of the ice as accurately as possible; a similar observation would be made at the ship, and a comparison of the notes would tell him what he wished to know.

"If it is as I suspect," said the commander, "we shall find that there is a more rapid movement of the ice to the south of us than there is to the north. The ice is turning, as we have seen by the change in the ship's position, and if we can learn the drift at the points indicated we can calculate with tolerable accuracy the distance we are from the land."

Everything was made ready, and early the next morning the two sledges got away on their journeys, each carrying the necessary tools and instruments for making the observations. Major Clapp and George went with one of the sledges, while Dr. Tonner and Fred had the other. The major's sledge made about seven miles to the north; but owing to the roughness of the ice to the south, and some ugly breaks in it, the Doctor found himself little more than four miles away when it was time to stop. Both camped on the ice, each using one of the hummocks for a shelter to protect the tent from the wind, in case it should come on to blow. Snow was melted by the aid of an alcohol lamp, and coffee was made in the same way; pemmican and biscuit were the solid part of the provisions, and it is unnecessary to say that the exposure and exercise gave everybody an admirable appetite.

George and Fred had their first experience of sleeping on the ice, and the novelty of it was a compensation for the discomfort. Each of the party had a sleeping-bag, which was nothing more nor less than a huge sack of deer-skin, amply large enough to hold its owner. To go to bed was to creep into the bag feet-foremost and then close the top, with the exception of a small aperture for the admission of fresh air. To get up, one had simply to creep out of the bag; and as they all slept with their clothes on, there was no toilet to be made other than a few shakes and twists to get the body into working order and the joints in their proper places.

Sleeping-bags are an indispensable part of an outfit for an arctic sledge journey. They have been used by every explorer from the days of Wrangell and Parry, and probably were employed by their predecessors. In addition to the bag there is a sort of coverlid of furs, which is spread over the feet of the sleepers after they have taken their places. The spreading of this protector is no easy matter, as it must be done when everybody is in his bag and has very little use of his arms. After being used a few times it absorbs moisture, which freezes as fast as it is taken in; the coverlid becomes like a piece of sheet-iron, and the same is the case with the tent and the sleeping-bags.

"It is a curious circumstance," said the Doctor, "that the sleeping-bag belongs alike to the frigid and the torrid zones. When I travelled in the deserts of Arabia we had bags of muslin in which we slept at night to shield us from mosquitoes; here we have bags of deer-skin with which to protect ourselves from the intense cold."

Breakfast was very much like the supper; at any rate, it consisted of the same provisions, but Fred managed to get up a change in it. "When I went to supper," said he, "I first took a bite of pemmican and then a bite of biscuit. For breakfast I began with the biscuit and followed with the pemmican, so that breakfast and supper are not the same after all."

Both parties were fortunate enough to find crevices where the field had recently broken and left only a covering of young ice a couple of feet thick. Cutting through this young ice they were able to make the soundings they desired, and also to use the lead for obtaining the direction and rate of the drift. As soon as they had carried out the orders of the commander they returned to the ship. One of the parties saw a bear, but the animal was not inclined to familiarity, and made off as fast as he could go. As an attempt to capture him would have caused delay, it was wisely decided to let him alone.

The result of the observations was given to the commander, together with notes concerning the character of the ice over which the parties had travelled, and the crevices where the soundings were made. Commander Bronson made a careful computation, in which he was assisted by Major Clapp and Captain Jones, and in a couple of hours arrived at his decision concerning the movement of the ice.

"According to my calculations the field where we are is resting against the land, or, at all events, is aground about twenty-five miles north of us. The current is bearing it in a circular direction, or rather in the segment of a circle, and if we go north the distance I have indicated we shall find solid ground, or perhaps a reef or shoal on which the ice has touched. If it were not for the haze which has filled the northern horizon for several days I think we should see the land easily."

"Then," said the major, "I move that we go in search of it. If we find land we shall add something to the geography of the world, as nobody has ever been here before."

His opinion was echoed by the rest, and it was at once decided to go in search of land.

The expedition was arranged like the one of the day before, with the exception that the party was to carry provisions for ten days, and the sledges were to travel in company. In their eagerness to be off they got away two or three hours before daylight, and made such good progress that they were nowhere to be seen when the sun came above the horizon. The commander was so busy with matters that required his attention that he did not have time to call through the telephone to Captain Girard, and tell him that the sledges had gone on a voyage of discovery! We have a suspicion that he did not wish the Frenchman to know anything about it until too late for a party bearing the tricolor to get ahead of the Americans.

With the early start, and their enthusiasm to help them along, our friends made nearly eleven miles before camping for the night. The next morning they were somewhat stiff and sore, but keen as ever for going on; George and Fred showed a great deal of energy in getting things ready for the start, and the drivers had their dogs harnessed and everything in place before the sun was up. Soon as it was fairly above the horizon the sharp eyes of Fred made a discovery which filled the whole party with excitement.

There was the land they had been looking for, and it was exactly in the direction and apparently at the distance predicted by Commander Bronson!

Everybody was in great glee at the sight, and needed no incentive to be off. They made the best progress they could, but there were so many hummocks and rough places that by noon the sledges were less than five miles from their camp of the previous night. A halt was ordered, and men and dogs rested from their labors. George was impatient to know something of the strange land they were approaching; and so he climbed to the top of the highest hummock in the neighborhood, and scanned the distant shore with a glass.

Having made out all that was possible, he looked to the south, to ascertain if he could see the ship. Suddenly a speck on the ice caught his eye; it was a speck of red, and was moving. Adjusting the lenses of the glass to bring the speck into focus, he was not long in making it out.

It was the tricolor, carried in front of the sledges from the *Gambetta*.

The young man came down from the hummock with the alacrity of a school-boy escaping from a hornet's nest, and in a few strides he was at the spot were his companions were halted.

"Hurry up! hurry up!" he shouted. "The Frenchmen are after us, and not more than three or four miles away."

No further incentive was needed for the American part of the expedition, but the dogs and their drivers were not so quick of comprehension. While they were preparing to be off again, George mounted a hummock to pick out the best road, and to his great delight he espied a stretch of smooth ice, which began not more than a mile from where they were, and apparently continued nearly up to the land.

This smooth ice did not lie directly between them and the shore, but farther to the westward. He reported it to the major, and the latter ordered the route to be changed so as to reach the level stretch, where the greater distance could be more than equalized by the superior speed at which they could travel. From that time till the edge of the smooth ice was reached, one of the party was constantly at the top of a hummock, or proceeding ahead of the sledges in order to find the best road; and we can be sure that they frequently looked behind, to ascertain if the Frenchmen were lessening the distance between them.

The major conjectured that the moving field had broken in such a way as to leave an expanse of open water which had been speedily frozen over, probably in a single night. There were ridges here and there, but nothing serious, and when they were fairly upon it the teams dashed merrily along. The major had taken a hint from Captain Hall and prepared a log, which he threw occasionally, to ascertain the speed they were making. It was difficult to have anything like an accurate estimate, as they were obliged to make frequent halts to remove tangles from the harness, and otherwise straighten out the teams. A dog-team will manage to get into a good many snarls in the course of a day's travel; it is a severe trial of the explorer's patience, but there seems to be no help for it.

The log was constructed on the principle of the log of a ship, and consisted of a fishing-line divided into knots and wound on a reel that turned freely on a handle in its centre. At the end of the line was an iron bolt weighing a pound or more, and serving the same purpose as the float on the nautical log. It was inconvenient to manipulate a sand-glass on board a dog-sledge, or to hold a watch with mittened hands to count the time; to get over this difficulty the major had practised counting "one, two, three," and so on up to ten, in almost exact unison with the beats of a

ON THE LEVEL ICE.

watch. With this contrivance he ascertained that the sledge sometimes went as fast as eleven miles an hour, but it rarely did so for more than a few minutes at a time.

They estimated that in their first hour on the ice they made fully six miles, and somewhat less than that distance in the second hour. By sunset they were within half a mile of land; but, unfortunately, their progress was again impeded by rough ice, which was piled on the coast in a way far from welcome to the anxious explorers.

ICE-LOG, LINE AND REEL.

CHAPTER XV.

THE LAND VISITED AND EXPLORED.—THE AMERICANS IN POSSESSION.—PERIL-
OUS JOURNEY OVER THE ICE.—THE SHIPS IN GREAT DANGER.

"WE mustn't let the *Gambetta's* people get ahead of us," said the
major, as the sledges came to a halt at the edge of the smooth ice.

"Suppose you and George go ahead with the flag," replied the Doctor, "while Fred and I look after the teams. We must be the first to
hoist our flag on the land, and claim it for our nation."

"All right," the major answered. "Get the flag immediately," he continued, turning to George, "and we'll show our friends of the *Gambetta* that
we have not forgotten Wrangell Island."

Action was suited to the word without a moment's delay, and the
major and George made the best possible speed to the shore. They had
a rough road among the hummocks, and through the broken ice, but
under the circumstances they made excellent progress.

Just above the point where they landed there was a rocky hill perhaps
a hundred feet high. Pausing a moment to take breath, and make sure
they were not pursued, George fixed his eye on the summit of this hill;
then, with an expression and attitude that would have done honor to the
hero of "Excelsior," in the act which Longfellow has made immortal, he
climbed to the summit and proceeded to place the American flag where
it could wave in the arctic breeze.

"I take possession of this land in the name of the President of the
United States!" said George, as he planted the point of the slender staff
in a crevice of the rock.

"And it shall be called President Land," added the major, who had
been obliged to ascend more slowly than his youthful companion.

"Wonder where our French friends are now?" said George, as the
ceremony of taking possession was concluded.

"They'll be along as soon as they can get here," was the reply, "and
perhaps they won't like it when they find we've got ahead of them."

The glass had been left with Fred, and so our friends had only their
14#

unassisted eyes to see with. They scanned the horizon in the direction they had come, but could not discover any indication of the French sledges.

"We'll leave the flag here for the present," said the major, "and see what we can do to help Fred along. There they are, struggling among the hummocks; see, there is a sort of lane right from the edge of the smooth ice close up to the shore, and evidently they haven't seen it."

George proposed to go and guide the sledges into the lane the major had pointed out; the latter was to remain and watch the flag, and also keep possession of the land they had discovered and annexed to the possessions of the United States. The major approved the suggestion, and away went the youth down the hill, but hardly with more rapidity than he had climbed it.

The sledges were quickly guided in the right direction, and by dusk the whole party was on shore. The tent was put up at the foot of the hill, and to make the possession of the land beyond question, a flag which Fred drew from the baggage was hung above it, and waved a greeting to the one on the summit of the hill.

"Two souls with but a single thought," said the Doctor, as he looked at Fred and George, who stood admiring the banners they had spread to the breeze.

"Yes," responded the major. "If two heads are better than one, why are not two flags, even though they be small?"

"They're large enough to hold President Land against all comers," said George, "and I don't care now how soon our French friends come along."

Fred scanned the expanse of ice with his field-glass, but the growing darkness impeded his vision; he could see nothing of their rivals, and as all hands were heartily weary, they proceeded to get supper and prepare for sleep. The dogs were fed by their drivers, and aided by the alcohol lamp the party was soon provided for as liberally as circumstances would allow. Soon as supper was over they crawled into their bags, and slept soundly till early in the morning.

Fred was the first to rise, and immediately on getting out of the tent he looked to see if the flags were where they had been left. Both were unharmed, and when satisfied on this point the young man took his glass, and climbed the hill to ascertain what had become of the party from the *Gambetta*.

They were at the edge of the rough ice that had given the Americans so much trouble the day before, and were just starting in among the hummocks to make their way to the shore. Evidently they were ignorant of the existence of the lane which had been discovered from the hill-top the day before, and were in the same error that had befallen the Doctor and himself. Without a moment's delay he descended the hill, and went out among the rough ice, to put the Frenchmen in the proper way. In a little while they were in the right road and safe on land; they pitched their tent about three hundred yards from that of the Americans, not from any spirit of unfriendliness, but in order to keep the dogs from fighting. The party from the *Gambetta* graciously accepted their defeat in not being first on land, but promised to be ahead of the Americans the next time anything of the kind was undertaken.

IN CAMP.

It seemed that they were not able to get over the smooth ice until after sunset, and the latter part of their ride across it had been done rather slowly, for fear of accidents in the growing darkness. When they reached the rough ice they saw the case was hopeless, and the Americans were certainly ahead of them in getting to land. Very sensibly they spread their tent where they were, and waited till morning before going on.

It was decided that the two parties should act together in exploring the newly discovered land; and as the Americans had given the title to it, the French should have the right to name the highest mountain. It was further agreed that all mines of gold, silver, or other valuable product of the earth, should be the joint property of the two expeditions, and no concession to work mines or till the soil should be valid without the signatures of the captains of the *Vivian* and *Gambetta*. Fred suggested that it would be well to arrange for the establishment of an army and navy, and also for a police force to maintain order in President Land, but his idea did not secure speedy adoption. It was agreed, however, that the government of the country must be republican, and the inhabitants would have the right to make their own laws without danger of interference from the home authorities.

These preliminaries settled, it was agreed that the exploration should be made to the westward by the party from the *Vivian*, while the *Gam-*

betta's people would examine the country east of the camp. One entire day was to be allowed for the exploration; if either party was detained from camp overnight, it was to be understood that a serious accident had happened.

The ground was too rough for the sledges to be of any use, and consequently they were left at the camp, together with everything else not needed for the day's journey. During the remainder of that day the region around the camp was examined, and the next morning both parties made an early start. Of course the dog-drivers remained at the camp to keep the dogs from straying, but all the rest of the party went to explore the land.

It did not take long for them to decide that the scheme for the government of the country would be of little use, as the inhabitants would not submit to it. The only residents they could find were bears, foxes, and other wild beasts, and a republican form of government has never been popular among these creatures. They are autocratic in their dispositions, and generally adhere to the principle that might makes right.

Fred got a shot at a white bear before they had gone half a mile from camp, but the animal made off altogether too fast for anybody to follow. Then the rifle was handed to the Doctor, but no game was discovered for some time. There was very little vegetation, only a few mosses and stunted shrubs, and our friends were unanimously of the opinion that it would not pay to attempt to colonize the country. Back of the camp, and perhaps a couple of miles inland, there was a hilly ridge about three hundred feet high. It was quite steep, and composed of broken shale, which made it difficult of ascent. The Doctor and Fred climbed to the top of the ridge, while the major and George proceeded along its base.

Back of the ridge was a broad extent of ice which proved to be a glacier, the first that Fred had ever seen. Dr. Tonner shouted his discovery to the major, and then followed along the ridge to find a good point for venturing on the surface of the ice. As there was nothing to be seen at the base of the ridge, the major and George climbed up to join their companions, and then it was decided to cross the ice, or at least make an investigation of its character.

The glacier was evidently an ancient and permanent one, as the sides of its channel were worn into precipices by the long continued flow of the river of ice. It was no easy matter to get fairly on the ice, owing to its broken character at the edge, and our friends walked a considerable distance before finding a satisfactory spot. There were deep fissures in the ice, and as the party was unprovided with the proper apparatus for glacier-climbing, it was necessary to proceed with great caution.

CROSSING A CREVASSE ON A BRIDGE OF ICE.

At length a bridge of ice seemed to promise secure footing, and one after another they ventured upon it. George slipped when nearly over; fortunately he fell on the side where the depth of the fissure was only a few feet, and escaped without injury. On the opposite side there was a sheer descent of some thirty or forty feet, and the consequences of a tumble there would have been serious.

Close to the ridge the ice was dirty, and mingled with the *débris* of rock and earth it had gathered in its contact with the wall that kept it in place, but towards the centre the appearance changed to a pure white. Evidently the air was not filled with dust in this locality, or the surface of the glacier would have revealed it. George thought the bank of the glacier offered an excellent spot for building a summer-house, as the site was a cool one, and the expense of having the ice-carts call every morning would be avoided.

Fissures were numerous, and some of them were concealed by freshly fallen snow, which greatly increased the danger. The major ordered a return to the land at the first favorable opportunity, and their intention of crossing the glacier was abandoned. Following down two or three hundred yards they found a place where the solid ice touched the wall of rock and enabled them to set foot on the earth again.

From this point it was decided to follow the glacier to its mouth, if not too far away. The fall was so slight that the surface was apparently level, but still there must be a fall in order to give the mass a movement onward. There was no living thing on the surface of the glacier, but in a little valley enclosed by some of the hills which formed the ridge the Doctor saw a herd of musk-cattle plucking the very scanty herbage that grew there. Creeping around, so as not to alarm them, he managed to get a shot at close range, and brought down one of these animals of the far North. The rest ran away at the report of the rifle, and at the apparition of the strange beings that rose from the ground as soon as the shot was fired.

"Now that we have a musk-ox," said the major, "what will we do with it?"

The question was a perplexing one. As they were unable to carry the meat to camp, and had no means of cooking it where they were, it was decided that they would return that way if practicable, and take enough of the meat to camp to have some fresh steaks for supper, provided the bears and foxes did not come upon the prize in their absence.

As this is the first of these animals that we have seen, we may as well give a description of him.

The musk-ox is peculiar to the polar regions of America, and its range is confined to the Arctic Circle, or very near it. It is twice as large as the reindeer, and when full grown is little if any smaller than a cow two years old; it has strong horns that bend around the head like those of the wild sheep of the Rocky Mountains, or wild goat of the Himalayas, and its body is covered with long hair to protect it from the cold. The flesh when fat is not much unlike beef, and has an agreeable flavor; but when the animal is lean, it has a strong smell of musk which only a ravenous appetite can overcome. Expeditions in the arctic regions have frequently relied on the musk-ox for their supply of fresh meat, and in several instances these animals have been the sole support

A MUSK-OX.

of parties for several months. They are not easy to approach, and can run very fast in spite of the shortness of their legs.

So much for the musk-ox, which our friends left with a sigh, and the Doctor half regretted having wasted a bullet upon. "What a pity he did not come down to our camp to be shot," said Fred, "as he would then have been handy for us to use. The only proper way of hunting is to bring in your game alive, and then kill it when it is wanted."

They traced the course of the glacier to the sea, but found nothing of consequence after walking five or six miles. Then it was time to return, and they decided to follow the shore back to camp—or rather the Doctor and the major did so, while the youths went to bring in the steaks for supper. The walking was not so easy along the shore as it was at the ridge farther inland. A good deal of the ground was covered with snow, and all the hollows were filled with it; generally it was hard enough to bear the weight of a man, but this was not always the case, and whenever it gave way the walking was laborious.

In some places the shore sloped from the ridge down to the water, or rather to the ice, while in others it was steep and precipitous. Wherever there were any cliffs there was a great number of birds, and their tameness showed that they were not accustomed to the visits of man. There were gulls, auks, eider-ducks, lumme, and several other members of the feathered tribe, but it was too early in the season to find their nests. Ten or twelve

ducks were obtained by knocking them down with stones, and the major
said he could have killed a hundred in this way if he had wished to do so.
Here and there, where the ground sloped to the water, they found pieces
of drift-wood, and when they reached the camp the major was rejoiced to
find that the dog-drivers had had the forethought to gather enough wood
during the day to make an excellent fire.   Thus the cooking of their food
was provided for, and they were not long in getting the ducks ready for
broiling.   The youths arrived a few minutes after the major and Doctor
had reached camp, bringing as much of the meat of the ox as they could
well carry.

DUCKS ON PRESIDENT LAND.

In a quarter of an hour or so the French explorers appeared, and were
welcomed with a loud cheer by the Americans.   They had been about ten
miles to the eastward, over ground similar to that traversed by the Americans, but somewhat more broken, and their progress had been stopped by
a ridge of rocks and a glacier which they were unable to cross without
the proper appliances for ice-travel.   Just beyond the ridge was a conical
rock two or three hundred feet high, and so far as they could ascertain it
was the most elevated point in the neighborhood.   One of the officers

THE "DEVIL'S THUMB," NEAR MELVILLE BAY.

made a sketch of the rock, which he named the "Butte Napoleon;" the major said it resembled the "Devil's Thumb," at the entrance of Melville Bay, which had been so named on account of its fancied similarity to an enormous thumb pointing in the air. Near the base of this ridge a seam of coal was found, and the indications on the surface showed that it was apparently of great extent. George and Fred at once suggested the formation of the "Vivian-Gambetta Coal Company, Limited," but the party was altogether too weary from the day's exertions to draw up the articles of incorporation.

The *Gambetta* party had been successful in hunting, as they had killed a bear which proved both young and fat, and what was of more consequence, he was shot within less than half a mile of camp. The skin was utilized as a sledge for transporting the meat to the sea-shore, and by the time the sun went down all the explorers were at their tents. The Americans divided their ducks and beefsteaks with their French allies, and the latter returned the compliment with an abundant supply of bear-meat, for feeding the dogs from the *Vivian*. Men and dogs went to sleep with full stomachs—an excellent preparation for the fatigues of the return journey to the ships.

In the morning there was some difficulty in getting the sledges on the ice again, as there was a movement of the field along the shore. During the night a strong breeze blew from the south-west, and an hour or so after it set in the crashing and grinding of the ice along the shore showed that it was in motion. Cracks and narrow lanes were opened in two or three places, and a good many huge blocks were forced upon the beach. It was evident that the explorers ought to get back to the ships as speedily as possible, or they might find themselves altogether cut off from retreat by the breaking up of the ice.

A practicable spot was found close to the French tent, and, without waiting for breakfast, all the teams started over the route they had come a couple of days' before. Following the lane already described, through the rough ice, they reached the smooth field and then halted for rest and food. The remains of the supper of the previous evening served for the morning meal, with the addition of pemmican and tea; the dogs looked wistfully on, but it would have been contrary to custom to feed them immediately before the long run which they were to make. Soon as breakfast was over the journey was resumed; but it was not accomplished as quickly as the outward one, owing to several cracks in the ice, over which it was necessary to lift the sledges. Before the line of hummocks was reached the ships were plainly discernible, and each had a large flag flying, to enable them to be made out as easily as possible. The major thought the position of the ships had been changed considerably since the party left them, and the Doctor agreed with him. It seemed that they were farther to the east than before, and evidently the drifting had increased during their absence.

When they reached home again they were welcomed with all the honors. Both ships were dressed in flags, a salute of two guns was fired by the *Vivian* and a similar one by the *Gambetta*, and the crews were ranged at the gangway to greet the travellers with three ringing cheers. Commander Bronson said he had been watching for their return since morning, and the movement of the ice had caused a good deal of alarm for their safety. A man had been kept in the crow's-nest with the most powerful glass the ship possessed, to watch out for them and report their approach; and the same precaution had been taken on the *Gambetta*. The lookout on the latter ship was the first to announce the return of the sledges, and therefore the French captain was consoled, to some extent at least, for the march the Americans had stolen on him in starting ahead of his party, and taking possession of the land before his people could get there.

It was late in the afternoon of the second day from land when the sledges reached the ships, and the wearisome journey was ended. The best supper that could be provided on board the *Vivian* was ready for our friends, and they sat down to it with the keenest of appetites. During the progress of the meal they told the story of their adventures, and of the addition they had made to the geography of the arctic regions. After supper Fred proceeded to designate on the map the position of President Land; the point where the sledges reached it was set down as latitude 83° 24′ north, longitude 115° 10′ west. It was known to extend about ten miles east and west from that point, but of its area to the north they were entirely ignorant.

The breeze continued to blow from the south-west, and by morning it had increased to half a gale. The ice heaved and cracked in many places, and the progress of the field to the north and east was more rapid than ever. Everybody was on the alert, and the developments of each hour were looked forward to with the greatest anxiety. The dogs and sledges were taken on board the ship, but the casks of provisions that had been placed there in the event of the sinking of the *Vivian* were allowed to remain, as they might be needed at any moment. While it was desirable to be prepared for the loss of the ship, it was equally necessary to be ready to float away in her in case she should be released from her icy prison. The boats were made ready for launching; clothing, provisions, and equipments were piled close to the rail, ready to be thrown out at a

moment's warning; and those who were not on duty went to sleep with
their clothes on and their knapsacks by their sides.   It is hardly necessary
to add that, under the circumstances, nobody slept soundly.

Discipline was carefully maintained.   The watches were changed as
regularly as though the weather was of the finest and the ship were sailing across the Pacific under the steady influence of the trade-wind.   As
the day advanced, the movement of the ice increased; a little past noon
a large crack opened from the bow directly ahead, and another parallel to
it a hundred yards away.   About the middle of the afternoon the man in
the crow's-nest called out "*Land!*" and of course everybody was full of
anxiety to see it.

COAST SCENE IN THE ARCTIC CIRCLE.

It was fully half an hour before it could be made out from the deck,
and then only faintly.   From the course they had been drifting it was
evident that the land in sight was the region lately visited by the sledges;
and if they continued to go on as they were then proceeding, they would
be close upon it by the following morning.   The Doctor went to the
crow's-nest, and was quite positive he could recognize the "Butte Napoleon" from the description and drawing of the French officers.   It was
thought that the land was about fifteen miles distant, and in the course
they were drifting they would pass to the eastward of it.

Some of our readers may wonder that they were so near the land before seeing it. It must be remembered that the island was covered with snow, except in a few places, and consequently its appearance was almost identical with that of the ice-fields which surrounded it. The weather was hazy, and a clear horizon was the exception rather than the rule; and furthermore, the land was not sufficiently elevated to be visible at a great distance, even if all the other conditions had been favorable.

"Well, we can't go ashore just now," said the Doctor, when he returned to the deck, "and it's lucky we embraced the opportunity when we did."

"Yes," responded the major, "and it's luckier that we embraced the opportunity to get back again. If we had remained there another day it is doubtful if we would have returned at all."

The subject was not a pleasant one for contemplation. Nobody liked to think what would have been their fate if left on that desolate and hitherto unknown island, and the conversation took another turn.

"If we go on in this way without accident," said the commander, "we may be at the pole before the middle of summer. But I confess I don't understand it altogether."

"Nor do I," said Captain Jones, who had just joined the group. "Here is the ice threatening to break up in the beginning of May, fully two months before we have any reason to expect it. It looks very much as though we were on the borders of the Polynia of the Russians, and the barrier was about to divide, and let us into the open polar sea."

"At any rate," replied the commander, "we are beyond the latitude of any previous navigator, and must not be surprised at anything. By to-morrow noon we will be north of the 84th parallel of latitude, which has never yet been passed by man. Parry turned back at 82° 45'; Hayes at 81° 37'. Captain Markham, of the British Expedition of 1876, reached the highest point yet attained, 83° 20' 26.'' In 1881 the United States ship *Alliance*, in search of the *Jeannette*, went along the coast of Spitzbergen to 80° 10' north, and longitude 11° 22' east. And here we are, within six degrees or three hundred and sixty miles of the pole! If we can—"

A call from the lookout aloft arrested their attention. Captain Jones mounted rapidly to the crow's-nest, and then, with more excitement than was usual with him, he shouted to Commander Bronson.

The latter lost no time in ascending to the captain's side. The rest of the party waited breathlessly below while their superiors were observing the state of the ice, and the conditions ahead of the drifting floe. After what seemed hours to our friends, but was really less than twenty minutes, the commander returned to the deck, leaving the captain aloft.

"The way we are now drifting," said he, "will carry us close to what appears to be a point of land projecting to the eastward of the 'Butte Napoleon.' The ice is being forced on this point, and we can see it heaving and breaking, and piling up as it is pushed onward by the wind and current. Outside the point the floes are much broken, and our position is a perilous one. If we drift upon the point we shall be hopelessly wrecked, unless something little short of a miracle should save us; if we

A SHELTER FROM THE ICE.

clear the point we shall be in danger from the floes that are crashing against each other, and our hope must rest in the unusual strength of our ship. As we are going we can hope to clear the point, but may not do so; the *Gambetta* will certainly clear it, but then she will be in the peril I have mentioned from the breaking of the ice."

The casks of provisions were hoisted on board and piled close to the rail, where they could be thrown overboard in case of necessity.

The sun had set, and the twilight of the arctic was upon them. "Shall we ever see the sun again?" was the question which each asked himself as he watched the disappearance of the orb of day.

The captain descended from the rigging, and the party retired to the cabin. They could plainly hear the creaking and groaning of the ship as the ice moved around her, and occasionally there came a sound louder than usual which told of the extraordinary strain upon their floating home. There was little conversation at supper, and as soon as the meal was over the commander said they must get what sleep they could during the night, and be prepared to leave the ship at any moment. The same precautions were taken as on the night before, but every one realized that the peril was more imminent, and escape from the ship was by no means indicative of an escape with life.

There was little sleep on the *Vivian*, and the same was doubtless the case on the *Gambetta*. All were anxious for the morning, and for hours and hours it seemed to Fred and George that the darkness was without end.

EFFECT OF AN ARCTIC GALE.

CHAPTER XVI.

ESCAPE FROM THE ICE.—IN THE OPEN POLAR SEA.—STEAMING AND SAILING TO
THE NORTH.

WITH the first blush of dawn our young friends were on deck.   Fred
recalled the lines in one of his school-books:

> "The night, the long, dark night at last
>   Passed fearfully away.
> 'Mid crashing ice and howling blast
>   They hailed the dawn of day,
> Which broke to cheer the whaler's crew,
> And wide around its gray light threw."

The *Vivian* was standing upright in the ice, as she had stood for
weeks, but the *Gambetta* was heeled over so that her yards almost touched
the water.   The point of land, concerning which there had been so much
anxiety on the previous evening, was about a mile away, on the port side
of the *Vivian*, and the ice was piled upon it in great masses, which appeared in some places hundreds of feet in height.   It was an immense
relief to know that the ship had weathered this miniature cape, and they
had not to contend with the horror of being dashed upon it.   And oh!
welcome sight, which they had not known through all that long winter,
beyond the jutting point there was an expanse of open water!   True, it was
encumbered with cakes of ice that stippled its surface as far as the eye
could see, but compared with what they had known during their imprisonment, it was like a pellucid lake in the mountains.

Around them the ice-field was cracked and broken in many places,
and several lanes of water were visible.   The telegraph line connecting
the ships had been taken up soon after the return of the explorers from
the island, and when the increasing wind made it probable that the ice
would move more rapidly to the northward.   The route where the wire
had been stretched could be traced over the mounds of ice, except in two
or three places where there had been extensive breaks in the field, and
some of the mounds had altogether disappeared.   Communication between

the ships was conducted by signal-flags; when the *Gambetta* heeled over, our friends expected every moment the announcement that she was sinking, but as she displayed no signal, it was concluded that there was no immediate danger.

They drifted with the ice as before, but appeared to move in a circuitous direction, in consequence of the edge of the field impinging on the land. Suddenly there was a loud crash, and the ice split in front of them, directly in line of the crack which had opened the evening before. The land-ice, as we may call it, swung away from the ship, while the rest remained practically in its former position; then the *Vivian* heeled over, broke loose from the floe, righted to an even keel, and was afloat!

NEAR THE ICE.

The captain ordered the engineer to get up steam as soon as possible. The fires were ready for lighting, and in a few minutes a dense volume of smoke was pouring from the funnel.

The lane in front of them widened as the floes swung apart from each other, and though the water was full of floating cakes, it was comparatively open and suitable for navigation. Pending the readiness of the engines to propel the ship, the sails were spread; their influence was quickly felt, and almost instantly the *Vivian* was forging ahead, with the water rippling beneath her bows.

In spite of the peril of their position, with the ice on three sides and the land on the fourth, Captain Jones called for three cheers as the ship began to move. Officers and men responded with all the vigor of their lungs; whatever danger might threaten them, it was a great delight to be free once more, and they signified their feelings by the energy with which they cheered. As the last cheer died away the *Gambetta* rose from her reclining position to an even keel; the *Vivian* fired a gun and ran up a flag in token of congratulation, to which the French ship responded in the same manner.

The lead showed ten fathoms of water; the captain ordered the helm aport, so that the *Vivian* could reach the expanse of water formed on the lee side of the point of land we have described. In a little while there was sufficient steam for turning the screw, and with engines to aid the sails the *Vivian* soon found a harbor.

At the same time the *Gambetta* was in motion. The ice did not open as readily around her as around the *Vivian*, for the reason that it was not drawn to one side by its contact with the land; but a lane formed, through which she crept slowly forward, partly through the aid of engines and sails, and partly by the efforts of her crew. The men were sent out with ice-anchors, which they made fast under the direction of an officer stationed in the cross-trees; as soon as an anchor was fixed it was drawn in by the steam-winch, and thus the ship was slowly advanced. Finally, only a narrow line of ice separated her from the clear water; this was blown up with a can of powder, and then by hard pushing with her engines the *Gambetta* was afloat in the harbor that held the *Vivian*.

Afloat and uninjured after all the peril they had passed through! It was an occasion for rejoicing, and as the *Gambetta* swung parallel with the *Vivian* and slowed her engines, the yards of both ships were manned by their crews, and the cheering that went up from the throats of those happy sailors must have astonished the listening bears and musk-cattle on President Land. Never before were the echoes of that harbor awakened by human voices, nor yet by the guns which fired a salute, each ship to the other, in congratulation over their release from imprisonment in the ice-field and the perils of the escape.

They were in unknown waters, with the land close aboard; consequently it was necessary to proceed with caution, and the ships moved with only enough speed to give steerage-way. The *Vivian* was in advance, and nearer shore than the *Gambetta*, and therefore in more danger of taking the ground; she kept the lead going steadily, but in no place did it show less than six fathoms, and there was no danger except from hidden rocks or shoals.

The bay was about four miles in length from the point of the peninsula which had served to break up the ice, and the next projection to the north. Its depth was something more than two miles, perhaps two and a half, and in the direction the wind was then blowing it was well sheltered. The farther side was terminated by a promontory or foreland which closely resembled the North Foreland of Frobisher, at the entrance of the bay named after the enterprising mariner of the early days of arctic exploration. The waves were breaking at the foot of this promontory, and beyond it the ice was pressing northward under the influence of the wind and current. As an attempt to pass out of the bay might bring the ships into the ice again, it was deemed prudent to anchor, and make an investigation with the boats before proceeding.

Down went the anchors for the first time in many weeks, and the chains rattling through the hawse-hole was a welcome sound. Then a boat was lowered from the *Vivian*, and another from the *Gambetta:* the

THE NORTH FORELAND.

Vivian's boat rowed to the side of the *Gambetta*, and it was hastily agreed that she should proceed to investigate the condition of the water as far as it could be seen from the top of the promontory. Meantime the *Gambetta's* boat would take soundings in the direction of the foreland, and as far beyond it as would be safe to venture.

George and the major were assigned to the work of exploration with the boat's crew from the *Vivian*, and away they went in the direction of the land. It was easy enough to row over the water, but not so easy to find a landing-place.

Apparently the tide was out, and the beach was concealed by an ice-collar eighteen or twenty feet high, exactly similar to the ice-collars which explorers in other parts of the arctic seas have described. A rope with an ice-anchor formed part of the boat's equipment; this anchor was thrown over the ice, and after several failures it caught and held firmly.

Two men pulling upon it with their entire weight were not able to move it, and then the most nimble of the sailors climbed up and assisted the others to follow. Two men were left in the boat, and the rest of the party ascended the promontory.

CLIMBING AN ICE-COLLAR.

Their attention was attracted to the vast numbers of birds that filled the air, and flew so close to the explorers as to be easily knocked down with sticks. George wanted to stop long enough to get a supply for the ship, but the major commanded that no delay should be made, as the birds were altogether a secondary consideration.

They had an hour of the hardest kind of climbing to reach the top of the hill, as the broken shale which lay in many places retarded their footsteps and frequently compelled them to fall on hands and knees. George was the first at the top, where he waved his cap and gave a loud hurrah; evidently his progress was noted from the ships, as the *Vivian* dipped her flag three times in honor of his achievement, and the *Gambetta* did likewise.

The view beyond the hill was encouraging, as it revealed a wide strip of open water between the land and the pack of heavy ice which spread away to the eastward. This water extended as far as they could see, and the major decided without hesitation that it would be quite safe to venture into it. In front of the hill the ice-pack was not more than a quarter of a mile from land; the indications were that there was plenty of water between the foreland and the ice, though this could only be made certain by actual soundings.

Descending the hill they took a route different from the one by which they went up; on their way down, when near the base, they had the good-fortune to come upon several nests of the eider-duck, of the variety known as the "king," which breeds earlier and farther north than the common eider. The birds were just beginning their period of nesting; no nest contained more than one egg, with the exception of two or three which

THE LUMME OF THE NORTH.

had two eggs each. The major said the eider-duck usually lays from five to seven eggs, and does not begin incubation until about the end of May.

They gathered all the eggs they could find, and managed to get nearly three dozen. They killed eight or ten ducks by knocking them down with sticks, and on reaching the boat they found that the sailors had secured as many more by the simple process of striking them with the oars when they flew or swam near the boat. Several lumme and auks had been taken in the same way, and when the boat returned to the *Vivian* it had a good supply of food for the cabin table.

George was surprised to find that the egg of the eider-duck is about twice as large as a hen's egg; and when the harvest of the day had passed through the hands of the cook, he decided that the eggs were as delicious as they were large. While the party was discussing the novel dinner, Captain Jones said these eggs were considered the greatest of all delicacies by the Labrador fishermen; and in the season when they were obtainable the whalers in the far North had all they wanted to eat. He said he had frequently gathered fifteen or twenty dozen in half an hour or so on the islands where the ducks have their breeding-places, and that the down from the nests paid them handsomely for their work.

George's curiosity was aroused, and he wished to know more of the process of obtaining down from the eider-duck.

"I can't tell you exactly," replied the captain, "as I have never studied the habits of the bird very carefully; but I believe that when the eggs are laid the female plucks the down from her breast and places it around and beneath them. After she begins incubation the male bird deserts her, and when she has occasion to leave the nest in search of food, she pulls the down over the eggs to keep them warm during her absence. If the nest is robbed of eggs and down, she finds another mate and begins the work over again; and if she is robbed a second time, she seeks a new mate. As she has stripped her breast of all its down to supply the two nests, the third is supplied by her last companion.

"The down from a nest will fill your hat, but it doesn't weigh more than an ounce, and generally less. I have seen nests that yielded two or three ounces, and have heard of some that contained half a pound of down, but I never saw them, and very much doubt if anybody else ever did."

The captain further said that the down was worth three or four dollars a pound in the English market, and was highly prized on account of its lightness and warmth.

While our friends were absent on land another boat had been making a survey of the harbor under the charge of the Doctor and Fred. They had taken soundings in several places, finding plenty of water for anchoring within a hundred yards of the shore, and made a tracing of the shore-line, together with the bearings, both true and magnetic. They named the place "Bronson Bay," in honor of their commander, and with the assent of the major the promontory which the latter had ascended was designated "Clapp's Cliff," in commemoration of the event of the day.

Meantime the crew of the *Gambetta's* boat had made soundings to the front of the foreland, and found plenty of water; they were in some danger from the waves, which broke rather furiously at the base of the steep rock, but by keeping well out from the shore they escaped accident. It was decided to steam around the foreland and into the open water beyond it, and as the *Gambetta* had made the soundings she took the lead.

VIEW FROM TONNER'S ISLAND.

Steaming slowly as before she made the passage without hinderance, and then the *Vivian* followed. Once around the foreland they had plenty of water; and though it was full of fragments of ice, like the bay they had just left, there was not enough to trouble them. Keeping a sharp watch for shoals and rocks, throwing the lead continually, and holding themselves as far from land as the ice-pack would permit, the vessels kept on for some twenty miles or more, when they were stopped by another projection of land. The ice-pack was crowded close up to this projection, and was so dense that it was not deemed prudent to venture into it without further investigation.

Again they anchored, and this time the fires were drawn, in order that there might be no unnecessary consumption of coal. Besides, it was the end of the long arctic day, and everybody was sufficiently tired out to need a rest.

The next morning there was great activity on both ships. Each of them sent a boat to land, and another to explore the bay where they were anchored; the land parties were provided with rifles and shot-guns, as well as scientific instruments, and were instructed to bring in any game they could find, in addition to determining the position of the bay and the character of the water beyond, if any could be seen. The *Vivian's* boat was the first to get away, but it was thought proper to allow the *Gambetta's* people to be first on shore, inasmuch as they had given the *Vivian's* party the exclusive occupation on the previous day.

Without following the movements of all the parties in detail we will see what they accomplished.

The bay was simply an indentation in the land, about twenty miles long, sheltered from southerly and north-westerly winds, and other winds between them to the west, but open to all others. It was named "Girard Bay," in honor of the captain of the *Gambetta.*

At the northern end of the bay there was a steep cliff or bluff about three hundred feet high, which was named "French Head," to commemorate the nationality of the flag that was unfurled from its summit.

The position of French Head was found to be latitude 84° 31′ north, longitude 114° 45′ west.

About four miles south of French Head the bay was studded with rocky islands, of which only two or three could be visited, on account of the ice that filled the channels. The Doctor and Fred climbed to the top of one of these islands (which was named in the Doctor's honor), and the young man made a sketch of the scene while they rested from the fatigue of the ascent.

The party that ascended French Head reported that the pack-ice filled the horizon to the eastward, and there was no hope of escape in that direction; but there was open water north of the cliff, and the coast seemed to trend away to the westward. If they could manage to pass the cliff, it was the opinion of the officer in charge of the observation that they could go at least twenty-five miles, and perhaps twice or three times that distance, without obstruction.

At one time the ice seemed inclined to sweep away from French Head and allow them to pass. Steam was ordered on the ships, and the signal of recall for the boats was set; but before they could return, and the vessels got ready to move, the ice closed in again.

The parties were not especially successful in hunting, as they saw nothing larger than birds. The fact was they had no time to spend in sport, as they were chiefly occupied with their observations. The second day of their stay in Girard Bay was principally devoted to hunting; and as the birds were very tame, they were knocked down by hundreds. The crews of both ships had an ample repast from this source of supply, and so did the dogs, though the latter would have preferred fish or beef. They bolted the birds, feathers and all, and when a dog had finished his ornithological breakfast he had a fringe of feathers around his muzzle which seemed to change him into a hitherto unknown specimen of the canine race.

FRENCH HEAD.

One of the hunting parties came back with a report of the existence of a channel just back of French Head, which might let the ships through into the open water to the north. They had entered it from the little group of islands explored by Dr. Tonner and Fred, and in their chase for birds they ascended it a mile or more. The tide was running through it very gently, but enough to show that there was communication between Girard Bay and some other body of water.

A couple of days were spent in exploring this channel, a boat going from each ship for that purpose. The result of the exploration was that the channel was found a dangerous one for the ships to enter; it was narrow in many places and quite tortuous, and there were several ugly rocks along the way. The passage was possible, but very hazardous, and it was determined not to attempt it until all chance of escape around French Head was hopeless.

For nearly a fortnight the ships remained at anchor in Girard Bay, waiting a favorable opportunity to continue their journey. All the scientific men of the expeditions were busy with observations on the flora, the fauna, and other productions of President Land, and on the character of the rocks, the traces of miocene and pliocene formations, and other things that interest the geologists and students of natural history. George and Fred were of great assistance to their elders in making the records of the observations, and in packing away the specimens of the products of this hitherto unknown land.

One afternoon the wind chopped suddenly round to the westward, and gradually increased as the hours went on. By six o'clock it was a strong breeze, at nine it was a high wind, at twelve it was half a gale, and by three in the morning it was a full-fledged gale "with its coat off," as the captain expressed it.

Each ship put out an extra anchor, and everything was made snug aloft. "I think something 'll come of this gale," said the captain, "and we must make the most of it."

Evidently "something was to come of it," as the force of the wind carried the ice out to sea and left the front of French Head quite free of it. Here and there scattered fragments were visible, but nothing to impede the progress of a ship.

For twenty hours the gale blew steadily, and was of the kind that shaves the hair from the back of a dog, or removes the shoestrings even when properly tied. Then it subsided as slowly as it had risen; the fall of the barometer was more moderate than is the case in southern latitudes, and it did not begin until an hour or so before the cessation of the gale.

Now was the opportunity for the ships!

When the tempest had reached the condition of half a gale the fires were started in the furnaces of the ships, and by the time it was down to a high wind they were ready to proceed. Up came the anchors, and in a little while the *Vivian* and *Gambetta* had rounded French Head and were steaming through "International Reach," the name which had been given to the stretch of water beyond the promontory.

EXPLORING THE CHANNEL.

"Didn't I say something would come o' that gale?" said Captain Jones, as they steamed northward. "How I wish we had a good chart of this reach, so that we could go ahead at full speed. It's less than four hundred miles to the North-pole, and who knows but what we've got an open road to it?

"I guess it's the same here as it is in Smith's Sound," he continued. "From the looks of things we've got the land-water same as we have it there. Frequently, when the sound is full of ice, there's an open strip along the western side, and not a few ships and boats have made their way north through that water."

Yes, they had the land-water, and what was more, the strip widened as they went north; or, rather, the land trended away to the north-west, while the edge of the ice-pack seemed about on a due north-and-south line. As they hauled away from land the sounding-lead showed a steady deepening of the water. Five miles from the shore-line they had thirty fathoms, and then it was deemed safe to increase the speed to eight knots. But all the time the lead was kept going, and a sharp lookout was maintained in the crow's-nest, on the cross-trees, and on the bows. Occasionally the lead indicated the shoaling of the water, and whenever this was the case the pace was reduced to little more than steerage-way until the soundings deepened again.

"There's one thing in our favor," said George to Fred, as they were looking over the ship's side and studying the line of the coast they were passing, "we are in no danger of collision with other ships trying to cross our track."

"Don't be so sure of that," was the reply. "Who knows but we may encounter a ship that has forced its way through the ice above Smith's Sound and is making for the pole, just as we are. The same conditions that have favored us may give somebody else a similar chance."

George admitted the possibility of such an event, but was still inclined to the opinion that they would have plenty of sea-room.

Observation at noon showed they were in latitude 85° 10' north, longitude 113° 50' west. Only three hundred miles to the pole!

The advancing season and their high latitude had dispelled the arctic darkness. Daylight was continuous, and there was no necessity for lying by for the night, since practically the night had ceased to exist. But for the convenience of chronology they continued to talk of day and night the same as in more southern latitudes, and we will follow their custom.

By noon of the second day, after they had passed French Head, the land was nothing more than a faint line along the western horizon, while the ice-blink to the eastward showed that the pack was still in their neighborhood. The wind was steady from the west, and as a prudential measure the fires were extinguished, and the ships relied altogether upon their sails.

The farther the ships went from land the less numerous were the sea-birds; but not so the whales, which were visible in great numbers. Dozens of them were in sight at once, and they did not appear disturbed by the presence of the ships. Evidently they were ignorant of the destructive propensities of man, as they played around the ships, and sometimes were altogether more familiar than was desirable. Several times, after diving, they came up beneath the bows of the *Vivian*, and were so near that they could have been harpooned from the ship. Once a whale scraped his back against the vessel's keel, but fortunately for our friends he seemed to treat the affair as a joke, and did not resent it. While the thickness of the *Vivian's* sides might have saved her from injury, it would have been a serious matter if he had dashed at her with the immense momentum of his huge body.

"What a place for a whaler!" said Captain Jones, as he looked at the huge cetaceans playing in the waters. "It beats the old days of the Okhotsk Sea and Scammon's Bay, when a ship could fill up in a month and go home. Some of 'em are good for two hundred barrels, and they're all to be had for the taking."

"Sail ho!" shouted the man in the crow's-nest, and the captain's dream of the whaler came to an abrupt termination.

CURIOUS APPEARANCE OF THE SUN.

16

CHAPTER XVII.

ICEBERGS AND GLACIERS. — LAND AGAIN. — "LA TERRE LAFAYETTE." — THE
"VIVIAN" AT THE POLE.

"THE last place in the world for a sail!" exclaimed the captain, as he
sprang into the rigging, and mounted with the agility of a cat. "It's
a Yankee pole-hunter, or one of those Scotch whalers from Dundee, I'm
sure."

Of course there was great excitement in the party on deck during the
captain's absence aloft, and all sorts of conjectures were made, and various
theories propounded. The captain eyed the strange sail through a glass
for at least a quarter of an hour; then he scanned the horizon in every
direction, again looked intently at the sail for ten minutes or so, and finally
closed his glass and returned to the deck.

"It's no sail at all," said he, with a mingled expression of satisfaction
and disappointment on his face. "It's an iceberg, but it looks so much
like a ship under full sail that I don't wonder the lookout was deceived.

"It's a big one, too," he continued, "and we shall probably see more
of 'em. It's larger than any berg we've come across yet, and I'm curious
to know where it came from."

A couple of hours later another iceberg was reported, and some time
afterwards another.

By observation and dead-reckoning, when the sail was announced, they
were within less than two hundred miles of the pole. The presence of
the icebergs reduced greatly the probability of an unobstructed voyage to
the point where there is neither latitude nor longitude.

The iceberg first seen was about four points off the port bow, while
the second was almost dead ahead. It was not considered advisable to
change the course of the ship in order to look at one mountain of ice,
when another could be reached without any divergence. The *Vivian* held
her way, and in due time reached and passed the second iceberg; it was
so nearly in her course that she was obliged to turn aside a little in order
to keep at a respectful distance.

As well as they could estimate its size, it was fully half a mile long and a third of a mile broad; an enormous belt seemed to encircle it, as though the layer of snow in one year had been different from what preceded and followed it. This appearance is not at all unusual in icebergs; Captain Hall describes one of exactly the same formation, and says he gave it the name of "the belted iceberg," on account of its enormous girdle.

THE BELTED ICEBERG.

The part of the berg below the water was much broader than the portion above, and accounted for its ability to float in the depth they were navigating. Just as they were in front of it a mass "as large as a church" broke off from one side and fell into the water with a loud splash. The wave it created caused the *Vivian* to pitch and roll as though in a heavy sea.

"You see the advantage of not going very near those fellows," said the captain. "If we had been close up to the side of that berg we might have been swamped."

Everybody could see the force of the captain's assertion, and there was no inclination for a nearer view of the white-robed stranger. Naturally they discussed the origin of the bergs, and wondered whence they had come.

"I think," said the captain, "we shall find land before long, and that it contains glaciers which have given birth to these bergs. It's a pity we could not explore President Land more thoroughly than we did; it would be interesting to know whether it had more glaciers in it than what we saw there."

There were many fragments of ice floating in the water; in fact, during all their voyage in the polar sea thus far, they had never been entirely free from them. After passing the bergs we have described, the number of floating fragments increased, and it began to look as though the way to the pole was far from being an open one.

The weather changed for the worse; it became colder, and the sky was frequently overcast. Once in a while a snow-squall set in, and made it impossible to see far ahead; at such times the ice was decidedly dangerous, and it became necessary for the ships to shorten sail.

"After all," said Commander Bronson, while they were passing through one of these squalls, "we could not expect a long continuance of the fine weather that followed the gale. The polar regions can hardly be unlike the rest of the world; storms and calms follow each other, and so we may expect an offset to the weather that has favored us."

The squall lasted for an hour or more, and then the sky became clear again. The wind continued favorable, and by varying her course now and then the *Vivian* managed to make good progress and avoid all injury from the ice.

The captain's prediction was realized, for within less than twenty hours after he made it land was sighted. It proved to be somewhat more mountainous than President Land, and as the *Vivian* approached it the front of a glacier was plainly to be seen at the end of a triangular bay. An iceberg which had recently broken off was lying inside the entrance of the bay and nearly filled it; the berg appeared to be resting on the ground, and the captain said it would be necessary for a good deal of it to be melted away by the sun before the rest could float and find its way out to sea.

They coasted along the land, looking for a good point to send a boat on shore, as the bay where the iceberg lay was not considered favorable. At length an opening was seen through a cliff, and as there was good anchorage in the vicinity, the *Vivian* furled her sails and came to a stop. The *Gambetta* continued, with the evident intention of sending a boat on shore at another point and making the exploration as extensive as possible.

Great flocks of birds were seen on the cliffs, and while the boat with the Doctor and Fred was gone to explore the land, another carrying the major and George went to lay in a stock of game for the table.

A SNOW-SQUALL AMONG THE ICEBERGS.

They rowed along towards the base of the cliff, and as they did so a sound reached their ears like the rumbling of a railway train or the fall of a cascade. It increased as they approached the cliff, and finally became so loud that they could hardly hear each other. The noise was made by the birds that had just begun their period of nesting, or, as George expressed it after seeing the way the birds lay their eggs, "their period of rocking."

"You observe," said the major, "that the face of the cliff consists of a series of steps or ledges from one to two or three feet deep. These birds are the lumme, which we saw on President Land, and they are common through all the arctic regions.

"The female lays only one egg, and this she deposits on the bare ledge of rock. Look at the creatures and see how they are stowed away there."

George looked, and saw that the birds were sitting close together, with their heads outward, but they were not keeping very quiet. In some places they were packed in solid rows, and so near were they to each other that where the ledges were narrow and frequent they almost hid the face of the rock from view.

"The female bird can only cover her egg by placing it upright," the major continued. "This she does with her bill, and then she sits down on it and waits for the hatching. If she doesn't keep quiet she may topple the egg over the ledge, where it is broken by the fall, and then she is eggless.

"When she has lost her egg, she watches her chance to steal another. The birds are obliged to leave their eggs occasionally in search of food, and when one does so she generally finds on her return that some other bird has stolen her property and is sitting upon it. She accuses somebody of the theft, and there is a fight; and that's what all that noise is about.

"Sometimes the fight becomes general, and dozens of birds will be engaged in it. In the tumult many of their eggs are rolled over the cliff, and the losers content themselves by stealing the first they can seize. For this reason one of these lumme rookeries is the noisiest place you can imagine."

The first shot sent a great many birds into the air, and for a time it looked as though a cloud had come between the boat and the sun. Each shot brought down several birds, and the work did not require any exercise of skill. In a little while they had all the boat could carry, and then made the best of their way back to the ship.

As there was no probability that the shore-party would return for several hours, Captain Jones decided to change his anchorage and send out two boats to secure more birds. The *Gambetta* anchored two or three miles farther north than the *Vivian*, and sent a boat on shore; then she followed the *Vivian's* example and sent two boats after lumme, so that the flocks were a good deal disturbed.

SHOOTING LUMME.

Two or three hours sufficed to supply both ships with all the birds they wanted. The lumme is less desirable than the duck as an article of food, but he is a great deal better than no bird at all. Officers, men, and dogs had all the lumme they wanted, and the feast was enjoyed by all concerned.

The shore-parties had been ordered not to remain on land more than ten or twelve hours, and to return immediately in case of a signal to do so. A snow-squall arose, but was of short duration, and as there was enough to do in examining the coast where the ships were lying, the explorers on land were allowed to stay the full time allotted to them.

Twelve hours after their departure Fred and the Doctor returned; they were pretty well tired out with their excursion, and had excellent appetites for the dinner which awaited them. They reported that the land was principally a mass of rock, and they had been able to go only about two miles from where they left the boat. They had gone to the rear of the cliff, which they estimated to be not far from five hundred feet high, and found that there was a range of hills in the interior, bordering a broad valley filled with a glacier. It was the same glacier they had seen in the bay, and was much wider where they saw it than at its entrance into the sea. Through an opening in the hills they could see another glacier, but could give no estimate as to its extent.

Of course they hoisted their flag at the highest point they reached, and allowed it to wave for several minutes in the arctic breeze. The Doctor gave the name of "Mount Lincoln" to the peak, but the naming of the land, of whose extent they could not be certain, was courteously left for their French allies.

As soon as the boat returned from shore the *Vivian* made sail, and hoisted the signal "we wish to communicate." The *Gambetta* remained at her anchorage, and the *Vivian* stopped again within five hundred yards or so of her consort. Meantime, while the *Vivian* was changing her position, the *Gambetta's* boat returned, and the Doctor went on board the French ship to compare notes, and ascertain what name would be given to their latest discovery.

Captain Girard felt highly complimented at the politeness of the Americans, and after a brief conference it was decided that the new land should be set down on their chart as "*La Terre Lafayette*" (Lafayette Land). The position was fixed at latitude 87° 10′ north, longitude 112° 50′ west.

Less than three degrees from the pole!

The French explorers had discovered a glacier, evidently identical with the one seen by the Doctor and Fred. They had found the rocks very difficult of ascent, and though keeping a sharp lookout for bears, musk-oxen, and other animals, they had seen none. One of the Frenchmen found the tracks of a bear, but the animal that made them was evidently far away. At all events he did not show himself, and the party returned without any trophies of the chase.

Then the Doctor returned to the *Vivian*, and the two ships filled away on their voyage to the North. It was understood that they would follow the coast unless it trended too far to the westward, but neither was to be hampered by the movements of the other. As far as they could see, the coast-line was about north and south, and if it continued in that direction it would not carry them out of their way.

On they went, but unforeseen difficulties arose. They had not been three hours under way when a dense fog set in, and compelled them to lay to. What with the ice and the unknown coast it would be dangerous to go on; any moment they might come in collision with an iceberg or be dashed on the rocks, and either fate was not to be risked. The fog lay thick about them for several hours, and when it lifted, the *Vivian* was unpleasantly near a jutting headland, which terminated in a mass of rough and ugly rocks. The *Gambetta* was about a mile to the eastward, and close under her lee lay a huge iceberg, towards which the ship was slowly drifting. Evidently the escape was a narrow one for both navigators!

The sounding-lead showed a depth of eighty or a hundred fathoms in some places, and not more than half that amount a short distance away. The bottom of the sea was as uneven as the land in its neighborhood, and any minute they might come on a rocky islet, with no shoals around it to give warning of its proximity.

The fog cleared away and they made sail again. When they had gone three or four miles, the *Gambetta* suddenly backed her sails and made signal "I am aground." The *Vivian* answered that she would go to the assistance of her companion, and as soon as she could get up steam she moved to within half a cable's length of the stranded ship. Meantime the *Gambetta* had made steam, and a cable was passed to the *Vivian*. The latter pulling and the former backing with all the force of their engines, the *Gambetta* was soon afloat and apparently uninjured.

"Lucky it wasn't a rock instead of a shoal," said Captain Jones, as they dropped the *Gambetta's* cable and saw it pulled on board. "I think we want water more than land, and we'll give the shore a wide berth."

The *Vivian* headed off in a north-easterly direction, and the *Gambetta* did likewise. In a couple of hours they had a hundred and fifty fathoms under their keels, and no sign of rocks or shoals. Then Captain Jones ordered the northerly course to be resumed, but commanded the officer of the deck to maintain their present distance from land. "If you find we're making it closer than ten miles," said he, "you will steer to the eastward. Keep a sharp lookout for islands or icebergs, and give 'em all the offing they want."

Steaming cautiously along when the weather favored, and slowing down or stopping altogether in fogs or squalls, the ships advanced to the north. In clear weather the land was distinctly visible over the port side, but too far off for detailed observation. It seemed to be a series of cliffs and headlands, with now and then a stretch of comparatively level land of two or three miles. George thought he saw a house at the base of one of the hills, but a careful observation showed it to be a mass of rock curiously shaped like a human habitation. Fred was not to be outdone in discoveries, and excitedly announced that he had found a church overlooking a small village at the edge of one of the sloping plains. But the telescope brought him to grief as readily as it had disappointed George; the church and village were clusters of large rocks, evidently deposited by a glacier or swept down by a flood in ages gone by.

Every few miles the white face of a glacier was visible, and the origin of the icebergs that abounded in the waters was no longer a mystery.

All things have an end, and this voyage to the North-pole was not to be an exception to the rule. Three days after the grounding of the *Gambetta* there was unusual excitement on board the *Vivian*, and we may presume that the same was the case on the French ship.

The ship's position was announced as latitude 89° 30' north, longitude 111° west. The pole was only thirty miles away!

But this was not all. On their left the land seemed to terminate in a conical mountain eight or ten thousand feet high, and from the top of this mountain a column of smoke and steam floated away on the wind.

"Who would have thought there was a volcano at the pole?" said one of the youths, as he gazed upon the novel spectacle.

"Better, a good deal, than Symmes's Hole," remarked the Doctor, in reply. "Better for us, at any rate."

"Please tell us about Symmes's Hole," said George. "Who was Symmes, and what was his theory?"

"John Cleves Symmes was born in New Jersey about 1780," Dr. Tonner answered, "and died in Hamilton, Ohio, in 1829.

"He was a captain in the United States Army, who fought bravely and honorably through the war of 1812, and was afterwards engaged in supplying the troops on the upper Mississippi with provisions. For the last ten years of his life he devoted himself to the elaboration of his theories concerning the formation of the earth, and making them known to the public by lectures and pamphlets."

"Was he what they call a 'crank' in these modern times?" one of the youths inquired.

"It is not always easy to define the boundary between the scientific theorist and the crank," answered the Doctor, "and so I cannot answer your question by a simple 'yes' or 'no.'

"Captain Symmes believed that the earth was a hollow globe, open at the poles, the southern opening being somewhat larger than the northern one.   According to his theory the shell of the earth was about a thousand miles thick, and the northern opening two thousand miles in diameter. Take an orange four inches in diameter, with a very thick rind, cut holes at top and bottom, each of them one inch across, scoop out the interior till only the thick rind is left, and you have a fair idea of the shape of the earth according to Captain Symmes."

"But what did he have on the inside of his globe?" said Fred.

"The inside was composed of land and water, like the outside," was the reply.   " It was warmed and lighted by the sun shining in through the openings, first at one end of the earth and then at the other.   The waters flowed through these openings, just as the currents flow on the outside, and his theory was that only by such a formation of the earth could the equatorial, Gulf Stream, and polar currents be satisfactorily accounted for.   The inhabitants of the inside of the earth, if there were any, lived on a concavity, just as we live on a convexity, and they had land and water in about the same proportions as ourselves.

"Captain Symmes brought forward a formidable array of facts in support of his theory, and he had a great many followers.   His ideas were based on scientific reasoning, however incorrect may have been his deductions, and his pamphlets were read with interest at the time.   He delivered his lectures in various parts of the country, principally in the west; in the winter of 1826–27 he lectured before the faculty of Union College, and was listened to with profound respect by the well-known doctors, Knott and Wayland.   Ridicule was excited by the peculiarity of his theory, and 'Symmes's Hole' became a by-word; but there is no doubt that he was a man of intelligence, honor, and integrity.   He secured the attention of the scientific and scholarly men of his day, and was so confident of the correctness of his theory that he offered to command an expedition to verify it."

At times the clouds closed in upon the volcano and concealed it from sight, and at others only the sharp cone at the summit was visible.   Our young friends longed to go on shore and be the first to ascend this hitherto unknown mountain, but the suggestion was not favorably received. "We will visit the pole first of all," said Commander Bronson, "and then, if circumstances favor, we'll explore the land in the vicinity.   The opportunity to get to the pole does not come every day."

They left the smoking mountain behind them as they moved onward towards the north.   Before them the sea was stippled with fragments and patches of ice, but there was no indication of solid earth.   The *Gambetta* was abeam of the *Vivian*, and about half a mile distant; as the land began to recede, Captain Jones observed that the cloud of smoke from the French funnel was becoming more dense, and the ship was increasing her speed. Just as he did so the fog fell around them, and the *Gambetta* was hidden from sight.

"The Frenchman's trying to beat us to the pole," said the captain, as he sprang to the speaking-tube communicating with the engineer.

A VIEW THROUGH THE CLOUDS.

What he said to the engineer was not audible to those on deck, as they were too far from the bridge to hear distinctly, but its effect was to increase the speed of the *Vivian.* As soon as the steam could perform its work the screw was making its maximum number of revolutions every minute. The captain caught the first puff of a breeze on his cheek, and instantly gave the order for making sail. In five minutes the sails were filled, and away went the *Vivian* at the highest speed she had made since passing the icy barrier.

"We'll show him a trick or two," said the captain, displaying more excitement than was his custom. "We got that breeze just in time, and if we can lead him a couple of miles before the fog lifts he'll have hard work to make it up. A stern chase is a long chase."

The man at the wheel had plenty of occupation. The lookouts were continually announcing cakes of ice, and the captain had to think quickly in giving his orders. For two or three hundred yards around the ship there was comparatively clear vision, but beyond it they had to trust to good-fortune. The smaller cakes were not heeded, but the larger ones required to be treated with respect, for fear of serious consequences.

For more than an hour this excitement continued, and then the fog lifted. There was the *Gambetta*, with her engines working at their best, but she had neglected to make use of her sails; the result was she was fully a mile astern of the *Vivian*, and before she could follow the latter's example and spread her sails another half mile had been lost.

And the pole was less than ten miles away!

"Good-bye, sweetheart, good-bye!" said the captain, waving his hand in the direction of the *Gambetta*. "The American flag will be the first to float over the pole."

Land was announced on the port bow. The captain mounted to the crow's-nest, and soon descended with the report that there appeared to be an island in the direction indicated. As well as he could make out, it was a mass of conical peaks with a volcano in the centre; but considering that it didn't cover the pole, he was not concerned about it for the present.

To the surprise of every one, the disappearance of the fog was followed by the disappearance of the ice. Hardly a speck was visible in front of them, and there was no hinderance to their progress. As there was no chance that the *Gambetta* could pass them, the sails were taken in one by one, but they were only partially clewed up, lest their rival might steal a march on them by an unexpected slant of the wind. Occasionally the engines were slowed a little to enable the crew to take soundings, but as no bottom could be found with thirty fathoms of line, it was considered safe to go ahead again at full speed.

The elements combined in favor of our friends, as the clouds and fog rolled away and gave them a clear horizon all around. The horizon seemed farther off than usual, but whether this was the effect of imagination, or the peculiarity of the atmosphere, or because the earth is flattened at the poles, nobody could say. Whether the sun was stationary or not, as Captain Hall claimed it would be at the pole, they were then unable to determine, but with the activity that prevailed in the use of instruments, a speedy solution of the problem was likely. All the quadrants and sextants that the ship contained had been brought on deck, and were being applied to every use of which they were capable. Of course there were no stars to aid them while the sun was shining, but fortunately the moon was in the heavens, and proved of great assistance to the navigators in determining their position.

Whales and seals played about the ship in great numbers, and flocks of birds filled the air. The pole was far from being a scene of desolation, so far as animal life was concerned; the captain endeavored to be calm, but when the whales in their total absence of fear lazily rolled on the surface within fifty yards of the *Vivian*, he could not help thinking what havoc he would make if his mission had been for oil instead of science.

When the chronometer indicated twenty-two minutes past three o'clock in the afternoon (Greenwich time) of the ninth day of June, the *Vivian* described a circle in the Arctic Sea, and then stopped her engines. The captain announced that they were exactly over the North-pole.

The ship was dressed in bunting, the American flag being at the fore, and the tricolor holding the place of second honor. The sailors mounted the rigging and gave three hearty cheers, the guns fired a salute in honor of the achievement, and while it was in progress the flags were dipped three times, and then three times again. The *Gambetta* ranged along-side and joined in the demonstration, and when the noisy part of the ceremonial was over the crew were mustered on deck, and officers and men stood with uncovered heads while Commander Bronson read, with deep feeling expressed in his rich voice, the following

PRAYER AT THE NORTH-POLE.

Written for the use of Captain Hall's North Polar Expedition, by Rev. Dr. Newman, of Washington, to be used only on reaching the Pole.

Great God of the universe! our hearts are full of joy and gladness for all Thy marvellous goodness unto us. We have seen Thy wonders upon the deep, and amidst the everlasting hills of ice, and now we behold the glory of Thy power in this place so long secluded from the gaze of civilized man. Unto Thee, who stretchest out the north over the empty place, and hangest the earth upon nothing; who hath compassed the waters with bounds until day and night come to an end; we give Thee thanks for what our eyes now behold, and for what our hearts now feel.

Glory be to God on high, and on earth peace, good will towards men! We praise Thee; we bless Thee; we worship Thee; we glorify Thee; we give Thee thanks for Thy great glory, O Lord God, our heavenly King! God the Father Almighty! Praise Him all ye His works. Praise Him sun, moon, and stars of light. Praise Him ye heaven of heavens, and ye waters that be above the heavens. Praise the Lord from the earth, ye dragons and all deeps, fire and hail, snow and vapor, stormy winds fulfilling His word; praise Him frost and cold, snow and ice, day and night, summer and winter, seas and floods. Praise Him all ye rulers and peoples of the earth. Let every thing that hath breath praise the Lord. Glory be to the Father, and to the Son, and to the Holy Ghost, as it was in the beginning, is now, and ever shall be, world without end.

In Thy name, O Lord, we consecrate this portion of our globe to liberty, education, and religion, and may future generations reap the advantage of our discoveries. Bless the nation that sent us forth; bless the President of our great republic; bless all the people of our favored land, whose national banner we now wave over this distant country.

And now may the God of our fathers guide and direct our returning footsteps to those who wait to greet us with joy in the homes and land we love. May no evil befall us; no sin stain our souls; no error lead us astray from Thee and duty. Hear us for the sake of Him who hath taught us to pray: Our Father who art in Heaven, hallowed be Thy name; Thy kingdom come; Thy will be done on earth as it is in heaven; give us this day our daily bread; forgive us our trespasses as we forgive them who trespass against us; lead us not into temptation, but deliver us from evil; for Thine is the kingdom, the power, and the glory forever. Amen!

"NE PLUS ULTRA."

CHAPTER XVIII.

DISCOVERIES AT THE POLE.—LEAVING THE POLAR SEA.—ESCAPE THROUGH THE ICE-BARRIER.

FOR a description of the land discovered by the *Vivian* as she approached the pole, and of the scientific observations made by both ships during their stay in the open polar sea, we must ask the reader's indulgence. We are permitted to state, however, that nothing out of the usual order of things was found there. Disappointment awaits those who have supposed that the North-pole is nothing more than a flag-staff firmly set in the earth at the point where there is neither latitude nor longitude. One of the sailors of the *Vivian* was possessed with this idea, which he expressed in the hearing of Frank. The young gentleman good-naturedly endeavored to undeceive the illiterate mariner, and made the following explanation:

"The word 'pole,' as applied to this part of the earth, does not mean a staff or pole of wood. It is derived from the Greek πόλος (polos), which means a pivot or axis, and is supposed to be the pivot on which the earth turns around once in twenty-four hours."

"But I don't see any pivot at all," responded the sailor; "and if there's a shaft for the world to turn on, it seems to me there ought to be a gudgeon for it to turn in."

Fred abandoned the attempt to give instruction in physical geography to one who was so literal; he contented himself with the reflection that the sailor was not alone in believing that the axis of the earth is something more than imaginary.

Disappointment also awaits those who have imagined that the open polar sea is more like the tropics than the arctic regions. It is warmer there than farther south, as had been established by the observations of several explorers previous to the *Vivian's* voyage, but it is by no means like the Gulf of Mexico or the Sea of Arabia, as some writers would have us believe. The birds that fly to the north make their summer homes and their nests on the islands of the polar sea, but at the approach of winter they retreat to the southward, like the feathered inhabitants of Greenland and Labrador.

Birds are very abundant on all the islands of the polar sea, as navigators have long believed through observing the vast numbers that fly northward. There is no one to disturb them, and they can breed in perfect security, so far as the presence of man is concerned. The arctic foxes may trouble their nests occasionally, but

AN UNWELCOME VISITOR.

the number they can devour, in the egg or out of it, can make no perceptible impression on the size of the flocks. The fox goes long distances in search of food, and generally knows where it is to be obtained. It is probable that he exists through all the islands of the far North, and might tell the story of the pole if he could speak or write.

One day George made a suggestion, which was adopted by Commander Bronson, and also by Captain Girard as soon as he heard of it.

"Here are these birds all about us," said George, "and they'll go south at the end of their breeding season. Suppose we catch as many as we can, and mark their wings with the date of our reaching the pole, and the name of the ship; we can do this when there is nothing else to occupy our time; and, besides, it will not draw our attention from the scientific work, as the catching and marking can be done by the sailors. If we should be so unfortunate as not to escape from this polar sea, or be delayed here for a winter or two, perhaps one of these birds will be the means of telling how far we came to the north.

MARKING A CARRIER-PIGEON.

"They mark the wings of carrier-pigeons in the way I propose," he continued, "and it will be an easy matter to do so with these birds. Of course there is not one chance in a thousand, or even ten thousand, that one of them will fall into the hands of anybody who will find the mark, and know what it means; but that is a risk we must take."

Stamps similar to those used in post-offices were prepared from movable types, giving the names of the ships and the dates of their reaching the pole; after that time, whenever a bird not needed for food was taken, the mark was placed on his wing and he was liberated. Indelible ink was used for the stamping, so that the mark could not be washed out by the sea-water. The birds objected to the business, and frequently the sailors were scratched and bitten in a way that would have discouraged persons less hardy than they were after their winter in the ice. The men considered it capital sport, and while the exploring and surveying parties were busy on the islands, the sailors occupied themselves with the conversion of geese, ducks, mollemokes, auks, lumme, and other feathered denizens of the polar regions, into carrier-pigeons.

On one of the islands where they were looking for birds, the major and George found a vein of excellent coal coming out close to the water's edge. The discovery was reported to Commander Bronson and Captain Girard, and an examination of the specimens showed that the coal was identical with what the *Vivian's* bunkers had been filled when she left San Francisco.

Already there had been anxiety at the consumption of fuel, and this discovery was of great importance. The ships were taken into the little bay where the coal was found, mining operations were begun, and in a few days every available place on the *Vivian* and *Gambetta* was filled with fuel.

As the end of July approached it became necessary to consider the future. Should they pass a winter in the polar sea or make their way out at once, if possible?

The ships had remained nominally in company after the coaling was completed, though frequently out of sight of each other among the islands around the pole, or driven apart by the winds. It was understood that when separated they would endeavor to meet again at the spot where they last exchanged signals. It was further understood that if a ship was not at the rendezvous four days after the last exchange of signals, she would not be there for four days more; but unless she was there at the end of the second four days, she was detained by accident or stress of weather. The plan worked very well, and at each meeting notes of the surveys were exchanged, and much valuable information was obtained relative to the winds and currents, by means of simultaneous observations in different localities.

On the 26th of July they made a rendezvous in front of the volcanic island which was discovered when the ships first approached the pole. It was a collection of sharp conical peaks, of which the central one was an active volcano. Ordinarily there was little more than a thin cloud of smoke and steam pouring from its summit, but when the *Vivian* approached it on the 26th of July it was more active than usual.

A VOLCANIC ERUPTION.

"It looks as though we might witness a polar eruption," said Fred, as they regarded the volcano from the deck of the ship.

"Yes," replied George, "a pyrotechnic display in honor of our farewell."

As they drew near they found the violence increasing. Columns of smoke and steam rose high in air, and formed a dense cloud above them; ashes fell on the *Vivian's* deck, and with the aid of their glasses they could see stones ejected with great force, as though thrown from a cannon. A stream of lava poured down the side of the mountain, and reached the sea at the end of a narrow bay at its base. There were loud reports, resembling the crashing of whole batteries of artillery fired at once, and altogether the scene was like what may be witnessed at the eruption of a volcano in more accessible regions.

Both the youths desired to go on shore, and asked the permission of the commander to do so. But the request was refused, and strict orders were given that no boat should leave the ship except for communication with the *Gambetta*. There was nothing peculiar about this polar eruption, and it was not deemed prudent, under the circumstances, to risk an accident which might prove very serious.

The *Gambetta* met the *Vivian* at the time and place agreed; Captain Girard came on board the *Vivian* with two of his officers, and there was a conference of an hour or more on the subject of their future movements. It was agreed that no good was to be gained by spending a winter in the Arctic Sea sufficient to compensate for the attendant danger, and it was advisable to get out of it before the advent of the season of cold and darkness.

"There are two routes we can follow," said Commander Bronson: "we can try that by Spitzbergen, or the one through Smith's Sound.

"If we enter the ice-barrier, by following the meridian of Greenwich," he continued, "we shall come very nearly upon the track of Parry, where he found the ice drifting south almost as fast as he progressed to the north."

"*Très bien*," remarked Captain Girard.

"And by following the meridian of 60° west," Commander Bronson responded, "we shall strike the ice-belt in the line of the farthest northing of the Nares expedition of 1875–76. Then if we are fortunate in finding a passage through the barrier we shall enter Robeson Channel, and thence go through Kennedy Channel to Smith's Sound. Once there we have a well-known route before us through Baffin's Bay, Davis's Strait, and the Atlantic Ocean, to an anchorage in New York harbor."

"*C'est magnifique*," answered the French captain. "*Je propose les deux routes.*"

Commander Bronson thought well of the proposition, and it was arranged that the *Gambetta* should endeavor to find her way out of the polar sea by the route of Spitzbergen, while the *Vivian* would seek the passage through Smith's Sound. Each would carry despatches and letters for the other, and, in order to give time for their preparation, the ships were to meet four days later, at or near latitude 87° north, longitude 30° west. At that point they would separate, and each was to make the best of its way homeward.

For the next four days writing materials were in great demand on board the *Vivian*, and we may be sure the same was the case on the *Gambetta*. The letters and official despatches were carefully enclosed in a rubber bag, whose outside bore in conspicuous letters the address of the Navy Department, Washington. It was to be delivered to the American consul at the first port of Europe reached by the *Gambetta*, and forwarded thence to its destination.

The ships met as agreed, the letter-bags were exchanged, and then each steered away on its own course. Flags were dipped and guns fired, and the officers and men of both vessels cheered themselves into a condition of huskiness before the freshening breeze carried them out of each other's hearing. Would they ever meet again?

Just beyond the 86th parallel a large island compelled the *Vivian* to make a *détour* to the eastward, and when she turned again to the south she found the ice increasing in quantity. Careful observation showed that it was drifting to the south, and the gallant craft boldly entered the pack, and trusted herself to be carried where it chose to take her.

Steam was raised on the engines as soon as the *Vivian* entered the ice, and every advantage was taken of lanes of water, or breaks in the pack, to work the ship to the south. The pack was not a close one, and the skill of Captain Jones as an ice-pilot, combined with the efficiency and perseverance of his officers and crew, gave a good result. By the noon observation on the 5th of August they were in latitude 84° 35′ north, longitude 60° 10′ west. Seventy-five miles farther they would be at the highest point reached by the Nares expedition.

The ice now closed in, so that the engines were of little use, and the fires were put out. The usual precautions for escape in case of the loss of the ship were taken, and the deck was piled with provisions, clothing, and materials for a journey over the ice, in the same way as on the previous winter. For the present there was no great danger, as the ice was not as heavy as that which surrounded them to the north of Herald Island. But it was proper to be prepared for anything that might happen, and everybody was ordered to have his knapsack ready at his side whenever he lay down to sleep.

To describe the experience of our friends in the ice-pack would be telling over again the story of their drift to the northward, before their release in front of President Land. Their progress was slow, often not more than three or four miles a day, but sometimes it reached fifteen or twenty miles. On the 20th of August the coast of Grant Land was in full view, and on the 23d a sledge expedition was sent out in charge of Major Clapp, with instructions to visit the land and seek the traces of previous navigators.

According to the calculations they were close to Cape Sherman, and the little harbor where the *Alert* passed the winter.

The major was accompanied by Fred and two sailors, with a team of fifteen dogs and one of the drivers; these dogs were all that remained of the original forty. Some had died of disease, others had strayed from the ship at different times, and four had jumped overboard while the *Vivian* was cruising in the polar sea.

The major was instructed to observe carefully the bearings of the ship, and during his absence a large flag was kept constantly flying. He reached the land after about forty hours' travelling, and found that their calculations were correct. A cairn supposed to have been erected by the *Alert's* crew was discovered; but though it was carefully taken down, no record could be found. The major killed a musk-ox in good condition, and the whole party was regaled upon the flesh of the animal. Choice steaks were reserved, and brought back in sufficient quantity to supply the cabin table for a single dinner.

The expedition was absent three days and a half, and in the mean time the *Vivian* drifted about fifteen miles to the south. The season was so late that the chance of getting through Smith's Sound was very doubtful; already the weather was cold, and the young ice, wherever there were any open spaces, formed to a thickness of two inches in a few hours when the wind was not blowing.

On the 1st of September they were fairly within Robeson Channel. For a week the ice seemed to be very nearly stationary, and Commander Bronson determined to look for a good place for passing the winter, as it was pretty certain that Kennedy Channel would close before they could reach it.

Under the influence of a strong wind from the north, the pack broke sufficiently to allow the ship to be warped through several leads close up to the eastern shore. A favorable opportunity offered to get the *Vivian* into Polaris Bay, and it was promptly embraced; immediately afterwards the ice shut in solidly to the south, and it was decided to pass the winter where they were.

The *Vivian* was laid up about a mile from where the *Polaris* passed the winter of 1871–72, and there she remained until the following July. She was housed over in the same way as on the previous winter, and a high bank of snow was built around her. This bank of snow is a great protection against the cold, and makes a great economy of fuel during the long hibernation. The Hudson's Bay and other northern whalers invariably surround their ships with snow while lying up during the winter, and sometimes they give the embankment the appearance of a miniature fort.

Fred and George were greatly interested when they learned they were at the scene of Captain Hall's last winter in the far North. As soon as they could obtain permission they visited his grave, which they had no difficulty in finding through the description by Captain Tyson. They found

GRAVE OF CAPTAIN HALL.

that the board originally placed there had been blown down by the wind, and the inscription almost wholly obliterated. The brass tablet, which was placed at the foot of the grave by the Nares Expedition, was undisturbed. The tablet was prepared in England, and the inscription closes with the words, "Erected by the British Polar Expedition of 1875, who, following in his footsteps, have profited by his experience."

Another board was prepared, with a copy of the inscription taken from the old one, as follows:

TO THE MEMORY OF C. F. HALL,
LATE COMMANDER OF THE NORTH POLAR EXPEDITION,
DIED NOV. 8, 1871.
AGED 50 YEARS.

When this board was ready all the officers and sailors of the *Vivian* who could be spared from duty went in procession to the grave of the zealous explorer, and solemnly placed the memorial at the head of his last resting-place. All were silent while Commander Bronson pronounced a brief eulogy in honor of the man whose earnestness, perseverance, and endurance are familiar to all those who have studied the history of arctic explorations. Their memories went back to that sad occasion in the long darkness of the arctic winter when the crew of the *Polaris* buried the remains of their late commander. Here is the account in Captain Tyson's journal:

"*Nov.* 11.—At half-past eleven this morning we placed all that was mortal of our late commander in the frozen ground. Even at that hour of the day it was almost dark, so that I had to hold a lantern for Mr. Bryan to read the prayers. I believe all the ship's company was present, unless, perhaps, the steward and cook. It was a gloomy day, and well befitting the event. The place, also, is rugged and desolate in the extreme. Away off, as far as the dim light enables us to see, we are bound in by huge masses of slate rock, which stand like a barricade, guarding the barren land of the interior; between these rugged hills lies the snow-covered plain; behind us the frozen waters of Polaris Bay, the shore strewn with great ice-blocks. The little hut which they call an observatory bears aloft, upon a tall flag-staff, the only cheering object in sight; and that is sad enough to-day, for the stars and stripes droop at half-mast.

"As we went to the grave this morning, the coffin hauled on a sledge, over which was spread, instead of a pall, the American flag, we walked in procession. I walked on with my lantern a little in advance; then came the captain and officers, the engineer, Dr. Bessel, and Myers; and then the crew, hauling the body by a rope attached to the sledge, one of the men on the right holding another lantern. Nearly all are dressed in skins, and, were there other eyes to see us, we should look like anything but a funeral *cortége*. The Eskimos followed the crew. There is a weird sort of light in the air, partly boreal or electric, through which the stars shone brightly at 11 A.M., while on our way to the grave."

Lest we might weary our readers we will pass briefly over the *Vivian's* second winter in the ice. The ingenuity of everybody was taxed to the utmost to make the long night pass without the inroads of physical and mental disease among the officers and crew, and it is our pleasure to record that the effort was successful. Hunting parties were organized whenever

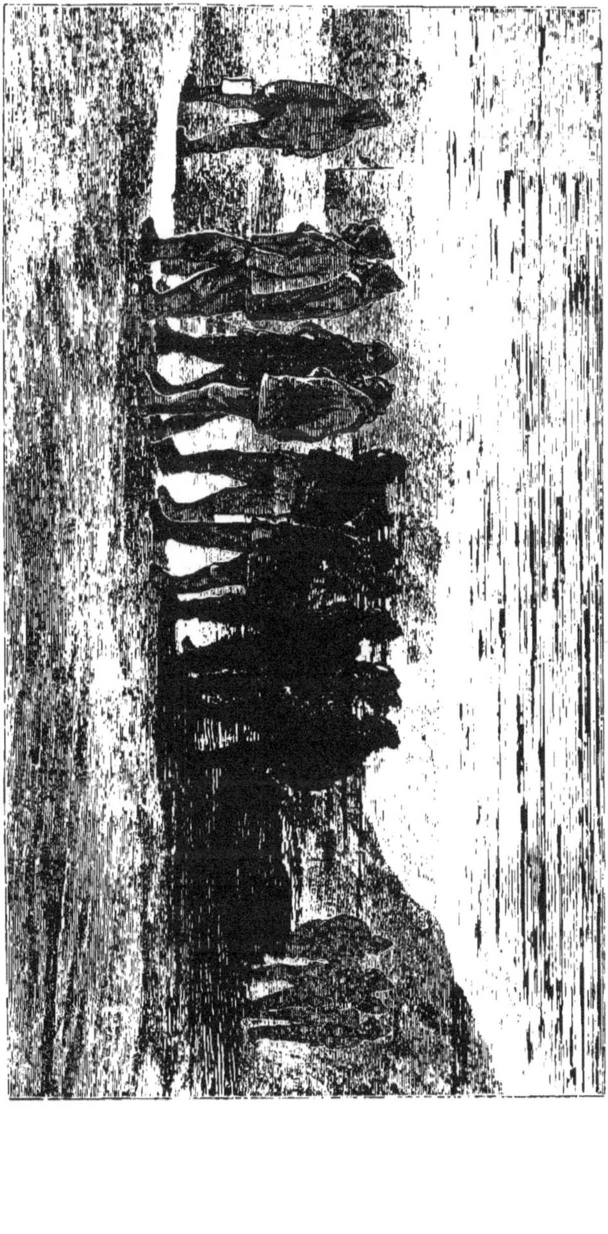

THE BURIAL OF CAPTAIN HALL.

circumstances favored; there were skating, leap-frog, base-ball, and other games in the open air; theatrical and other entertainments were given, as in the previous winter; classes were organized for instruction in various branches of education; lectures were delivered; and altogether, as the chronicles record, "the season passed off pleasantly." There was not a single case of serious illness in the entire crew, and nobody "sulked" or became despondent. What an improvement over the experiences of arctic wintering a hundred years ago!

The spring came and then the summer, or rather the spring ran so quickly into summer that it required a quick observer to note the period of transition. When the sun returned above the horizon, several expeditions were sent out to explore the interior of the country; but they added nothing of consequence to the data of previous navigators. A sharp lookout was kept for the first sign of open water, and after the middle of June no one was allowed to go far from the ship.

By the 1st of July there was open water both north and south of Polaris Bay, but the ship still remained in her winter position. The ice-drift had begun some time before, and the movement through Robeson Channel into Hall's Basin, and thence into Kennedy Channel, was continuous. On the 3d of July the ice in the bay broke in many places, and on the morning of the 4th the *Vivian* was free. The anniversary of American independence was henceforth to be doubly remembered by every individual of the ship's company!

The wind carried the ice out of the bay, and the *Vivian* followed it. Until the head of Kennedy Channel was reached, the water was comparatively clear; steam was ordered on the engines, and with its aid they made good progress and passed Cape Morton, at the end of Petermann Peninsula. Beyond this cape the channel was thickly blocked with ice, and the engines were powerless to force the vessel through it.

Captain Jones watched his opportunity and made fast to a floe, in a position similar to that taken by the *Vivian* when beset in the ice off Herald Island. Thus protected from danger of a "nip," the vessel drifted south with the ice through Kennedy Channel into Smith's Sound, the speed varying from one to one and three-quarter miles an hour. On the fourth day after leaving the winter position the *Vivian* was fairly in Smith's Sound, and the opening of the ice allowed her to make use of her engines once more.

She passed near Rensselaer Harbor, where Dr. Kane wintered with the *Advance* during 1853–55. Here she was caught again in the ice, and drifted through Smith's Channel past Port Foulke, a well-known name in arctic

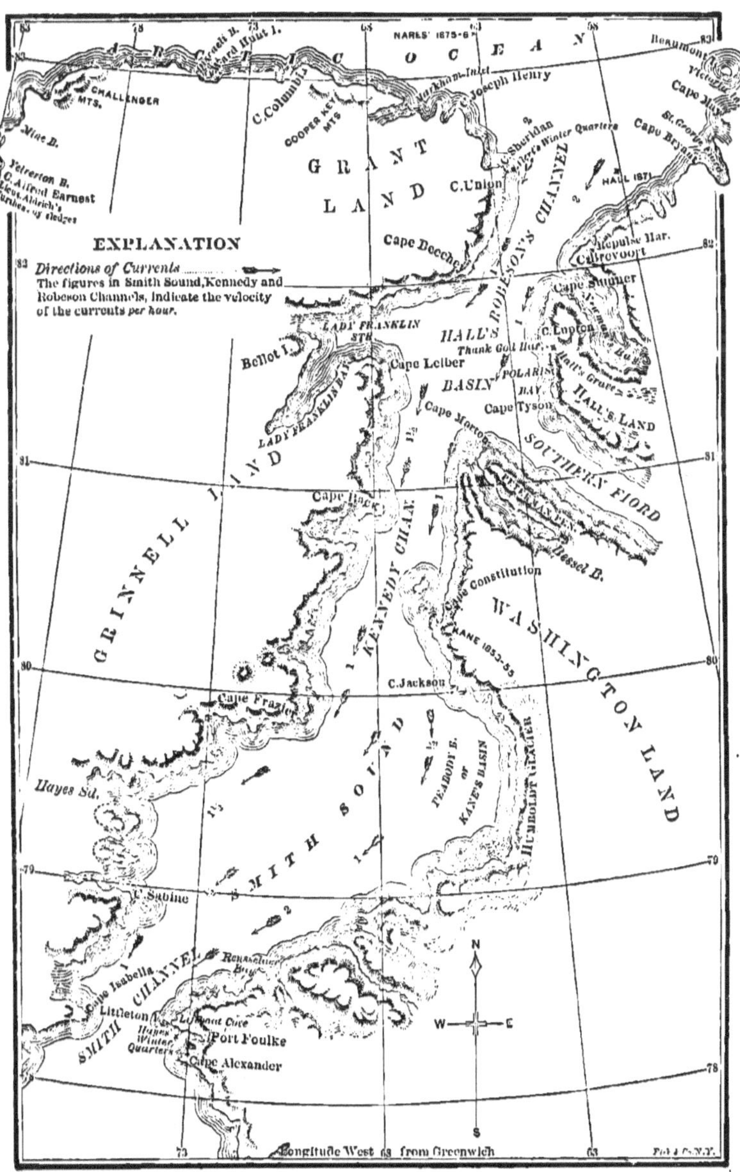

MAP OF SMITH SOUND, AND KENNEDY AND ROBESON CHANNELS.

chronology. It is the place where Dr. Hayes wintered in 1860–61, in the schooner *United States*. From that point he made a sledge journey over the ice, and reached latitude 81° 37' north. Dr. Hayes was a firm believer in the open polar sea, and down to the time of his death he entertained the hope of one day reaching the pole by way of Smith's Sound.

DR. I. I. HAYES.

Littleton Island is at the narrowest part of Smith's Sound, in latitude 78° 24' north. Of late years it has been a place of deposit of coal and stores for exploring expeditions, and it contains a post-office where ships may obtain information of each other. Commander Bronson desired to visit the island, and accordingly the *Vivian* steamed into a little nook not far from the scene of the loss of the *Polaris*, and nearly opposite Lifeboat Cove, where Dr. Kane found shelter. As the *Vivian* dropped her anchor, two skin-clad forms came out from among the rocks a quarter of a mile away and advanced to the water's edge. Soon as a boat could be lowered the commander and Major Clapp went on shore, and were eagerly welcomed by "the whole population."

The inhabitants included the two individuals already mentioned, the first strangers our friends had seen since leaving the coast of Siberia. They proved to be Innuits or Eskimos, and luckily one of them had worked on an American whale-ship, and could speak enough English to make himself understood. He and his companion had come over from the main-land two or three days before, and were preparing to leave when they saw the *Vivian*.

They guided our friends to a heap of coal, which had been left there the previous year by an American supply-ship, in accordance with the arrangements mentioned in the early part of this book. It was protected from the weather by a roof of flat stones, and on one side of the roof were painted the directions for finding the "Littleton Island Post-office." Appended to the directions were the words, "don't allow natives to accompany you."

Signal was made for another boat to come ashore, and in a few minutes it was dancing over the water and among the cakes of ice, bringing Dr. Tonner with Fred and George. The situation was quickly explained, and while the youths went with the natives to see the spot where the *Polaris* went ashore, the elders of the party sought the post-office.

It was a hole in the solid rock, about a foot square and two feet deep. To its mouth was fitted an iron door, fastened in its place with cement, and so solid was the construction that no tools possessed by the natives could make an impression on it. The surface of the door was studded with the heads of bolts; turning two of these one quarter round, according to the printed directions issued by the Navy Department to arctic exploring ships, and then sliding two others from the sides towards the centre, Commander Bronson unlocked the door of the safe where the letters were concealed.

The contents of the safe were taken on board ship for examination, and the door was relocked. The bolts were rusty, and the operation had required fully half an hour, which was well employed by the youths. Accompanying the natives, they had visited the spot where Captain Buddington, and those of the crew of the *Polaris* who were not left on the ice-floe with Captain Tyson, had passed the winter. The English-speaking native, who answered to the name of "Jack," said he was at the island when Captain Buddington and his party sailed away in the two boats they built from the timber of the *Polaris*.

He said the white men passed the winter on the island, living in a house they erected on shore, and fitting it up with bunks brought from the ship. In the spring the natives came there, and pitched their tents close by, so that "Polaris Camp" had for a time a lively appearance.

Before Captain Buddington left he gave the wreck of the steamer and everything on shore to the chief of the Eskimos, but shortly after the transfer the steamer broke loose from her moorings in a gale and drifted out to deep water, where she sank. The natives were obliged to content themselves with what was left on shore, but they mourned earnestly the loss of the ship and the abundant store of wood of which she was constructed.

POLARIS CAMP.

CHAPTER XIX.

THE SIGNAL SERVICE STATION.—FROM LITTLETON ISLAND TO UPERNAVIK.

EVIDENTLY the post-office on Littleton Island was not extensively patronized, as it contained only three letters and a newspaper, the latter more than a year old. The letters were for the use of any one who choose to read them; they recorded the visits of exploring ships, but there was no news of special interest to our friends. There was a memorandum concerning the signal service party under Lieutenant Greely, which is known to the readers of the newspapers as "The Greely Colony."

Commander Bronson read this paper carefully, and then explained as follows, partly in his own words and partly from the notes:

"Lieutenant Weyprecht, of the Austrian North-pole Expedition, recommended that a ring of observing stations should be placed around the pole, as near as was consistent with safety, for the purpose of making meteorological observations for the period of one year. His plan included the joint action of several nations, and at the three International Polar Conferences, held at Hamburg, in 1879, at Berne, in 1880, and at St. Petersburg, in 1881, the programme and details were settled. At the last meeting it was decided to delay the beginning of the enterprise from 1881, as first proposed, until 1882. Preparations had been made in the United States, however, for carrying out the original programme, and in the summer of 1881 two expeditions set out, one for the northernmost point of Alaska, under Lieutenant P. H. Ray, the other, under Lieutenant A. W. Greely, for Discovery Harbor, Lady Franklin Bay, 81° 50' north latitude, and 65° west longitude, 500 miles from the pole. The other ten stations selected were Fort Ray, north of Manitoba, by the British; Cumberland Island, north of Hudson's Bay, by the Germans; Goodhaab, Greenland, by the Danes; Jan Mayen Island, by Austria; Spitzbergen, by the Swedes; Bosskopp, near North Cape, by Norway; a point near the White Sea, by Finland; Nova Zembla, by the Russians, who had another station at the mouth of the Lena River in Siberia; and Dickson Haven, near the mouth of the Yenisei River, by the Dutch.

"The Dutch expedition failed to reach its destination, having been caught in the ice in the Kara Sea. Observations were made during the winter, however, and the party made their escape when their vessel sank, on the breaking up of the ice in the following summer.

"The most northerly of these stations was manned by officers and men of the United States Signal Service, under command of Lieutenant Greely, and they went there in the summer of 1881, a year in advance of the rest. The expedition was carried to its destination on the steamer *Proteus*, and it was agreed that a ship should be sent to its relief in the following year, or in the summer of 1883 at farthest."

"Then they have all been taken away by this time," one of the youths remarked.

"Not yet," was the answer. "Lieutenant Greely was to start south by the 1st of September, 1883, if no help reached him before that time, and it had been arranged that the relief steamer should land stores at Littleton Island on her way up. Thus, in case of the loss of the steamer, he would accomplish his retreat in boats or on sledges, and feel sure of finding stores at Littleton Island. But this memorandum says the relief steamer, the *Proteus*, the same that carried him north in 1881, did not stop here on her way north, and she was crushed in the ice before she could reach Lady Franklin Bay. Her crew returned to the south, and thus there was no communication with the men who had passed two winters in this very high latitude."

"And what became of them?"

"Hopes and fears are about equally balanced," was the commander's answer. "We may believe that Lieutenant Greely remained at Lady Franklin Bay for a third winter, and found sufficient food by killing musk-cattle, bears, seals, and walruses before winter set in; or we may think he started south, was relieved by the Eskimos of Cape York, and reached the Danish settlements of Northern Greenland. Then there is ground to fear that he and his men endeavored to carry out the programme laid down for them, but perished of hunger on reaching Littleton Island and finding that the promise of a deposit of provisions had not been carried out. Of course there has been a court of inquiry; everybody concerned is endeavoring to shift the responsibility on the shoulders of somebody else, and with a fair prospect of success."

"What a pity we did not know about it when we were on our way south!" one of the youths remarked.

"It is indeed," answered the commander, "as we might have searched the bay and perhaps found the members of the observing party; besides, we could have renewed our stock of fuel. There is said to be a fine seam of anthracite coal at Discovery Harbor; some say it is the finest in the world, and could furnish an inexhaustible supply for all the wants of navigation."

"A very small seam would supply all that will be wanted for navigation here," said Captain Jones, "and there is no chance that it can ever be carried to another market."

"Well, at any rate," responded the major, "Lieutenant Greely did not suffer for want of fuel."

"No, it was the existence of this vein of coal that caused the selection of Lady Franklin Bay as an observing station. You may be sure there have been plenty of denunciations of the selection since the mishap of 1883, and dozens of scientific men can demonstrate that it was unwise.

"Public attention has doubtless been roused by this time, and you may be sure there will be plenty of relief sent in the summer of 1884, perhaps when it is too late. Some of the ships used for whale or seal fishing will be bought or chartered, and sent here as soon as the season will permit."[*]

A record of the visit of the *Vivian* was prepared, and then the whole party returned to the island, carrying the letters and paper that had been taken from the strong-box in the rock. The most interesting reading to our friends, apart from the account of the signal service, was in a letter from San Francisco, printed in the newspaper which was found in the box. It gave a long account of the outfitting and departure of the *Vivian*, and her voyage across the Pacific Ocean. It said the latest news from her had just arrived by a whaling ship, which received a bag of letters from the *Vivian* in the vicinity of Herald Island. "According to what I can learn of the contents of the letters," said the writer of the communication, "the *Vivian* was about to enter the icy barrier in the hope of finding her way to the pole. Perhaps she will come out through Smith's Sound, or by way of Spitzbergen, and it is to be hoped the government will keep a sharp watch for her, as it did for the *Jeannette* in 1881."

"Perhaps we shall meet a relief expedition before we get far from here," said the commander, as he finished the printed letter. "Who knows but they will send to this very island to find us?"

"And we're ready to be found," said the major, "although we are not sadly in need of relief."

---

[*] The author earnestly hopes to be able to add a note, at the end of this volume, announcing the safety of the Greely party. Though not without misgivings, he believes they remained at Lady Franklin Bay during the winter of 1883–84, subsisting on the products of the country, as already indicated, and came south in the spring to meet a relief party at Littleton Island or Upernavik.

"If you see an opening in the ice, and a chance of getting away from here," said the commander to the captain, as they started for the shore again, "fire a gun and hoist the recall signal. We'll come back in a hurry, and you can trip the anchor as soon as you see us on our way.

ESKIMO IN WINTER DRESS.

"We might take some of this coal," he continued, as they reached the land, "but I don't think we'll need it as badly as some that may come after us. We've enough to get to Upernavik, unless we have a hard time in the ice on our way down."

They returned the letters and paper to the box, and with them the record of the *Vivian's* visit. Then they closed the box again, according to the directions, and restored the Littleton Island Post-office to its original condition. Of course they had been joined by their Eskimo friends as

SEPARATION OF THE "POLARIS" AND THE FLOE PARTY.

soon as they landed, but these fellows had been judiciously taken to one side, and kept there by Fred and the major while the box was being closed.

Then they looked around for traces of the visit of any of the Greely party, but found none. Evidently nobody had lived on the island since the crew of the *Polaris* wintered there, with the exception of the wandering Eskimos who had occasionally visited it for a very brief stay.

A gun from the steamer attracted their attention, and they hastened to obey the signal. When they reached her side she was ready to start, and before they had mounted to the deck the water was churned into foam by the screw.

"There's an opening in the ice around the point," said the captain, "and I want to make the most of it."

"Make it as fast as you like," answered the commander; "you can't go south too rapidly for us.

"It was not far from this point," said he, "that the *Polaris* separated from the floe party, as described by Captain Tyson in his narrative. The ship was drifting south with the ice, and was about opposite Littleton Island on the fifteenth day of October. A gale arose, the ship was nipped by the ice, and there was great fear that she would be crushed and sunk. Boats and provisions had been placed on the ice in anticipation of such an event, and while Captain Tyson and eighteen others were engaged in arranging things, so as to save as much as possible, the ship, to use his words, 'broke away in the darkness and was lost to sight in a moment!'

"It was in the night, and a fearful snow-storm was raging. Some of the men were left on small cakes of ice, but were gradually brought together by their shipmates, who made good use of the boats for this work. When all were assembled the boats were hauled on the ice, and everybody sought what shelter he could get till morning.

"It was in this way that the remarkable voyage of Tyson and his party on the ice-floe had its beginning. Fortunately there were several natives with Captain Tyson who understood how to catch seals, and it was on seal and bear meat that the shipwrecked mariners mainly lived until they were rescued. Let us hope that we may not have to repeat their experience by a journey on an ice-floe."

As the *Vivian* steamed away from her anchorage, she was followed a short distance by one of the natives whom they had left on shore. He was an object of great curiosity to our young friends, as they had not yet seen an Eskimo in a skin canoe.

The skin canoe, or *kyack*, of the Eskimo is very much like the *baidar* of the inhabitant of North-eastern Siberia, both in shape and the material of which it is constructed. It is made of seal-skin stretched over a frame, and is sharp at both ends; it curves almost in the form of a bow from stem to stern, and the occupant sits in a hole near the centre. The skin that forms the deck is drawn tightly around him, so that he suffers no injury if the water breaks over the boat.

The natives go fearlessly on the water in these apparently frail boats, and will often venture where the white man hesitates with his stronger construction of wood and iron. To propel this craft they have oars, or paddles, with blades at both ends; the blades are dipped alternately in the water, and the little *kyack* goes along at a wonderful rate.

AN ESKIMO AFLOAT.

"They perform curious feats with these *kyacks*," said the major, as the party were looking over the side of the ship and admiring the dexterity with which the native handled his little craft.

"They will turn somersaults in the water," he continued, "and keep it up a dozen times in succession."

Of course this assertion caused some surprise, and the major went on to explain:

SOMERSAULT IN A KYACK.

"It is proper to say that only a few can do it, and they never make the attempt unless a friend is present with his *kyack* to render any needed assistance.

"I once saw a Greenland Eskimo perform it. He turned over and over till we thought he did not intend to stop, and felt himself well paid for the feat with the present of a pocket-knife. One moment he was completely under water and the next above it, and he was so well secured in his place that only his hands and face were wet. The danger of the performance lies in the risk of his paddle breaking while he is under water, and also the chance that he may make a false stroke.

"Another trick they perform is for a native to run his *kyack* over another without injury to either. This he does by dashing forward at the greatest speed and passing the bow of his own boat over the centre of his friend's, just in front of where its owner sits. There is less liability to injury to either craft than to the occupant of the one that is overrun; a little miscalculation may send the point of the *kyack* through the man, who is so bound in his place that he cannot get out of the way."

The steamer turned the point of Littleton Island and put her prow in the direction of Baffin's Bay. The ice covered the water to the eastward, close up to the Greenland shore, but along the western side of the strait there was open water, and the *Vivian* went through the loose pack without much difficulty. It was ten or twelve hours before she was fairly out of the ice, and where she could get along without using her engines.

The fires were extinguished and the ship proceeded under sail, passing Ellesmere Land and North Devon without hinderance. Off the entrance of Lancaster Sound the ice became thick again and the fires were rekindled.

From Lancaster Sound the *Vivian* headed south-easterly across Baffin's Bay, and five days and four hours after she left Littleton Island she was within twenty miles of the coast of Greenland, in latitude 73° 35' north, longitude 56° 25' west.

"We are now," said the captain, "in the latitude of Tossac, and directly in front of it. It is the most northerly inhabited spot on the globe, not counting the dwellings of Eskimos at Cape York and other points. It consists of a single frame house with several huts and tents. The owner is a Dane, and has command of the northern district of Greenland; he rules over a vast territory, and his most numerous subjects are bears, seals, and other denizens of the regions of ice."

"How far off are his neighbors?" somebody asked.

"It is about fifty miles from Tossac to Upernavik" (U-*pern*-a-vik), was the reply. "The latter is the capital of a district of the same name; the district extends from latitude 70° to 74°, and includes some eight or ten settlements, each with a local governor and a few other inhabitants. In some of these settlements the governor is the only white inhabitant, and if he has any family his wife is pretty certain to be a native.

"Dr. Hayes describes the Governor of Karsuk," the captain continued, "as a native of Denmark, who was married to an Eskimo woman and lived in a hut rudely constructed of earth and stones; but it differed from

THE MOST NORTHERN HOUSE ON THE GLOBE.

the native huts around it in having a section of government stove-pipe sticking through the roof, and in being lined with pine boards obtained from the chief of the district at Upernavik. No other house was permitted to be as elegant as the governor's, and by comparison with the rest it might be called a palace.

"In the common houses the family and the dogs lived together, but the governor had a separate residence for his dogs a short distance from his own. His house had a window, while the others had none; and while the single room of his dwelling was sixteen feet by twenty, the others were only eight feet by twelve. The governor had no trouble to maintain his authority with the few natives under his control. They paid the taxes in oil and seal-skins with great promptness, and altogether conducted themselves like well-disposed subjects.

The government purchases all the whalebone, oil, narwhal-ivory, eider-down, and other products of the region that the natives have to sell, and pays for them in money, or in goods from the storehouses."

"And they do one thing which other governments might imitate to advantage," said the major; "they sell to the native anything he wants in the way of food, clothing, tea, coffee, or other goods, with the single exception of spirits. All traffic in spirits is forbidden, and thus the natives are not in such a condition of demoralization as those of the Siberian coast. It is a pity Russia will not follow the example of Denmark, and forbid the traffic in spirits in her Siberian ports and among the natives."

"The rule of Denmark in Greenland has been of the most paternal and conciliatory character," added Dr. Tonner. "Its object has been to make the natives useful subjects, instead of keeping them in a state of dependence; they are encouraged to be industrious and provident, and as they find their rulers set them a good example, they have nearly all embraced Christianity."

George wished to know something of the Greenland form of government.

"Greenland is a province of Denmark," was the reply, "and the capital is at Julianshaab, near the southern extremity of the peninsula. It has a population of about seven thousand, and is divided into twelve districts; the inhabitants live along the coast, as the interior is quite unfit for human beings to dwell in. The governor lives at Julianshaab and has general jurisdiction over the country, but his power is far from absolute. The six northern districts are united into one inspectorate, and the six southern districts into another. Each inspectorate is controlled by an 'inspector;' the governor at Julianshaab cannot overturn an inspector's decrees, though he may secure his removal. Each town or hunting-station can send a representative to the parliament which meets at Julianshaab;

the government is therefore one in which the people have a voice, and any matter, however trivial, may be brought up for the consideration of parliament.

"Dr. Hayes visited the parliament house while the distinguished body was in session. He says, 'The house is a one-story plain building, about sixteen by twenty feet, and built of pine boards. There is a single room inside which contains a long table flanked with rough benches, on which the parliamentarians sit. There are twelve members of parliament, and the thirteenth seat at the head of the table is occupied by the pastor of Julianshaab, who presides over the sessions. The members are dressed in seal-skin trousers and Guernsey frocks, and such a thing as a coat to

THE GOVERNOR'S RESIDENCE.

cover the broad suspenders which cross the back would seem to be un-known.'

"The government presents a cap to each member as a badge of office, and this cap must be worn while parliament is in session. It is made of scarlet cloth, with a broad gilt band around it; on the front of the cap are the royal emblems of Denmark, and above them the insignia of the colony of Greenland, in the shape of a polar bear standing on his hind-legs. The air of the legislative hall is redolent of fish, and nearly all the transactions relate in some way to fishing or hunting, generally the former.

"For example: while Dr. Hayes was present at the session a native came to present a petition. He had lost his *kyack* while fishing, and produced evidence that it was crushed by the ice. He had a family to support, and no means of living since he lost his boat. Parliament considered his case, and sent him to the government storehouse to work at eleven cents a day; his wife was allowed to draw a small allowance of food for

A GREENLAND PARLIAMENT IN SESSION.

herself and children from the storehouse every week, and the value of it was to be charged to the account of parliament.

"There were several cases in which men had lost their boats or fishing implements; where the accident was not caused by their own carelessness, and the sufferers were thrown out of employment by their losses, they were reimbursed by the parliament. The reason of this is that it is desirable to keep the people from idleness; and, furthermore, the public revenues are increased by the industry of the inhabitants. In some cases the money is not given, but loaned to the applicant for relief, and he is allowed to repay it in one or two years."

"But suppose," said Fred, "a man repudiates his debt, and doesn't pay at all, what will the government do about it?"

"If he does so from further misfortune," was the reply, "and the facts are shown, the time for payment is extended; but if his refusal to pay is based on idleness, or unwillingness to meet his debts, there is a very effective way of bringing him to terms."

JULIANSHAAB, CAPITAL OF GREENLAND.

"What is that?"

"The amount of the loan is deducted from what he brings to the government storehouse for sale; and if this plan fails, he is not allowed to buy anything there on any terms. The government has the only shops or stores in the country, and it is impossible to obtain tea, coffee, sugar, bread, guns, fishing implements, ammunition, or anything else, except at its warehouses. The obstinate man can't hold out long under these circumstances. Crimes are very rare in Greenland; small ones are punished by fines, and in capital cases the accused is sent to Copenhagen for trial.

"They have here an excellent system for encouraging industry. The government buys everything the native has to sell, and pays him in money or goods as he may prefer. There is a certain standard of prices for

SHIPS LOADING WITH KRYOLITE AT IVIKTUT, GREENLAND.

every article brought in by a native until he has reached a certain figure; above that figure there is a sliding-scale of higher prices as an inducement to industry.

"Perhaps you may not fully understand me. Well, suppose the standard price of seal-skins to be ten cents, and that each man is expected to catch a thousand seals every year; he gets ten cents for each skin, whether

he brings in a thousand or only a hundred. But for every skin between
one thousand and twelve hundred he receives twelve cents; between
twelve hundred and fourteen hundred, fifteen cents a skin; and between
fifteen hundred and two thousand he receives twenty cents a skin, or
double the first standard. These are not the exact figures, but are given
to illustrate the system."

George wished to know when this plan was adopted, and how long
Greenland had been under the control of Denmark.

"In the year 1781," said the Doctor, "the Royal Greenland Fishing
and Trading Company was formed on much the same plan as the Hudson
Bay and the East India companies. It received a charter giving it the
exclusive control of commerce in Greenland and the management of the
natives; fortunately the company was in the hands of men who thought
more of doing good among the savages than of making money. Its profits,
while fair, have not been large, and the prosperity of the people has been
carefully looked after. Spirits and other injurious things have been ex-
cluded, and no foreigner is allowed to trade with any Danish subject in
Greenland. The natives have all the civilization they need, and for more
than a century everything has gone on peaceably."

Here the conversation was interrupted by the announcement that they
would soon be in the harbor of Upernavik, unless prevented by accident.

ENTERING A HARBOR IN GREENLAND.

CHAPTER XX.

SIGHTS IN GREENLAND.—NEWS FROM HOME.—END OF THE VOYAGE.

AS they neared the shore Fred espied a boat of a different construction from the *kyack*, but evidently of native manufacture. It was coming out of a narrow passage near one of the islands, and the crew was evidently having a good time, to judge by the laughter that rung over the water.

Fred called the attention of his friends to the novel craft, and wondered what it was.

"That is an *oomiak*, or women's boat," said the captain. "If you permit an Irish bull, you may say it is manned by women."

"Do you mean that all the crew are women?" asked the youth; "there are six or eight at the oars, and one in the stern with the steering-oar."

AN OOMIAK.

"Those at the oars are certainly women," replied the captain, "and the other may be either a man or a woman. This is how it happens:

"The *kyack* that you saw at Littleton Island is a man's boat, and women are not allowed to use it. The open boat, such as you see, is only for women, and a man would consider himself disgraced by being one of its crew. He might sit in the stern and steer the boat, but it would be contrary to custom for him to handle an oar."

"Anyway it is a comfortable looking craft," replied the youth, "and the women seem to understand perfectly how to manage it."

"They are very expert in the management of the *oomiak*," was the response, "and are accustomed to it from infancy. The boat is apparently frail in construction, but it can sail well, and is of great use to the natives for purposes of transportation. A *kyack* is intended for hunting and fishing, and has no place for carrying anything more than its occupant, while an *oomiak* can hold a great deal of freight."

Further investigation led to a description of this style of boat.

The *oomiak* may be anywhere from fifteen to forty feet in length. It consists of a framework of poles securely lashed together with thongs of seal-skin, and held apart at the top by thwarts which serve as seats. The bottom is flat, and has a rude floor, but a stranger must step very carefully to keep his feet from going through the bottom.

When the framework is ready it is covered with seal-skins, and as no single skin can be large enough for a boat, there must be a number of skins sewn together. The women perform this work with sinews, and they do it so well that not a drop of water can leak through. The frame is turned bottom upward and the covering is spread over it, and fastened to the rail with strong thongs. When the covering is put on it is moist; it shrivels as it dries in the sun, and becomes hard as leather, but it is so full of oil that it has a very slippery feeling. It is impervious to water, and will last a long time unless brought against hard substances. When it dries it becomes translucent, and when you are a passenger in an *oomiak* you can see how deep you are in the water without looking over the side.

The next day Fred had an opportunity to inspect an *oomiak* which was drawn up on the beach at Upernavik, and also to have a near view of its crew. It is safe to say he was fully as much interested in the latter as in the former.

The crew consisted of seven young women, six of them "before the mast," while the seventh was the commander. Their costume was the funniest that the youth had ever seen worn by a boat's crew, and he was quite sure it would make a sensation among the young ladies of his acquaintance who are fond of rowing.

The dress was of furs and skins. Beginning at the feet, there were long boots of seal-skin reaching to the knee, where they met pantaloons of the same material; the boots were of various colors, and some of them quite tastefully painted, and the trousers had bright stripes on the side or

in front, formed by sewing in pieces of leather of bright hues.   Above
the trousers was a jacket, with a bright stripe just below the waist, and
terminating at the throat in white fur or some other ornamental material.
The hair was gathered in a knot at the top of the head, and altogether the
costume of these Greenland boat-women was by no means unhandsome.

THE OOMIAK AND ITS CREW.

Fred asked what were the uses to which this boat was applied.   He
was told that it carried the governor wherever he wished to go in the
neighborhood; and when the men went out hunting or fishing in their
kyacks, the women frequently followed in the *oomiak* to bring home the
game or fish that might be obtained.   "They go long distances," said his
informant, "and the women do not hesitate to go out in any kind of
weather."   Ordinarily the boat is rowed by its crew, but it has a mast,
and when the wind is fair a sail is spread and the breeze utilized.   If the
owner can afford to buy canvas for his sail, it is made out of that material;
but if he cannot endure the expense, the sail is made of seal-skins.

There are two anchorages at Upernavik, one being an open roadstead,
where ships have no shelter from southerly or westerly winds, while the
other is a landlocked harbor.   The former is directly in front of the settlement, and is used by ships that intend to remain only a few hours; the
latter is behind the town, and beyond a rocky ridge, but, though giving
perfect shelter to ships, it is not very easy to enter.   Captain Jones decided to anchor in the outer harbor until they could communicate with
the governor, and determine whether they would proceed at once or remain a few days.

Major Clapp and Dr. Tonner went on shore as soon as the *Vivian* had anchored, and made a call upon the inspector. The latter said he was expecting ships from the South, but none had arrived, with the exception of two or three Scotch whalers who had gone forward to look for whales in Melville Bay. The yearly ship from Copenhagen would be due in a few days—in fact, she might arrive at any moment—and meantime the strangers were welcome to anything in his power to give them.

He was greatly surprised on learning the route by which the *Vivian* had arrived at Upernavik, and heartily congratulated our friends on their success in reaching the pole. He said that a supply of provisions and five hundred tons of coal had been left there the previous year by an American war-ship, for the use of any exploring expedition that might need it, and especially any ship from the United States.

UPERNAVIK.

The major and Doctor returned to the *Vivian* with the information they had obtained. Commander Bronson said he thought no one could have a better right to the coal than themselves; he had expected to find coal at Upernavik and was not disappointed. The engineer reported that they had less than seven tons remaining, and therefore a new supply would be very acceptable.

The *Vivian* immediately proceeded to the inner harbor, and in a little while was safely anchored where no ordinary wind could disturb her. While she was being taken from the outer to the inner anchorage, Commander Bronson went on shore with the major to pay a visit to the inspector, and arrange for such assistance as they could have for taking in coal. Fred and George occupied their time in an inspection of Upernavik, and as the place was small it did not take long.

The inspector's house was, as might be expected, the most elaborate building; but even that was not large. There were about twenty other houses, all occupied by Eskimos, and altogether the town had less than a hundred inhabitants. There were a good many dogs wandering about; some of them were inclined to familiarity not of a friendly nature, but by vigorous flourishing of sticks and flinging an occasional stone they kept the brutes from doing harm. The houses were anything but cleanly in appearance, and neither of the youths had any desire for a permanent residence in Upernavik.

Back of the settlement, and on the slope of the ridge separating it from the inner harbor, is the cemetery. There are crosses and stones to indicate the position of the graves, and little enclosures (or mounds) of stone. Very little vegetation can be seen at Upernavik, and the ground is so hard that there is rarely any attempt to dig deeply to form a grave. Bodies are placed on the surface and covered with stones: unless the work is thoroughly done, the remains become exposed in course of time. The youths found one of the coffins nearly uncovered, and through its broken lid the occupant could be plainly discerned.

The inspector returned the visit of the officers of the *Vivian*, and remained to dine with them. Most of the men of Upernavik were away in pursuit of seal or walrus, and the inspector said he would not be able to give any assistance in loading the coal beyond showing the best way of getting around the harbor. There were two whale-boats in the harbor, which he kindly loaned to the captain; the latter said that by using these boats he could easily load in two or three days all the coal he needed for getting to New York.

A hundred tons of coal were taken on board by using the whale-boats as barges, and towing them back and forth between ship and shore. While the coaling was in progress the inspector asked Commander Bronson and his officers to take tea with him; the invitation included Fred and George, and was gladly accepted by all concerned.

The house was comfortable, though not large, and our friends passed a delightful hour in the society of the host and his family. They had tea and coffee, and a variety of little cakes and good things prepared by the lady of the house, together with some canned fruits which came from Europe or America. They were particularly struck with the flowers which were kept growing in the windows of the house, and learned that every inhabitant of Greenland who can afford it keeps an abundance of living plants in his dwelling. Dr. Tonner said he had observed the same thing in Siberia, where the homes of people in comfortable circumstances often resemble conservatories.

THE INSPECTOR AND HIS FAMILY.

When the coal was all on board, and farewell visits had been made to the governor's house, the order for departure was given. Just as the anchor left the bottom, and the ship was beginning to move, a native came paddling his *kyack* into the harbor in great haste, and yelling at the top of his voice.

It was not easy to make out his meaning, but a streak of smoke on the sky served as an interpreter. A steamer was coming!

The engines were stopped, and the anchor dropped once more to the bottom. The cloud of smoke increased, and in a little while a steamer flying the American flag came in sight in front of Upernavik and cast anchor in the outer harbor. The crew of the *Vivian* cheered lustily as they caught sight of their national banner, and there were tears of joy in the eyes of our young friends. Our country's flag is a most welcome sight when we are far from home and in a foreign land. Especially dear must it have seemed to those arctic explorers after their sojourn of two long winters in the regions around the pole!

THE NEW ARRIVAL.

It was a ship of the United States Navy, and as soon as the anchor was dropped she sent an officer on board the *Vivian*, with a letter-bag addressed to Commander Bronson. And what recent dates! Twenty-two days from New York! It seemed to carry them home in an instant, and for a while some of the party forgot that they were yet in the far North and within the Arctic Circle.

There were letters for everybody—for Fred and George, as well as for the elders of the party, and also for the junior officers and the crew. For an hour or more there was silence on board the ship as the seals were broken and the contents of the missives eagerly devoured.

The majority of the letters were private, and therefore we will not examine them. Fred wondered how it had been found out that they were coming that way, and why a ship had been sent to meet them at Upernavik. A slip cut from a newspaper and enclosed in one of his letters told the story. It read as follows:

"It will be remembered that in October of last year a wild-goose was killed on Lake St. Charles, near Quebec, which had the words "*Vivian*, North-pole, June 9, 18—," stamped on the feathers of one wing. As the *Vivian* was known to have gone in search of the pole, the stamp is supposed to indicate the accomplishment of her object. It was thought she would return by way of Smith's Sound, if possible, and the Government will send a steamer in the hope of meeting her at one of the Greenland ports early in July. Letters intended for this ship should be sent in care of the commandant at the Brooklyn Navy Yard not later than June 10th. The steamer will proceed north as far as may be consistent with safety, and if no news is obtained of the explorers, it will return to New York during the month of September."

So it was one of the carrier-pigeons, improvised according to George's suggestion, that gave the news of the *Vivian* and her successful voyage to the North-pole!

Both ships remained at Upernavik long enough for the *Vivian* to receive a plentiful supply of all the provisions she needed for her voyage to New York. They sailed together, but were separated in a gale just after passing Cape Farewell, at the southern extremity of Greenland, and did not meet again until they were off Fire Island, about forty miles from Sandy Hook. Almost side by side they crossed the bar and entered the capacious harbor at the mouth of the Hudson River, made a brief halt at Quarantine, and then continued on their course till they dropped anchor between the Battery and Bedloe's Island. The *Vivian* thus completed the voyage from the Golden Gate to Manhattan Island by way of the northwest passage and the polar sea.

Four days after her arrival a telegram from Granton, Scotland, announced that the *Gambetta* had reached Reykjavik, in Iceland, and after taking coal and stores would proceed to Havre. The youths could not understand why the telegram should be dated at Granton until the major informed them that there was a line of steamers between that port and Reykjavik. "We shall probably receive letters from our French friends," said he, "as soon as the mail can bring them, and also the letter-bag we intrusted to the *Gambetta*. They would be very sure not to miss the steamer to Granton."

Sure enough, the Liverpool steamer, a fortnight later, brought the *Vivian's* letter-bag for the Navy Department, and also a packet of letters in care of the postmaster of New York. The packet was to be delivered

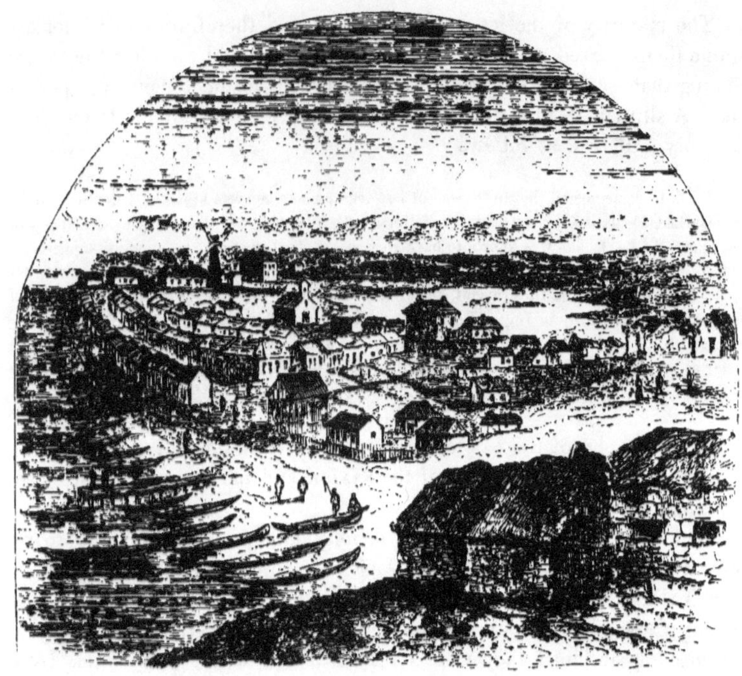

REYKJAVIK, ICELAND.

to Commander Bronson, or any officer of the *Vivian*, or held to await the arrival of that vessel. Among the letters was one for George from the young officer who assisted him in the preparation of "Parry and Paris." With George's permission we translate the material part of his friend's missive:

* * * * * * * *

"After separating from the *Vivian* we steered south-east, and reached the meridian of Greenwich about latitude 85°. There we encountered much ice, and hesitated two or three days before entering the pack, which contained so many bergs as to be very dangerous. At last we found an opening in the pack, and worked our way slowly through the lanes and among the floes to latitude 84°. There the pack closed in upon us, and we had a narrow escape from being crushed between two enormous floes. With a great deal of difficulty we sawed and blasted away the ice sufficiently to reduce the pressure, and bring the vessel to an even keel.

"We found that the ice was drifting southward, the same as in Captain Parry's sledge journey, and for some time we had hopes that it would enable us to get out before the close of the season. But our progress was so slow that the end of August found us in latitude 81° 20′ north, longitude 20° east, and it became necessary to look for winter-quarters. On the 1st of September the ice opened sufficiently to enable us to enter a small bay in the most westerly of the 'Seven Islands,' and as soon as we were inside it closed again. We had hoped to reach Hecla Cove, where Parry's ship remained during his attempt to reach the pole, but this was impossible, owing to the drift of the ice.

"We passed the winter in much the same way as the previous one, but missed greatly the company of our good friends the Americans. We were in less danger from the ice than before, on account of the shelter which our bay afforded, and we were able to make hunting excursions on the ice. We found that the Dutch navigators had been there before us, and on the rocky shores there were the skeletons of unfortunate sailors who had died there. The solid ground makes it impossible to dig a grave, and the only mode of sepulture is to place the coffin on the ground and cover it with a few stones. Sometimes even this was not done, and in course of time the skeletons became fleshless through the action of the winds and the intense cold.

"In the spring we had some hunting experiences, and made sledge journeys over the ice to the northern extremity of Spitzbergen, but discovered nothing of importance. We were all glad when the breaking up of the ice released us, and the drift carried us to the westward. We escaped from the ice-fields without serious injury, and then sailed past the island of Jan Mayen to Iceland. We tried to land on Jan Mayen, but were prevented by the fog, which made it extremely dangerous to seek a harbor. From Jan Mayen we sailed to Reykjavik, and here we are once more in communication with the civilized world. We hoped to learn something about the *Vivian* on our arrival here, but are disappointed; we shall look for letters from you when we reach Havre, and feel confident that you will not be far behind us in reaching home."

*   *   *   *   *   *   *   *

Letters had been sent to Havre, bearing the congratulations of the *Vivian's* party to all on board the *Gambetta*, immediately on the publication of the despatch from Granton; consequently each expedition learned of the safety of the other. And so ends the story of

THE "VIVIAN'S" VOYAGE.

INTERESTING BOOKS FOR YOUNG PEOPLE.

THOMAS W. KNOX'S WORKS. 8vo, Cloth. Copiously Illustrated.

    THE BOY TRAVELLERS IN THE FAR EAST. Five Parts. $3 00 each.

        PART I. ADVENTURES OF TWO YOUTHS IN A JOURNEY TO JAPAN AND CHINA.

        PART II. SIAM AND JAVA. With Descriptions of Cochin-China, Cambodia, Sumatra, and the Malay Archipelago.

        PART III. CEYLON AND INDIA. With Descriptions of Borneo, the Philippine Islands, and Burmah.

        PART IV. EGYPT AND PALESTINE.

        PART V. CENTRAL AFRICA.

    THE VOYAGE OF THE "VIVIAN" TO THE NORTH POLE AND BEYOND. Adventures of Two Youths in the Open Polar Sea. (*In Press.*)

    HUNTING ADVENTURES ON LAND AND SEA. Two Parts. $2 50 each.

        PART I. THE YOUNG NIMRODS IN NORTH AMERICA.

        PART II. THE YOUNG NIMRODS AROUND THE WORLD.

CHARLES CARLETON COFFIN'S WORKS. Four Volumes. Copiously Illustrated. 8vo, Cloth, $3 00 each.

    THE STORY OF LIBERTY.   THE BOYS OF '76.
    OLD TIMES IN THE COLONIES.   BUILDING THE NATION.

INDIAN HISTORY FOR YOUNG FOLKS. By FRANCIS S. DRAKE. Copiously Illustrated. 8vo, Cloth. (*In Press.*)

THE HISTORY OF A MOUNTAIN. By ÉLISÉE RECLUS. Illustrated by L. Bennett. 12mo, Cloth, $1 25.

THE CATSKILL FAIRIES. By VIRGINIA W. JOHNSON. Illustrated by ALFRED FREDERICKS. Square 8vo, Illuminated Cloth, $3 00.

WHAT MR. DARWIN SAW IN HIS VOYAGE ROUND THE WORLD IN THE SHIP "BEAGLE." Illustrated. 8vo, Cloth, $3 00.

COUNTRY COUSINS. Short Studies in the Natural History of the United States. By ERNEST INGERSOLL. Illustrated. 8vo, Cloth. (*In Press.*)

FRIENDS WORTH KNOWING. Glimpses of American Natural History. By ERNEST INGERSOLL. Illustrated. 16mo, Cloth, $1 00.

THE ICE QUEEN. By ERNEST INGERSOLL. Ill'd. 16mo, Cloth, $1 00.

WHO WAS PAUL GRAYSON? By JOHN HABBERTON, Author of "Helen's Babies." Illustrated. 16mo, Cloth, $1 00.

THE FOUR MACNICOLS. By WM. BLACK. Ill'd. 16mo, Cloth, $1 00.

MILDRED'S BARGAIN, AND OTHER STORIES. By LUCY C. LILLIE. Illustrated. 16mo, Cloth, $1 00.

NAN. By LUCY C. LILLIE. Illustrated. 16mo, Cloth, $1 00.

NEW GAMES FOR PARLOR AND LAWN. By G. B. BARTLETT. 16mo, Cloth, $1 00.

JAMES OTIS'S STORIES. Illustrated. 16mo, Cloth, $1 00 each.
  TOBY TYLER; OR, TEN WEEKS WITH A CIRCUS.
  MR. STUBBS'S BROTHER. A Sequel to "Toby Tyler."
  TIM AND TIP; OR, THE ADVENTURES OF A BOY AND A DOG.
  RAISING THE "PEARL."

CAMP LIFE IN THE WOODS; and the Tricks of Trapping and Trap
  Making. By W. Hamilton Gibson. Illustrated by the Author. 16mo,
  Cloth, $1 00.

THE TALKING LEAVES. An Indian Story. By W. O. Stoddard. Illustrated. 16mo, Cloth, $1 00.

DIDDIE, DUMPS, AND TOT; OR, PLANTATION CHILD-LIFE. By
  Louise-Clarke Pyrnelle. Illustrated. 16mo, Cloth, $1 00.

W. L. ALDEN'S STORIES. Illustrated. 16mo, Cloth, $1 00 each.
  THE MORAL PIRATES.
  THE CRUISE OF THE "GHOST."
  THE CRUISE OF THE CANOE CLUB.

HOW TO GET STRONG, AND HOW TO STAY SO. By William
  Blaikie. With Illustrations. 16mo, Cloth, $1 00.

SOUND BODIES FOR OUR BOYS AND GIRLS. By William
  Blaikie. Illustrated. 16mo, Cloth, 40 cents.

THE HISTORY OF THE UNITED STATES NAVY, FOR BOYS. By
  Benson J. Lossing, LL.D. Illustrated. 12mo, Cloth, $1 75.

FRENCH HISTORY FOR ENGLISH CHILDREN. By Sarah Brook.
  Edited by George Cary Eggleston. Illustrated. 12mo, Cloth, $1 00.

THE ADVENTURES OF A YOUNG NATURALIST. By Lucien Biart.
  With 117 Illustrations. 12mo, Cloth, $1 75.

AN INVOLUNTARY VOYAGE. By Lucien Biart. Illustrated. 12mo,
  Cloth, $1 25.

HENRY MAYHEW'S WORKS. Illustrated. 16mo, Cloth, $1 25 each.
    THE BOYHOOD OF MARTIN LUTHER; or, The Sufferings of the Little
  Beggar-Boy who afterwards became the Great German Reformer.
    THE STORY OF THE PEASANT-BOY PHILOSOPHER. (Founded on the
  Early Life of Ferguson, the Shepherd-Boy Astronomer.)
    YOUNG BENJAMIN FRANKLIN. A Story to Show how he Learned the
  Principles which Raised him to be the First American Ambassador.
    THE WONDERS OF SCIENCE; or, Young Humphry Davy (the Cornish
  Apothecary's Boy who became President of the Royal Society).

SCIENCE FOR THE YOUNG. By Jacob Abbott. Illustrated. 4 vols.:
  Heat.—Light.— Water and Land.—Force. 12mo, Cloth, $1 50 each.

ROUND THE WORLD; including a Residence in Victoria, and a Journey by Rail across North America. By a Boy. Edited by SAMUEL SMILES. Illustrated. 12mo, Cloth, $1 50.

THE SELF-HELP SERIES. By SAMUEL SMILES.

SELF-HELP. 12mo, Cloth, $1 00.—CHARACTER. 12mo, Cloth, $1 00.—THRIFT. 12mo, Cloth, $1 00.—DUTY. 12mo, Cloth, $1 00.

THE BOYHOOD OF GREAT MEN. By JOHN G. EDGAR. Illustrated. 16mo, Cloth, $1 00.

THE FOOTPRINTS OF FAMOUS MEN. By JOHN G. EDGAR. Illustrated. 16mo, Cloth, $1 00.

HISTORY FOR BOYS; or, Annals of the Nations of Modern Europe. By JOHN G. EDGAR. Illustrated. 16mo, Cloth, $1 00.

SEA-KINGS AND NAVAL HEROES. A Book for Boys. By JOHN G. EDGAR. Illustrated. 16mo, Cloth, $1 00.

THE WARS OF THE ROSES. By JOHN G. EDGAR. Illustrated. 16mo, Cloth, $1 00.

POLITICS FOR YOUNG AMERICANS. By CHARLES NORDHOFF. 12mo, Half Leather, 75 cents.

GOD AND THE FUTURE LIFE. The Reasonableness of Christianity. By CHARLES NORDHOFF. 16mo, Cloth, $1 00.

THE THOUSAND AND ONE NIGHTS; or, The Arabian Nights' Entertainments. Translated and Arranged for Family Reading, with Explanatory Notes, by E. W. LANE. 600 Illustrations by Harvey. 2 vols., 12mo, Cloth, $3 50.

STORIES OF THE GORILLA COUNTRY. By PAUL B. DU CHAILLU. Illustrated. 12mo, Cloth, $1 50.

THE COUNTRY OF THE DWARFS. By PAUL B. DU CHAILLU. Illustrated. 12mo, Cloth, $1 50.

WILD LIFE UNDER THE EQUATOR. By PAUL B. DU CHAILLU. Illustrated. 12mo, Cloth, $1 50.

MY APINGI KINGDOM: with Life in the Great Sahara, and Sketches of the Chase of the Ostrich, Hyena, &c. By PAUL B. DU CHAILLU. Illustrated. 12mo, Cloth, $1 50.

LOST IN THE JUNGLE. By PAUL B. DU CHAILLU. Illustrated. 12mo, Cloth, $1 50.

OUR CHILDREN'S SONGS. Illustrated. 8vo, Ornamental Cover, $1 00.

THE HISTORY OF SANDFORD AND MERTON. By THOMAS DAY. 18mo, Half Bound, 75 cents.

YOUTH'S HEALTH-BOOK. 32mo, Paper, 25 cents; Cloth, 40 cents.

STORIES OF THE OLD DOMINION. From the Settlement to the End of the Revolution. By JOHN ESTEN COOKE. Illustrated. 12mo, Cloth, $1 50.

THE HISTORY OF A MOUTHFUL OF BREAD, and its Effect on the Organization of Men and Animals. By JEAN MACÉ. Translated from the Eighth French Edition by Mrs. ALFRED GATTY. 12mo, Cloth, $1 75.

THE SERVANTS OF THE STOMACH. By JEAN MACÉ. Reprinted from the London Edition, Revised and Corrected. 12mo, Cloth, $1 75.

FRED MARKHAM IN RUSSIA; or, The Boy Travellers in the Land of the Czar. By W. H. G. KINGSTON. Illustrated. Small 4to, Cloth, 75 cts.

SELF-MADE MEN. By CHARLES C. B. SEYMOUR. Many Portraits. 12mo, Cloth, $1 75.

THE LIFE AND SURPRISING ADVENTURES OF ROBINSON CRU-SOE, of York, Mariner; with a Biographical Account of DEFOE. Illustrated by Adams. Complete Edition. 12mo, Cloth, $1 00.

THE SWISS FAMILY ROBINSON; or, Adventures of a Father and Mother and Four Sons on a Desert Island. Illustrated. 2 vols., 18mo, Cloth, $1 50.

THE SWISS FAMILY ROBINSON — Continued: being a Sequel to the Foregoing. 2 vols., 18mo, Cloth, $1 50.

DOGS AND THEIR DOINGS. By Rev. F. O. MORRIS, B.A. Illustrated. Square 8vo, Cloth, Gilt Sides, $1 75.

TALES FROM THE ODYSSEY FOR BOYS AND GIRLS. By C. M. B. 32mo, Paper, 25 cents; Cloth, 40 cents.

THE ADVENTURES OF REUBEN DAVIDGER; Seventeen Years and Four Months Captive among the Dyaks of Borneo. By J. GREENWOOD. 8vo, Cloth, Illustrated, $1 25; 4to, Paper, 15 cents.

WILD SPORTS OF THE WORLD. A Book of Natural History and Adventure. By J. GREENWOOD. Illustrated. Crown, 8vo, Cloth, $2 50.

CAST UP BY THE SEA; or, The Adventures of Ned Grey. By Sir SAMUEL W. BAKER, M.A., F.R.S., F.R.G.S. 12mo, Cloth, Illustrated, $1 25; 4to, Paper, 15 cents.

HOMES WITHOUT HANDS: Being a Description of the Habitations of Animals, classed according to their Principle of Construction. By the Rev. J. G. WOOD, M.A., F.L.S. With about 140 Illustrations engraved on Wood by G. Pearson, from Original Designs made by F. W. Keyl and E. A. Smith, under the Author's Superintendence. 8vo, Cloth, $4 50; Sheep, $5 00; Roan, $5 00; Half Calf, $6 75.

THE ILLUSTRATED NATURAL HISTORY. By the Rev. J. G. WOOD, M.A., F.L.S. With 450 Engravings. 12mo, Cloth, $1 05.

BOOKS ON THE ARCTIC REGIONS.

HALL'S ARCTIC RESEARCHES. Arctic Researches and Life among the Esquimaux: being the Narrative of an Expedition in Search of Sir John Franklin, in the Years 1860, 1861, and 1862. By CHARLES FRANCIS HALL. With Maps and Illustrations. 8vo, Cloth, $5 00; Half Calf, $7 25.

HAYES'S LAND OF DESOLATION: being a Narrative of Observation and Adventure in Greenland. By ISAAC I. HAYES, M.D. Ill'd. 12mo, Cloth, $1 75.

TYSON'S ARCTIC EXPERIENCES: containing Captain George E. Tyson's Wonderful Drift on the Ice-Floe, a History of the Polaris Expedition, the Cruise of the Tigress, and Rescue of the Polaris Survivors. With a General Arctic Chronology. Map and Ill's. 8vo, Cloth, $4 00.

PARRY'S VOYAGES. Three Voyages for the Discovery of a Northwest Passage, and Narrative of an Attempt to Reach the North Pole. By Sir W. E. PARRY, R.N. 2 vols., 18mo, Cloth, $1 50.

RICHARDSON'S ARCTIC EXPEDITION. Journal of a Boat-Voyage through Rupert's Land and the Arctic Sea, in Search of the Discovery Ships under Command of Sir John Franklin. By SIR JOHN RICHARDSON, F.R.S. Illustrated. 12mo, Cloth, $1 50.

BARROW'S ARCTIC VOYAGES. Voyages of Discovery and Research within the Arctic Regions, from the Year 1818 to the Present Time (1840); with Two Attempts to reach the North Pole. Arranged from the Official Narrative. By SIR JOHN BARROW, F.R.S. Map. 12mo, Cloth, $1 00.

LAMONT'S SEASONS WITH THE SEA-HORSES; or, Sporting Adventures in the Northern Seas. By JAMES LAMONT, F.G.S. With Map and Illustrations. 8vo, Cloth, $3 00.

WRANGELL'S EXPEDITION TO THE POLAR SEA. Narrative of an Expedition to the Polar Sea, in the Years 1820, '21, '22, and '23. By Admiral FERDINAND WRANGELL, Russian Navy. 18mo, Cloth, 75 cents.

TYTLER'S NORTHERN COASTS OF AMERICA. Historical View of the Progress of Discovery on the more Northern Coasts of America. By P. F. TYTLER, F.R.S. With Sketches of the Natural History of the North American Regions. By JAMES WILSON. 18mo, Cloth, 75 cents.

POLAR SEAS AND REGIONS. Discovery and Adventure in the Polar Seas and Regions. By Professors LESLIE and JAMESON, and HUGH MURRAY. Illustrated. 18mo, Cloth, 75 cents.

UNCLE PHILIP'S WHALE FISHERY. The Whale Fishery; or, Conversations with the Children about the Whale Fishery and the Polar Seas. By UNCLE PHILIP. 2 vols., 18mo, Cloth, $1 50.

HARPER'S YOUNG PEOPLE.

An Illustrated Weekly for Boys and Girls. 16 Pages.

SOME OPINIONS OF THE PRESS.

The regular visits of this beautiful weekly come like rays of golden sunshine into the family circle.—*Zion's Herald*, Boston.

HARPER'S YOUNG PEOPLE is a noble storehouse, well stocked with good things, grave and gay, for the whole household of children—from the wee ones to the boys and girls well on in their teens. Parents can make no mistake in subscribing for the current year, that their little ones may have a yearly round of joy.—*From the "Sunday-School Journal," edited by the* REV. JOHN H. VINCENT, D.D.

In its special field there is nothing that can be compared with it.—*Hartford Evening Post.*

It conveys information and amusement to all, and many a teacher will know better how to instruct her class after having perused its pages. It is one of the peculiarly admirable publications of the day.—*Philadelphia Record.*

HARPER'S YOUNG PEOPLE is the best of all the weeklies for children. — *Evening Chronicle*, St. Louis.

An inexhaustible reservoir of humor, instruction, and entertainment for the young people of the family. Its tone is unexceptional, and it will be found an admirable present for the juveniles.—*Indianapolis Journal.*

HARPER'S YOUNG PEOPLE has now come to be one of the most attractive and excellently edited juvenile periodicals of the day.—*Independent*, N. Y.

The grand success of this beautiful and instructive illustrated weekly for young readers is the best proof that it fills a needed place. No magazine of its kind has ever come into such boundless popularity in so short a time.—*Chicago Inter-Ocean.*

The illustrations form a whole art gallery in themselves, and a gallery that contains some gems worthy of preservation by the people of the most cultivated taste in pictures. —*Brooklyn Times.*

Subscription Price, $2 00 per Year.

Postage Free to all Subscribers in the United States and Canada.

☞ *A Specimen copy sent on receipt of a three-cent stamp.*

BOUND VOLUMES OF HARPER'S YOUNG PEOPLE.

Volume I. *out of print.* Volumes II., III., and IV. may be had of the publishers. Price $3 00 per Volume. The Volumes begin with the First Number issued in November. Each Volume contains over 800 pages and about 700 Illustrations, and is bound in Ornamental Cloth, with Frontispiece and Index.

There is entertainment enough in its eight hundred and odd pages of stories, sketches, poems, puzzles, and pictures to fill up the evenings of a whole winter. It is good, wholesome entertainment, too, and will both amuse and interest the juveniles.— *Philadelphia Inquirer.*

We know of no book better calculated to interest and instruct the young than the fifty-two numbers of this popular illustrated weekly. It contains a vast amount of good reading of the most varied character. * * * All that the artist's skill can accomplish in the way of illustration has been done, and the best talent of the country has contributed to its text.—*New England Journal of Education*, Boston.

If we had a dozen children, and could only buy one Christmas gift to be divided among them, our choice would certainly fall on this book that has so many beautiful pictures and quaint stories pressed between its handsome covers.—*New Orleans Picayune.*

Its wealth of stories, sketches, poetry, pictures, puzzles, and correspondence form a collection of intellectual treasures, the possession of which will make any boy or girl in the land "as happy as a king," and which, by reason of its moderate price, is within the reach of all who wish to have it at their command.—*Baltimore Gazette.*

PUBLISHED BY HARPER & BROTHERS, FRANKLIN SQUARE, N. Y.